DARKEST BEFORE DAWN

Book #3

The Veil Series

Pippa DaCosta

ISBN: 1500996572

ISBN-13: 978-1500996574

Paperback Edition.

US Edition.

Version 1.

www.pippadacosta.com

Chapter One

It's not every night a bloodied and disheveled Prince of Hell shows up on my doorstep with an orphan girl, demanding I keep her safe before vanishing into thin air. But that's exactly what happened when I first met Dawn.

I'd worked up a sweat scrubbing demon blood out of my suede boots. The day hadn't gone well. My work as a *free*lance Enforcer had seemed like a great idea at the time, especially the 'free' part. The Institute had answers I needed, but I was beginning to feel more and more like their blunt instrument. Demons hear *Enforcer* and don't want to sit and talk about their options. I killed more demons than I talked down, and being half-demon myself, my choice of profession gnawed away at my resolve. I was having a crisis, which was part of the reason I was scrubbing my boots with all the gusto of someone trying to wipe clean a guilty conscience.

Jonesy, my cat, wove around my ankles, determined to distract me, but it was the delectable voice of the Prince of Greed that finally caught my attention. I flicked my hair out of my eyes, tossed my ruined boot and scrub brush into the kitchen sink, and glared across the lounge at the TV.

On screen, Akil had poured all of his raw masculinity and charisma into a relaxed posture at the end of a plush crimson couch. He'd dressed impeccably in a dark suit that probably cost the same as a year's rent for my new apartment. He hadn't aged a day in the fifteen years I'd known him and still managed to pull off the slick thirty-something routine with masterful perfection. Never mind that he was an immortal chaos demon, spat out of creation at the same time as the earth. Nobody cared about that. All they saw was a professional businessman who had an answer for everything and could charm the scales off a snake.

"Not all demons are good, of course." He smiled, and the woman interviewing him raised her plucked eyebrows. "That wasn't what I was implying. I wanted to merely stress that demons are as varied and diverse as people." Whatever he'd been asked, he wasn't in the least perturbed. You couldn't ruffle his princely feathers as easily as that. I should know. I'd ruffled his feathers—or rather, his leathery, lava-veined wings—once or twice.

Akil's host drew a tight smile across her lips. "What about yourself?" She uncrossed her shapely legs, shuffled back in her high-backed seat, and then re-crossed her legs again. A murmur rippled through the unseen audience. Akil's smile hitched up at one corner, and a few feminine jeers from the audience lifted the mood. The host smiled and tucked her hair behind her ear. "Well? Everyone wants to know why you decided to come forward as the spokesperson for the demon community."

"Jenny." He purred her name like it was forbidden. I arched an eyebrow as Jenny squirmed in her seat. "It was necessary. Someone had to do something. Things couldn't go on as they were. The good people of Boston need answers. They need to know we're not terrifying monsters, just... misunderstood."

I snorted a laugh.

Jenny glanced at her audience and back to Akil. "Many of us here have seen the rather blurry news footage of you protecting Boston from the... Lah-Kar–"

"Larkwrari demon." Akil helpfully provided the correct pronunciation, the word rolling off his tongue with an ancient accent I'd never fully pinned down. Given his bronze skin tone and hazel eyes, people often assumed he was Italian or perhaps from somewhere further afield, somewhere hot and exotic. They were right about that. Before he'd come out as full-blood demon, very few had witnessed his true appearance and lived to describe him in detail, although there were a few pixelated images currently going viral on the internet. The women swooning in the audience would run screaming if they knew him as Mammon, Prince of Greed.

"Yes. That was two months ago," Jenny said. "Are we likely to see more events such as that one in Boston Gardens?"

"It's highly unlikely. That situation was extreme..."

I bowed my head and turned my back on the TV. I'd been at the Gardens during the 'event' they spoke of. In fact, Akil wouldn't have been able to save the city without me. But where he'd walked into the spotlight afterward, I'd slunk into the shadows. I hadn't seen him since. Nor had I seen or heard from Stefan, the half-demon who had caused the tear in the veil which protects this world from the netherworld, thereby letting the Larkwrari demon through. When it was all over and I realized I was on my own, I'd agreed to work freelance for the Institute as long as they stayed out of my life. So far, so good. On the surface, everything was fine, but scratch off the veneer, and I still struggled to cope with the emotional fallout from that day.

Jonesy, my cat, leapt onto the kitchen counter and nudged my arm with a rumbling purr. I tickled behind his ear. "I know, buddy. Don't worry. I'm not going anywhere." I'd abandoned Jonesy once before, around the time Akil had torched my old apartment building in an effort to flush me out of hiding. Yeah, not all demons are good. I'd yet to meet a good demon, and yet the people seemed to buy what Akil was selling.

Two booms against my front door frightened Jonesy enough for him to skitter off the counter and dart under the coffee table. They were the kind of knocks the police give you before kicking your door in.

I already knew who stood outside my apartment. His radiating warmth seeped beneath the door and crept inside my lounge. The framed modern art adorning each of my apartment walls served a purpose: the anti-elemental symbols locked down elemental power. Plus, he couldn't get in without a personal invite. Even knowing I was protected, I still felt a trickle of fear raise the fine hairs on my arms. I liked to call it fear because the alternative—desire—didn't sit well with my human half.

"Go away," I called. The Akil on the pre-recorded TV interview was still busy charming his audience. He had them laughing now, smiles all 'round. Even Jenny had warmed up to him. A dash of color brightened her cheeks. I grabbed the remote and switched off the TV.

"Muse, this is important," Akil said, his voice muffled behind the closed door.

"Then call me." I moved a few steps toward the door and stopped. "I tried to call you, and you ignored me." That had grated. It had taken me weeks to pluck up the courage to call him so we could meet and talk about Subject Beta, about the princes, about everything he should have told me before, and he'd blanked me like one of his fangirls.

"You need to open this door." That delicious voice eased beneath my defences and wove into my thoughts.

My chest tightened, and I clenched a fist over my heart. I had the essence of a demon shrink-wrapped around my soul, a vengeful necrotic parasite feeding and polluting my insides. I preferred to call the thing a parasite because, if I used his name, it made it too real, too fucked up. Akil probably had the means of removing it. When he'd tried, I'd shut him down. Letting him help felt too much like trusting him, and that was something I could never do again. I had no desire to trade one demon's hold for another. Occasionally, the dark thing hitching a ride in me decided to make its presence known, and now was one of those times.

"Akil, please... just go." I winced as the dark pulsed out of time with my heart.

"I need your help."

Dammit. He knew just how to push my buttons. "You're a capable guy. Figure it out." I moved close enough to the door that I could reach a hand out to open it, but I held back, fingers twitching.

"I have. That's why I'm here. You don't need to invite me in. Just open the door."

I wasn't inviting him in. I'd tried that once. He'd subsequently attempted to kill me. We had a complicated relationship.

I reached for the door handle as my demon unfurled inside me, awakened by Akil's presence. Her purr rumbled through me, making her desires perfectly clear. Everything about Akil flicked her switches, but I was the one calling the shots. Plus inside my apartment, she could no more manifest outside my skin than he could call his power. The symbolic artwork on my walls held her back.

When I opened the door, the verbal assault I'd prepared fizzled away in a gasp. Akil's torn claret shirt hung askew, and his suit pants were blood splattered. He had scuff-marks across his cheek and forehead. Blood dribbled down the side of his face. His normally hazel eyes brimmed with liquid fire. All of that I could have dealt with, but it was the young girl cowering behind his leg that surprised me the most. Her wide chocolate eyes peeked out at me as she clutched a stuffed rabbit to her chest, its faux fur matted with blood.

"What did you do?" I growled at Akil.

He narrowed his flame-filled eyes at me and then crouched down to face the little girl. Akil, his hands clasped around the little girl's upper arms, looked her in the eyes and said, "I'm sorry you witnessed... that. I had no choice. Muse will protect you. She's more formidable than she looks." I gasped, open mouthed, at the both of them.

The little girl blinked and clutched her bunny tight against her chest.

"I must leave you now." He smiled and toned down the fire in his eyes. He couldn't do much about the blood and his general disheveled state, but she didn't seem to notice. "Do as Muse says. Promise me."

"Okay. Will you come back?" she asked in a tiny, mouse-like voice.

Akil took too long to answer. I glared at him. "Yes, he'll come back," I snapped.

Straightening, Akil gave the girl a slight shove in my direction. She took a few steps inside and peered over her rabbit at my lounge as though looking at an alien world.

I flung my attention back to Akil. "What the hell, Akil?" I hissed, reining back my tone to avoid rousing my neighbors.

"Do the right thing, Muse." The softness of his tone set off alarm bells in my mind. "I know you will."

"You can't just turn up after two months and dump a little girl on me. I don't know how to look after children. What am I supposed to do? Who is she? Why do you look like you've gone ten rounds with a Hellhound?"

Akil ran a hand through his mussed hair, and I saw it tremble. How could I not? Akil didn't behave like this. He was the suave bastard on TV, not the beaten-up wreck at my door. "Just keep the demons away from her."

I gulped back a rising knot of panic. "What? Why are demons after her? She's just a little girl."

"As were you. Once." He glanced down the hall. A door-lock rattled; one of my neighbors had decided to investigate the commotion in the hallway.

"Akil..." I warned, lowering my voice to a stage whisper, "are you telling me she's a half blood?"

He met my stare. "Do the right thing."

"Is everything all right, Charlie dear?" my neighbor, Rosaline, asked, her English accent neat and clean. I poked my head around the door and gave her a sweet smile. A delightful sixty-something widow, she couldn't help caring too much about the lost cause next door – me. We'd bonded over tea. She made a mean lemon drizzle cake.

"Everything's fine, Rosa. I was just talking with my friend here... Not to worry. I'm sorry if we disturbed you."

"No-no..." She grinned and gave me a quaint royal wave. "As long as you're okay, my dear. Oh, would you mind taking a look at my television? I can't seem to change the channels. All I get is the Discovery channel, and I've had just about enough of rampaging wildebeest for one day."

"Yup, sure thing. Will do..." I waved and watched her plod back inside her apartment. When I turned to face Akil again, he'd made himself scarce.

I uttered a curse and then remembered my young guest and cursed again for swearing in front of a child. The little girl didn't seem to hear anyway. She wore a slip of a dress, several sizes too big for her skinny little body. Her socks were mismatched, and her black patent leather shoes scuffed. I moved around her. She blinked wide doe-eyes up at me. Her flushed cheeks, pink lips, curly mouse hair, and oval face suggested an age of eight or nine years, and I inwardly cringed. I had no idea what I was supposed to do with her. Thankfully, the demon smacking into my apartment window distracted me from that thought.

I jerked around and saw a dark shadow slam against the window, leaving oily imprints on the glass and rattling the frame. Another clattering boom against the adjacent window snapped my attention across the lounge. Claws scratched at the glass, setting my teeth on edge. I couldn't quite see the demons—too human to focus on their ethereal forms—but whatever they were, they didn't appear to be able to break through. My symbols worked their magic. I had a few seconds of smug satisfaction and then I heard a raucous cry coming from my bedroom. Jonesy blurred across the floor with a yowl, and following behind came a heaving cloud of black smoke. I'd left the bedroom window open.

My demon came to me like a blast of hot air from an oven. She'd already been lurking at the back of my mind, now she butted up against my skin. The protection symbols prevented me from summoning all of her. I couldn't use my element, but I had enough fire in my veins to see the prehistoric creature inside the miasmic shadow. I'd seen it before. They patrolled the night sky in the netherworld, and they also made an appearance in most dinosaur reference books. Palaeontologists called them pterosaurs, better known as pterodactyls. Demons called them *venatores – hunters.*

It teetered forward on its winged arms and legs, claws scratching against my hardwood floors, and cast its beady-eyed glance around. It let out an ear-piercing screech. The little girl squeaked behind me and scurried into the corner of the room where she ducked down and tried to hug herself into a tiny, insignificant ball.

I pinned the hunter in my sights and snatched a kitchen knife from the rack. We were equally matched in height—which isn't saying much—although its claws and beak full of razor-edged teeth gave it the distinct advantage. It screeched at me, the brittle sound like a clatter of cymbals.

"I already have demon blood on my boots," I growled. "I'd really prefer it if I didn't have to wash it off my walls as well."

It swung its elongated head and tried to get a fix on the girl behind me. Skittering to one side, it flapped its wings and snapped its jaws, unconcerned by my threat. Another of its companions slammed against the lounge window, jarring the glass. The hunter jerked its head, acknowledging its companion's idiocy. I used its distraction and bolted around behind it. Attacking it head on would get me a face full of sharp teeth. Snatching its left wing, I used my own momentum to swing around behind it. Its beak swung around after me, the two of us pirouetting before I plunged the kitchen knife into its leathery hide. I still had hold of its wing and yanked as it bucked away. The knife slid out with a *sloosh.* Blood spurted. Its beak snapped at me, close enough to taste the fish-oil stench of its breath. I recoiled, ducked, and as it snapped over my head, I thrust the knife into its neck and tugged its throat out with a grunt of exertion. The hunter whipped around, wings flailing and claws tearing at the gaping wound. It stumbled and staggered about the lounge, rearranging my furniture, and collapsed across my coffee table.

I dashed for the bedroom and slammed the window closed. Outside, the dark sky writhed with hunters. Any witnesses would see a cloud of black smoke against the night sky. Nothing too alarming.

I stepped back from the window and became acutely aware of the cooling demon blood plastering my top against my skin. I grimaced and walked gingerly back into the lounge, clothes chaffing. The hunter still lay sprawled across my coffee table, its blood dripping off the edges and pooling on my floor. How to dispose of a demon in

Boston? Call the Institute, but that would mean answering a lot of questions about who my little guest was.

She'd gone. The corner she'd been cowering in was empty, and my apartment door hung ajar. I lunged for the door and remembered I was covered in blood. Quickly, I tossed the knife into the kitchen sink and tore off my clothes while retrieving some jeans and a tank top from my bedroom. I was still tugging on my boots and doing up my fly as I stumbled from my apartment and hurried down the stairs.

Akil had left her with me, and within the space of five minutes, I'd lost her. If she got outside, the hunters would tear into her. I staggered down the last few steps and brushed by Lacy, another of my neighbors.

"Hey, Charlie, are yah okay?" her Boston accent chimed.

"Yeah, all good..." I tossed a wave over my shoulder, heading for the main door and then stopped and turned. "Did you see a little girl come by here?"

Lacy gaped at me. She was dressed for a night out in matching tartans and lace up Doc Martin boots. Her faux fur jacket was so white it would have glowed under UV. Not much shocked Lacy, but she'd lost her voice now. I'd forgotten to wash the blood off my face. She gestured at me, mouth open. "Is that...?"

"Oh, it's not real." I grinned brightly. "I was playing dead with my... erm niece. Y'know. Ketchup." Family members played dead with ketchup and kids, didn't they? I was sure I'd seen it on TV.

She screwed up her face, not believing me for a second. "Yeah, she went outside. Do you need some help?"

"Nope. I'm fine. We're fine. Which way did she go?"

"Toward Sidewalk Cafe."

"Thanks." I didn't wait around for more questions and just hoped I'd remembered to shut my apartment door. If anyone saw the demon draped over my coffee table, I'd have a whole lot of explaining to do, not to mention losing my deposit. I'd only been in the apartment a month and was technically meant to be making a good impression.

Early Friday evenings in Boston were as busy as weekday rush hours. I lived in the heart of South Boston, a rejuvenated district currently undergoing something of a popularity revival. Southies liked the friendly neighborhood atmosphere of the place and feared the desirable ambiance had attracted too many well-to-dos who would spoil what made the place special. I couldn't comment, being a newbie myself, but I did like the close-knit community. It felt like home, and for me, that was a damn miracle.

The many cafes and bars of East Broadway were opening for the evening, but the sidewalk was still clear enough for me to spot the little girl weaving her way through the tourists and after-work crowds. I glanced up at the sky and immediately saw the flock of hunters passing overhead. They had all the finesse of the black smoke from *Lost*, and I winced. If this went public, my boss at the Institute, Adam Harper, would lock me down and take away my freelance status. I had to control this. Dealing with Demons was, after all, my day job.

I didn't have my Beretta Pico sidearm or my Enforcer ID. I just looked like a crazy half-dressed woman with blood on her face chasing down a little girl. Could the situation get any worse? Breaking into a run, I raced through the crowd, muttering apologies as I brushed a few arms and bumped a few shoulders. I caught glimpses of the girl's ringlets and shiny black shoes, but she was quickly pulling away, able to thread herself through the crowd unnoticed.

A hunter's clattering battle cry trilled above, right before it dove toward the sidewalk. Someone screamed, also noticing what they'd see as a peculiar cloud rushing downward. I saw the hunter, its wings tucked in, beak open. It would slam into the little girl and make short work of her fragile human flesh. I couldn't let that happen. I summoned my demon's strength, releasing my mental hold and allowing her influence to flood through my body. She broke over me, pooled fire in my heart, and flushed my veins with ethereal energy. Still running, I lifted a hand and called to the heat slumbering in the buildings on either side of the street. Boston, like all cities, was a reservoir of heat. Human activity generated more than enough heat for me to play with. Answering the call, my element sloughed off the buildings and flooded the earth at my feet. Spooling it around my arm, I cast it outward, sending a whip-like tendril of fire over the heads of the crowd. Flames licked over the hunter and washed over the body of the beast, embracing every inch of it. It screamed an air-shattering cry and then tumbled out of the sky and thumped against the sidewalk, narrowly missing the unsuspecting crowd.

I didn't have time to explain to the gawping people what was happening. They would already know it was demon related. The news and events of late had prepped them, but that probably didn't make it any easier to witness.

I dropped off the sidewalk and ran along the road, casting another bolt of fire into the sky where a second writhing mass of darkness dive-bombed the fleeing girl. "Hey!" If I could get her to stop, I could turn and deal with the hunters in one go.

She veered left down a narrow, one-way street. The malicious black smoke funneled after her. A quick glance behind told me we were virtually alone. I called all of my demon and let her ride over my flesh, consuming every part of me. My one ruined wing burst from my back. My element draped me in flame. I stopped, planted my feet firmly on the cobbles, and thrust my hands skyward, launching with them a storm of orange and blue flames. The hunters scattered, but chaos fire has an intent all of its own, and they soon found tendrils of flame licking up their limbs. Jagged fragments of pain thumped me in the chest. I grunted. My power stalled. *Damn parasite*. With a snarl, I doubled my efforts. The black cloud burst apart from within and lit up the sky in a mass of fire strikes. Burned hunters slapped against the road. Some bounced off cars, setting off half a dozen alarms. I'd never been very good at subtle.

I finished off a few stragglers with some well-aimed fireballs and then jogged down the street, shaking off my demon with each step, returning to my normal, if slightly disheveled state. When I finally found the girl curled tightly into the crook of an old tree, I was myself again, complete with blood splatters.

I saw the whites of her eyes and tried to offer her my best, most friendly smile. In the distance, sirens announced the arrival of the authorities, and no doubt the Institute would be included in that response. I crouched down and offered her my hand.

"It's okay. The man who brought you to me, Akil—he was right. I'll keep you safe, but you gotta stay close to me."

She blinked and hugged her bunny.

I needed to get back to my apartment where the symbols would hide us both from demons. If I could get home and clean up the mess waiting for me, then maybe the girl might open up and explain just what the freakin' hell was going on. I'd call Akil too. I had no idea what he expected me to do that he couldn't, and his 'do the right thing' explanation wouldn't cut it.

"What's your name?"

She blinked again, and her lips tightened. She didn't trust me, and I couldn't blame her. I had no idea what she'd witnessed with Akil, but given the fifteen minutes we'd spent together, I'd have a hard time trusting anyone if I was her.

"Shall we do this properly?" I shuffled a bit closer. "My human name is Charlie, but my real name is Muse." I held out my hand, inviting her to shake it.

"That's a funny name." A slight netherworldly accent slurred her words.

"Yeah, a not-so-funny guy gave it to me."

"I have a funny name too."

"Oh, and what's your name?"

"Dawn." She held out her rabbit. "This is Missus Floppy."

"Dawn is a lovely name." I shook Floppy's paw and then Dawn's tiny, cold hand. "I'm very pleased to meet you both. Would you like to meet my cat, Jonesy? He loves tickles behind his ears."

Dawn clutched her bunny against her chest once more and smiled. "Okay, Miss Muse."

Chapter Two

Adam only left the safety of the Institute complex when
the world was about to end or I was involved. I wasn't
surprised when he filed in behind the clean up crew. I
leaned against the kitchen cabinets, arms crossed, watching
the blue-overall-clad Institute employees surround the dead
demon in the middle of my lounge and set about removing
its carcass and copious amounts of drying blood from my
apartment.

Adam gave the room a visual assessment, his gaze
lingering on the framed symbols as though inspecting them
for any errors. He took his time, observing his crew doing
what they did best. He would look at me when necessary,
not before. While I waited, I watched him, knowing he
could feel my gaze crawl over him. A substantial man,
both in demeanor and presence, he dressed casually in blue
jeans and a blue-striped shirt. Suits weren't him, despite
spending the majority of his days behind a desk. His
graying hair should have been too long for a man of his
middle-years, but he somehow made it look distinguished.
His fawn colored eyes instantly disarmed anyone who
didn't know him. He'd smile and ask you how your day
was, right before he went for the jugular. He and I didn't
get along.

Finally, after five minutes of rising tension, Adam
turned those deceptively warm eyes on me. "I assume
you're the fire demon who ran down the street in plain

sight of half a dozen CCTV cameras and upward of fifty witnesses?"

Usually, he'd wait until he had me in his office before laying down the Institute law. Tonight, I was getting the no-holds-barred treatment.

Jonesy sat next to me on the kitchen counter, twitching tail dangling over the edge. My cat was an excellent judge of character.

"Would you prefer I let the flock of hunter demons eat the unsuspecting commuters?"

"I'd prefer discretion, Muse."

One of the blue-suit guys moved toward my bedroom. I tensed. "Nothing in there. It's all out here." The guy glanced at Adam, who nodded, and returned to the tacky pool of dark blood spreading across my floor.

Adam arched an eyebrow and crossed the room to my kitchenette. "I'm loath to think you're hiding something from us."

"There's nothing left to hide, Adam." I made a point of meeting his stare. He wouldn't think I was laying it on thick. This was how we always danced.

"Have you heard from Stefan?"

Now, I did flick my gaze away. "No."

"David Ryder?"

"No."

Stefan and Ryder had vanished after the event at Boston Gardens, and it remained an open wound between myself and the Institute. In fact, I believed Adam only kept me on to see if either Stefan or Ryder resurfaced around me. They hadn't. The last time I'd seen Stefan, he'd accused me of killing his sister. He thought I'd deliberately drugged him to subdue his demon and believed I'd sided with his nemesis, Akil. I'd left Stefan with Ryder as he struggled to contain his demon half, and I'd helped Akil drive the Larkwrari demon back through the tear in the veil. Ryder would keep Stefan safe. Either that, or Stefan would lash out and kill him. Given the madness that had come over Stefan since his lengthy stay in the netherworld, I hadn't ruled it out. That thought—among many others — kept me awake at night.

"Need I remind you, we have authority over your living arrangements and career?"

I ground my teeth. Hate is such a strong word. I liked to think myself incapable of true hate, but I was only half-human, and my demon hated Adam Harper with every netherworldy cell in her body. It was only because I'd made a deal with Ryder not to torch the Institute or spontaneously ignite Adam that I'd refrained from doing both.

"Why were the hunter demons here?" he asked.

I shrugged. That was a good question, and the sudden change of direction caught me off guard. "They must have been sent by someone who knew where I lived."

"Wouldn't your protection symbols hide you from any such threat?" He nodded toward my framed prints with the swirling interwoven markings.

He was right. Those symbols kept me off the demon radar. "What can I say? They found me. I dealt with it."

Any number of demons could have sent the hunters after me. Demons despised my half-blood nature, detested Enforcers, and had all taken my general lack of willingness to die as an affront to their demon egos. Hell, even Akil had sent demon-nasties after me in the past, although he appeared to have resolved his homicidal tendencies since I'd literally sucked the life out of him. My immortal brother could have sent them, but I'd learned assassins weren't his style. Valenti was more likely to run me through with a sword. He liked his sibling-rivalry up close and personal.

I shuddered and shoved thoughts of my half-brother to the back of my mind. Of all the crap I had to deal with, I really didn't need the specter of Val occupying my thoughts.

Besides, the hunters hadn't been after me. They'd wanted the girl, and Akil had led them straight here. Adam wasn't to know that, so I played dumb and shouldered the blame.

He waited for me to offer up some sort of explanation that he was happy with, but when it became clear after several minutes of silence, that I had no intention of elaborating, he made his excuses to leave. "Next time, Muse, dial down the fires from hell. I have enough trouble trying to manage demon sightings all over the city. I don't need one of my Enforcers in the headlines, especially a hybrid."

"Yes boss," I grumbled with zero conviction.

It took the Institute team an hour to wipe my lounge clean. Glad to see the back of them, I hurried them out the door with the disinfectant still drying and immediately checked on Dawn. She sat perched on the end of my bed, legs dangling over the edge and didn't look as though she'd moved since I'd told her to stay-put and stay quiet.

"Who was that?" She followed close behind me as I returned to my now-spotless lounge.

"They're not the type of people you want to be getting involved with, given their history with half bloods." I glanced down at Dawn. She stood inside my personal space, peering up at me, Missus Floppy loose in her hand. "That is what you are, right?"

"What's a half blood?"

Okay, we really needed to talk. "Are you hungry?" I asked with a smile.

She nodded.

"Chill out on the couch, and I'll make us some food." She skewed her wary gaze to the couch, regarding it suspiciously. "Sit. It won't bite."

She crossed the lounge with tight steps and hitched herself onto the couch. Curling herself into a tight ball, she sunk into the cushions as though hoping they'd swallow her up.

I flicked on the TV and channel surfed to something non-offensive, watching Dawn's eyes widen to absorb the images.

I checked my fridge for food and found it distinctly lacking. I couldn't cook. I'd tried it once. Or rather, Akil had attempted to teach me, but I'd struggled with the whole idea of heating up a stove when I could use my element. Needless to say, toast is flammable, and eggs explode when heated using chaos energy. Who knew? Akil had found it highly amusing while I'd considered myself a failure. Things had changed since then, but I still shied away from cooking.

Two microwave meals it was then.

"You're safe here, Dawn." I prepared the frozen meals. "As long as you stay inside these markings, the demons can't find you."

"They did before."

I glanced back at her. She was watching a wildlife program about chipmunks, overlaid with dramatic music. "The symbols only work on higher demons, the big guys with conscious thoughts. Some of the lesser ones can still get through, if they know what they're looking for. Plus, I left the window open. Don't do that. It gives them an in. Same with the front door. So we just have to stay here until we figure out what's going on."

The microwave pinged. I managed to turn the desiccated peas, carrots and shoe-leather meat onto plates so they looked partially edible and carried them over to Dawn.

She didn't bother with cutlery and dove right in with her fingers.

"Careful, it's hot." She didn't seem to care. Eyes darting between chipmunks and her plate of food, she tucked in as though I'd served her a gourmet meal. I watched her closely, finding myself transfixed by this quiet little girl. Why did Akil have her? What had happened to him? Why leave her with me? Why were the hunters after her? I wanted to demand answers from her, but I wasn't that heartless. The interrogation could wait.

I reached out and swept a lock of her curly hair behind her ear. A trickle of my element seeped outward, as it sometimes did around demons. It happened often enough that I barely noticed it. It wasn't invasive, just a curious touch, but Dawn jerked back and glared at me as though I'd slapped her.

I snatched my hand back. "It's okay." I'd felt a little stirring of the energy slumbering inside her. She was a half blood. Had she been full-demon, my skin would have crawled by now, plus she wouldn't have been able to enter my apartment. Now that I'd sensed the power in her, I knew for certain she was like me. "We're the same, you and me."

"The man who saved me, he says you're strong."

He would, I thought. Demons only care for power, and considering Akil was the Prince of Greed, he liked nothing better than overflowing chaotic energies. "He *saved* you?"

She blinked. "He told me not to tell you."

That sounded more like Akil. I smiled. "It's okay. You can trust me."

She shook her head, ringlets bobbing. I wasn't going to push it. Not yet. But I needed answers. If Akil was using this little girl to get to me, I'd take my overflowing chaotic energies and use them to go nuclear on his ass.

"Do you think you can trust Akil?"

She shook her head. Good girl. "He's strong too." Her eyes unfocused, and what little color she had drained from her face. "I don't want to go back," she whispered.

"You don't have to go anywhere you don't want to. I promise you that." I took her dainty hand in mine and gave it a squeeze. She squeezed back, eyes glistening. There were memories in my head just like hers. I knew what it meant to be a half blood abomination among demons. If Dawn had endured half of what I'd been subjected to, she was lucky to be alive, never mind coherent.

The parasitic demon knotted around my heart tightened. I sucked in a sharp breath, tugging my hand from Dawn's to clench it against my chest. It never let me forget its existence.

My cell phone rang, providing a welcome distraction from the hideous creature hitching a ride inside me. I left Dawn watching the chipmunks and answered the call.

"Charlie, it's Detective Coleman." His fast footfalls punctuated the background drone of traffic. A car door slammed. "Dead demon call just came in. I'm about to head down to a penthouse in Battery Wharf to seal it off— the usual—and thought you'd want to know."

"Hey," I drawled. "I'm fine. Thanks for asking." Coleman worked homicide at Boston PD, but he also got burdened with cases of suspected demon involvement. I was on his speed dial as the phone-a-friend for anything suspiciously inhuman. "Why would I want to know?" Battery Wharf was an exclusive luxury apartment complex. Not somewhere you'd expect a demon to turn up dead, but things were changing. Demons were everywhere, so the press said.

"Well, for one, you're the Institute, and I'm obliged to tell the Institute when one of your ki— when a demon turns up dead."

I caught that little slip of the tongue but let it go. "Noted. And?"

"You're acquainted with the apartment owner. Akil Vitalis."

Chapter Three

I left Dawn in Rosa's doting hands and rode along with Coleman to Battery Wharf.

Akil owned property all over Boston. I knew of a handful of apartments and townhouses, but I wagered that he had dozens more hidey-holes he hadn't told me about. He'd spent much of the last eighty years building up a financial portfolio consisting of mostly property, but also shares in several corporations. The Prince of Greed had his finger on Boston's financial pulse, much to the irritation of the Institute, who had so far failed to catch him embroiled in anything illegal. Luckily for Akil, being a demon wasn't against the law. Yet. Akil was meticulous when it came to his business persona. So much so that, when I trapped him on the other side of the veil for six months, his businesses continued to operate without the head of the snake. When he got back, he stepped back into his suit —no tie—as though nothing had happened.

But something had happened at Battery Wharf, something he hadn't planned for. His luxurious penthouse apartment with its floor-to-ceiling windows, marble tiles, granite countertops and hardwood floors, had been scorched by fire. Nothing had actually gone up in flames, from what I could tell, but something had flash-burned through the lounge, dusting the décor with soot. Smokey imprints swirled across an otherwise crisp white ceiling.

Coleman followed me, watching my reaction. He knew I had a 'relationship' with Akil, but he didn't know the details. I'd told Coleman exactly what the Boston PD needed to know. Akil was a Prince of Hell and not to be fucked with unless they wanted to get their fingers burned. Prior to my revelation, they—like everyone else in this city—thought Akil was every bit the charming and successful businessman who happened to have volunteered for the role of demon ambassador. Nothing was ever that simple with Akil.

A few uniformed cops trailed in behind while I wandered. Outside the windows, Boston Harbor glistened in the sunlight. I'd spent many an hour on that terrace, watching the boats below. This apartment was different from the others he owned. Akil only came here when he needed time to think. This was his city bolthole. Modern furniture married with chic accents, creating a timeless quality where old married new, much like its owner.

I scanned the lounge area. Two empty wine glasses stood proudly on the coffee table. On the floor, as though kicked off in a hurry, lay a pair of women's high-heeled shoes. My sightline followed the discarded shoes to the body sprawled in the doorway to the master bedroom. Thankfully, not Akil's body. He was immortal, but I'd learned his human vessel wasn't. When Coleman had mentioned a body, I'd guarded myself against the possibility it could be Akil. When I found myself looking at the slippery gray skin of a female demon laying face down, a relieved sigh slipped from my lips.

I crouched down beside the corpse, noting the fin running down her spine and the four-inch stab wound in her lower back. I tilted my head to get a good look at her face. She had whiskers, like those on a catfish, and her lips pulled back into a cod-like grin. Considering her human vessel had been stunning, her demon was grotesque. I knew her as Carol-Anne. She'd once tried to kill me— what demon hadn't?

"Your thoughts?" Coleman tucked his hands in his coat pockets. In the bright apartment, his face had the same creamy pallor as the dead demon's.

I straightened and stepped around her body into the bedroom. "Her name is Carol-Anne. I knew her. She's the owner of The Voodoo Lounge, a demon club in Charlestown." The bedroom's white ceilings, pale blue walls, and mahogany floors gave the impression of understated luxury. The bed sheets were knotted, pillows scattered. I stepped onto a plush white rug and felt it squelch beneath the soles of my boots. Pools of water glistened on the hardwood floors. I touched the bed sheets and rubbed the moisture from my fingertips. "She was a water elemental. Pretty high on the food chain."

The last time I'd seen her, she'd been on her knees in front of Levi, the Prince of Envy. He'd been sent to collect and escort me to my father, Asmodeus. I'd managed to delay Levi's plans, but the threat still hung over my head like Damocles' sword.

"The water damage seeped through to the below apartment. That's how we got the call. She's a water elemental, huh. And what element is Akil Vitalis again?"

He already knew the answer, but I played his game. "Fire."

Coleman scratched his chin. I'd been teaching him the finer points of elemental chaos demons, at least the details I knew, which were woefully lacking since Akil wouldn't take my calls. "How well do you know her?"

I glanced back at Coleman standing in the doorway. He was tall and wiry thin, trading strength for speed, and coiled as tightly as a spring. He regarded me as though he might have to slap some cuffs on me, and that prospect didn't please him. Thankfully, as this was an all-demon incident, I outranked him. It didn't stop his cop instincts throwing up warning flags though.

"Not very. When I went off the rails a few months ago, I went to the Lounge looking for help. She was there. She put me in touch with someone. That's all I saw of her."

Coleman dug into his coat pocket and took out a pack of gum. He popped two pieces into his mouth and chewed. A week ago, he'd declared he was giving up coffee. The gum helped. "Why's she here?"

"I have no idea." The fact she'd been on Levi's payroll and now lay face down in Akil's apartment didn't bode well. The princes weren't supposed to meddle in the machinations of their princely brethren. And it looked as though Akil had gone beyond meddling, straight into provocation. Why? Did it have something to do with the half blood girl in my apartment?

"Charlie... C'mon." He arched an eyebrow, warning me that he'd recognize a lie. "You know Akil..."

I glanced at the bed and wondered why Carol-Anne would have been here, in the bedroom. My mind jumped to all sorts of conclusions, some of them graphic, none appealing. "Maybe they're an item. Hell, I don't know." Thoughts of exactly what Akil and Carol-Anne might have been up to in the bed lodged in my head. I grimaced. Water and fire didn't mix, but that doesn't mean it didn't happen. I had fire in my veins and had been briefly involved with Stefan, an ice demon. It should have been wrong—every part of my half-demon nature should have been repelled by Stefan— but damn, it had felt so right. Akil and Carol-Anne? I shivered. Stranger things had happened. Not that I should have cared. Akil could do what he pleased. It was none of my business.

Coleman gave up waiting for me to explain and shook his head, lifting his hands in surrender. "Well, as this is demon, it's not my problem. I thought I'd do you the favor of giving you first refusal before the Institute comes down on this like the NSA at a hackers' convention. Have you seen Akil recently?"

My memory flashed on the image of an amber-eyed and disheveled Akil at my door. "Not since the Garden event." I'd been lied to enough that lying to anyone else grated against my better judgment, but Coleman didn't need to get involved.

He held my gaze, trying to stare the truth out of me. Cops must have that universal expression stamped into their DNA. He couldn't be sure I was lying, but it wasn't his call to make. Adam, however, would grill me until my juices ran clear.

"Thanks for calling me."

Coleman nodded. "Sure."

I did my duty and called the Institute while Coleman listened in and then waited for them to swoop down before the press got wind of it and Akil's sexy-as-sin picture could be plastered all over the tabloids. He wouldn't like that. His halo would slip in the eyes of the Boston public. Never mind that his tarnished halo hung on devil horns. I needed to speak to him. Leaving bodies in his apartment wasn't his style, but then neither was saving little half-blood girls. Unless you counted me. Did saving young impressionable girls twice in fifteen years make it a trend if the rescuer is immortal?

I dialed his number on my cell but didn't get a reply. I called Rosa and checked on Dawn. She was sleeping, and Rosa was happy to watch her for me. Hanging up, I nodded at the Enforcers inviting themselves into Akil's apartment and readied myself for the interrogation.

Chapter Four

Adam was thorough. He suspected I was lying and tried to talk me round in circles, but I'd been in the hot seat before and knew how he operated. I argued that the hunters showing up and the dead demon in Akil's apartment happened to be a coincidence. He knew it was bullshit, of course, but I didn't falter, and eventually, he released me. I asked him for a week off, citing stress as my motive. He just about choked on his reply, but he couldn't refuse me, not without risking me quitting on him. Again. For some reason, he didn't want to get rid of me, and I couldn't quit, not if I was going to find out the truth about Subject Beta—a.k.a. me.

The fresh bite in the air and bleeding sky told me it was almost dawn when I got home. After apologizing profusely to Rosa, I found Dawn asleep in my bed—a tiny fetal bump beneath the sheets. I collected a spare pillow and quilt and sprawled on the couch, holding out little hope that sleep would come. *It* didn't allow me to rest. As the quiet of my apartment settled over me and the comforting sounds of Boston faded into the background, the parasitic demon clutching my heart awoke.

He crawled out from my insides like a spider nursing its web. Seeking tendrils of darkness groped through my mind and invaded my thoughts. Alive, Damien had been a wretched, blood-thirsty murderer who derived pleasure from pain. I'd been sold to him, a worthless half blood, a plaything, and he'd used me in every way imaginable and in some ways unimaginable. Akil had saved me the first time, but when Damien returned, he'd found new ways to torture me. He'd tied his very essence to mine, and when I'd killed him, his soul—or whatever the fetid thing inside of his carcass had been—had ported over to me. It struck at my heart, sunk its barbed claws in, and made itself a new home.

Nights were impossible. My dreams, when they came, resembled poisonous recipes of blood, desire, and savagery. They weren't tangible enough to hold on to when I woke, and for that I was grateful, but their filthy residue lingered during the day, soiling my thoughts, and they were getting worse.

Dawn touched my face, abruptly waking me. I heard the echoes of my scream in my ears and felt wetness on the pillow. As I blinked, a few more tears escaped. Dawn climbed onto the couch and wriggled beneath the quilt beside me. She snuggled close, head tucked beneath my chin. I didn't try to stop her. After a few minutes, the tremors rippling through me slowed, and the tears dried on my cheeks. A little of my element curled around her, drawing her close. She couldn't have known about the demonic tumor inside of me, but she didn't need to. She would have her own horrors stalking her dreams. I closed my eyes and prayed that the pain and horror of Dawn's past was over, that she'd escaped at a younger age than me. I hoped she would never have to endure half the things I did.

Chapter Five

Leaving Dawn in my apartment while I went looking for Akil made my gut squirm, but taking her with me would be an equally bad idea. Reminding myself she was safer inside than anywhere else, I left her with the TV and some snacks and locked the door behind me. I hesitated. If I took her with me, I'd at least know she was safe, but if she still had the hunters after her, we'd soon find ourselves fending off a repeat attack, and Adam wouldn't let it slide again. If the Institute got hold of her, she could kiss any hope of freedom goodbye.

I rented a car with cash, removed the battery from my cell, and tucked my Beretta Pico gun into its holster inside my coat. You can't be too careful when the Institute has eyes on you. It took all morning driving around Boston to tick off the properties I knew belonged to Akil. Most, he'd rented out. Others were empty. It had been a long shot, but there was one last thing I could do.

Summoning a demon is easy. It's what you do with them when you have them that's tricky. A little blood, a focal point, and an invitation extended to their many names is all it takes. It only works for higher demons, and more often than not, they're mighty pissed at being yanked out of their daily routine. Summoning a prince was tantamount to inviting a great white shark into a cage in your front room and then getting into the cage with it. I tried not to make a habit of summoning demons, mostly because I spent my life running from them. But Akil had gone AWOL, leaving me little choice.

I couldn't summon Akil in my apartment, not with Dawn there. I wanted frank answers to direct questions and suspected Akil would lie with Dawn hovering around my legs. I also needed some way of tempering his power, just in case he took offense at my summoning him like a pet. There was only one other place I could go where there were protection symbols on the walls and where prying eyes couldn't penetrate: Stefan's old workshop.

Stefan had restored cars when he wasn't stalking misbehaving demons for the Institute. He kept a workshop not far from Ryder's place. I'd visited both in the last couple of months, but neither Stefan nor Ryder had returned, and the workshop remained untouched with tools strewn around. An old Dodge Charger hunkered in the center, waiting for someone to put it back together again.

I used the key Ryder had given me almost a year ago and opened up the workshop only to find it empty. I hesitated in the doorway. I'd expected to see the chassis of the Dodge in the middle of the floor and the walls plastered with various tools and equipment. But it was all gone. Venturing inside, I checked the office and found it stripped bare. No furniture, just scuffed walls and dust bunnies. I walked through the back door and into the den. I already knew it would be empty, but seeing it naked where before it had been an Aladdin's cave of weapons seemed so final. Even the symbols that should have been spray painted across the walls had been scrubbed off and painted over. The bare bulbs illuminated an empty windowless room. My heart sank.

He's not coming back...

I'd always assumed Stefan would return to Boston. He'd been through hell—literally. Trapped beyond the veil with his impeccable control slipping, the death of his sister, and after my so-called betrayal, it was to be expected that he would need time out to regain control of his demon. But he would come back. Now though... He certainly wasn't coming back to his workshop. The place was cold, all traces of his life gone. Slouching, I puffed out a sigh. I missed him more than he'd ever know.

With heavy steps, I turned and yelped.

Stefan leaned against the doorframe, brittle-blue eyes sparkling. His faded blue jeans sported a few frayed tears that could pass as deliberately fashionable. But knowing him, they were probably the result of a demon getting too close for comfort. His Timberland boots had been scuffed raw. A midnight blue V-neck sweater hugged his athletic physique. His clothes were casual, but his stance was not. He'd crossed his arms over his chest and glared a narrow-eyed stare. The rakish smile I'd come to love was nowhere in sight. Instead, his lips were pursed into a thin line. His platinum blond hair was shorter than I remembered but still long enough to slide my fingers through. A memory of doing just that distracted me. I blinked rapidly before skipping my gaze away.

"What are you doing here?" His cold voice reminded me of how we'd last seen one another. We'd fought. I'd flung fire, and he'd thrown ice-daggers.

"I... er..." I'd come to summon Akil. The truth was a bad idea. He thought I was in cahoots with Akil when nothing could have been further from the truth. I should lie, tell him anything, but the thought of lying to Stefan just felt outright wrong. I'd never lied to him and didn't want to start now. "I..."

"Never mind," Stefan bowed his head, releasing me from his penetrating stare. "You should leave. I'll need your key."

I looked down at the key in my hand. Just a key, but it felt as though it should mean something more, like I was letting the last piece of him go. "Stefan—"

"Nothing you can say will change anything that happened, so don't waste your breath."

My throat tightened. How had things gotten so bad between us? "I was going to say, I'm pleased to see you're okay..."

He shoved away from the door and, within a few strides, stood in front of me. He plucked the key from my hand and met my eyes. "I'm not okay, Muse." His hand closed into a fist. "Don't tell the Institute you've seen me."

"I wouldn't—"

He turned and strode out the room, leaving me staring at the empty doorway. I shivered as a thread of cold air unraveled around me. I hadn't seen him for two months, I hadn't even known if he was alive, and that was our reunion conversation? Like hell, it was.

I jogged after him, anger flaring heat through my veins. "Hey." He stopped, boots scuffing the dusty floor, but he didn't turn. My breath misted, a reminder of the volatile nature of his element. It hadn't always been that way. "I don't deserve this." Was that a tremor in my voice? So much for conviction.

His shoulders tensed. I found myself readying for an attack by spilling a little heat into my fingers. The temperature in the workshop plummeted. The air I breathed tingled through my clenched teeth and burned my lungs.

He turned his head, but didn't look at me. It was more of a cursory acknowledgement. He hesitated, about to speak. Whatever he had on the tip of his tongue, he let it rest there and walked away for the second time.

"Stefan, wait..." I followed and stepped out onto the narrow backstreet, shielding my eyes from the sun's glare. A late 60's style Dodge Charger had been parked outside the workshop, leaving just enough room for cars to pass behind it. It had a glossy new coat. "Are you leaving for good?"

He tugged open the driver's door. I caught a glimpse of black leather seats with red piping before he got inside and slammed the door behind him. I wanted to yank that door open and yell at him to demand he listen to me, just for a few seconds, just long enough to make him understand why I'd done the things I had. But I didn't move. We would fight. It was clear that nothing I could say would end well.

He turned the engine over, and the throaty V8 grumbled to life. He was leaving. I might never see him again, and yet I didn't have it in me to stop him. Maybe because he was right. I shouldn't have brought Akil back. Never mind that I had to to free Stefan. I shouldn't have pumped Stefan full of a drug that inhibited his demon (also done to protect him). I should have stopped my owner from killing Stefan's sister (as though I hadn't tried).

The car growled as he turned it around at the end of the dead-end street then cruised back to where I stood. He opened his door and climbed out enough to peer over the roof at me, expression harsh, eyes cold. "I'm sorry we met, Muse. Don't come looking for me. It's not safe."

I'm sorry we met... I tried not to reveal the depth his words cut through me and shrugged a regret-laden shoulder. "Fine." Did he hate me that much? An emotional knot tightened my throat. I clamped my mouth closed, pinching my quivering lip between my teeth.

He waited, perhaps expecting more of a fight. He was right. No words could change the past. He glanced away, looking toward the main street, the exit, his way out. The time for redemption slipped past, and he ducked back inside the car. Had he glanced at me, I might have found the courage to say something to stop him, but he hadn't glanced back. He didn't even say goodbye.

He gunned the engine and spun the rear tires on the Dodge before it hooked and lunged away from the workshop, away from me. At the end of the street, the tail lights blinked red, and the engine roared once more before he peeled the car into traffic and disappeared out of sight.

I trembled and blinked back brimming tears. Screw him. I didn't need him. I didn't need anyone. It wasn't as though I cared about him or regularly dreamed about the cooling touch of his element easing through the blazing heat of mine. I certainly didn't want to remember how it felt to have his protective embrace pulling me close or how my name tumbled breathlessly from his lips when we lost ourselves in one another.

With a snarl, I turned and slammed a fist into the workshop door. Pain lanced up my arm. I hissed and spat my anger until most of it had fizzled away, leaving me nursing bruised knuckles as I trudged back to my car.

Chapter Six

Stuck in traffic, I jabbed at the buttons on the radio, trying to find some music that might take my mind off the bitterness Stefan had left behind. A track with a fast beat and minimal lyrics did the trick. Drumming my fingers on the steering wheel, I squinted through the drizzle on the windshield at the red tail lights blooming ahead of me. The wipers sloshed back and forth, adding an intermittent squeak. An autumn storm hunkered over the city. The oppressive gray skies suited my mood.

My plans hadn't changed, but if I was going to summon Akil I'd need somewhere secure and private to do it. The only place left was my apartment. Even if I did manage to summon him, I couldn't trust his answers. *Focus on the facts*, I told myself. I knew someone or something had attacked Akil. It took a lot to wear him down to the point where he didn't bother to heal himself. Or he was faking it. If I assumed everything I'd seen and heard in those few minutes he'd introduced Dawn had been true, then he'd either stolen the girl from someone who'd squared up to him, or he'd been more interested in protecting Dawn than himself. My instincts told me he was protecting her, but my instincts were all screwed up when it came to Akil.

I grumbled a frustrated noise and jabbed at the radio again.

I knew Carol-Anne and Akil had been having something of a civilized conversation, enough to warrant a glass of wine together. She'd kicked off her shoes, so things had gotten cozy. They'd moved the party to the bedroom and made it as far as the bed, if the drenched sheets were any indication. But something had gone wrong—at least for Carol-Anne. They'd fought... Mm, that didn't ring true. Carol-Anne was formidable, but she wasn't in the same league as Akil. She shouldn't have been able to rough him up. I'd seen him slam her down on The Voodoo Lounge bar without so much as dislodging an immaculate hair. But they *had* fought in his apartment. The scorch marks and sodden floors testified to that. *So Akil kills Carol-Anne, and then shows up at my place with a little girl who just happens to be a half blood?* Had Dawn been with them the whole time? Or had Akil collected her after killing Carol-Anne? And what did he expect me to do with her that he couldn't already do himself? He had access to resources on both sides of the veil, whereas I only had my wit and penchant for trouble. I was missing something.

The traffic inched forward. My windshield wipers squeaked. I eased my rental car into motion, rolling closer to the car in front of me. Leaning away from the door, I tried to get a better view of what caused the jam. The side window exploded inward. Shattered glass dashed my face and pummeled my clothes. I let out a startled squeal as a clawed hand the size of my head reached in and made a grab for my arm. I lunged away, twisted in the seat, and angled myself so I could shove off the door and shimmy backward into the passenger seat. The thick arm plunged inside the car again. A purely demon growl bubbled up my throat. I kicked out, striking the hand with the heel of my boot. It recoiled and then struck again, snatching knobby fingers around my ankle and yanking me toward the window.

The gearshift dug into my lower back, twisting me awkwardly, grinding against my spine. I spat a curse and kicked the hand with my free foot. The demon made a wet snarling sound, something like a bathtub full of water gurgling down a drain, and then drove his gnarled face through the window. He grinned, his gaping mouth too large for his misshapen pug-face. The passenger door wrenched open. A cool breeze wafted over my face, dashing my hot cheeks with rain. Briefly, my mind registered the rain tasted salty, then a dry, pitted arm hooked around my neck—skin rough like tree bark—and hauled me backward out the car. My leg slipped from the boot the pug-faced demon had hold of. I had a moment of weightlessness, right before my new assailant slammed me down on the hood of a car. My head thumped against metal. My teeth jarred. A net of white noise cascaded in front of my vision. Unconsciousness loomed. I blinked and tried to refocus, but the vast bulk of the rough-skinned demon blotted out the daylight. He pinned me beneath one branch-like forearm and leaned all of his weight into my chest. My ribs compressed. I tried to heave him off me, but my puny human hands barely closed around the girth of his muscles.

"Bears-the-flood," he growled around yellow teeth.

"Huh?" I grunted.

"Where half blood?" Clearly this demon didn't have much need to polish his human speech. He was probably fresh from the netherworld.

Screw this. I met his flat eyes and blazed heat through my limbs. My demon woke, her awareness fixed as sharp as lasers on our attacker. "You'd better hope you just look like you're made of wood..."

I inhaled, drawing in heat. Woody must have sensed me soaking up the elemental energy. He straightened, easing off my chest, and eyed me curiously. He'd underestimated me. One of these days, the demons would stop making that mistake, then I'd be screwed. But not today. I grabbed my gun, flicked the safety off, aimed, and fired in the time it took Woody to blink. A hole punched through his cheek, cricking his head back. He growled, and swung his stare back to me. I fired again. The gun jumped, and the round smacked into its chest. Another shot. He staggered back, arms flailing, eyes wild. Considering I'd just planted three bullets in his head and chest, he didn't seem all that concerned.

I fired once more for luck. He bumped back against my rental car and let out a roar that barreled down the jam-packed street. Bullets clearly did little more than piss him off. I lifted my free hand and coiled a thread of energy around my fingers. A smile hooked into my lips. A trickle of glee shivered through me, further arousing my demon-half. I flung a bolt of heat at Woody's chest. Fire blanched over him on impact. He wailed like a banshee and ran, slamming into stationary cars and ricocheting off moving ones. My smile died as I saw a member of the public using his cellphone to film the entire screw-up from inside his car. Dammit, Adam would be on my back again.

The remaining pug-faced demon sprang onto the top of my car, denting the roof as he landed on all fours and bellowed a roar loud enough to rattle the car windows. He looked a lot like a gorilla, if they came hairless, sporting forked tongues and blood-soaked eyes. He lifted my boot, waggled it, and launched it at my head with surprising accuracy.

I ducked, swept my left hand in a tight circle, and coiled energy around me. Fire burst into existence, gathered up my arm, and enclosed my hand. I aimed the gun in my right hand, figuring I might as well hit pug-face with all I had. The occupants of the car I was sprawled on gawked through their windshield. At least they weren't filming. I winked, the trickle of glee swelling into something more akin to lust for the hunt.

Pug-face sprang. I lashed out, casting a line of liquid heat, thrusting behind it a rush of energy that slammed into the demon mid-leap. The gunshot cracked the air. The demon lit up like a bonfire and jerked as the bullet punched through his gut. Pug-face landed hard against the side of the car, jolting me and the passengers, then dropped with a dull thud against the road.

Sliding off the hood, I counted two flaming demons sprawled on the road. Black smoke churned skyward. Several onlookers had left their vehicles, but none ventured too close, not while the fires still blazed. I shook off the tingling excitement, retrieved my boot, and made a quick exit. There was only so much damage control I could do, and no amount of bull crap about escaped animals from the zoo was going to mask my very public display of power.

***

It didn't take long to reach Southie on foot. I hadn't been far away when the demons had attacked. In all likelihood, whoever pulled their strings had been watching the main routes around the last known location of their hunters. Whoever it was, they obviously suspected Dawn was in my care. Maybe someone who knew I was connected to Akil?

I walked around the block a few times and took a few random shortcuts, checking over my shoulder for tails. Demons didn't do subtle. They stood out in a crowd simply by trying too hard to be human. They moved with a fluid grace, each step, each gesture, weighed and measured. They stalked like predators fixed on their prey. I wasn't being followed.

By the time I reached my apartment building, my soaked clothes stuck to me, and my hair clung to my face. My back and head ached, muscles tightening as bruises bloomed. Being half demon didn't make me any less squishy. When my demon rode me, I was tough, my human skin and clothes, protected beneath her otherworldly armor of elemental energy. But that's only when I was powered-up. Otherwise, I was just as fragile as everyone else. It was a trait my old owner had enjoyed exploiting. That same owner now pulsed inside me.

I jogged up the steps in my apartment building to my floor and dug into my pocket for my keys.

"Hey, Firecracker."

My stride faltered. Ryder leaned against the wall outside my apartment, looking every inch the returning tomcat. He chewed on a tooth pick, thumbs tucked into his cargo pants pockets. The black shirt might have looked smart on anyone else, but he'd somehow managed to crease it so the cotton resembled crepe paper. Even the creases had creases. He'd grown his hair out since I'd last seen him. Mocha locks scuffed his old-soul-eyes and curled around his stubble-dashed cheeks. He looked older than his mid-thirties, due in part to life's assault on him.

I'd never asked about his past, and he didn't ask about mine, but I had eyes, I'd seen a story on his face, and I'd listened when he thought I wasn't.

"What the hell are you doing here?" I unlocked my apartment door.

"Nice to see you too."

"They're watching." I grumbled, shoving open the door and suggesting he enter with a short hand gesture.

"When aren't they?" He sauntered inside. His shirt bunched around a concealed gun at the small of his back, and I wondered if he was here on business. Ryder looked like something the cat dragged in, but he'd been one of the best Enforcers Boston had until he'd vanished with Stefan.

Closing the door, I tossed my keys on the kitchen counter top. The TV was on. An empty bowl and plate sat on the couch. I checked the bedroom and found Dawn sitting below the window, teasing Jonesy with a thread of cotton. She looked up and acknowledged me with a tight smile. My cat didn't acknowledge my presence, his allegiance decided.

When I turned around, Ryder stood behind me, eyebrow arched. He plucked the toothpick free and pointed it at Dawn. "Whose kid is she?"

"That's what I'm trying to figure out." I eased the door closed and returned to the kitchen to fix myself a coffee. Thick. Black. With a mountain of sugar.

"You look like crap, Muse."

I could trust Ryder not to mince his words. "Thanks." I grabbed two mugs and clattered about my little kitchen. I liked to take my frustrations out on inanimate objects.

"You have blood on your cheek."

I swiped at my face. Ryder mirrored me, indicating I should aim higher. "You shouldn't be here." I peered into the shiny kettle at my reflection, spotted a splatter of demon blood below my eye, licked my thumb, and wiped it off. "If the Institute see you—if they think you're here..." I shook my head. "I've got enough to deal with right now. Speaking of which..." The water in the kettle simmered. Leaning back against the counter, I swept my damp hair off my cheeks. "Is there such as thing as salty rain?"

He managed to simultaneously frown and smile. "How the fuck should I know? Do I look like a weatherman?"

An unexpected pang of loneliness assaulted me before I could chase it away. Damn, I'd missed his surly no-bullshit stance on life. "Dammit, Ryder. Where have you been?"

His slid his gaze away and moseyed around my apartment. "Nice place." It didn't take long before he noticed something on the floor. He crouched down and scratched at the wood grain. Rising, he cleaned the substance from beneath his nail and flicked his gaze back to me. "Make a habit of inviting demons over?"

"Yeah, actually. Wednesdays are movie nights. They bring the snacks." His lopsided grin drew the slither of a smile across my lips. "Ryder, I could have done with you around." I hadn't realized how much he'd meant to me until he'd pulled the vanishing act. Ryder was still technically my handler, and mentor. While he'd reported my progress to the Institute, he'd also taught me how to shoot, where to aim on various demons, and how many f-words you could ram into a single sentence. Since the only other teacher I'd had was Akil, Ryder's no-holds-barred method of teaching had been… enlightening.

He pretended to admire the framed symbols on my walls. "Nah, you're fine. You don't need me. Never did."

I dropped my gaze. He didn't know about my former owner caged inside me. I could never tell him. His loyalties lay with the Institute, and the fact I was compromised wasn't something I wanted Adam knowing. "Are you staying?"

"Can't."

I swallowed an unexpected sadness. When had I become so lonely? "It's Stefan, isn't it?"

Ryder drew in a breath and winced before meeting my gaze. "He ain't doin' so good."

I'd gathered that when he'd turned his workshop into a walk-in freezer. I clenched my jaw and clamped my hands against the edge of the counter top. "When are you leaving?"

"Tonight." He scratched his chin with his thumb, frowning. "Are you in some kinda trouble?"

"Not yet."

He glanced at my closed bedroom door. Dawn's giggles bubbled from behind it. "Shit, Muse. Is Akil still sniffing around?"

"Actually, no. He's MIA."

Ryder's expression darkened as it always did when Akil's name came up. "Tell me what's goin' on."

I told him everything that had happened since Akil had appeared with Dawn. He listened, making the obligatory noises when I mentioned Akil. By the time I'd finished, the frown on his face had turned disapproving. "Don't trust her."

"Dawn?" I scowled. "She's just a little girl."

"A little girl dumped on your door by a Prince of Hell. Whatever he did to get her, it weren't pretty if he was cut up."

I bit back my denial. Ryder was right. As much as I wanted to believe Akil had left her with me for good reasons, there was no denying his absence was suspicious. "She's a half blood, like me."

Ryder nodded. "All the more reason to stay clear. You've been through enough. You don't need to deal with Akil's baggage. Hand her over to the Institute."

A ripple of heat bloomed inside me. I ignored it for the sake of friendship. "How can you say that? You know what they'll do to her, right? You said it yourself once. You know what they did to Stefan. He despises them."

"He hates Adam and what the Institute did to him under his father's orders. There's the difference. She's dangerous—"

"Like I was—"

"Like you all are. Fuck, Muse. I saw you pump a Prince of Hell full of enough power to turn him into something not even demon—something... god-like. I watched you and Stefan go at each other, calling god-knows what from the netherworld, and I've seen what it's done to him. Half bloods are dangerous. Don't try to sell me some crap about control. That lil' girl you got in there..." He jabbed the toothpick at the door. "The safest place for her is behind bars at the Institute."

I placed my coffee very carefully down on the counter. My element pulsed in an unpleasant wave, breaching my control and then receding as I drove it back. "I can't believe I'm hearing this from you." They'd locked me behind bars. Twice. I would have despised them for that even without my history of abuse.

"What if she can call the kind of power you can, huh? What if Akil knows that, and he's left her here to hurt you like a goddamn Trojan horse?"

"He wouldn't. He's different."

Ryder gave me a sharp look. "Don't defend Akil."

I pressed my lips together and ground my teeth. "He really wouldn't hurt me." Was I convincing myself as much as I was Ryder?

"Why? Tell me why he wouldn't screw with you again? You're his weakness. You can drain him dry. You think he wants you walkin' around lordin' that much power over him?"

"You said it yourself. Yeah, I can drain him, and I can feed him more energy than he can handle. In the netherworld, you didn't see what I did. I... I killed a lot of demons, and it changed how he looks at me." I tried not to think about how I'd turned a crowd of demons to ash, mostly because of how I found the memory to be disturbingly comforting.

Ryder blinked, but my revelation only gave him a few seconds pause. "Jesus, Muse. I didn't come here to hear you spout off about Akil's sudden change of heart. He's all demon and a stone-cold killer, or have you forgotten how he murdered your friend? Sword through the chest because the guy was in the way? You saw it, Muse, with your own eyes. You read that blade and saw Akil kill Sam."

A shattering pain sparked across my chest, drawing a hiss from between my teeth. Heady emotions often gave my parasitic owner a waking jab. The guilt I felt over Sam's death provided more than enough emotional fuel.

I pressed my hand over my heart and tried to suck in a breath around the pain. "Get out."

"Sure," Ryder said, mistaking my grimace as one of anger. He headed for the door. "Y'know, I told Stefan you aren't what he thinks." He tugged the door open and glanced back at me. "Don't make a liar out of me."

The second the door closed behind him, I fell against the counter. My trembling arms barely held me up. I couldn't catch my breath. With each throb, the tightness around my heart increased, shortening each gasp until the edges of my vision darkened. I willed myself not to collapse, not with Dawn there. I had to keep it together. But the dark hungered. Echoes of Damien's laughter resounded through my head. I'd stabbed him, torn out his throat, and burned his body from the inside out, and still he'd laughed. My stomach hitched, trying to eject my breakfast and with it the demon rotting away my soul. *Damn him back to hell.*

Ryder burst back into my apartment. "Institute. And they ain't for me." He strode across the lounge, eyes pinched with concern as he saw me struggling to stand upright. "Shit, Muse, what the–"

"I'm fine."

He dug into his pocket and handed me a set of keys and a wad of cash. "Take my car," he said, softer this time, "It's the beat up Mustang parked 'round the back. They'll be tracking yours. Don't use ATM cards. From what you tell me, that lil' girl is too hot to stay here. Get her out of town. Do what you've gotta do."

He squeezed my shoulder. Ryder didn't do physical expression of friendship; this was serious. "What about you?" I found my voice. "They'll take you in."

"They know everything already." His lips twisted as though he'd tasted something foul. "I'll tell 'em I was waitin' for you to come back. I got it covered. Go." He'd been keeping the Institute informed of Stefan's progress. I should have known. I could see the truth in his eyes. He wasn't happy about it, but it was his job, and Ryder was, first and foremost, an Enforcer.

After grabbing Dawn, the three of us hurried out of my apartment and down the hall to the fire exit. I shoved open the door and blinked as the stairwell lights flicked on.

Ryder hung back. "You'd better know what you're doing, Muse."

"Don't tell them." I clutched Dawn's hand in mine. "Don't tell them what's going on. Not yet. Let me figure out how to keep her safe. If I can't, I'll take her in."

Footfalls hammered on the stairs. Ryder frowned but nodded a silent agreement, then dug into another pocket and tossed me a cell phone. "Emergencies only. I'm in the contacts. Call if yah need me." He strode away to face his colleagues.

Beat up were two words for the '66 Mustang. Another couple were: *scrap metal*. Once pale blue, now sporting three rust-red donor car doors, it sat on fat Firestone tires and chipped chrome rims. The interior hadn't fared much better. Embossed ponies galloped over torn leather seats. Knots of loose wires dangled below the dash, and when I turned on the ignition, the dials didn't respond.

I turned the keys and prayed the engine had seen more loving care than the body. The V8 grumbled to life. The car coughed, belched a puff of black smoke, and found its rhythm.

Dawn whimpered in the passenger seat. "Hang on," I told her, catching a glimpse of two Enforcers in the rear-view mirror. I eased the car away from the curb, trying to appear inconspicuous. They noticed us immediately. Both started running. One palmed a gun. The other chinned a cellphone.

Ramming the car into gear, I jammed the throttle open and lurched the Mustang forward. Ryder had taught me a few things about driving fast. We'd often raced each other to demon incursions. I was no street-racer, but I could handle a little excessive speed.

"Put the belt on." Wrenching on the steering wheel, I swung the car onto Dorchester Street. The Mustang loped into lane. Tired suspension gave the car an unhealthy amount of body roll and threatened to break away the rear end. I planted the throttle and accelerated hard. A few cars behind us, a silver Ford Taurus swung out of the side street and carved its way through the light traffic.

"Dammit."

Dawn secured her belt and hunkered down in the passenger seat, her rabbit pulled close.

"It's gonna be fine," I muttered, mostly to myself. By running, I'd already ticked off the Institute. Just as long as they didn't know why I was running, Dawn might stay off their radar. Running was her only chance at a normal life.

At an intersection, I swung the car left, bumping over the uneven road surface and fighting the steering wheel. We sped on, through a roundabout, following Old Colony Avenue. Parked cars choked the roadside, while ahead, a stream of traffic slowed my approach to the expressway. I glanced in the mirror, spotted my tail screeching through the intersection, dropped a gear, and bumped the Mustang over the inlaid stones between the lanes. The car bucked and twitched into oncoming traffic. Dawn let out a squeak. I swung the wheel and peeled back into the correct lane, planting my foot to the floor. With a throaty roar, the Mustang gobbled up the road.

Behind, the gray Ford knotted in traffic. I wove around slower cars. The greenery of Joe Moakley Park opened up to my left, the railway tracks and expressway to the right. Just a few minutes more and we'd be on R93 out of town.

A wall of red tail lights flared ahead. I slammed on the brakes, sensed the car breaking loose, and pumped the pedal to try to control the skid. The fat tires squealed and bellowed smoke. I turned the wheel into the slide, prayed we didn't hit anything, and held my breath. The Mustang rocked to a halt sideways behind the jammed traffic, body panels untouched.

I puffed out a breath. "You okay?"

Dawn chewed her lip and nodded. A squeal of tires snapped my attention back to the road. The incoming Ford slammed on its brakes and attempted to pin us in. I caught a glimpse of the driver. Jenna Sparks. Enforcer. A colleague. We'd traded small talk a few times in the Institute cafeteria. Raven-black hair, cut close against a face too sharp to be considered beautiful. Fine cheekbones, full lips, fearless brown eyes. And she was tenacious as hell.

Ramming the Mustang into reverse, I twisted in my seat, and plowed the car backward off the road. We trundled over a grass median and down onto a slip road.

The undercarriage let out a nasty cry as it scuffed the road. Yanking on the wheel, I swung the Mustang around, so we faced the right direction, and dug around for first gear.

The Taurus bumped over the median after us.

The gears made a mangled, gnarling sound, protesting at the rough handling. I pumped the clutch and forced the stick into gear. Any gear. The Mustang sprang forward, throwing me back into the seat. Engine roaring, we built up some speed. But so did the Ford. As it drew up alongside, I shoved Dawn's head down. "Stay down."

Jenna glared at me through the window. She pointed, suggesting I might like to pull over. Yeah, that wasn't going to happen. I tightened my grip on the steering wheel and rammed the Mustang against her immaculate Ford. Screaming metal-on-metal briefly deafened me. The Ford veered off before coming right back and sideswiping us.

"Hold on!" I locked my hand around the parking brake and tugged. The rear end of the Mustang locked up and swung us sideways, helped by a quick jerk of the wheel. The Ford sailed on. We came to a halt facing the wrong way into oncoming traffic. I found a gear, planted the throttle once more, and played chicken with startled drivers until we burst out onto the Old Colony again, heading back toward my neighborhood.

Taking random turns, pushing the car to its limits, I only slowed when my mirrors were free of Enforcer vehicles. By then, we'd carved up half of South Boston. I'd lost the Institute for now, but they had my scent. I had to get out of the city and fast.

Chapter Seven

We got onto the expressway headed north. "You okay?" I asked Dawn. She hardly moved, just gazed out of the window, shoulders slouched while her thoughts were clearly elsewhere. "It's not always like this."

"Why did we run from them?"

Focusing on the road ahead, I considered how best to describe an international company that controlled and killed demons without terrifying her. "The Institute protects people from demons. They're good at what they do. But if you happen to be a demon, or even half demon, they're not the most friendly bunch."

She fell quiet. I prodded the radio, but like most of the Mustang's instruments, it was dead. As we lost the daylight, I considered my options. Unknown demons wanted Dawn. Akil had left her with me for a reason. I wasn't getting any help from anyone. It was just the girl and me. Ryder believed she was a trap. I couldn't blame him for thinking the worst. Akil was fond of ulterior motives. But Dawn was a half blood. Akil knew I'd understand.

"We're going to one of Akil's houses. I've not been there for a while." Years, in fact. "I... used to live there when I was younger. It's nice. We'll be safe at Blackstone." *Maybe*, I added silently. "Are you hungry?"

She shook her head and leaned against the door. Her mop of curls obscured her face, but I saw her lip quiver and tore my gaze away. What horrors had she seen at the hands of demons? Had she had a succession of owners like me? Did they beat her and violate her?

"Do you want to talk?" I asked carefully.

"No, Muse."

Something behind her voice sounded suspiciously like a warning. I backed off. I hadn't spoken of my past, not in detail, not to anyone. When Damien had returned, I'd told the Institute what they needed to know. Not even Akil knew it all. Demons are nothing if not vicious.

* * *

Akil's rural house was situated in Salem, New Hampshire, a forty-minute drive north of Boston, tucked inside the embrace of an ancient forest, like a fortress behind a barricade of trees. You'd never know Blackstone existed. Elaborate black iron gates designed to look like creeping vines guarded the mile long driveway. I knew every inch of those gates intimately. I'd crafted them. There was a track around the back, if a person was willing to drive another twenty minutes out of her way. The gates were padlocked, as I suspected they would be, so we took the long way around.

Designed by a European architect back in the early 1990's, Blackstone had matured well. Given its forest location, you'd expect to see a sprawling cabin, not the glass-fronted modern structure with its wing-like profile. Built into a slight incline, the split-levels cascaded down to a small lake. As we approached, much of the building's sophisticated design was buried beneath darkness. The Mustang's headlights raked over the stone and timber walls. Dawn eyed the sprawling structure with suspicion.

"Wait here." I left the Mustang. Gravel crunched under my boots as I headed for the side door. None of the lights came on, and besides the whisper of a breeze through the trees, the house and forest were quiet.

I knocked and rang the bell, but I didn't expect an answer. Walking around the double garages, I ventured into the dark around the back of the house and fumbled around a log-pile in the hope the spare key was where it always used to be. I'd been locked out before. Akil regularly disappeared without warning and after I'd spent a night on the doorstep, we'd stashed a key. Shifting logs around, I found it and returned to the side door.

Once inside, I flicked the lights on and entered the alarm code: the date I'd stepped through the veil for the first time and begun my human life. The musty air was cold and still, the big house as empty as a mausoleum. I ventured through each of the rooms, flicking on lights as I went. Sheets covered the furniture. A thick layer of dust coated what had once been smooth granite, polished marble floors, and glass surfaces.

I'd learned how to be human inside Blackstone's walls. My first good memories were forged in the grounds. Dawn would be safe at Blackstone as I had been.

Dawn wandered cautiously through the ground floor while I booted up the heating and security systems. The house was wired up like a bank vault and built with protective elemental symbols etched into the foundations. Discreet CCTV cameras fed images back to a basement control room. Six bedrooms, five bathrooms, three reception rooms, vast kitchen, deck and basement game room. Blackstone was more than enough house for Dawn and me. Too much, I realized, when I tried to find her again.

I eventually located her standing in the lounge, her tiny body dwarfed by the huge black granite fireplace. "Hey."

"This is his home?"

"Akil's? Yes. When he saved me from Damien—my owner, this was where he brought me. It's real nice in daylight. Probably seems a bit daunting right now." I crouched down beside her. Her gaze absorbed the room, eyes curious. "Nobody will find us here. Tomorrow, I'll go into town and grab us some clothes and groceries."

She turned in a slow circle. Her eyes darted as she assessed every inch of the lounge. "Why don't you call him Mammon?"

Because I tried not to associated the two. And Mammon scared the hell out of me. "It's the name he's chosen for when he's in human form. A long time ago, he went by *Ah-keel*. Now he's shortened it. Modernized it, I guess."

"But he's not human."

It wasn't a question, but I confirmed it anyway. "No. Not at all human."

"What are we?"

I smiled warmly. "I like to think of myself as human. But we're half way between demon and human. We're both and neither. We're different and lucky. We get to choose what we want to be."

"I don't feel lucky."

I hesitated, struggling to find the right words. Our gazes met. She patiently waited for me to elaborate. "Dawn, you don't have to tell me anything if you don't want to, but I think I know what you've been through. It's okay. Things will be better now. Akil saved me, and I think he's done the same for you."

"But he's..." Her eyes focused over my shoulder, her gaze distant. "He hurt my owner," she said quietly.

She'd seen him as Mammon. It explained the questions. "He is very dangerous. Don't ever forget that." I might like to heed my own warnings. "Dawn, what was your owner's name?"

"Carol-Anne."

I'd been right. Akil and Carol-Anne had fought. He'd taken Dawn for himself. *Prince of Greed, remember.* Not so long ago, he'd wanted my demon and the power repressed behind my weak human shell. Of course, he'd told me it was all for my benefit. He'd lied. Fifteen years ago, he'd stolen me from my owner just as he'd stolen Dawn from Carol-Anne. It seemed Akil was collecting half bloods.

I watched for any sign the girl was distraught at the memory of Akil killing Carol-Anne, but she blinked innocent eyes up at me with no trace of sorrow, just wide-eyed anticipation. "He set you free."

"Does that mean Akil's my owner now?"

"No." I smiled, forcing back a sudden urge to growl. "Nobody owns you. We don't have to be owned. You've been lied to, Dawn. We're strong—stronger than them." I lowered my voice to a conspiratorial whisper. "We're even more powerful than the princes."

Her eyes widened, and her little mouth parted in a silent 'O'. I smiled and gently squeezed her shoulder.

"But... But... I'm not... I don't..."

"It's okay. I was surprised too. I can help you, Dawn. I think that's why Akil brought you to me. We'll talk some more tomorrow. For now, let's get some rest."

She nodded and hugged her rabbit in the crook of her arm.

Chapter Eight

I shouldn't have taken Dawn to the mall. I doubted my decision the entire way there, while checking the skies for hunters and the rear view mirrors for Institute cars. Yes, it was idiotic, but I understood what it was like to be caged. Returning to Blackstone roused memories of my rebirth as a gangly teenage girl. Akil had opened my eyes to the world. I wanted to do the same for Dawn, even if that meant putting her in danger. Freedom is only mourned by those who no longer have it. Those who've never known it don't have that luxury. She didn't know what she was missing, but I did, and I wasn't keeping it from her for another second.

These were the first days of the rest of her life. Later, I would teach her how to draw from the veil in order to protect herself. She didn't yet have the maturity to handle that much power, but I could show her what it meant to be a half blood. I would teach her how to look out for herself, and maybe, if we were lucky, we'd have some fun.

Salem was a sprawling town with suburban-style residential areas. Dominated by Canobie Lake, it also boasted one of the largest malls in New Hampshire, and that's where we were headed. Parking up at Rockingham Park Mall, I stashed my gun in the glove box, noticing Ryder's phone inside. A text message blinked onscreen. From Stefan.

Answer your phone

As Dawn's wide eyes drank in the sight of the mall, I checked the calls list and found four missed calls from Stefan and one voicemail. I sat back in the driver's seat and humphed a disgruntled noise. Stefan had made it clear he wanted nothing to do with me, and the cellphone was Ryder's. I shouldn't even be poking around his messages... Although he had given me the phone, so technically it wasn't snooping. Right?

I tucked the phone into my pocket and gave Dawn a bright smile. "C'mon, let's shop."

* * *

We didn't have much cash. Ryder had given me enough to survive for a few days, but I was fast eating through that. Once it was gone, bankcards were out of the question. I'd worry about it then. Right now, I had to teach a little girl about retail therapy. Hell knew she could do with the distraction. My first stop had been a new set of clothes for me: jeans and a lightweight V-neck white wool sweater. I'd hastily changed into both, stuffing my blood-splattered clothes back into the bag. I'd also grabbed a charger for Ryder's cell. The pre-weekend crowd had swelled, and I didn't fancy explaining to security why I looked like I'd been in a fight with a mincer. After securing Dawn a Hello Kitty dress more befitting a nine-year-old girl, complete with shoes that fit, we roamed the mall. For fifteen minutes, Dawn stuck to my side, wide eyes darting back and forth, absorbing the crisp white lines, glistening floors, and shining glass. When we arrived at the central staircase, her mouth fell open. Sunlight streamed in through the domed glass ceiling. Her eyes traced the graceful fall of the stairs until the steps flared at our feet like the train of a wedding dress.

"It's a palace." Without taking her eyes off the stairs, she reached up and took my hand. I closed my fingers around hers and felt the feather light touch of a smile lighten my lips. I'd done the right thing in bringing her here. Never mind the risk, it was worth it just to see the wonderment on her face. She said little as we walked, but her eyes glistened like jewels when we passed stores and joined streams of people.

Grande latte in one hand, half a dozen bags in the other, I waited in line to pay for the Krispy Kreme donuts I'd just spent the last five minutes convincing Dawn to try. She still stayed close, but occasionally, she'd break away and dash over to something that had caught her eye.

The tills chimed, and the chatter of the crowd ebbed and flowed around me. My thoughts wandered. Now that Dawn and I could relax, I needed a plan. The Institute suspected I was up to something, but they didn't know about Dawn. That was good. If she stayed at Blackstone, she'd be safe enough. I couldn't stay with her though. I might be able to wring another weeks' vacation out of Adam, citing post-traumatic stress from the garden incident. He'd buy it with suspicion, but he didn't have a choice. That gave me two weeks to figure out why the demons wanted Dawn and how I was going to shake them off our tails. The hunters had been the first wave, but the two demons that attacked me in traffic were smarter. They'd deliberately targeted me. Whoever wanted her had upped their game.

What was so important about Dawn? Half bloods were generally considered worthless abominations. Those not killed at birth were sold to demons further down the pecking order as playthings, curiosities. Only a handful of demons knew the truth about half bloods. Akil was one. A shard of pain twisted in my chest. Damien had been another, but he'd only figured it out with help. Carol-Anne may have known, but she was dead, so I could scratch her off the list of suspects.

The line to pay inched forward. I shuffled my bags around and took a generous sip of latte.

Stefan knew about half bloods, and of course the Institute were the foremost authority on half bloods this side of the veil. They'd studied Stefan like a lab-rat until he'd been old enough and strong enough to tell them where to shove their experiments. But the Institute didn't employ demons, and neither did Stefan.

The only place I could think I might discover something was Carol-Anne's club, The Voodoo Lounge. The club sat at the heart of Boston's demon population.

She must have had acquaintances that could tell me something about Dawn or about why Carol-Anne had visited Akil. I'd met her demon doctor, Jerry a few months before when he'd tried to help me with some control issues. He'd seemed like a fairly reasonable guy, and with Carol-Anne gone, there would be a demon reshuffle in the hierarchy of that neighborhood.

I stepped up to the cashier's desk, digging my hand into my pocket for the cash to pay. A creeping sense of discomfort peeled across my skin, raising the fine hairs on my arms and sprinkling shivers down the nape of my neck. I froze and slowly turned my head. The line behind me consisted of bored shoppers. Someone rattled off a one sided conversation into a phone. A woman had hold of her two toddlers and was laying down the parental law. A man slouched near the back of the line, shifting awkwardly from foot to foot and peeking ahead, eager to get his shopping done.

I scanned further back, along the streams of shoppers flowing back and forth through the store.

"Ma'am?"

"Yeah." I dug out the cash and handed it over. What the shoppers behind me couldn't see was how I eased an elemental touch outward, reaching my senses beyond the apparent in search of the demon that had tripped my internal alarms.

Dawn twitched and swung her head around. I shook my head as she looked as though she might ask me why I'd flicked the demon switch.

Donuts paid for, I scooped up the bag and coffee and ushered Dawn from the store into the mall fairway. I kept walking, eyes scanning the crowd. The demon was here somewhere, and it was powerful. Shivers swept through me, adrenalin aiding my fight or flight response. I could feel its gaze on me, sense its penetrative touch, and a sickening deadweight of dread balled in my stomach. I recognized the touch of power. Fear rolled over me and scattered butterflies low in my stomach.

Dawn's nervous gaze checked mine every few steps. I mustered a smile, but she wasn't buying it.

I shoved by shoppers and wove between loitering groups, trying not to break into a run. A few people muttered in my wake. Hot coffee splashed over my hand, but I barely noticed. My heart thumped in my chest, and my breaths came fast. *Run.* I wanted to. But if the demon I sensed was who I thought it was, then running wasn't going to do a damned thing to save us.

"Muse?"

"It's okay. It's probably nothing." She would feel the touch too, but she might not recognize it as powerful.

I found the food court and planted Dawn at a MacDonald's table close to the wall. I dropped into the chair opposite her, leaned back, and scanned the faces around me. Demons stalk. In a crowd like this one, they could be spotted simply by the way they moved. Seventy percent of human communication is non-verbal. We're constantly in motion. Demons don't understand the intricacies of being human, mostly because they don't spend long enough in their human-suits to care.

I watched the crowd for any sign of someone standing perfectly still or a figure walking toward me, chin down, eyes up, but I couldn't place any demon, and within five minutes, the sickening fear and crawling sensation passed.

I slumped in the chair and closed my eyes. When I reached for my lukewarm coffee, my hand shook.

I'd faced Hellhounds. I'd drained a Prince of Hell of his element. I'd summoned and controlled enough raw elemental energy to level a city. And I regularly tracked demons and bumped them back across the veil, or worse, but very little struck fear into my soul like my brother, Valenti.

"Is it gone?" Dawn asked.

I nodded and eyed her over my coffee. Her flushed cheeks and light fluttering breaths suggested fear, but the look in her eyes didn't. When she smiled, it wasn't the nervous flitter of a smile I'd seen from her before, but a pearly-white grin. There was almost a predatory glean to her expression. She blinked and puffed out a sigh. "That was fun."

Fun? I chuckled. Right. She obviously hadn't met my brother. "We should get back to Blackstone."

Chapter Nine

The drive back to Blackstone was slow going. I threaded my way around various backstreets and roads to nowhere in an attempt to flush out any tails. It wasn't likely to do me much good. Val didn't drive. Such mortal means of transportation were beneath him.

How had he found me? *It might not be Val,* I told myself. Whoever that demon was, he may not even have been there for me. Maybe a demon lived in Salem and fancied a coffee or a new pair of shoes. It could have been a coincidence. Nobody could know I was in Salem. Although if anyone could sense me, it would be Val, as we had the same blood in our veins, courtesy of our father, Asmodeus.

Why would Val be here? Had it been Val? Why didn't he show himself? My brother didn't lurk. He was too proud for that. Had it been Val, he'd have just walked right up to me and said whatever he had to say. No, it couldn't be him.

By the time we returned to Blackstone, I'd convinced myself the phantom demon hadn't been my brother. That didn't stop me from checking the tree line around the driveway and house as I emptied the groceries from the car.

At least inside we were relatively safe. Val couldn't enter the home without an invitation, and even if he got inside, the hidden marks on the walls would prevent him from calling his power. On those terms, I could rest easy.

Dawn broke into a huge grin at the sight of the donuts. She plucked a pink ring donut free and took a generous bite. Her expression exploded with a sugar rush of glee.

"Good, huh? I told you." Shrugging off my jacket, I placed Ryder's cell on the countertop. The lure of the voicemail message called to me. I tapped my nails on the counter and chewed my lip.

Dawn sat at the breakfast table, chewing loudly, licking sugar from her fingers. "Can I have another donut?" she mumbled through a mouthful.

"Sure."

"They are amazing. I've never eaten anything like this. Why are they round?" She continued in a breathless rush of words. "How are they made? They taste like chaos, don't they? What's the hole in the middle for?"

I fell quiet and let her talk. My gaze settled on Ryder's cell. The last conversation I'd had with Stefan replayed in my mind. How had it come to that? Did he hate me? The parasite around my heart twisted. I winced.

Dawn lifted her gaze. "Are you okay?"

"Yeah..." I sighed. "I was thinking about a friend. He's a half blood like us. He taught me what we really are."

"Is he good?"

"Yes." My smile fractured and crumbled away. "I think so."

"Like Akil?"

"Oh, Akil isn't good." I poured some orange juice into a glass. "Y'know, you're right to be wary of Akil. He's a very complicated demon. He tried to hurt me once, but my friend, Stefan, saved me. Stefan... sacrificed a lot for me."

"What happened?"

"He trapped Akil on the other side of the veil. Neither of them could get back." I ran my fingers down the outside of the glass of juice and gathered up beads of condensation. "Time works differently there." Dawn nodded. She understood. "Six months passed, but for him it was more like years, and... he'd changed."

"I don't like it there."

"No, the netherworld is a harsh place to survive in, especially for us." Stefan had spent the equivalent of two years fighting to survive. When he'd stepped through the veil, his control over his demon had been faultless. When he came back, his demon controlled him, and I suspected he liked it. There's a certain freedom that comes when you release the demon. Reason, apprehension, doubts, they all fade away to nothing. It's addictive, that freedom, and it's dangerous. "As half bloods, we are responsible for a great deal of power. If we don't control it, it controls us."

Dawn plucked a donut free of the box and held it up, but her gaze wandered, and her eyes glazed over. "My owner wanted me to release my demon. She said the princes would be pleased."

A jolt of alarm shot through me. "The princes?" *Plural? More than one?* What I knew of them told me they never worked together. Ever.

Dawn nodded and took a bite out of the donut, muffling her next words. "She said I had to keep up with the others. If I was good, I could play with others like me."

"Others? Other half bloods?"

"I wasn't good." Dawn's gaze dropped. "I've never met the others—only you, Muse." She chomped the remainder of her donut and then with a grin asked if she could play with Missus Floppy.

I watched her run from the kitchen, in a hurry to get to her bunny. More half bloods. More princes. "Akil, you son-of-a-bitch, what the hell have you gotten me into?" In the absence of Akil's answers, there was only one other person who could help with a half-blood problem, but Stefan had made it clear what he thought of me.

I scooped up Ryder's cell from the countertop. I had to listen to it. Ryder had given me the phone. Maybe Stefan had been trying to contact me? I dialed the voicemail. *"Ryder, hey man, where are you? The workshop is empty. Muse was there..."* Stefan paused. Was that a growl? When he continued, his voice had gained a jagged edge. *"I thought it would be easier. You were right. I can't do this. I need... Just call me."*

I replayed the message. Definitely a growl. He still had the demon brogue, a deeply gruff accent from his time in the netherworld. It hadn't been so apparent when I'd seen him at the workshop. He'd deliberately hidden it from me.

I lowered the cell and glared at it before scrolling through Ryder's contacts, breezing past Ryder's Spare—which I assumed would be the cell Ryder had on him—and hovered my thumb over Stefan's number. I suspected I knew how this call was going to go. It would be awkward, stilted, and painful. He'd tell me to get lost. He clearly didn't want anything to do with me. But I couldn't give up on him. We needed to talk. There was a time I'd have told him anything, and although it had been brief, our time together had meant something. He'd said the same, right before accusing me of plotting with Akil. Surely, if I could just get him to listen... If we could get past all the horror, which had somehow drowned us both...

My thumb twitched over the call button. He'd cleaned out the workshop. He'd told me not to contact him. *I'm sorry we met.* I clenched my jaw and ground my teeth. He believed I was his enemy.

I jabbed Stefan's number. The cell rang twice.

"Ryder, get your ass back here—"

"Stefan."

A brittle silence snapped down the line. For a second, I thought he'd hung up.

"Muse." He said my name slowly, as though savoring it. I heard humor in his voice and something else, something rich and heady like hunger. I shivered and heard his audible intake of breath. "Why do you have Ryder's cell?" The hunger had gone. His voice was flat. Cold. Controlled.

"We need to talk."

"I've said everything I need to say."

"Then shut up, and let me talk." I tapped my nails on the counter. "I just—"

"Where's Ryder?"

"At the Institute probably."

Stefan muttered a curse. "Why do you have his cell?"

"He helped me ditch the Institute."

"Why do you need to ditch them?"

"Can we talk?"

"What are we doing now?"

"This isn't talking," I grumbled. "It's an interrogation."

"What do you think is going to happen, Muse? That you're going to explain what you did and everything will go back to the way it was before?" The demon slur crept into his words, deepening his voice with a touch of power. "Nothing you can say will change the past. If you need someone to talk to, why don't you run back to Akil? I'm sure he'll welcome you with open arms."

"Stefan." I swallowed back the urge to scream at him. "I get that you're grieving, okay. But this isn't my fault."

He barked a laugh. "You're joking, right?"

I curled my fingers into my palm and clenched my hand into a fist. "What happened to us? I thought..." I drew in a deep breath. "I never wanted to hurt you."

"Then we're even. Get over it. Don't call me again."

"Stefan, wait. Can we meet? Please."

He fell quiet. I listened hard. Had he hung up?

"You know where I am. You've always known." He ended the call.

I threw the phone onto the counter and planted my hands either side of it. Goosebumps sprinkled up my arms. A trickle of power bloomed inside me, responding to the sudden chill in the air.

Of course I knew where he was. I'd always suspected he'd be at the lake house, tucked away in the White Mountains a few hours drive north of Boston. I should have gone to him. I told myself I'd give him time. It had been two months. But time wasn't going to change anything. I knew that now. The longer this went on, the further apart we'd drift.

I straightened and glanced down the hall. Dawn was chatting to her bunny somewhere. I could hear her delicate, one-sided conversation.

I didn't want her to see how jaded Stefan was. She needed time away from demons to start building a life. I wasn't even sure Stefan would help her. For me, he wouldn't. Ryder would turn her over to the Institute. He'd made that clear. Akil had abandoned her with me. I was her only chance at freedom, and I would have to help her alone. I needed more information. Carol-Anne was the key. Someone at her club must know about Dawn. Tomorrow, I was going back to Boston.

Chapter Ten

"Don't open the door for anyone. Don't go outside. Don't worry if I'm not back by the time it gets dark. I've left some games out for you. Don't stick your fingers in any sockets." I stood at the door, car keys in hand. Dawn had nodded dutifully to everything I'd said, but to be sure, I repeated, "Don't go outside." As long as she stayed inside, Val or any other higher demon couldn't get to her.

"I won't. Promise." She grinned. "Cross my heart, and hope to die. Bake a demon in a pie."

Good girl. She was learning.

I left her alone at Blackstone and felt the first inkling of what it might be like to be a parent. The worry. Dawn seemed so small and the world so intent on harming her. I didn't know a damned thing about bringing up kids. It's not something I'd ever thought about. As far as I knew, I couldn't have kids. Being half demon wrecked the necessary plumbing. But when I left Dawn all alone at Blackstone, the concern nearly had me turning around again and abandoning my visit to The Voodoo Lounge.

The drive back to Boston didn't take long, despite my lane-swapping and erratic driving to check if I was being followed.

Carol-Anne's club, The Voodoo Lounge, was closed until further notice according to the sign on the door. I left the car in the club's parking lot and walked the block to Jerry's veterinary clinic. The walk gave me enough time to clear my head and to think like an Enforcer. Jerry knew

Carol-Anne. She'd referred to Jerry as *her* property. *He must know something of use.*

A few minutes later, I sat in Jerry's waiting room between a Siberian husky with a cone collar and a poodle with a bandaged paw. The potent odor of antiseptic tickled my nose, but it didn't mask the scents of dogs, cats, sawdust, and urine. The floor squeaked under the assistants' feet.

Jerry stalked through a back door behind the reception desk like death arriving at a wake. Did I imagine the animals falling silent? A cat hissed from behind me. I caught a glimmer of recognition in Jerry's gaze when he saw me. Towering over every other person in the room, he had to duck through doorways. His obscenely taut muscles strained against his shirt, but his tattoos were his most striking feature. The all-black interwoven anti-elemental symbols covered his face, arms, and I assumed they smothered the rest of him. They reminded me of New Zealand Maori tattoos. He'd told me once the tats kept him safe from demons. Combine the daunting tattoos, his size, the deep voice he dragged up from the depths of his soul, and he could make babies cry at ten paces.

Apparently though, he was the go-to guy for pet problems.

Jerry left the room a moment later, and the animals resumed their fidgeting. A nurse handed me a note telling me to meet him around the back in twenty minutes.

Discarded couch cushions, trashcans and fast-food bags choked the alley behind the clinic. Gulls keened overhead, and the Boston traffic hummed in the background as I waited for Jerry to emerge.

"I don't know anything," Jerry said by way of hello as he opened the back door. His bass voice rumbled around the alley. He closed the door and folded his arms, creating a wall of stubborn masculinity.

"C'mon, Jerry. Help me out." I gave him my most beguiling big eyes routine, but his flat expression didn't change.

"I already told the Institute what I know. I don't want you hanging around here, Muse. It's bad for business." He didn't mean the pedigrees inside the clinic.

Okay, time to cut the crap. "Why did Carol-Anne meet with Akil?"

Jerry ran a hand over his buzz cut hair. He sported more hair from the stubble on his chin than the hair on his head. "Is this on the record?"

I didn't answer immediately. If I pulled the Enforcer card, I could threaten to take him back to the HQ, and that was something he would avoid at all costs. Demon doctors had reputations to uphold, and it wouldn't do for him to be seen hand in hand—or in cuffs—with the Institute. But I liked Jerry. Hell knew why. I didn't want to lie to him.

"No, this is me asking because Akil has dumped me in the crap, and I'm trying to dig my way out of it."

Jerry narrowed his eyes, scrutinizing me for weaknesses. "She had a visit from a prince, the one that can't decide if he's a guy or a gal."

Oh hell, that was Leviathan. He liked to appear as male or female, often altering his appearance and gender from one moment to the next in a deliberate attempt to unbalance those around him. I locked my expression down. "When?"

"Three nights ago. Demon chatter spooked my clients. When the princes come out to play, the little guys run for the hills."

"What did he want?"

Jerry's shoulders bobbed in a shrug. "He'd come to collect something. Before you ask, no, I don't know what it was. Carol-Anne was nervous—a good nervous. Being one of his subjects, she jumped at any chance to please him. Water finds its way to water, right?"

I only knew of Levi because he'd tried to take me back to the netherworld. To my father. As it stood, I was on borrowed time. "Did you tell the Institute this?"

"Yeah, they were fishing for something juicy, so I gave it to them. There's nothing they can do anyway."

"Well, no, but Carol-Anne was found dead in Akil's apartment. They've been gunning for Akil for years. If they can prove he's broken human laws, they'll use it as an excuse to pool their resources and force him out of Boston."

A grin creased the tattoos around his mouth. "I'd pay to see that show."

Yeah, I worked for the Institute and doubted their abilities in a straight fight with a Prince of Hell. "Lucky for Akil, murdering another demon isn't against the law. Yet." Not that any prison could hold him.

"Are you sure Akil killed Carol-Anne?" One of Jerry's dark eyebrows quirked.

"I saw the crime scene. There wasn't any sign of a third person present, demon or otherwise, but no, I'm not sure about anything right now."

"So what's the crap he's dumped you in?"

I wondered how much to tell him. I could trust Jerry about as far as I could throw him. "Did Carol-Anne spend much time in the netherworld?"

"Not as much as most. She's like Akil. She *was like* Akil. Damn, I know you didn't like her, but she wasn't all bad, y'know, for a demon." Jerry leaned back against the wall. "She kept the trouble-makers out of town and made sure those who came through were at least capable of living this side of the veil."

"She aided the demon immigrants?"

"Yeah. You know what it's like. They don't just turn up on this side of the veil and walk into human lives. They need help blending in. Carol-Anne was a big part of that."

Maybe she helped half bloods too. "Is there anyone she worked with who might have a grudge against her? Someone who might want her out the way?"

"Demons? No. They needed her. People? Maybe. Ever since Akil came out as all-demon, folks around here have started asking questions, pointing fingers. The streets aren't safe for demons right now. I heard talk of a vigilante group—"

"Did you ever see a little girl with her? About eight or nine years old?"

Jerry didn't move. He breathed and blinked, but otherwise, he tried exceptionally hard not to give himself away. I waited.

"Maybe. Her niece or cousin or something."

"When we first met, you told me you'd only ever seen one half blood before, a man so ruined that even you couldn't save him. Was that true?"

He sighed. "Carol-Anne brought him to me. Poor bastard. I did what I could..."

"Why did Carol-Anne have a half-dead half blood?"

He dragged a hand across his chin and cast his gaze skyward. "Y'know, I don't ask questions of demons. That's how I've survived this long. I just patch 'em up and send them on their way."

"That's the only other half blood you've seen besides me?"

He met my gaze for a few beats and didn't say anything. "I'd love to help you, Muse. I would. I like you, even though your ice-cold friend turned my place into Santa's grotto. How is he, by the way? I saw what happened at the gardens, heard a few things on the grapevine afterward..."

"As far as I know, he's fine. I haven't seen him."

"Tricky things, half bloods." He shoved off the wall and opened the back door to his clinic. "Take care of yourself, Muse. I know one thing. If there are princes involved, you should stay out of their way." Jerry's smile softened his hard-as-nails persona.

"I wish I could." I smiled my own half-hearted smile. "Maybe they should stay outta my way?"

He chuckled, the sound of his laughter soft and delicious. "Maybe."

Chapter Eleven

The weather turned during the trip back to Salem. Blue October skies dulled to a dirty gray, and the wind blustered enough to sweep fallen leaves across Blackstone's driveway. I climbed from the Mustang and took a moment to check my Pico handgun before tucking it neatly in its holster. The wind whipped my hair about my face. As soon as I lifted my gaze, an elemental touch crept around my ankle and coiled up my leg.

It wasn't a touch I recognized, but it was demon, and that could not be a good thing. I closed the car door, kept my hands free at my sides, and walked calmly toward the house. Each step that made contact with the gravel brought with it another explorative touch. I couldn't see elemental energy unless I summoned my demon, but I could feel it. Each elemental touch varies depending on the demon. Like a handshake. But this one was different. The element was different. It didn't have the tingle of ice or the warmth of fire. Nor did it have the smooth sensation of water. The more it probed, the more my skin crawled. Whatever element it was, it tripped my human senses into fight or flight mode.

I reached out a hand for the door handle, and the metaphysical touch of fire skittered down my back. My skin prickled, and my chest tightened. *That* touch, I knew.

"Sister."

I gasped and clutched at the door handle, safety so close.

"Face me while I address you." His voice was rich with so much power he could whisper and silence a room.

Self-preservation screamed at me to dash inside, slam the door in his face and hide, but he was as fast as wildfire. He'd be on me as soon as my human body broadcast my intentions. It took every molecule of courage I possessed to turn and face my brother. He stood a few strides away, rapier pointed against Jenna's back. The Enforcer's wide blue eyes pleaded. She was on her knees, hands bound behind her back, mouth gagged with a strip of leather. She wasn't escaping, and from the panic in her eyes, she knew it.

Val's thin lips flirted with his perpetual smile that never quite made it to his molten silver eyes. He was adorned in various snug-fitting leathers—likely skinned from demons by his own hand. I counted two daggers sheathed inside his long, demon-skin coat. He'd have more concealed on him.

The wind tugged at the long braid of white hair cast over one shoulder and mussed his snow-white bangs. His eyes locked on me, rooting me to the earth. If I looked into his eyes long enough, I'd feel the touch of his element crawling inside me. Both born of fire, we shared the same blood. The same prince was our father. I'd always feared Val knew me better than I knew myself. When he looked upon me, it was always with disdain, as though he'd searched my soul and found me wanting.

I pinched my lips together and drew in air through my nose. "Alright." My fingers twitched at my sides. "Let's talk."

"Call the half blood to you."

I swallowed. "What half blood?"

Val's fine eyebrows furrowed. "Muse..." He jabbed the tip of the sword into Jenna's back. She grunted and arched away from the point of the blade. "I have no qualms when it comes to killing humans. This female serves a purpose. She lives because you have something I require. Hand over the half blood, and I shall release this *Enforcer.*" He spat the word *Enforcer*, disgusted that such a word should pass his lips.

I made the slightest of movements to reach for my gun when Val's eyebrow arched. I froze my hand. He observed with detached interest: a predator looking down from the top of the food chain. None of this mattered to him. It was merely a way to pass the time. His face held no hint of emotion, and despite the hint of a smile, he wasn't amused. Just indifferent. We were all ants to him, insignificant and fleeting.

But I had something he wanted, and as long as Dawn stayed inside, he couldn't get to her.

He stood statuesque against a gust of wind, hair and coat flailing. "Your options are slim. I kill the Enforcer. I kill you. I wait for the half blood to come out. I have an eternity of patience at my disposal. Or you call her, she leaves with me, and you and this female walk away."

"Why do you want her? I thought you were in the business of selling half bloods, not collecting them." The venom in my words surprised even me. "What's Dawn to you? Why do you even care what happens to her? You've never cared for anything, especially half bloods."

"Care?" he scoffed. "Is that what you believe me here for?" He tilted his head a degree and smiled. "You are a remarkable fool."

My heart thumped so loudly I was sure he could hear it. The pulsing pollutant inside me twisted and writhed. Gritting my teeth didn't subdue it, but I refused to show Val how screwed up I was. I could still draw from the veil and potentially drain him the way I had Akil, but not before he ran Jenna through.

"Thinking of draining me like you did Mammon?" A single eyebrow ticked as he caught me flinching. "Yes, I am aware of your talents. Very little surprises me."

"Must be dull."

His fine eyes narrowed. "If you attempt to siphon my element, I will end this miserable human's existence and savor your subsequent death. Think carefully, Muse. The half-blood girl is nothing to you."

"But she is to you." Why would Val want her? What was I missing? My fingers tingled with the electric dance of energy. I wanted to summon my element, pluck it right out of him and drain him of every last drop. If I could do it to a prince, surely I could do it to my brother.

"I am her custodian. She belongs to another. You are in my way."

"Carol-Anne, her owner, is dead."

"I will not explain my actions to the likes of you. Call her out, and I will let you live."

He could kill me. He wanted to. My brother's beautiful eyes sparkled with the knowledge of a hundred ways he'd end my life. He would have calculated how long it would take to run Jenna through and cross the distance between us. I could run, but he was faster. I could summon my element, but he'd be on me the second I flicked the demon switch in my mind. He already knew I was flirting with power. He'd feel the heat shifting in the earth beneath us. That sword of his would find a home in my chest before I could blink.

"Does our father, Asmodeus, know you're doing this?"

Val tensed. His amusement fizzled away, leaving his expression stone cold. "His name upon your lips insults him. You are not worthy."

"Why? Does it bug you, Brother, that we share the same blood?"

He threw Jenna face down on the dirt and planted a boot on her back, pinning her. She let out a muffled cry that he quickly silenced with the point of his sword against the back of her neck. A gust of wind rippled his coat and teased through his hair. He looked every part the netherworldly brother who had stalked my dreams since my childhood. He had sold me to the demons. He was the one who orchestrated my life of slavery. It all started with him. That knowledge helped steel me.

"Forget Jenna. Kill me. That's what you want. That's what you've always wanted. My life offends you. It must be even worse now that Asmodeus wants me..." A thought brightened my fear-addled mind, realization widening my eyes. "Ah, you can't kill me, can you? *Father* wants me alive."

Val's pale face contorted in a manner that no human face could mimic. His cheeks hollowed, jaw lengthening, eyes sinking as his glare gathered shadows. A snarl rolled leisurely across his lips. His disgust for me was evident in that ripple of his lips. I'd always known he hated me, but the magnitude of revulsion on his face stoked my natural fear. He shoved back, away from Jenna, and lowered the sword to his side. "The very fact I must converse with you is beneath me. I would prefer to run my sword through your pitiful flesh and be done with you."

At least I knew I was right. I snickered. "You have to share Asmodeus's affection with a half blood. Ouch. I bet that's dented your rep back home, huh?"

"Affection?" He spat. "Your ignorance insults me." Val's outline blurred. I blinked, trying to refocus, but it wasn't my eyes fooling me. He was changing, revealing his true form. Snarling lips rippled over crescent fangs. Vast, glossy black wings burst from his back and arched either side of him, reaching out to enclose us like the night closing in. His clothes fizzled away, revealing moon white skin and hair in perfect contrast to those midnight wings.

I thrust my demon into my body and took a step forward. Watching through demon eyes, I witnessed the full glory of my demon brother. He appeared more human than most full-blood demons, more human than me in all my demon glory, a trait that should have rendered him weak among his own kind. His defined immortal body glowed from within, turning him into a terrifying yet awe-inspiring beacon of power. His power swelled in the air—not just the element we shared, but something more potent. Raw chaos energy. It pressed against my skin and slid across my tongue while I breathed it in. His presence filled a space bigger than the driveway. He was everywhere, reaching through me, around me. Jesus, he wasn't just any demon, he was the firstborn son of Asmodeus, and I was out of my league.

He hunched low, spread his sleek wings wide, and hissed.

My breath caught. My fire spluttered. I was nothing next to him. He was immortal. Ancient. And I'd seriously pissed him off.

A gunshot shattered my trance. Val flinched and recoiled, distracted by the splash of blood burning crimson on his milk-white chest. He skewered Jenna with his blazing glare. She must have worked her restraints free, because she had a gun cupped in both hands, aimed squarely at his chest. He moved faster than I could track, morphing into a blur of black wings and tumultuous energy. He threw Jenna down against the hood of the Mustang and loomed over her. She struggled to bring the gun down between them. He let her writhe for a few seconds, a slither of delight lifting his lips, before he clamped her wrist against the hood of the car behind her and grinned into her face. She instantly stopped fighting. Her eyes widened, and her lips parted. Her whole body slumped as though the steel I'd seen in her had melted away. Her tongue darted across her lips. That wasn't defiance in her eyes. Desire simmered there now.

I launched myself at him. He couldn't kill me. I had the advantage. At least in theory.

Val didn't even look up. His dark wings swept back, corralling me into their embrace. The second their duck-down softness touched the fire of my flesh, the fight drained out of me. I dropped to my knees, smothered in a warm, comforting darkness. Sleep suddenly seemed like the best idea I'd had in days. I yearned to close my eyes, curl up in the caress of his wings, and drift in an ocean of black.

The parasite on my heart pulsed. I jerked. It's poison inside my soul leeched outward, wrapping around my limbs and bleeding strength into numb muscles. I gulped a lungful of cloying power-ridden air and summoned fire. Heat devoured my flesh, broke over me, and spilled outward in a hungry wave.

Only when Val's wings opened and released me could I see again. He turned, swept his wings behind him, and lunged. His shoulder hit me square in the chest. I let out a grunt and tried to twist away, but he clutched my arms, and we both tumbled to the ground. He fell on me, crouching like an animal prowling up its fallen kill, wings high above him. The wind whipped his hair about his face. His eyes burned with a light so white, it almost appeared fragile. I knew I should be fighting him, but my body didn't want to obey the mental screams to hit the bastard with everything I had.

He smiled a true smile, not the ghost-like smiles he's favored me with before. This was real. It was wicked. Divine. Delicious.

He leaned in so that his terrible eyes were all I could see. "Sister..."

His voice plucked desire from my depths and summoned it to the surface of my flesh where it flushed across my skin. No, this wasn't right... He lowered himself against me. Where his fevered demon skin met the lava-veins of mine, a static blast of power scattered through me. I bucked and twitched, fighting, recoiling, wanting, but not wanting. I shoved at him then sunk my fingers into his shoulders and pulled him against me. He was doing this to me. I didn't desire him. I couldn't stand to be within two feet of him. I was scared of him. Of everything about him. He terrified the broken little girl who cowered inside of me. Oh, but I wanted his wings around me. To feel him ease inside me and fill me up until I came crying his name.

My lips tingled. The urge to taste him, to ease my swollen lips, pushed at my denials. Need pulsed between my legs.

"Half-blood filth..." he whispered into my ear. His lips brushed my skin, feather-light. "I have you. I may not be permitted to kill you, but there are other pursuits worse than death, as you are aware. I will make you beg for more. Only when I am the air you breathe, the thoughts in your mind, the sensation embracing your skin, will I discard you."

No-No! My eyes fluttered closed. I was drowning in him and had no hope of escaping the weight of power pushing into my pores and suffocating my thoughts. The dark inside burned through my veins, but it wasn't enough. I wasn't demon enough to beat my brother.

"Muse...?" Dawn.

I turned my head and saw her standing by the back door of the house. Her rabbit hung limp by her side. Her ringlets bobbed around her head. Then Val's wing came down, and I couldn't see anything but the embrace of darkness. It felt like home.

Chapter Twelve

Cold water thrown in your face must be one of the most unpleasant ways to wake up. The splash shocked me like a jolt of electricity. I sat bolt upright. My demon immediately tried to burst from my skin but instead butted up against it. Where the hell was I?

Jenna planted a hand on her hip and glared down at me.

My cheek stung. Had she hit me too?

"Good. I thought you were never going to wake up." She glanced about us, prompting me to do the same.

We were in the lounge at Blackstone. "Dawn?" I shoved off the couch and managed two steps before my vision flooded with black. I fell back into the couch and blinked my vision clear. My head throbbed, and my stomach rolled.

"If Dawn's the little girl, she's gone. The demon took her."

Rubbing my temples, I groaned. "When?"

"Hours ago. You've been out cold most of the night."

Val took her back to the netherworld. I promised to protect her, and failed. I sunk my hands into my hair and spat out a curse. "I have to go after her."

Jenna rolled her eyes. "Yeah, well, better you than me. That's one demon I don't want to see again unless he's stone cold dead." A dash of color touched her cheeks, and considering she had a healthy bronze glow to her skin, it took a lot for her to blush. She licked her lips and skewed a glance at me. We shared a flicker of recognition. She'd felt his power too. "What is he?" she asked, a hint of reverence lifting her voice.

"I have no idea. I thought he was like me. All hellfire. But he's not..." He had heat. He blazed white with an abundance of it, but he also messed with my head on a level I didn't even want to acknowledge. He wielded a different kind of heat. A body of heat. The heat of wanton desire. I recalled, in gut-churning precision, the touch of his nakedness, and it felt wrong, so very wrong, but my body didn't think so. Holy hell, I'd lusted after my own brother. Saliva pooled in my mouth. My empty stomach flipped at the thought of what might have happened. I growled, disgusted and appalled with myself. "Did he do... anything to me?"

Jenna's brown eyes met mine with a peculiar fierceness. Her brow tightened, and her lips pressed closed. "No. He fled with the girl."

"Val is a full-blood demon. He's Asmodeus' son," I said softly, remembering Stefan's words. "Asmodeus is the Prince of Lust." Of course Val would screw with my head. It was in his DNA. It wouldn't have been so bad if I didn't actually *want* to experience his touch all over again. How could my own body betray my mind? I'd lusted after my brother, and by the look on Jenna's face, so had she. "Are you okay?"

She'd glazed over, focused on a spot somewhere beyond the lounge windows. "Yeah..." Running a hand back through her hair, she shook herself, and met my gaze. "Thanks to you. If you hadn't jumped him when you did, I'd have let him do anything to me right there on the car." She grimaced and turned away. Jenna was a fighter. I'd seen her take down demons twice her size with roundhouse kicks and short, sharp jabs. She was an imposing figure and a damn good Enforcer. Val'd had her salivating at his feet in seconds.

"You're lucky to be alive." So was I. It was only the ominous, if distant, presence of my father that prevented Val from killing me. If a demon as powerful as Val was concerned with adhering to the wishes of our father, just how bad was Daddy-dearest?

Jenna drew in a deep breath and nodded. "So what now, Muse?" She plucked her gun from inside her coat and checked the chamber. "I need to report this to the Institute." Ejecting the magazine, she gave it a once-over and rammed it home again.

I winced. There was no way I could stop her from talking, short of tying her up.

She took my delay to reply as her cue to explain. "I followed you up here. Your brother caught me watching you at the mall." She licked her lips again and wiped a hand across her mouth. "The Institute knows I'm here. If I don't check in, they'll send a team."

Akil would already be pissed that Enforcers had crawled over every inch of his Boston apartment. If I brought them to Blackstone, he'd probably send the Hellhounds after me.

"Okay. Alright. I just need... some time." Val followed Jenna here from Boston. I was sure of it. He couldn't have found Dawn or me hidden inside Blackstone's walls, so he'd tracked Jenna after she'd tried to tail me. Maybe I should have listened to Ryder. Had I handed Dawn over to the Institute, at least she'd be on this side of the veil. She'd have a chance. In the netherworld, where Val had surely taken her, they'd tear her apart and remake her into something damaged beyond repair.

"You wanna tell me what's going on?" Jenna asked stiffly. "Why you ran from us in Boston? Who the girl is? What you're hiding?"

I didn't have much choice now. I'd lost Dawn. I had to get her back. Could I go to the netherworld and face my brother alone? I wasn't a coward, but I did have some sense of self-preservation. And even if I got her back, what then? Val would come after me. I didn't relish the idea of another family reunion. I needed help. "Stick around, and you'll get your answers. I have to summon a Prince of Hell. Wanna help?"

Jenna looked at me as though she wasn't sure if she'd heard me right. "Don't do things by halves, do you Muse?"

"Not anymore." I grinned.

Chapter Thirteen

I glued a candle to a salad plate, using its own molten wax to stick it fast, and placed it on the floor in the center of the lounge. We'd pushed the furniture up against the walls, giving me plenty of space to work.

Jenna handed me a kitchen knife. "You've done this before?" She swallowed with an audible click, wiped her hands on her leggings, and stepped back.

"Summoned a demon? Yeah, a few times. I've never summoned a prince though."

"You think he'll tell you about Dawn?"

Crouched beside the candle, I dragged the sharp edge of the knife across my palm, wincing as it stung. Blood pooled inside my clenched hand and dripped onto the plate. "Maybe. I don't know. We'll see. Stay back. I don't know how he'll react to you. Don't say or do anything unless I tell you to."

She backed up against the wall. "What if it goes wrong?"

Her voice quivered. She was afraid, and so she should be. The princes were formidable, myth-like nightmares. Few this side of the veil had ever seen one. Fearing the Seven Princes of Hell was healthy. She didn't know I'd given up being afraid of Akil, that he needed me to pump him full of power and I needed him to free me of the demon consuming my soul. We had a mutually beneficial relationship. "I can control him."

"Yeah, but what if..."

"If it goes wrong, blow out the candle. With the focal point gone, there's nothing to anchor him here."

"And he can't go full-demon on us, right?" Seeing her haunted wide-eyed look, I began to doubt having her here was a good idea. "We tried to summon a high ranking demon once at the Institute. It was a bloodbath. If he's, y'know, all demon, he might try to– " Her hand hovered over her sidearm.

"Not with the symbols in these walls. He'll just be Akil. Relax, Jenna, you're making me nervous."

I turned my attention to the candle and watched the flame writhe on its wick. "Mammon, One of The Seven, a First, Prince of Greed, Guardian of the Dark, Son of Chaos, *Master of Lies*," —my own addition–he'd earned it— "I, Muse, invite you to share with me this place and time. You will not harm me. By our element, I summon you."

The air trembled. An electric thrum of energy danced around us, invisible, but distinct enough to vibrate against my skin. I straightened slowly and glanced behind me. I'd been caught out before. It was daylight outside, but inside, the shadows lengthened, crawled up the walls, and consumed the light, plunging us into shades of gray. This was new.

Jenna caught my eye. I gave her a reassuring nod. She stood still, breathing slowly, waiting.

The electric charge strumming the air tightened across my skin. The fine hairs on my arms and down my neck prickled. He was coming. I swallowed. I wasn't afraid. He'd be pissed I'd summoned him, especially in front of a witness. Well, he'd have to swallow his pride. I'd had enough of fishing for answers to questions I didn't understand. It was time for him to tell me the truth.

Reality peeled apart in front of me, opening a jagged tear between this world and the netherworld. A blast of superheated energy rolled over me. I staggered back and shielded my face. When it passed, Mammon knelt on one knee in the center of the room. Horned head bowed, he held his leathery multi-jointed wings extended, their tips brushing the walls. Dust rained from his obsidian body.

His corded muscles shimmered with a slick layer of energy. Darkness throbbed around him, remnants of the netherworld air clinging to its prince.

Shit. I hadn't expected him to appear as a demon. Say what you will about demons, but they know how to make an entrance. This was his house. Perhaps he'd rigged it so only he could summon his power inside the walls.

Mammon lifted his head. His eyes swirled like pools of lava. Red embers fizzled across his cheeks and skittered across his square jaw before settling beneath his skin. He pulsed with fire, veins throbbing red. Sweltering heat poured off him and over me. Perspiration beaded at my hairline. I wondered how Jenna was holding up but dared not look away. Looking away would be a sign of submission.

"Blackstone..." His coarse voice resonated, grumbling around the room and through my thoughts. "You brought her here..." Those fire-filled eyes narrowed on me. I didn't have a hope of reading his expression. His face resembled a human man's but hardened and exaggerated, as though carved from black granite.

"Mammon." I inclined my head. It wouldn't hurt to offer some respect.

His head jerked. He sniffed the air and swung his head to the side. Jenna stood perfectly still, hands flattened against the wall. Mammon's rumbling laughter filled the room. She cringed, but stood firm. Jenna wasn't the type to run. If she did run, Mammon would likely lunge for her. He dragged his gaze back to me and finally straightened. His chest glistened with blood. Streams of it ran down his thighs and pooled at his feet.

He grunted, acknowledging what I'd seen, and then shook himself all over, beating his wings. Hot ash blasted my face. I hissed and buried my face beneath the crook of my arm. Only when the heat passed could I look up. He'd hunkered down. His immense body trembled. His flesh tore open, rippling and contorting. Chaos energy licked over me, tugging on my demon. Mammon's presence faded, and Akil fell forward, naked and bleeding, landing on his hands and knees.

I dashed to his side and dropped to my knees. "What happened?" He rolled his eyes up to me. I cupped his cheek in my hand. He leaned against my touch, seeking comfort. "Akil... please... Tell me what's happening." He shivered, teeth clenched. Jesus, who had done this to him? I pulled him close and cradled his head against my chest.

"Did you do the right thing by the girl?" he growled.

I brushed tendrils of his blood-soaked hair away from his face. "I lost her. Val has her." He closed his eyes and shuddered. I pulled him against me. "Dammit, Akil. Tell me what's happening." I couldn't even summon my own power to help heal him. The marks in the walls prevented it. I tried anyway, but my demon pushed against my skin, unable to break free.

"Find her."

"I will. What does Val want with her?" I closed my arms around him and listened to his ragged breathing. The metallic odor of blood and the burned rubber smell of the netherworld burned my nose and throat.

"She is too powerful." Pain wracked him. He jolted in my arms, teeth locked. "You must get her away from your brother. He will deliver her to Levi."

"I will..." I stroked my hand down his arm and felt him wince. "Who's doing this to you?" He tensed, his muscles turning to stone in my arms. His voice was failing, fading in and out. I clasped my hands on his cheeks and searched his half-closed eyes. "Akil, stay awake. Who's hurting you?"

"Levi..." His eyes closed.

"Akil..." He fell limp in my arms, but he breathed. He wasn't dead. Not yet. If his vessel died, Akil as I knew him would be gone. Mammon would craft himself another avatar, but he wouldn't be Akil. I'd lose him. I needed him to get Damien out of me. I needed him, dammit.

"Muse, the candle..." Jenna approached.

The little candle flame flickered, as though disturbed. It twisted and writhed on its wick and then, with one final splutter, snuffed out. Immediately, Akil's weight lifted. His body dissolved right there on my lap. He just misted away to nothing. I snatched at my own breath and pressed a hand to my chest where the parasite throbbed around my heart. Akil was dying. Val had Dawn. Levi was torturing Akil, likely for information on Dawn's whereabouts. I couldn't save them both alone. I needed help. I needed the smartest, most badass demon hunter this side of the veil.

Jenna looked to me for our next move. "We need back-up." I climbed to my feet and strode from the room. I collected Ryder's cell and car keys and left the house with Jenna in tow.

We drove in silence toward the Salem mall to collect Jenna's car. Fury burned through my veins, flaring hotter as my thoughts darkened. I would protect Dawn. I'd promised her that much. And Akil... How dare Levi torture him? He had no right. Akil was infallible. A smug bastard he might be, but he didn't deserve that. What if Levi killed Mammon's vessel, killed Akil?

"Akil means a lot to you." Jenna leaned an arm against the passenger door and watched the leafy tree line blur past.

I glared ahead and tried to imagine what she thought she'd seen: a Prince of Hell dying in my arms and no doubt the terror in my voice. "No. I need him. There's a difference," I replied flatly. She'd witnessed Akil's true form and looked him right in the eyes. More than that, she'd held his stare. That took balls. She obviously had a pair. I liked her all the more.

She turned her head and watched me. "What on this earth do you need a Prince of Hell for, Muse?"

Good question. The answer was mine to keep.

"What the hell are you?"

I had some witty retort on my tongue about a half-baked mistake, but it twisted in my mouth and died on my tongue. She'd seen me go demon. I'd deterred Val's magnificent wings, albeit briefly. I'd bowed to a Prince of Hell and gathered him into my arms. She'd probably read the reports from the Garden event, where I'd funneled pure energy into Akil. As far as she was concerned, I had a Prince of Hell on a leash. She didn't know I had another demon shrink-wrapped around my heart or that I could wipe out a city if I put my mind to it.

I shrugged a shoulder. "I'm just me. Caught in a storm."

Jenna watched me closely. She was an Enforcer, trained to eliminate the demon threat. So was I, technically, but I was demon first. My allegiance didn't rest with the Institute, and it never would. I worked for them—for Adam—because I needed answers. Jenna saw through my act and witnessed the demon in me staring right back at her.

She didn't say another word, and once at the mall, she retrieved her car. We drove back to Boston in convoy. Her car loomed in my mirrors the whole time.

Chapter Fourteen

We pulled up outside the lake house a little after midday. Jenna climbed from her car, talking into her cellphone. She shivered, reached inside the car, and pulled out a buff colored trench coat and shrugged it on. She strode away from her car like a woman in charge. I'd reassessed my impression of her over the last few hours. She was Institute, through-and-through. She probably never doubted herself while scrubbing demon blood out of her boots. She and Ryder would get along like a house on fire.

I took a few moments to absorb the serene surroundings. Sunlight sparkled on the lake to my right. The body of water lay embraced by sentinel pines as far as the eye could see. Frost-brittle grass crunched under my boots as we approached the white weatherboard house. Here, I'd learned how to draw from the veil. Here, Stefan had lied to me. Here, Akil had tried to kill me. Here, hidden in the metal memories of a sword, I'd witnessed Akil murder my friend. For somewhere so beautiful, it held many ugly memories. But there was good too. Among the embrace of trees, Stefan had taught me how to summon my element from beyond the veil. He'd opened my eyes to the truth.

As we approached the house, Jenna ended her call.

"What did you tell the Institute?"

She tucked her hair behind an ear. "That I'm still tailing you. Which I am."

"You didn't mention Akil or Dawn?"

"Not yet."

She would though, and soon. "Did you tell them where we are?" We stepped up onto the wraparound porch and stopped outside the side-door.

"No." She frowned at our surroundings. "I don't know where we are. In the middle of moose country, by the looks of it." She tightened her coat around her. "Is it always this cold here?"

I knocked on the door. There were no other cars parked alongside the house. Maybe nobody was home. I'd decided not to call ahead. It would only make the inevitable conversation worse, if such a thing were possible.

"Who we meeting?" Jenna asked, stamping her feet and breathing into her cupped hands.

"A friend."

"Another prince?" She arched an eyebrow.

I smiled. "No, I don't generally socialize with the princes if I can help it. They tend to want my head on a stake."

"Unless it's Akil."

I winced. Even mentioning Akil's name here set my teeth on edge. Nerves fluttered in my chest, stirring my parasitic hitchhiker. Speaking Akil's name around Stefan felt like throwing gasoline on a bushfire. This wasn't going to go well. I knew that and tried to steel myself against the inevitable.

I opened my mouth, about to ask Jenna to let me do the talking, when Stefan jerked open the door and rested his forearm on the jamb. He skipped an analytical gaze from me to Jenna. His piercing eyes narrowed a fraction. Jenna made a small, pleasantly surprised noise in her throat.

"Jenna..." He smiled easily. "How's the wrist?"

Flirtatious laughter peeled from her lips. "Fine, thank you. It took a good few months to heal. Messed up my aim for weeks. Had I known we were seeing you, Stef, I'd have brought a tub of Ben and Jerry's."

My demon bristled. If I had hackles, they'd have shot up. An angry hiss sounded at the back of my throat. I cleared it with a cough and gritted my teeth to prevent any more demon noises escaping me. I locked a bright smile on my face. "You know each other?"

Stefan turned his back on us and strode into the open-plan lounge. "Sure, Jenna and I were... friends before I had a surprise vacation in the netherworld."

I heard the hesitation in that word: *friend*. Whatever they had together was none of my business anyway. It's not like I had what some might call a relationship with Stefan or like I went to hell and back for him.

I crossed the threshold and immediately felt the press of the protective symbols painted on the walls. My demon shrank back, which would likely be a good thing, considering that I was having trouble keeping my bright smile alive and the various colorful curse words from breaching my lips. My demon was jealous. And surprisingly, so was I. Jenna knew what ice cream he liked. It bothered me. I didn't even know if he liked books or movies or what his favorite color was. If he liked take-out food or fancy restaurants. It hit me hard, the realization that Jenna knew him better than I did. They'd been friends. The one friend I'd had, Akil had killed. I had colleagues. I had acquaintances. I had lovers. But nothing real. Nothing lasting.

Jenna closed the door behind us. "I didn't know you had a place in the mountains, Stef."

Good. I knew something she didn't. Oh, god, what was I doing? This was ridiculous. So Stefan and Jenna may have been an item. It didn't matter. Of course he had a life before me. What did I expect? Besides, there were other, more important, priorities.

Stefan paused beside one of the two patterned couches huddled around a pine coffee table. His fingers danced lightly on the back of the cushions. "There's a lot you don't know, Jenna." He slid his gaze to me. "What do you want, Muse?" The pale blue of his shirt complimented his dazzling eyes. He'd rolled the sleeves up like it wasn't bitterly cold inside the house. Loose-fitting jeans implied a casual and calm persona. Almost. His power simmered around him. I couldn't see it, but it crackled in the air like an electrical current.

"I need to talk with you." To do this, to convince him to help me retrieve Dawn and Akil, I had to reel in my emotions. No matter what he said, I couldn't let my feelings rule me or allow my demon to distract me. *Forget the past*, I told myself. I needed him to help me. Forget everything that broiled between us, simmering the tips of my fingers, tugging on my control, demanding to be free.

"I thought we'd already had this conversation." Cool. Calm. No hint of anger. We were testing each other. That was good. At least I hoped so. I couldn't quite tell if, below the chilled-out exterior, he was about to launch into a verbal assault. He couldn't summon his demon, not inside the house. Maybe, if we stayed like this, we could have a civilized conversation, our demons packed away for a battle another day.

Jenna had stilled beside me. She couldn't see the power he carried, but her instincts would be prodding her subconscious. I froze the prefect expression of indifference on my face and looked at her. She glanced at me, back at Stefan, read between the lines, and sighed. "You know what, I'll take a walk around outside. It's warmer out there."

I kept my head bowed and listened to her leave. I might have felt guilty for pushing her away, if I hadn't remembered whom she worked for. The door clicked closed behind her, and I was alone with Stefan. The weight of words unsaid virtually suffocated me.

"Can't look me in the eye?" Stefan asked. "Guilty much?"

Anger sparked to life in my veins. I snuffed it out, closed my eyes, and took a deep, steadying breath. He would not bait me. When I opened them again, Stefan had moved a few strides closer. I opened my mouth, unsure where to start. I remembered what it was like to trace my finger down the line of his jaw and tease my fingertips across his lips. He looked back at me, unblinking, locked motionless as though encased in ice. A sliver of a smile hitched up one corner of his lips. It was subtle, just a hint of humor.

"Well?" he growled, his demon accent was rich and deep as molasses. He'd been hiding the accent from me at the workshop and from Jenna. My demon did a curious little purr inside my mind, rolling over like a cat falling over herself at the feet of her master. She wanted a piece of him. We both did.

I swallowed, waging my own internal battle to stay focused. "I listened to the message you left for Ryder."

"Prying? Wow, that's low."

The anger was back, all my own. My demon still wallowed in the restrained power he radiated. Torn inside, I battled on two emotional fronts. "I've had a rough few days. Cut me some slack." Pinching the bridge of my nose, I sighed. *Stay calm. Don't fight.*

He crossed his arms and regarded me coolly. Whatever he saw, it drained the tension from his body. "Alright, you've got ten minutes. Say what you gotta say and leave."

"I... er wanted to check that you were okay."

His gaze skipped away. He smiled. "Have you heard from Ryder?"

"No. He's a big boy. He can look after himself. *Are* you okay, Stefan?"

"Of all the things you could ask, that's your first?" He brushed a hand across his chin. "When the Larkwrari came through the veil, Muse, at the garden, it tore me apart. I held the veil open too long. It poured enough raw power into me that I should have leveled the city." His eyes told me he'd wanted to. I knew that feeling. "Or died."

I glared back at him. "Hurts like a bitch, doesn't it?" My gaze said, *yes I've taken in that much power and nearly died from it. What do you want? A fuckin' medal?*

He laughed softly. "Look at you, Muse. Standing here, thinking you're something hot. Must feel nice to have a prince on the end of your strings. Do you burn for him, Muse?"

He was hurting. I'd let him off the things he'd said at the statue, and I'd let it go now, but a time would come when I wasn't going to let it slide so easily. "Don't do this, Stefan. You're better than this."

"And how would you know? You had a few sharp things to say to me that night on the pier, right before I stepped through the veil for you. What was it? You never wanted to see me again. Well, you almost got your wish. Didn't think it through though, did you?" He smiled. His words were born of anger, but his tone was flat.

I watched his face. The smug smile sat firmly on his lips, and laughter danced in his eyes. I didn't see anger in his expression. He hid it perfectly. I was walking on thin ice. I lowered my voice, "You know I didn't want to hurt you."

His gaze wandered briefly. Perhaps the memories clouded his thoughts. Was he faltering?

I approached the back of the couch, deliberately keeping a barrier between us. "You said... you thought about me while you were trapped in the netherworld... That I meant something to you."

He chuckled and sunk his hands into his hair, sweeping the blonde locks back from his face. His eyes had brightened. His smile tightened, almost twisting into a sneer. He moved back and paced behind the opposite couch. "You did, once." He threw a glance my way, accusation in his eyes.

"Stefan..." I whispered. My breath misted in front of me. "I never stopped thinking about you."

His glacial eyes blazed. "Were you thinking of me when you screwed Akil? Every time since? I lost years, Muse. For you. To keep that pyscho-prince away from you and Nica. The second you get back, you're all over him. I wouldn't even care if it was just time. Two years, pfft," — he tossed his hands in the air "—it's nothing. But I lost so much more than that. So, please forgive me," he growled, "if I seem a bit tense."

"I know you're grieving. I miss Nica too."

"You have no idea." He snarled, turned on his heel, and stalked into the kitchen, out of sight.

I growled and shut down the acidic rage simmering in my gut. I wanted to march in there, yell at him, scream that I needed Akil to get Damien out of me, that I wasn't screwing Akil, to yell that I never wanted any of this. My hands clenched, itching to throw something, a few punches, maybe some crockery.

Slowly, I entered the kitchen and hung back in the doorway.

Stefan leaned forward against the countertop, his back to me, hands splayed on the surface, head bowed. "You can't be here. I can't stand this." His words grated as though he'd dragged them through hell to speak them.

"I'm sorry." His shoulder muscles tensed beneath his shirt. I'd once slid my fingers over those broad shoulders and pulled him close, so close I didn't know where he ended and I began. "For everything you think I did. Every day, I wanted to get to you, Stefan. I worked for Adam, did everything he asked. I hated every second of it, but I did it to get my demon back to go after you." He had to listen to me, to hear my words. I couldn't live with this any longer. Either way, he had to know my side. I had enough fetid darkness devouring my insides. I didn't need or deserve his hatred. I needed him to understand in a way I hadn't even realized until that moment.

"It doesn't matter." The muscles in his braced arms flexed like cables under strain.

A swell of emotion clogged my throat. "I'd have done anything to get to you. I never gave up. They said you were dead. I knew you weren't." I blinked back tears. The truth hurt. "I knew the netherworld would try to kill me. I knew Akil was there. Val too. I didn't care. Even after the things Damien did, how he destroyed me all over again, I came for you." Tremors rolled through my body. Memories flowed forth. I'd not dealt with the fallout from my time in the netherworld. The horrors I'd endured were still there, too close to the surface of my thoughts to hide from. My demon snarled at my weakness, despising my emotional humanity, but I didn't care. If Stefan would just look at me, he'd see the truth exposed on my face. "Please believe me. I never gave up on you, Stefan."

"You..." His breath sawed out of him. Veins of electric blue ice sparked across the countertop and snapped up the windows, cracking the glass. "You must."

He shouldn't have been able to draw his power. But he was. The air in the kitchen hardened against my skin. Ice frosted on my lips. I breathed in the burning cold. My throat tightened. My bangs collected diamond-ice. Frost dusted my lashes.

Stefan's outline rippled. My focus phased out as translucent wings of ice sprouted from his back. The sunlight cascading through the window refracted through those wings and scattered countless shards of light across the kitchen. The entire room sparkled. He turned. His demon glared at me through crystalline eyes. I couldn't see all of his transformation, just a superimposed ghost of what he truly was. Man and demon vied for the same space. My vision blurred. Power trembled beneath my feet and rippled through the air.

I stole a small backward step. Stefan abruptly appeared in front of me, filling my vision. He lifted a hand to touch my face. Dry-ice spiraled from his skin, rising like smoke. When his fingers brushed my cheek, the touch burned. I hissed and turned away. He was everywhere at once, the air I breathed, the thoughts in my mind, the embracing cold shrinking around me, closing into a deadly embrace. I couldn't breathe. Ice crawled across my tongue and down my throat. Instincts screamed at me to run. I looked into his eyes and fell into the power swirling there, caught in his crippling beauty.

"Back off!" Ryder pressed a gun to Stefan's temple. Swirling ice vapor teased around the muzzle, dusting the barrel as it crept toward the grip.

Stefan's eyes bored into mine. His cold leeched the heat from my body, drawing it out of my flesh. I was dimly aware of my seizure-like shivering, but it didn't seem to matter. My demon kept trying to break through. Her attempts felt like nothing more than a fly bumping against a window. Wrapped in ice, I was solid. Hard. Unbreakable.

"Stefan. You know I'll do it. Back away from Muse." Ryder cocked the hammer.

Stefan smiled. Ice cracked away from his lips. He moved back. Those glorious wings chimed. Snow trailed from their crystal-feathered edges.

Ryder grabbed me by the shoulder and shoved me back. "Get out!"

I stumbled backward through the kitchen doorway and bumped into Jenna, standing rigid, gun out, aimed at Stefan.

Stefan gleamed in the sunlight. Glorious. Godly. I couldn't tear my gaze away. The touch of winter coiled up my legs and slithered around my waist.

"Get it under control, pretty boy." Ryder drawled, a gun a few inches from Stefan's head. Ryder's grip trembled. Ice clawed over his hand.

Stefan still looked at me. The smile had frozen on his lips. He hadn't even blinked. And I knew now, it was a mask. His demon had complete control. He could draw from the veil with a single thought and kill us all where we stood. He might not even need the veil to do it. Just how powerful was he?

"Go." His demon voice splintered the layer of ice smothering everything in the kitchen. The windows shattered. Ice and glass exploded.

I ducked away and fled through the door with Jenna hot on my heels. Panting, we stopped by the Mustang and waited for Ryder to emerge from the open door.

Stefan had lost control. No wonder Ryder had said half bloods were dangerous. He'd been dealing with this.

"Is Ryder going to be okay?" Jenna asked. I nodded, teeth chattering too much to speak. She shrugged off her coat and handed it to me. I shook my head. "Take it before you get hypothermia or something."

"N-no. I'm okay." He wouldn't have hurt me, would he? Was that what he'd been doing? Was he killing me with cold?

Jenna threw her coat around my shoulders and bunched it beneath my chin. She smiled. "You're as stubborn as he is. Deal with it." She plucked her cell from the pocket and jabbed speed-dial.

"What are you d-doing?"

"I have to report this. He's out of control."

Ryder beat me to it. "No you don't. They already know." He ambled over, holstering the gun inside his jacket. It was Stefan's gun, the Desert Eagle, complete with entwined scorpions etched into the grip. Ryder saw me eyeing the weapon. "He recognizes it. Helps ground him. Dunno for how much longer though."

"Ryder... Why d-didn't you tell me?"

He nodded at the Mustang. "Get inside the car. I'll crank the heater up an' get you warm."

Obliging, I sat shivering in the passenger seat. Jenna sat in the back, eyes trained on the house, hand resting on her thigh, ready to go for her gun.

Ryder rested a wrist on the steering wheel, turned toward me, and peered at me in that way he did when I screwed up and we both knew it. "What are you doin' here?"

"I needed to talk to him."

"He could've killed you."

"I didn't know he was... like that."

Ryder raised his eyebrows. "You were in Boston when Stefan brought a snowstorm in summer, right? You remember the dragon-demon eyeing us all for lunch? Don't kid yourself, Muse. Did you think he was goin' to be able to brush it off?"

My shoulders dropped. I sunk in the seat. "Yeah," I said in a small voice. "He's Stefan."

"Not any more, he ain't."

My demon shifted and resettled. "He just needs time."

Ryder looked out of the windshield at the house. It looked serene in the sunlight, as it had when we'd arrived. "Yeah, well, the Institute hasn't decided what to do with him."

"He can't go back to Adam."

"Nope. They aren't daft. Stefan inside that place again? He'll make Damien's killing spree look like a fuckin' Sunday stroll. The ward-symbols don't stop him. Dunno why. They used to."

Even Akil couldn't get through those symbols. Could he? He'd summoned his true form back at Blackstone. What if the princes weren't affected by the symbols? What did that make Stefan? As powerful as Akil?

"You've been up here all this time. Guarding him? Protecting him?"

"Both. Until Adam issues the order to have him... dealt with."

"Killed."

Ryder didn't reply.

Would Ryder do it? Yeah, of course he would. He wouldn't hesitate.

I pulled Jenna's coat tighter around me. The shivers were subsiding, leaving me exhausted and miserable. "Maybe I could..." I shrugged. "I don't know... help him somehow?"

Ryder's left eyebrow shot up. "What, like you did just then? Muse, no offense, but you're the last thing he needs. You push all his demon buttons. Always have."

"Yeah, but I couldn't bring my demon to that showdown. It wasn't a fair fight. You don't get it." I glanced back at Jenna. She glared at the house, fingers twitching on her thigh. She wouldn't hesitate to kill either. "Nobody gets it. I have a demon in me. Like him. I control it every second of every day. Mostly. Not always, but more often than not. Stefan and me, we're the same."

"Right, and that's why I don't want you in there. I got enough trouble controlling one fucked up half blood, I don't need two." Ryder gave me the cold, hard, military-grade stare. "Don't even think it."

I sighed and looked away, wandering my gaze along the tree line. "I lost Dawn, the little girl. Val has her in the netherworld. Akil is–"

"In Boston, doin' his thing."

"What?" I snapped my head around.

"Yup. Demon chatter has him back on top, butterin' up Boston's too-rich-to-care and fending off fangirls too stupid to live."

"Are you kidding me?" I shrieked. Jenna spat a disgusted curse in the back. "He was bleeding-out in my arms a few hours ago."

Ryder gave me a discerning glare. "You do too much lookin' with your eyes when it comes to Akil."

"You think he played me?" I scowled.

"Well, geez, give the lil' firecracker a certificate." Ryder smiled. "I love yah, Muse, like a sister. But for fuck sake, stay away from Akil. He'll screw you over every which way but Sunday."

I clamped my mouth closed and frowned at the galloping pony motif on the Mustang's dashboard. Had Akil set me up to go into the netherworld, guns blazing, in a bid to rid himself of his competition? Levi. If he thought I had that much clout, he was going to be seriously disappointed. What about Dawn? He said she was powerful. He wanted her tucked neatly away, nice and safe, with me so he could manipulate us both later?

I puffed out a sigh. "Screw Akil. I have to find Dawn. I promised her I would." When I faced Ryder, his face had softened. "I can't let her live like I did, Ryder. She doesn't deserve that. Nobody does."

He nodded, understanding, and dragged a hand down his face. "You came here to ask Stefan for help?" He didn't need me to reply. He slumped back in the driver's seat. "Hate to break it to yah, Muse, but Stefan ain't much use to anyone. And if he can't control that thing inside him, he's as good as dead."

Stefan couldn't help. That left only one option for back up. And I was going to kick his demon-ass for screwing with me.

Chapter Fifteen

Akil was playing hard to get. Surprise, surprise.

I swung by his office and got blanked by the tight-lipped receptionist. I left a dozen messages on the three numbers he used. I tried his various houses. Nada. With each rebuttal, I fumed. He was screwing me over again. I'd kill him. I'd suck the life right out of him and shove him in Boston Harbor and see how he liked it. Twisted, sociopathic bastard.

By the time I got home, Jonesy glared green eyes at me, declaring me unfit to own a cat because I hadn't fed him for what felt like weeks. He twitched his tail and turned his nose up as I begged his forgiveness and unlocked my apartment. I was about to step inside when I heard laughter coming from two doors down. I knew that honeyed laughter. I'd suck the fire out of his veins and hand him over to Stefan.

I stalked up the hall and rapped my knuckles on Lacy's door, foot tapping.

Lacy answered, bright smile plastered across her face, half empty glass of red in one hand, hair mussed. "Oh, Charlie, you didn't tell me you knew Akil." She gushed. Lacy didn't gush. She wore wellington boots to nightclubs and white to funerals. She was not a fangirl.

I leaned out and peered around Lacy to pin Akil in my sights. He'd draped himself over her leather couch, looking like the cat that got the cream. His shirt gaped at the collar, revealing a tempting V of bronze skin. That smile could melt glaciers.

I put some serious heat behind my glower. How could he be sitting there, drinking her wine, warming her cheeks, while I thought he was dying in the netherworld?

Lacy giggled. "He was waiting for you, so I invited him in. I couldn't just leave him on the doorstep." She fanned her face, her black nail polish stark against her pale skin. She lowered her voice and said softly. "He's hot... I can't wait to upload this to my timeline." She yanked down her top, revealing the rise of her breast. "He signed me."

"Akil!" I snarled.

Lacy jumped. "It's cool. We're just friends, like. Right, Akil?" She turned and yelped. He stood an inch from her, towering over her young and impressionable person.

He handed her his wine glass. "Of course." He eased by her, deliberately brushing against her body.

She practically melted in a puddle of estrogen right there.

I stepped back, let him by, and watched Lacy give him bedroom eyes as he sauntered down the hall. "Go take a cold shower. Then call me when the wine has worn off so we can talk demon-protection."

She pointed a finger-gun at me. "Gotcha. You have awesome friends, Charlie."

I rolled my eyes but smiled. "Sleep it off."

"I won't be sleeping...." She let the door swing closed.

Akil leaned against the wall outside my open apartment door, arms crossed, eyes alight.

I planted a hand on my hip. "If you think I'm stupid enough to invite you in, think again, pal."

"That is not what I was thinking."

"I don't even want to know." I stalked down the hall, entered my apartment, and slammed the door in his face. Jonesy nudged my ankles. "Stupid, goddamn demons. I think he's dying. I'm the one trying to recruit Stefan to launch a raid on the netherworld. What the freakin' hell...? Ryder was so right. I should listen to Ryder more often. He has Akil pegged." I slammed cupboards and muttered a whole pin-board of expletives.

Only once Jonesy was chomping on his food did I stare at the closed door. Akil was still out there on the landing. I felt his heat creeping under the door. He wouldn't knock to get my attention. That was beneath him. He'd wait. Let me stew. He had an eternity to wait. Well, he could damn well wait. I'd die of old age before I let him in.

He knocked.

My thoughts came to a screeching halt.

"Muse, we need to talk."

I marched to the door and yanked it open. "You can start by telling me why you aren't dead."

He had the gall to look sorry, but it didn't reach those eyes. It never did. "Immortal?" He blinked.

"Ha-feckin'-ha. What, you got a sense of humor while Levi beat the shit out of you?"

Fire flashed in his eyes. "Careful."

"Or what?" Oh yeah. I was ready for this. *Bring it on, Prince of Hell.* I spread my arms. "You can't get me in my apartment, mister-I'm-dying-in-your-arms-come-save-me." I finger-walked the air. "So just mosey on back to the hole you crawled out of. I'm done."

His lips quirked. "Is that all you've got?"

"Hell, no. Stay away from Lacy. She's sweet. You're like the anti-sweet, whatever the word is for that."

"The devil."

I gaped then, quick as wildfire, asked, "Are you?"

"No, he's in Hollywood."

"Huh?"

"Satan."

I blinked and shook my head. "Whatever. Where was I?"

"Insulting me."

"Oh my god, yes. You're impossible. You're a murdering son-of-bitch. You get off on pain and control and fucking up peoples' lives. You lie through your teeth. You wouldn't know the truth if it crawled up your ass and bit you on the balls." *Oh yeah, I could get used to this.* "You have no idea about personal space. You're in my face the whole time. It's wrong. People don't do that.

People respect each other's boundaries. You stomp on boundaries. Also, you snore."

His eyes had softened to a green-flecked hazel. He worked his lips, as though trying to swallow something wriggly and alive. Inside, he was laughing and trying damned hard not to.

Anger fizzled beneath my skin. "You think this is funny?" I snorted. "You would. Your sense of humor is so dark, even the lesser demons don't get you."

"Charlie, dear, are you okay?" Rosaline's fine English accent stopped my tirade.

Akil choked off a laugh. "She's okay, Rosaline. Just voicing a few grievances. How is the television?"

"Oh, it's working perfectly. You're such a nice young man. I'm always telling Charlie how she should find herself a nice man."

Nice? I poked my head around the door. "Rosaline, you have no idea."

"You're very kind, Rosaline." Akil flashed her a smile. "But Mu-Charlie is too good for me."

Rosaline placed her hand over her ample bosom. "Oh, modest too." She was wearing lipstick. She never wore lipstick.

I retreated to my apartment and threw my hands in the air. "You fixed her TV?" We glared at one another as Rosaline's mutterings wafted down the hall. "You coerced my neighbors into inviting you in?"

"Yes."

"You're evil." I meant it. "If you hurt them, ever, I'll bring the fire down on you so hard you'll never be tangible again."

"Don't talk dirty to me, Muse." He stepped over the threshold and into my apartment. "I just might take you up on your promises."

My jaw just about hit the floor. He was in my apartment. I hadn't invited him, and yet, there he was. Panic scurried through the debilitating effects of shock. I mentally swatted it aside. Had I mentioned something about the truth, his ass, and other parts of his anatomy? I'd really said those words together in the same sentence to a

Prince of Hell. I blinked a few times, swallowed carefully, and flicked my hair out of my face. "You spoke to my landlord too?" I said, voice pitched too high to be nonchalant.

"Yes, I did. He said I could visit at any time. Polite gentleman, don't you think?"

My heart fluttered so fast I thought it might burn itself out. "What is wrong with people? Don't they watch the news? You're a demon."

"But I'm so charming on television." He quirked an eyebrow, and I had a hint right there of his grand plans.

This was unacceptable. "Get out."

"No." He closed the door behind him.

"Unlike my neighbors, I know what you are. I meant all those things."

"I don't doubt it."

"I don't want you here."

"Yes you do."

I snorted. "I really don't."

He moved so fast that all I got was a face of displaced air and then I was staring at his chest. I rammed both palms against him and shoved back. "No. No, I'm not doing this." I backed away. "You were bleeding-out in my arms, Akil!"

"You wanted answers. So ask questions."

I pressed my back against the cool apartment wall, grateful for the rigid stability. He stood in my quaint kitchen, looking somewhere between intrigued and mildly bored, the picture of sophisticated elegance in his obscenely expensive suit. Cufflinks reflected the light while his eyes captured it. Immortal. Ageless. Infinite. So toxic, he should come with a danger-of-death warning sign.

"What's Subject Beta?" I asked. Akil's eyes widened. He hadn't expected that question, and that's why I'd asked it. I hadn't forgotten about the file I'd skimmed on Adam's desk the night Nica died. I'd tried to meet with Akil during the last two months, and he'd eluded me. Until now.

He blinked, erasing all traces of his surprise. "Part of an Institute initiative to reproduce and utilize half-bloods."

My mouth fell open again. I scratched around my own head for my voice, but it was gone. It took me a few moments of blustering to say, "I'm sorry, what?"

"Subject Alpha is Stefan. You are Subject Beta. There are two others in Boston that I'm aware of."

My mouth worked, but no sound came out. My brain backpedalled. "Why?" I spoke so quietly I wondered if I'd spoken at all.

"You—or more specifically half bloods in general—are their secret weapon."

"You're lying?"

"No. I rarely lie. I merely manipulate the truth. I don't need to lie about the Institute. Everything about them offends. They meddle in the affairs of demons and believe themselves above the laws of nature. It is abhorrent." He delivered the last word with a disgusted snarl.

I hadn't expected this. Not only was Akil in all likelihood telling the truth—shocker—but the Institute had been watching me since I was born? "But... When? Val... Sold me... I thought..."

"Valenti controls the half bloods. All of them. He always has. You were to be sold to a nameless demon. That demon had plans to hand you over to the Institute in exchange for unhindered travel to this side of the veil. Val discovered the betrayal. He retrieved you and killed the demon who dared trade with humans."

I pressed my hands against the cool walls on either side of me. "Okay..." I'd always known my brother was responsible for my troubled upbringing, but I hadn't realized the Institute had a vested interest in me from such an early age. They'd bargained with demons to get their hands on me. How far did their reach extend? Was Akil in on it? I lifted my gaze. "Where do you come into all of this?"

"Do you mean how I saved you, taught you how to be human, gave you a lust for life, and you threw it all back in my face? That part?"

"No." Just had to remind me, didn't he. "How do you know all this?"

"How do you know about Operation Typhon?"

I narrowed my eyes at him. He knew everything in that handsome head of his. I'd been so afraid of him before, I'd never asked the horrifying questions. I hadn't wanted to know about the past. The future was all I needed. The problem was, you can't have one without the other.

"I read a file on Adam's desk."

He inclined his head and looked at me through dark lashes. "The ancient Greeks believed Typhon the father of all monsters."

"Adam." His name slotted into place like the missing piece of jigsaw.

Akil didn't reply. He didn't need to. "I make it my business to observe the Institute closely. I knew about you before you were born, when you were an idea, a chess piece on a figurative board. When Valenti decimated the demon for bartering one of his half bloods, I was intrigued. I asked myself why demons and humans alike were squabbling over half bloods. I watched. I learned. I waited."

"While I suffered?"

He held my gaze and moistened his lips. "I'm not perfect."

Laughter bubbled up and burst from me, turning from something light and jovial, to dark and menacing. The putrid thing knotted around my heart tightened. I choked back the insane hilarity and clenched a fist to my chest. I never expected the truth to hurt. My legs wobbled. I bowed over and planted my hands on my thighs, trying to control my breathing. I was used to being a worthless half blood, a demon plaything. I didn't expect anything from demons, only the worst they could do to me. But Adam had tried to buy me? And to know Akil had watched me all those years. While I'd been shoved from demon to demon, he'd eyed me from a distance. Everyone seemed to know all about me while I stumbled about in the dark, groping for answers.

"Who was my mother?" I asked softly, waiting for the tightness in my chest to pass.

"I don't know. I suspect she succumbed during your birth or was killed soon after. You father, Asmodeus, is brutal."

I looked up. "You knew about my existence before I was born, but you don't know who she was? Can you tell me anything about her?"

"No. I had other priorities. I avoid stalking human women, present company excluded, especially females under the wing of another prince."

"Do you think I'm maybe like her?" I didn't know why I asked. I'd never really thought about her before. I'd wondered, briefly, what it might have been like to have had a normal childhood, but pining over a past that could never have been wasn't for me. The future, that was me. I lived for tomorrow. I didn't ask questions. I didn't care. One foot in front of the other, always moving forward, always running headlong toward hope.

"I think..." he lowered his voice to a soothing timbre. "If she was anything like you, she'd have rained hell down on them all."

"You're damn right she would have." I straightened and pushed off the wall. I staggered somewhat, but Akil knew better than to reach for me. His dark eyes watched me approach him, drinking in my stride. I stopped inside his personal space, placed a hand on his chest, and stood on tiptoes to plant a chaste kiss on his cheek.

He turned his head and looked down at me as though trying to solve an exasperating puzzle. Surprise muddied the amusement in his eyes.

"You should try the truth on for size more often. It suits you."

Chapter Sixteen

I woke slowly, wrapped in body-hugging warmth. Opening my eyes, I watched dust motes dance in the sunlight pouring through the windows. The world was quiet, my thoughts soft and content. Jonesy purred in my ear. I had a few glorious moments where my ignorance really was bliss, and then reality punched me in the gut. Like when you wake and think it's a weekend, but it's not. It's a weekday, and you should have been at work an hour ago. Multiply that sensation by a hundred.

Akil lay behind me. His warm spicy scent filled my head and tingled on my lips. I tensed and stopped purring. I'd been purring? Gulping, I took mental stock of the situation. I had all my clothes on. We were on top of the bed covers, not tangled up in each other's limbs beneath them. I sighed out the breath I'd been holding. Why were we on my bed? Why hadn't he said anything? Was he awake?

His breath fluttered at my neck, sending a shiver trickling down my spine. He wasn't touching me, but his heat radiated as though I'd curled up in front of an open fire. A tickling tendril of heat crawled across my back, down over my hip, and wove around my thigh.

In all the years I'd lived with Akil, I'd never once woken up next to him in the morning. I'd woken to an empty bed. Every. Single. Time.

We'd talked last night until my voice was hoarse and my head full off Adam's treachery. Akil knew more than I could have imagined. Adam had learned about half bloods after falling for a demon held captive by the Institute: Yukki Onna, Stefan's mother. Adam did the dirty, she became pregnant, and gave birth to Stefan at the Institute under the watchful eyes of the Institute scientists. Adam vowed to protect Stefan, knowing his newborn son would be killed if Yukki returned with him to the netherworld. Adam planned to eventually return him to Yukki, but Stefan was no normal child. He had power, power Adam could control, mold, and utilize for the benefit of the Institute. Stefan was a weapon. Half bloods were more powerful than Adam or the Institute could have imagined. Operation Typhon was born.

I must have fallen asleep on the couch. Did I fall asleep on Akil? Had he carried me into the bedroom? My demon stretched inside me, casting out a ripple of heat. Akil's breath shortened. He was awake, all right.

"Shouldn't you be pulling the wings off flies or something?" I quipped. Fake bravado made substantial armor.

"What would that accomplish?" His breath brushed my shoulder.

"Why are you here?" I couldn't turn to look at him. If I did that, I didn't trust what might happen next.

"Did you know you purr in your sleep?"

"That's not me. It's my demon."

"It's... adorable."

I jolted upright. He lay on his side, head propped up on an arm, thankfully fully clothed, although his creased shirt rode up his waist revealing a tantalizing glimpse of bronze skin. "Okay, what's going on? This isn't you. First, you start telling the truth, and now you're all..." I gestured, grasping for the right word, "Nice. A Prince of Hell doesn't do nice. Where's the real Akil?"

"Lay back down, and I'll reacquaint you with him."

I sprang from the bed and wobbled to my feet. "Urgh, how long was I asleep?"

"Twelve hours and fifteen minutes."

I hadn't dreamed. The suffocating nightmares hadn't stalked me. I'd slept a whole twelve hours without waking in cold sweats with my own screams ringing in my ears. I pressed a hand to my chest. Damien was still in there, but he was quiet, still. Dormant. Had Akil's presence somehow subdued him?

"What did you do?"

A frown touched his face. "I was the perfect gentleman. You appear to have a very low opinion of me."

"Well, duh. You killed my friend. You tried to kill me. I'm more surprised that you aren't laying the power on thick and summoning my demon out of me so you two can tango."

He gestured with a flick of his hand. "Your delightful symbols won't permit me."

Did that mean he couldn't draw his power or just that he couldn't draw *her* out of me?

He straightened in much the same way big cats do, his languid movements unhurried and graceful. Once on his feet, he eyed me curiously. His hair was mussed and scruffy from twelve hours sprawled on the bed. His shirt gaped open and hung crooked on his muscular frame. He looked slept in, vulnerable, and very human, and it messed with my notion of the flawless, infallible, Prince of Hell.

He stepped closer, invading my space, and lay his hand over mine resting on my chest. "He consumes you from the inside." The honeyed roll of his words failed to mask the gravity of their meaning. "I know. I feel him. I witness his dark polluting your brilliance. If you wait too long, his essence will adhere to yours, and you will never be free of him. He will destroy the light in you."

I blinked up at Akil. "To get him out, I have to let you in... let you do the same to me as he did."

He inclined his head. "Not the same. It would be glorious. Would you rather he fester inside you?"

"I'd prefer to be free of both of you."

He trailed the fingertips of his left hand down the side of my face while keeping his right hand clasped over mine on my chest. "An infusion is a wonderful thing: an eternal bond between paired demons." He leaned in closer, shutting out my awareness of anything but him. A smile twitched his lips but didn't settle. The sparkling touch of restrained energy fizzled between us. A welcome warmth spread through my body, loosening muscle and chasing away the fears rattling in my head. Recognizing the seductive spell he'd cast, I balked and stepped back, but he moved with me, backing me against the wall. My demon reached for him, her snarl bubbling in my head when she could no more wrap herself around him than I could push him away. His fingers played lightly on my chin, tilting my face up. A lick of power strummed through me. "I will scrub the memory of Damien from your mind and soul. It will be..." His eyelids fluttered. The tip of his tongue darted across his lower lip. "...true ecstasy. You'd be free."

"Free of him, not you..."

He slammed a hand against the wall beside my head, rattling the windows. I flinched and gritted my teeth, but I held fast. He would not win this battle of wills. His rumbling growl was pure demon. Power bubbled up from the depths of his immortal presence and simmered dangerously in his eyes. He snared my gaze with his and bowed his head low enough that I could have flicked out my tongue to taste him. I reined my desires back, hands fisted at my sides. My demon paced behind mental bars. She wanted to pounce on him, tear his clothes off, and taste every delectable inch of his perfect body. She'd ride high on the ecstasy he offered. She didn't care for feelings or loyalty, and she didn't give a damn about control. She wanted to screw him until we shattered. I struggled to separate the sensations vying for supremacy. Her needs, my wants, the desire strumming beneath my skin—it all conspired to break me apart.

"You want me," he breathed. "All of me. You like what I am. You blame your demon—a weak excuse, Muse." With every word, his lips brushed mine. Heat sizzled beneath the feather-light touch. An impulsive urge to dart my tongue across his lips almost broke me. I bit my tongue and hoped the pain might anchor me. To taste him, to devour him, to explore every delicious inch of him... I'd been there before. I knew him intimately, and that only made self-restraint all the more punishing.

"You lie to yourself, Muse." The power beneath his words plucked my fears away as though they were insignificant. "You forget, I know you better than any man, or demon. Better than you know yourself." Filaments of fire sparked in his eyes. "I see your soul. I see the heat of desire burning in your eyes. Your need is wet between your legs." He lifted his hand from my chest and drove it lower, leaving a trail of heat. His fingers flicked open my pants buttons, his words punctuating each release. "You. Want. To. Fuck. Me."

Lust speared through me. I couldn't deny anything he'd said. It was all true. I dropped my head back against the wall and closed my eyes. He was right. I burned for him. My skin fizzled. My heart drummed a relentless beat. It was only by a tiny thread of stubborn denial that I clung onto control, but that thread was unraveling, slipping through my fingers. *It's just sex,* I told myself, *just like old times.* This was old territory. And yet it wasn't. I'd changed. Whatever this was, it was different and weighed down with meanings I didn't understand. I snapped my eyes open and clutched at his shirt, torn between pushing him away and dragging him close. I needed his hands to brand me and his lips to follow. The smile tugging on his lips told me he knew I'd lost.

"Akil..." *Stop...* But I couldn't say it. My demon rattled her bars and roared in my head. If she would just shut the hell up and let me think...

He pinched my lower lip between his teeth, letting it spring free as I sucked in a breath. His wandering hand found the wetness between my legs. A reluctant groan peeled from me. His fingers roamed. I whimpered and felt him smile against my cheek. "I will bury myself inside you," – deeper – "and free you, Muse."

A pent-up groan bubbled at the back of my throat, not quite free, and I slumped against him. "Damn you..." I snarled.

"Say yes. Accept me. Now." He leaned into me, his body a wall of hard muscle and otherworldly strength. His blunt teeth nipped my lips, my chin. He knotted his free hand into my hair and held me still, dark irises blazing with a halo of amber. Raw elemental power wrapped around me in an unseen embrace. I couldn't think through the roaring need and wave after wave of heat. I was aflame inside, barely human, a beast consumed by desires. My hips rocked against his fingers as they dove in and eased out. I was losing my mind.

"Get. Out." The words hurt to say. I wasn't even sure they were mine.

"No." He growled the word in a rushed kiss. The spicy taste of him danced on my tongue. I wanted more. I sunk my hand into his hair and plunged my tongue into a raw exploration of a kiss as though my life depended on it. I breathed him in, drank him down. His mouth roamed. His teeth nipped, sharper this time, rough with urgency.

A dart of control pierced my madness. Perhaps it was the memory of my owner's abuse or the remnants of him throbbing around my heart, but whatever its source, it blindsided me enough to release me from the crazed hunger. I planted both hands on Akil's chest and shoved him away. He staggered, snarled, and lunged. His heady scent danced on my tongue and sideswiped my denial. His arms clamped around me, biceps flexing. His body crowded mine. Steel and honey. So hard, so smooth. I teased my tongue down his jawline and down his neck where his pulse tapped a brisk tempo against my lips. I could almost taste the blood rushing through his veins. His muscles trembled beneath my hands. He wanted me. My body may have betrayed what I needed from him, but he was equally slipping into desire. It went deep, this madness. Did he realize how lost we both were? I tore his shirt open, nipped his shoulder, and dragged my nails over the taut biceps and down his toned arms. My demon roared. I growled, snarled, and snapped at her, driving her back. He was mine.

Akil tore my top over my head. His fingers speared into my hair and locked tight. He yanked me against him, releasing a savage groan against my neck that spilled a new wave of quivering heat through my body.

Jesus, he was unrefined, raw, and wild. I caught the gleam of the demon glaring back at me. Chaos caged. He wasn't a man. That being inside him, simmering just below his trembling flesh, was an eternal demon—not of this world, not belonging to humanity in any way. He was unreal, so far beyond my naive comprehension that I could no more hope to understand him than I could the workings of the universe.

"Stop," I breathed. My lust-soaked body belied my complaint.

"No. You need this. Don't deny it." He strangled a groan, the sound so wrought with bottled up lust that I couldn't help grinding my hips against his hardness. "Submit to me, body and mind," he ordered, fire in his eyes, power in his voice. An undoing spilled through my demon. Had it not been for my human half, I'd have been reduced to a mindless puddle of demon hunger at his command.

Where that molten stare wandered, my skin tingled. I couldn't breathe, couldn't see past desire. The smothering madness tore out all reason, but... "Akil?"

He growled low again, this time in warning. "Don't deny me." Need slurred his words. "Do not condemn yourself, Muse." His body shimmered behind a heat-haze. He pulled me to him, grinding the hardness of his cock against my hip. Another grunt of failing restraint slipped from him. I breathed out a pleasure-leaden moan and arched back. He held me tight, possessively, his hands smoldering against the small of my back. He trailed simmering kisses down my neck, lower, summoning fire in their wake. He hooked his fingers over my bra and tugged it aside. His lips burned. His tongue swirled around my nipple. I locked my hand in his hair and growled out a curse.

When his power sought mine, writhed through my skin and thrust toward my center, I immediately shrank away. Despair finally broke through the suffocating insanity. Akil would drive himself inside me, tear out Damien, and make himself at home. He would do to me the same as Damien had done: force his power inside and tear me open. I flinched and drew my humanity around me like a coat of armor. He couldn't have me like that. What Damien did to me was never happening again. Nobody could control me, beat me down, and drive me to my knees in submission. Ever again.

"I will never submit." My barely human speech betrayed my demon. She spoke through me despite the symbols on the wall. She was there, driving the lust out and glaring back at Akil's flame-filled eyes with nothing short of defiance.

I shoved his shoulder. He twisted back in against me, growling a warning.

"Stop." I clamped his face in both hands. "Just... stop. I'm not doing this with you."

He did stop. The world stopped too. I held his conflicted gaze and waited, not breathing. He wouldn't force me. He might be a beast inside that body, a creature of greed. He wanted, he yearned, he desired, but he'd never crossed that line. It was the only truth about him I could trust.

Finally, his eyes softened. He searched my face and with a sigh, planted a chaste kiss on my lips, and encircled me in his arms. The superheated lust we'd summoned dispersed. Seconds ticked on. Our panting breaths slowed, and our bodies cooled. The rapid beat of his heart corralled my runaway thoughts.

"I can't trust you." Humanity clipped my voice. I was back in the room and in control. But damn, he smelled divine: hot spices, sex and cinnamon. I drew in a deep breath and savored him because this wasn't happening again. He was my drug. An addiction. If I let him, he'd destroy me, and it was my choice to make.

He swallowed and stroked my hair back from my face, expression surprisingly calm. "You shouldn't."

"I don't think I can ever trust you."

"In which case, you had better become accustomed to sharing your soul with Damien." He peeled himself away from me. The sudden absence of heat released a wave of shivers through my body. He bent and scooped his shirt off the floor, gaze skipping to me as I watched him. He shrugged it over his shoulders, leaving it gaping, and gave me the raised eyebrow and wicked smile that sprinkled lust through my veins all over again. He knew the effect he had on me. Was there a Prince of Temptation? It should have been him. I slumped against the wall, cold but defiant. Akil raked a hand through his hair, eyes hardening. "The spirit which forms the soul can be changed, shaped, molded. Souls are akin to chaos in that respect. Make no mistake, your owner will destroy yours." He ruffled his hair, let his hand drop, and sucked in a wavering breath. "Your stubbornness will be your downfall."

"It's my choice to make." At least I didn't sound like I was about to collapse, even if I couldn't quite move away from the wall just yet.

Akil weighed my words. His smile had gone. While he buttoned up his shirt, I watched shadows gather into a frown on his face. "We have a half blood to find."

I nodded but couldn't find my voice until it occurred to me what had just happened. Ryder's words came back to haunt me. I did too much looking with my eyes, and Akil was made to seduce and manipulate. What had Akil told me once? His vessel was a trap, designed to lure and consume. The trembling of his formidable muscles, his sculpted masculinity, how impossibly perfect he appeared to be: it was an act. Even now, as a tiny bead of perspiration trailed idly over his rippled abs while his fingers worked the buttons closed. Every part of him was fake. Akil had played the 'nice' card in a bid to get me to submit to him.

My smile masked the downward tilt of my lips. "Oh, you're good."

He lifted his head, and his eyes narrowed, cutting me a scathing glance. "You must have me confused with another sociopathic demon."

"That's not what I meant, and you know it. All of this…" I flicked my hand. "The Prince Charming act... Mister Nice. You were screwing with my head." Yeah, it made sense now. *Butter me up with some truths, and then royally screw me over.* I lifted my chin and glared at him. "I thought we were beyond that crap. I guess I was wrong. You're still a lying son-of-a-bitch. You're not worth it."

Rage burned so quickly through his dark eyes that a blast of heat warmed my skin for a few seconds. A muscle jumped in his jaw. I'd clearly offended him, and my conviction stuttered.

"I've killed demons for lesser words, Muse." He turned and stalked toward the bedroom door.

Oh yeah, my words had hurt him. Well, that was unexpected. If he hadn't instigated the charming act to manipulate me, what had it all been about? Why was he being nice? I raked a hand through my hair. Nice I couldn't figure out. Nice disarmed me unlike anything else. Had he waltzed in here, all brutal orders and demands, I wouldn't have been surprised, and I'd have slapped him down much earlier. But he hadn't. Sure, he'd tricked his way into my apartment, but for him, that was par for the course. Something must have rattled him enough to bring him to me with answers on his lips.

I pushed away from the wall. "Akil, what happened in the netherworld? You were hurt. I didn't imagine that."

He stopped in the doorway, one hand resting on the jamb. He didn't look back. "Levi captured and tortured me for information on Dawn's whereabouts."

Just how powerful was Levi if he could reduce Akil to a bloody mess? "Did you tell him you gave her to me?" I asked quietly.

Akil's shoulders twitched. He chuckled, awakening the vestiges of desire tingling beneath my skin. "No. It takes a great deal more than physical pain to manipulate me."

"I lost Dawn anyway. You were tortured for nothing."

"On the contrary, I learned a great deal about Leviathan. Previously, I relied on Carol-Anne's ego to get what I wanted. I invited her to my apartment, feigning intrigue in her half-blood pet. Unfortunately, that didn't end well for her." Akil tilted his head and lifted his dark eyes to me. "Your brother took Dawn. As the custodian of half bloods, he will have returned her to Levi. And I know exactly where to find Leviathan." He paused, a thoughtful expression lightening his face. "Life really was quite tedious when the princes were forbidden to challenge one another." He didn't appear beaten. If anything, he made the fact he'd been tortured sound like foreplay.

It occurred to me that I'd been fooled by a bleeding Akil, as no doubt had Levi. "How did you get away?"

A wicked smile played on his lips, revealing sharp teeth. "You make the same mistake he did, assuming I was tortured under duress. Levi underestimates my abilities." His gaze told me never to screw him over, that he was the biggest, baddest, most manipulative demon out there. I believed him. And I'd just denied him a chunk of my soul.

I smiled right back.

Chapter Seventeen

Akil broke the lock on the door into The Voodoo Lounge and gave it a brisk shove, almost taking it off at the hinges. I followed him inside the empty club. Within a few strides, a void of darkness swallowed me. I had a sense of space. Quiet yawned wide. I quickly spilled some of my element through me. My vision shimmered. Monochrome grays and black molded into the ghostly shapes of the bar and dance floors.

Akil's eyes glowed red in the dark. I liked to think of myself immune to most demon appearances, but still I flinched a little. Lacy wouldn't have been so quick to let him sign her chest had she seen that look. *Who needs horns and a tail when you've fire in your eyes?*

I trailed along behind him. He knew exactly where to go. During his torture he'd learned that Levi's lair overlaid The Voodoo Lounge. The netherworld exists in the same space as our world, just not in the same realm. The veil acts like tracing paper. The hard pencil lines on one side—our landscape—scores through to the other side, creating a similar imprint. Related but different twin worlds. Boston is a barren, half-burned dead forest in the netherworld, but the landscape follows the same contours. Those points of reference don't change. Nobody had mapped exactly what locations in our world matched the netherworld's. Demons don't care for maps, and nothing human (besides a few half bloods) could skip through the veil to accurately survey the netherworld.

One of the back rooms in The Voodoo Lounge served as an entrance to Levi's personal warren—Akil's word. At the Lounge, Levi, the Prince of Envy had always been close. Just a veil away. We were about to hop through the veil and take a discreet look around for Dawn. I suspected there might be an element of revenge involved. Levi had taken Akil to his warren to torture him. Now Akil wanted back in on his own terms. But as long as we found Dawn, Akil could do whatever he wanted to Levi. I wouldn't hang around to watch.

"Are you going to tell me how cozy you and Carol-Anne got?" Despite whispering, my voice echoed through the empty club.

"Ah, you found her body. I suppose that means the Institute people were crawling all over my apartment."

"Yes. They didn't discover anything."

"Of course they didn't. Did you think I'd leave my financial accounts and plans for world domination where prying eyes could see them?"

I stumbled, alarmed, until he slowed and tossed a grin over his shoulder. Right. World domination. He was joking, wasn't he? "Were you sleeping with her?" I asked, determined to get a straight answer before he turned away.

He faced me, still smiling. "Why should it matter if I was sexually involved with Carol-Anne? I don't believe you and I are in a relationship, or are you about to correct me?"

This was awkward. I shifted from one foot to the other and wandered my gaze away. "Obviously, we're not."

His chuckle promptly stopped me from further inserting my foot into my mouth. "I wasn't, nor have I ever, been involved with Carol-Anne. I'd like to think you credit me with more intelligence and better taste."

I swallowed to try to moisten my suddenly dry throat. A change of subject was in order. "Detective Coleman called me when her body was discovered. He thinks I'm in cahoots with you."

"He's not the only one." Akil continued to stride across the dance floors, gait confident and shoulders proud.

He missed my eye-roll. "I'm not here for you. You think everything's about you. I'm doing this for Dawn."

"That is an important distinction."

Was he laughing at me again? I closed the distance between us as we hurried down the back hallway. Closed doors flanked either side of us. "Who else thinks I'm working with you?"

"They all believe you're working *for* me. Levi. Valenti. The entire netherworld. Although, perhaps not your father. Most demons—including the princes—are ignorant of the significance..." He hesitated a breath. "And Stefan."

Stefan's name on his lips drove an icicle through my heart, as I suspected he knew it would. He was right. Stefan did think I was in bed with Akil. I let it go. Now was not the time. "What significance?"

"Can we have this discussion another time?"

"No, you always say that when I'm getting too close to the truth. And there may not be another time. You're slippery." He stopped so abruptly I walked right into him and almost fell over myself.

He turned. "Slippery?" Amber swirled in his eyes. In the dark hallway in the empty club, he did the whole demon-bad-ass look a little too well.

Raking my hand through my hair, I recovered from falling over him. "Yeah, y'know... Difficult. Tricksy. I want my answers now before you disappear or volunteer for torturing again. How did you come back from that all flawless and..." I cleared my throat. "Er—y'know—pretty." I didn't want to admit how mind-numbingly sexy he was. Admitting I found him attractive felt too much like handing him a small victory. I crossed my arms. "When you were wounded a few months ago, I had to reach through the veil for the power to heal you."

His eyes widened at the memory. He liked it. "You think I'm *pretty*?" he asked carefully.

Now I was smiling. Some words just didn't sound right coming from him. I made a mental note to coerce him into saying obscure words like fluffy... or marshmallow. I snickered.

"Is our situation amusing, Muse? We're about to break into the Prince of Envy's warren, and you're giggling like a child."

"I'm sorry." I coughed and shook myself. "I'm just enjoying this mutual ground I seem to be on with you." It did feel good, though, poking a tiger with a stick.

He pressed his lips into a thin line and peered down at me as I tried to wipe the smile off my face. Once I'd regained my composure, he said, "I've been... different since you shared your element with me above Boston gardens."

"Different?" The way he said that one word, savoring it, rolling it across his tongue, it was a good different. "Are you going to elaborate?"

"No. What do you mean by mutual ground, Muse?"

Hello, warning-tone. I'd touched a nerve. I eyed him the same way he scrutinized me. I'd been afraid of Akil for the majority of my human existence. Afraid, in awe of, bewildered by. But now, I wasn't the cowering half blood afraid of Akil's shadow. I hadn't been since I'd drained him, and I would never be again. It was exhilarating, empowering, and I wondered if this was what freedom felt like. Or was it something far more seductive... like power?

A smile broke across Akil's face as he clearly read my thoughts in my expression. "And therein rests the significance I spoke of."

"I don't understand."

"You will." He opened the door.

A wall of water hit me square in the chest, blasted over my head, and slammed me against the wall. I thrust an arm out, searching for Akil's reaching hand, missed, and gasped before the torrent of water tore me away from him and flushed me down the hall.

Chapter Eighteen

I coughed, spluttered saltwater from my lungs, and lifted my head out of the puddle I appeared to be laying in. My hair clung to my face, obscuring my vision. I blinked. Green eyes the size of headlights glared at me through steel bars.

I yelped and scurried back. Pain sliced up my back, wrenching out another cry. I was caged on all sides, above and below. I couldn't stand, couldn't stretch my arms out without bumping the razor wire-wrapped bars. My demon reared up, but the second her intention to ride through me became clear, something rammed her back down and pinned her to the back of my mind with as much mental precision as a pin through a butterfly.

I snarled and clenched my fists against my temples. "Get out of my head!"

Wet laughter bubbled around the empty dance floor outside my cage.

I snapped my head up and glared through wet bangs at Leviathan. He filled the space between floor and ceiling with his serpentine bulk. A scaled tail coiled around my cage and disappeared down the hallway from which I'd been flushed. His huge upper-body resembled a human's insomuch as he had arms and a chest, but his head was all green-scaled sea-serpent, and those eyes pierced the gloom, spotlighting me in an emerald glow. I could never mistake the wet, sickly, touch of his mind inside mine.

His slick green snout snuffled at the bars. A forked tongue flicked out, tasting the air. I flinched away. Leaden pressure pulled at my arms. For a moment, I ignored it, more concerned with the demon the size of a school bus eyeing me up for lunch. But then I realized my hands appeared to move away from me of their own accord. *What the hell?* It felt like waking in the night with a numb limb. Commands left my mind, but my arms didn't obey. They stretched out. I watched, sickened and horrified, as I reached out and closed my hands around the steel bars of my cage. Snatches of pain twinged up my arms. The razor wire bit into flesh. Blood streamed over the back of my hands, down my arms, and dripped from my elbows, but I couldn't let go. My knuckles whitened.

Leviathan's vast serpent body sashayed, which I took to be an expression of pleasure.

"Get the fuck out of me!"

I heaved my body back. My arms snapped taut, but my hands refused to let go. Images started to pile into my mind. I couldn't stop them. This was my so-called talent. *Make her bleed; Make her read.* I could see the past in metal, any metal, but for it to work, I had to seal the link with my own blood. I jolted as though hit with an electric current.

A limp little girl cowered in the same space as me. So tiny. Her wet ringlets matted against her head. She trembled, whimpered, and clutched her rabbit against her chest. I recognized her tatty dress and mismatched socks.

Dawn.

My well-maintained reservoir of rage boiled dry inside me. I screamed at Leviathan with everything I had, but when the bellow broke over me and boomed from my throat, it didn't sound like any scream I'd voiced before. It was a pure, unfiltered, demonic roar of fury.

Leviathan's grip on my mind and body relaxed. He rippled back, body and tail undulating like waves on the ocean. He finally shook his demon away and stood before me in his human suit. Clad in snug fitting leather and interlocking steel plates, he was dressed for battle. He bristled with daggers and swords. A braid of auburn hair fell to his thighs and twitched like a cat's tail. His eyes glowed green. Haughty cheekbones pulled his lips into thin lines. He should have been handsome, but something in his perfection screamed alien, and my human senses recoiled.

Breathing hard with the sound of my own demon scream still ringing around us, I plucked my hands free off the razor wire. He was out of my body for now. I seethed so much that the water I crouched in simmered where it lapped against my clothes. Oh, I'd kill him—once I figured out how to summon my demon before he could pin her down again. He was so going on my revenge list.

"Greetings, half blood. You have gained power, I see. Asmodeus will be pleased."

"Asmodeus can go fuck himself." My demon lent my voice a throaty resonance, adding a threatening weight to my words, even if it was all bluster. I didn't take well to being caged. It felt too familiar, and if the memories bubbling to the surface of my simmering thoughts were anything to go by, anger was all I had to protect myself from my past. *Demons do so like their cages.*

Levi's thin lips twitched like eels. "Passionate too, and yet to look at, you're rather unremarkable. Physically and mentally fragile. Riddled with insecurity... However, I am beginning to understand why my courtly brethren have taken it upon themselves to take an interest in you. You were quite efficient dispatching the hunters I sent after Mammon and the lesser demons I subsequently sent for you. You obviously have hidden talents. Half bloods are quite the puzzle. I do so enjoy tempering your kind."

"You want to temper me? Let me out this cage, and we'll dance." He almost seemed to be considering it. "What? Asmodeus won't allow it? Are you his pet now? Aren't you meant to be a prince? You wanna talk about judging books by their covers? Did you take fashion tips from Legolas? You're all trussed up in leathers and blades, and yet I've not seen anything to imply you're an awe-inspiring Prince of Hell. From my humble cage, you look like a fantasy freak trying too hard."

Levi stalked closer and crouched in front of the bars, leathers creaking. He draped his long arms over his knees and cocked his head. A double-eyelid flickered across his eyes. He unashamedly raked his gaze all over me, and I felt the touch of it as though he rode his hands across my skin. It turned my stomach.

I spat excess saliva at his feet. "Coward. You couldn't handle me outside these bars. You're afraid of a lowly half blood, not even a full de—"

His hand shot through the bars and clamped around my throat, jerking me against the side of the cage. Razors cut into my cheek, my chin, neck, shoulder. If I could summon my demon, I'd tear open the veil and boil the water from his veins. But she was still strung up like a sacrifice inside my mind. She thrashed, but his mental grip held firm.

He shoved me back and watched me gasp air with no trace of emotion on his face. "If you were mine, I would take great pleasure in crushing your spirit." His double eyelids flickered again.

"But I'm not yours..." I wheezed, rubbing at my throat. "You really live up to your name, huh. Envious much?"

He straightened his lithe body. A shimmer of power washed over him, leaving him female. I smiled. I couldn't help it. What did he think he was going to accomplish by wearing a woman suit? She was just as unnaturally stunning, all wrapped up in leather and steel, like something out of Tolkien.

"Where is the young half blood?" she asked, siren-voice pitched high enough to rattle my skull.

I dabbed at the blood trickling down my cheek. "I don't know. I thought you had her. Wasn't that what all the blood-on-metal crap was about?"

"I did have her. I kept her in that very cage. My subject Carol-Anne was her guardian. Mammon wove a net of lies to entrap my subject and stole my half blood from me. He has quite the penchant for half bloods, it would seem. Carol-Anne should have expected as much from the Prince of Greed. She failed me and suffered the consequences. Her quick death was generous of me."

Levi killed Carol-Anne. It wasn't Akil? I hissed as saltwater washed over the cuts on my hands. The water level was rising. I searched around the gloomy dance floor.

Where was Akil? Water dribbled in through various cracks in the walls and around closed doors. I hated water, having almost drowned twice. Plus, my demon didn't play well with water elementals.

I tried to maintain my bravado even as I shivered in my flooded cage. "I thought you princes couldn't meddle in each other's business, some sort of mutual agreement not to piss each other off."

She-vi smiled a dazzling smile. "When it is convenient. The old rules are rarely upheld. Titles are shifting. Battlements are crumbling. Laws are worthless when those who uphold them also break them. Mammon is an opportunistic hunter. Do you deny it, Mammon?"

Akil peeled from the shadows behind Levi like a wraith. Now that he'd revealed himself, I could sense his familiar warmth in the air. He moved with predatory grace, head dipped, eyes up and locked on me.

"This gift of yours is quite the feisty half blood," She-vi crooned.

I hissed at Akil. "Bastard." I wasn't surprised. I'd completely given up being surprised when Akil screwed me over.

He stopped beside She-vi, not blinking, barely moving. His dark eyes narrowed by the smallest of margins. His lips tightened, and his shoulders bowed. I'd have to have been blind to miss the obvious disappointment. He seemed to catch himself revealing too much and shook his head, rebuilding the stoic mask. He straightened his shoulders and turned to Levi. "Contrary to what you both believe, I didn't bring Muse here for you. My last visit to your warren was somewhat... restricted." He smiled, his teeth too white, their tips sharper than normal. "You will not be taking Muse anywhere. I advise you release her from the cage before we have ourselves a disagreement."

She-vi looked at him sharply. "Do you dare deny Asmodeus his blood-spawn?" She laughed. "Oh, but you are so weak, Mammon. You think to challenge me for that?" She waggled a finger dismissively in my direction. "She is uncontrollable, virtually worthless, and infected by a degenerate demon by way of an infusion. Have you not tired of her by now? Your alliance with this half blood is foolhardy."

She-vi was either too proud or too blinded by her misconceptions about Akil to recognize his reserved posture for what it really was. I'd spent enough time with him to know his stillness was a prelude to an attack. Like a cat ready to pounce, he had her locked in his amber-fringed sights. While she ranted about how pathetic I was and how stupid he was, he studied her weaknesses. How could she not see it? I didn't get a chance to follow that trail of thought. Ice tugged at my fingers. Its greedy touch burned my skin. I plucked my hand free and looked down. Delicate threads of ice spiraled around the bars of my cage. I puffed out a breath. It plumed in front of my face. She-vi's fluidic voice echoed around the dance floor as a thin layer of ice crusted across the top of the rising water. It fractured and refroze almost as regularly as my own breathing. As it refroze, it thickened.

I shifted onto my knees and peered through the steel bars at the shadows. If Levi had unpinned my demon, I could have reached out with all my senses, but all I had was my human skillset, which in the gloom, was practically useless.

Akil and Levi were too engrossed in discussions to notice the ice crawling up the walls. Akil's smile had turned smug. He'd bowed his head, eyebrow arched. She-vi had a few scarce moments to reel in her attitude before he would clamp a hand around her throat and lay down some demon badass. A large part of me wanted to watch, but the ice continued to build. I twisted around, wincing as my clothes snagged on the razor wire. Spider webs of hoarfrost trailed from the lights. Icicles lengthened. Surely the two princes would notice.

They did. But it was too late.

I saw Stefan at the same time as Levi and Akil noticed him emerging from the shadows. Blue-eyes ablaze, red-leather coat sparkling with ice, he wasn't all demon, but wasn't far from it. Levi hissed a warning. The club exploded in ice. The world warped from liquid shadows to brittle, ice-white sculptures. In a fraction of a second, a shock of frost dashed across the walls, devoured the ceilings, washed over the bar, entombing both princes in crystal.

The bars of my cage shattered. Fragments of jagged steel blasted me. I hunkered down, curling into myself, sure the ice would consume me next.

"Muse..."

I lifted my head. Stefan held out a hand, his expression bleak and eyes fierce. This was it. The moment he'd finish what he started at the George Washington statue months ago. My parasite clenched around my heart, mimicking fear. Then Stefan smiled his crooked, wise-ass smile, and I let out a relieved breath. He was still Stefan. Not yet fully demon. I closed my hand around his. The chilling touch of ice wrapped around my wrist and threaded its way up my forearm.

He tugged me effortlessly to my feet. "C'mon... They won't stay frozen for long."

Akil and Levi resembled sculptures, one the striking representation of modern man, the other a warrior-woman—both frozen in the midst of a heated discussion. And both would be baying for blood once they thawed out. Streamlets of water cleaved valleys through Akil's sculpture. I'd wager you couldn't keep a fire demon frozen for long. Stefan slowed as we passed them. I couldn't quite see the expression on his face, but I heard his snarl.

"Do you know what you've done?" I whispered, hoping to distract him. Stefan and Akil had a history. They'd spent years battling in the netherworld. Demon to demon. There were a million reasons why Akil should suffer, and only two reasons he shouldn't. I needed him to free me of my demon hitchhiker. But more alarmingly, the thought of seeing him hurt knotted my insides with fear.

Stefan glanced back at my question and grinned. "Hell, yeah." His lust-for-life smile almost had me sobbing with relief. He really was Stefan. Stefan the Enforcer. The protector. The red coat, the swagger—he was back, just as he should be.

We burst from the Lounge into the night to find Stefan's gleaming Dodge parked half on the curb. I ducked inside the car. "They won't let this go."

In the driver's seat, Stefan gunned the engine, rammed the car into gear, planted the throttle, and swung away from the club, all in the space of about two seconds. "Let them come."

Coming from anyone else, that taunt might have been all bark and no bite, but there was nothing fake about the wildness in his eyes. Shit, he wanted the princes to come for him. I fumbled with the seatbelt. The last time I'd been in a car with Stefan, his driving had nearly killed me. Granted, we were being chased by Hellhounds at the time. I wasn't sure whether I'd prefer to be chased by the hounds or Princes of Hell.

"How'd you find me?"

"You still have Ryder's cellphone. He turned the GPS app on before giving it to you." Stefan caught my scowl. "He knew you were in trouble. He cares about you."

As we sped through the nighttime streets of Boston, I struggled to tear my gaze from Stefan. The light from the streetlights broke over his face. He appeared leaner somehow, unforgiving, refined. His eyes captured the light, fractured it, and splintered the color in his irises; aquamarine, amethyst, and sapphire. His eyes mirrored the colors of the veil.

After just a few minutes of white-knuckle driving, Stefan swung the car off the main stretch, bumped it up a curb, and stomped on the brakes. He flung open the door and jumped out. Did he always park cars like he'd stolen them? He tugged open my door, snatched my hand, and tugged me out. I yelped. "Hey—"

"Come with me." Eyes bright in the pseudo-dark of the city and breathing hard, he tugged me after him.

We passed through a gate into a leafy city park and climbed a dirt path to the top of a knoll. He released my hand as we crested the top. From our vantage point, the parkland sloped down to the water's edge. A glorious view of Boston Harbor sparkled in the distance. Beyond the inky strip of water some distance away, the high-rise buildings of the financial district glistened.

"Watch." Stefan descended between avenues of trees. An icy breeze whispered against my cheeks and kissed my lips. I smiled and pulled my coat tighter around me, wincing as my dozen or so cuts protested. It was beautiful, serene, an island of calm amidst the madness of my life.

Stefan lifted his arms, fingers rigid, coat rippling behind him as he walked. A carpet of ice bloomed beneath each step. Ice-strikes scattered and sparked in every direction, flooding the ground in white. Ice climbed trees, scampered up near-naked branches, and burst from their tips like crystal flowers. Snowflakes dallied in the air, but the sky was clear. They blinked into existence and danced around their master. He turned the world to winter with his every step and didn't look back. It was utterly surreal and completely spellbinding.

I ventured down the hill, almost falling on my ass too many times to count. Around me, the ice groaned, cracked, chimed, and sighed, drowning out the distant sounds of Boston. I shivered, teeth chattering, and summoned what heat I could find to fight the worst of the cold from my flesh.

Trees bowed over, weighed down by climbing vines of ice. Rime clawed at my boots. I had to pool more heat into my feet to keep it at bay. Stefan's ice was hungry, needy, like a living thing.

He reached the bay's edge at the bottom of a frozen avenue of trees. Ice gobbled up the black harbor waters ahead of him, only stopping its feast when he turned and smiled over his shoulder. I slipped, stumbled, somehow managed to stay upright, and cursed. One of his eyebrows arched. I scowled. "Hey, fire demon, okay? Ice messes with my chi."

He turned in a flurry of red coat and jogged back to me. "Well... C'mon... What do you think? You're impressed?"

"It's er..." I skipped my gaze over the avenue of ice while snowflakes landed on my lashes. Vapor rolled skyward, swirling and writhing higher to meet the flakes falling from a cloudless sky. The bitterly cold air tasted like minerals. He'd turned the park into a picture postcard of the netherworld. "It's stunning." *Like him.*

He gripped my shoulders, startling a tiny gasp from my lips. "You told me what it was like. You said you'd never give up your demon, that she's a part of who you are. I thought you were nuts."

His enthusiasm fixed a genuine smile on my face. "Gee, thanks."

"But I get it now." His grip tightened. "The Institute tethered me."

"Listen, about that... I know some things about Adam you should probably hear."

He cut me off with a sharp glare. "Not now." He pressed a cool finger to my lips. "Later." He stilled. Doubt, or maybe hesitation, crossed his face. Before I could discern which, he clamped my face in both hands. His boreal eyes shone, and for a breathless moment, I thought he'd kiss me. He didn't. He closed his eyes and eased his ethereal touch into me.

My demon snapped to attention. She flung herself into my flesh, staggering me with enough wanton energy that for the briefest of moments, I utterly lost my mind. Like lightening in the dark, power jolted through me. I sucked in a sharp gasp. Fire broke over my skin. My element surged, knocking my humanity aside in its rush to meet this new, overflowing source of energy.

I tugged back and severed Stefan's contact. The power he'd shared shut down, leaving me breathless and disoriented. "Holy hell, Stefan." I licked my lips. "You're like..." *Like the sensation I get reaching through the veil and tapping into the great reservoir of energy in the netherworld.* He felt like raw chaos. My demon wanted to roll over at his feet. It was unnerving and deeply erotic. Raw chaos standing within reach, all wrapped up in Stefan, ready to be undone. Words failed me. It was too surreal, too impossible. Too demon.

I backed up, not trusting my own thoughts or his. "This is all... great, but Levi and Akil will be looking for us, and you've just painted the park in ice, so y'know, we're not exactly hard to find. I need to get to Dawn. I promised I would keep her safe. She's a half blood girl, and she..." He stood frozen still. "She..."

His wings snapped into existence, elaborate flourishes of ice arching either side of him. They were huge and damned distracting, especially since they sang like distant bells. I gawked. I couldn't help it. His wings always rendered me speechless.

"Call your demon, Muse." His voice dropped to demon-tones, rich, dark, and dangerous. My own darker-half did an odd little trill inside my head, further distracting me. I was having a hard time remembering my own name, let alone the fact we were meant to be running away from immortal bad guys.

I suspected if I did summon my demon, I'd be seeing more of Stefan than his fantastical wings, and I wouldn't have a hope in hell's chance of controlling my dark half. "I'm not sure that's a good idea." Look at me, the sensible one. What was the world coming to?

His lips quirked. He flicked his wrist and produced a blade of ice.

I hiked an eyebrow up. "So what is this? Suddenly you're getting all pissy again. Why? Because I won't play?"

He moved as quickly as Akil ever has and hooked an arm around my waist, pulling me against him. "We've got some crap to work out," he whispered against my cheek.

I turned my head. His lips brushed mine. A rising tide of need warmed me through. It would be easy to let go, to forget it all and throw my arms around his neck and drag him into a kiss. Dawn was out there. She needed me. Whatever this was, it wasn't helping anyone. I knew one way of ending our dance. Mention of a single name should do it. "Like you not believing me when I tell you I didn't go to the netherworld to save Akil? I'm not involved with him."

His grip tightened. "Lies, I can smell him on you."

"I've never lied to you." A growl underscored my words just enough to add a threat. "And I never will. I know what lies can do. Believe me or don't. It's the truth.

The same as when I tell you I didn't mean to hurt you, or Nica."

He pressed the tip of the ice-sword under my chin. If it wasn't for the glimmer of humor sparkling in his eyes, I might have readied myself for the attack. "Words are cheap."

"You sound like Akil."

He bristled and pulled back, but the smile stayed. "Maybe I have reason to. Summon your demon, Muse. We're alone." He backed away. "You promised me a wild ride when you got your demon back, or was that a lie as well?"

I narrowed my eyes at him. "Back at the lake house, when you lost control, would you have hurt me?"

"I didn't mean for that to happen. I was... I just want to be free." He held out a hand. "Join me, just for a little while? C'mon, where's the fun in being different if we can't enjoy it?"

When he asked like that, I couldn't very well say no. "Oh, for hell's sake." I readied my stance in the snow and summoned my demon. She broke over me, enveloped my humanity in coal-black armored skin, and peered through my eyes at the ice-king before us. He'd shrugged off his humanity, clothes and all. Holy hell. He was nothing short of an angel, a deadly, razor-edged, diamond-eyed angel framed by wings of shattered crystal. Looking upon his true form, I had to wonder if he was ever meant to be a part of this world. He was clearly netherworldly, right down to the intricate fractals swirling beneath his skin. A curious chattering rattled through my teeth, the sound purely demon and one I had no hope of curbing.

"You want to fight it out? Fine." I didn't have a hope of beating him. He had more power rolling off of him than Akil. I unfurled my ragged wing and gave it a flick. Frankly, next to him, I looked like something that ought to be put out to pasture and shot. "Winner gets—" I flung a blast of fire at his face, turned on my heel, and darted toward the nearest frozen tree.

He snapped into existence in front of me, moving too fast for my eyes to track. I gasped, jerked back, and skidded, somehow managing to stay upright, but it wasn't pretty. He hunkered down and rolled the ice-sword in his hand. The glint of mischief in his eyes tugged a broad fang-filled smile across my lips. Backing up, I called to the slumbering city heat. It rushed into my body, burning away my doubts. Laughter peeled from my lips. I spun heat and energy around my arm and threw it over my skin, igniting a shield of fire. "Take your best shot, Frosty." Spreading my arms, I reveled in the embrace of my element.

He straightened, and took a few strides toward me. A short sharp jab stung me in the right butt cheek. I jumped. "Ow!" Ice daggers hovered in the air around me. He had all the fancy tricks. I flung my arms out, releasing a blast of heat in all directions, instantly melting his brittle daggers.

He summoned more with a chuckle. I swatted those like flies. We danced, his ice and my fire. After a while, I forgot the little girl I was meant to be saving and the princes, who by then had to be hunting us. I didn't care that cracking ice and raging fire would attract unwanted attention. I was lost in the freedom of the demon, riding by her side and happy to neglect reality while I played. Our game of fire and ice was a rollercoaster I had no control over. At some point, the moments blurred into a stream of motion and sensation. As demon, I knew only the thrill of the hunt, the chase, the capture, the wild and breathless anticipation. It was glorious, but in the clash of chaos, the threads of my tentative control unraveled.

We were laughing, teasing, snapping and growling like wolves at play: deadly, yet tamed. Ice rained, and flames spiraled around us. I was demon and free.

A wave of ice splinters rolled across the ground. My snarl quickly turned to laughter. He lunged. So did I. We clashed in a shower of opposing elemental sparks. "Freedom..." He panted. "Feels good, doesn't it."

I surged my element into him, seeking out the well of power at his center. He hissed as though burned and faltered, falling away from me. I had a few tricks up my sleeves too. I strode closer. He backed away. I pushed in deeper, seeking, reaching, entwining. He snarled and slammed into me. We tumbled to the ground in a panting, sizzling tangle, sprawled like spent lovers.

"What did you just do?" he asked, dragging his gaze along my thigh, down the concave of my waist, and over the rise of my breasts.

I felt his appraisal like a cool breeze across my hot demon skin, and an electric sizzle of power strummed through me, fluttering desire low in my abdomen. If he didn't notice the physical change in my demon body, he'd sense it. "Maybe I'll teach you sometime if you teach me how to control fire like you control ice."

He shook crushed ice from his hair. "I'd like to." His eyes turned serious as he reached a hand up and placed it carefully over my heart. His all-demon cool blue touch fizzled against my fire-veined skin. He sucked in a breath and toned down his own power, then gently eased his element through me, into the darkness slumbering at my core. I knew what he sensed as soon as I saw his handsome face cut into a scowl: Damien, my unwanted hitchhiker.

Stefan shrugged his demon off in one graceful roll of his shoulders. He was just Stefan again. Fully clothed, virtually normal but for the cerulean glare. I dropped my head back on the frozen earth and closed my eyes. My demon sauntered off to the back of my mind, dumping me back into human flesh. My clothes scratched against my skin, heavy and restricting. A small part of me pined for the freedom again. *Just let go...*

"It's the soul-lock you feel. When I stabbed and burned Damien, he didn't die. He made himself a new home in me." The words made it sound so simple. Nightmarish memories broiled.

Eyes still closed, I concentrated on the warmth of Stefan's hand resting on my chest. "I... didn't realize," he said. "That day was..." He didn't need to say it. I knew exactly what that day had been. I relived it constantly in my dreams.

"He lives in me. Every breath, every heartbeat, I share with him." I hadn't told anyone. Damien was my dirty secret. When I finally opened my eyes, I found Stefan watching me with a curious muddle of emotions on his face. Confusion, definitely. There was sympathy too.

"That's why you need Akil," he said softly.

"Yeah, Akil can fix me. But it's not that simple. I don't trust him. Part of me thinks he would take Damien's place. He's never said he wouldn't." The words began to flow easier now. It felt good to finally breath life into the fears I'd harbored for so long, as though sharing the horror relieved some of the burden. Is this what it felt like to have a friend? Someone I could share my secrets with? Someone who would listen without demanding something of me in return?

"You're right. Akil will take Damien's place if you let him. He's all demon. He wants you. He wouldn't let a little thing like free will get in his way." Stefan put on an alarmingly similar portrayal of Akil, right down to the netherworldly accent, "*It's too late, Muse. It is done, you must get over it.*"

I laughed and punched Stefan on the shoulder. This really wasn't funny, and yet, with Stefan, I almost felt as though it could be. He chuckled dryly, but his light laughter faded as his gaze fell to his hand resting over my heart. An unhurried quiet fell over us. His hand rose and fell with the rhythm of my breathing, and I recalled when we'd last lain that close, lost in one another, as though nothing could ever tear us apart. How wrong I'd been.

"Muse..." His breath hitched. He looked away. "Those things I said that day at the statue—I was out of line." When he faced me, renewed fierceness burned in his eyes. "I was afraid, and angry... I wasn't thinking clearly. I still can't think straight. Since I've been back, I can't focus... The demon rides me the whole time. I..." He licked his lips and closed his eyes, exhaling a weary sigh.

The insults he'd hurled at me by the Washington statue had stung, not least because his words had cut close to the truth. I closed my hand around his. When he opened his eyes, the sadness on his face struck me like a physical blow. I understood. I always had. Fear clamped around my heart. Fear for him. For us. I tightened my grip on his hand. It would be okay. Together, we were stronger. I opened my mouth to tell him as much when a floodlight washed over us from above. A helicopter swooped low. The downdraft whipped up snow and ice, virtually blinding me. Stefan hissed and tore his hand from mine.

"DEMONS. STAY WHERE YOU ARE. YOU WILL NOT BE HARMED."

His wings flared wide. He rose to his feet with leisurely grace and walked into the helicopter's downdraft. The wind tore at his coat, but he stood proud, wings held high against the maelstrom. A dozen red laser spots danced on his coat. Black-clad Enforcers spilled from the trees. Stefan flashed me a smile, but it wasn't the light-hearted grin I loved. That smile was hungry and filled with sharp teeth. The sight of it spilled liquid ice into my veins. Before I could draw breath to warn the Enforcers, he dropped into a crouch, spread his wings, and snarled.

Chapter Nineteen

"He killed seven Enforcers." Adam sat behind his desk, hands steepled in front of him. Jenna and Ryder flanked me. "Impaled two."

Squirming in my seat, I averted my eyes, focusing over Adam's shoulder. "You were going to kill him."

"That was not our intention." Adam's broad shoulders slouched. His bloodshot eyes spoke of the same level of weariness I felt in my bones. "We hoped to capture him."

"All the more reason for him to lash out."

"He murdered his colleagues in cold blood."

I didn't need reminding. Not only had I been there to witness Stefan's actions first hand, I'd been at the debriefing where a dozen monitors replayed the fantastical footage of a fire and ice demon throwing down in a winter wonderland in the center of Boston. I'd squirmed in my seat then too. Witnessing my demon half deliver the elaborate display of power in a room filled with Enforcers stamped a fat target on the back of my head. I'd felt their gazes burn into me. Adam had glowered at me—not the footage—during the entire meeting.

A kid had filmed the entire showdown on his cellphone. If that wasn't enough, I now sat in front of Adam's desk, hemmed in by two people who quite possibly had me on their hit lists. Jenna and Ryder hadn't said a word. Ryder wouldn't meet my eyes.

"What were you and Stefan discussing prior to my squad's arrival?" Adam asked.

I blinked and dragged my thoughts back into the room. He meant the part on the home movie where Stefan lay over me, hand on my chest. It had looked intimate on screen, and it was, but not in the way they'd all assumed.

Adam sat very still, radiating calm authority. The only time I'd seen him rattled was when I'd brought up the subject of Stefan's mother. He looked at me with those fatherly eyes, and I almost wished I could tell him all about my conversation with Stefan and how my sick bastard of an owner coiled around my heart even now. Adam looked like he'd listen—right before he'd shoot me up with PC34 and toss me in a cell.

"Sex," I said, hoping to disarm him.

His expression tightened. "After the vast amounts of energies the two of you had summoned, you wouldn't be talking about sex, you'd be having it."

My plan backfired. I cringed. A flush of heat warmed my face.

Adam removed his glasses. He pinched the bridge of his nose and exhaled a deep sigh. "I owe you an apology."

That got my attention. "Huh?"

He slid his glasses back on and leaned back in his seat. "You have more control than I've given you credit for. I underestimated you, Muse."

Yah think? I frowned. He had to be going somewhere with this uncharacteristic praise.

"The fact is," he continued, "half bloods are all about one thing: control. Stefan has lost all control. He is no longer viable and must be destroyed."

"What?" I glanced at Ryder and Jenna. Both stared through stoic masks straight at Adam. They knew this was coming, and they didn't care. "You don't mean that. He thought you were going to hurt us. He didn't mean to kill anyone. He just reacted." Nobody in this room was listening to me. "He's your son, Adam. Doesn't that mean anything to you?"

"I lost Stefan when he stepped through the veil eight months ago."

A snarl curled my lip. "You lost Stefan the moment you decided to turn him into a weapon. How old was he when you abandoned him to the Institute scientists? Did he even know a normal life before then? Did he ever have a father who loved him?"

Ryder flicked his keen eyes to me. Yeah, that's right. I know all about Stefan's past and more.

"That monster you toyed with in the park, Muse, wasn't my son," Adam replied, as cool as ice.

"He was the real Stefan, you ignorant bastard, and if you cared at all you'd realize that."

"Stefan wouldn't have killed innocent men and women doing their jobs, trying to protect the people of Boston." Adam cut his gaze to Ryder. "Ryder? Jenna? Would you disagree?"

"No," Ryder drawled. "He nearly killed me escaping the lake house."

This was a witch-hunt. "But he didn't kill you. He could have, and he didn't. He came for me."

Ryder twisted in the seat, jaw set and stare rigid. "Muse, that thing in the park ain't Stefan no more." His voice quivered with unreserved anger. "He's unstable. He killed good people back there."

"I'd have done the same, backed into a corner like that."

Ryder gave me a dry look. "No. You wouldn't. And you know it."

Maybe Ryder was right. Maybe I wouldn't have. What did that mean? Stefan had killed the Enforcers in an instant. After he'd smiled at me, a wave of fragmented ice burst from him, instantly freezing anything it came into contact with. The helicopter had pitched and plummeted into the harbor. The sounds of twisted metal were only matched by screams of agony from the fallen. His ice hadn't touched me. He knew exactly who to target. I'd watched, numbed by shock, and then he'd vanished, leaving behind a landscape of blood-stained snow.

They believed him out of control. What they didn't know—what nobody but me knew—was that he'd never been more in control. He knew exactly what he was doing. He was free.

I lifted my gaze to Adam and narrowed my sights on him. "Subject Alpha is no longer viable, huh? Put him down like a lab-rat, and then what? Buy another half blood for Operation Typhon? They're worthless anyway, right? Or maybe summon Yukki-Onna and screw her again. Keep her locked up here while she gives birth to your demon spawn."

Adam ground his teeth behind tight lips. He swallowed and spoke his next words with precise care. "Ryder, Jenna, you're dismissed. I want your written conclusion on my desk in an hour. Ryder, you will lead the team tasked with Stefan's termination."

The two Enforcers stood and left the office. Neither acknowledged me. I leaned forward in my chair. "Don't want them to know about your dirty little secret?" Adam wasn't squeaky clean in all of this. I wasn't going to let him sit back in that damn chair and order the death of his son like he was a saint, doing the heroic thing.

"Operation Typhon was a failed experiment. It was never approved."

I smiled. "Mm, so what happened? You went ahead anyway? Unofficial-like?"

He leaned in his chair and rested a hand on his desk, rubbing his fingers together as he considered his words carefully. "Who gave you this information?" He asked like he was enquiring how my day went, as though the answer was irrelevant. I knew that tone. It meant I was cutting close to the truth.

"There are two others like Stefan and me..."

Adam flinched. A smiled slashed across his lips. "What else do you know?"

"You named me Subject Beta while I was still an infant. You tried to buy me from some nameless demon, but my brother stopped the deal. You told me my employment was inevitable. You've been watching me, monitoring me, even when I was with Akil. I saw the pictures. You must have been waiting for Akil to tire of me or for me to get away from him before you made your move." I paused, giving him time to deny it. He looked back at me, reserved, calculating. I was right. Hate burned like bile in my throat. "I had five years on my own. What stopped you from recruiting me then?"

"You'd learned a great deal from Akil. Things I couldn't teach you, especially as Stefan was becoming difficult. I couldn't trust my son to teach you what was required. You weren't ready. We'd seen no evidence of your power. At that time, Stefan was our only benchmark. We didn't know if you possessed the same level of power as he did. So I continued to monitor you closely."

My heart fluttered. Everything Akil had told me was true. "How closely?"

"You were untested, raw and naive, and still very much under Akil's protection." He paused, steeled his gaze, and said, "I sent in a handler." He leaned forward. "The man you knew as Sam Harwood worked for me. His real name was Jason Bywater. Akil learned of my plans and killed him in front of Stefan as a warning to me, I suppose. Stefan knew nothing about Sam's real motives, but he reported the incident to me. I had hoped Sam—Jason would stay in place for several years. He was a good operative..."

As Adam's voice trailed off. The bottom fell out of my world. I was sitting there, bolstered by the facts, all geared up for a verbal fight, ready to pry the truth out of Adam, but he'd just slapped me down and wrenched my happy little five-year-folly out from under me. Sam, my friend, a big part of the only *normal* life I'd ever had, was a lie. Sam wasn't even called Sam. The guy I'd shared beers with, movie nights, weekends away—his whispered promises, gentle touches, and easy laughs were all lies. A jagged shard of emotional pain sliced through me. I had to get out of Adam's office before I killed him. My fingers itched. My demon snarled. I slowly, carefully, rose to my feet. Violent tremors twitched through me. The urge to burn Adam from the inside out very nearly tore my control out from under me. I could taste ashes on my tongue and feel the burn in my fingers. "You were right..." I growled, sounding more demon with each breath. "Be grateful I have control, Adam, because at this very moment, my instincts are screaming at me to boil your insides."

He didn't move, just sat behind his desk and observed with clinical detachment. "There's a war coming, Muse. My actions were justifiable in the grander scheme of things. You need to decide whose side you're on."

"I'd rather side with the demons than you." In that moment, I envied Stefan his freedom to kill.

I strode from Adam's office. Rage boiled the blood in my veins. The Institute buzzed around me: hallways filled with people devoted to protecting humans from the demon incursion. Phones shrilled too loudly. Snippets of conversations drifted by as I broke into a jog. I had to get away. I barged by several people and heard them hiss in pain. Elemental heat rolled off me. I had to get out.

"Muse." Ryder blocked my path.

I snapped my head up and tried to veer around him. He caught my arm and hissed, releasing me with a flurry of curses.

"Don't come near me." My head swirled. The demon roared. I staggered and ran.

"Muse! I have to stop him. Don't get in my way."

I burst from the warehouse building, trailing fire in my wake and almost cried with relief when my demon stepped into my skin. The sweet release she offered robbed me of the flood of emotion breaking over my mental barricade. Sprinting, hard and fast, I ran away from the Institute and their treachery. My five years of freedom was just another cage. An illusion. When would it be over? When did I get the chance to live my life as I wanted? When could I be free of demons and people like Adam, and Levi, and Val, my father, Damien, the netherworld, every-fucking-thing that wanted to kill me or screw me over? I just wanted the truth. Was that too much to ask? Did I not deserve it?

Sobs bubbled from my lips. I laughed a vicious peel of laughter. Dripping liquid fire, I ran harder. The dark inside bloomed, wrapping oil-slick tendrils of power through muscle and flesh, tightening, consuming, feeding. I staggered and fell against a car. Flames spilled across the hood and arced over the roof. The fire hungered, and seeking freedom, it roared higher. I danced back and admired the firelight licking the air. A cruel smile twisted my lips. The fire was free. I could taste its joy and sense its unfettered lust. It was free, and it called to me to join it. *Burn it. Burn them all.* A shout shattered my reverie. Backing up, I swept my heated gaze over the crowd surrounding me. I read the fear and disgust in their animated expressions and agitated states. But I couldn't hear them over the roar of the flames. Half-crazed whispers filtered through raging inferno. *Burn them. Their hatred will know terror.* A flick of my wrist, and the fire would respond. They wouldn't escape. I could kill them all in an instant.

"Get away!" I snarled. Fire dripped from my fingertips.

I reached for the veil, unable to stop myself. I ached to feel the power coursing through my veins. I was a coward, seeking peace in oblivion, and I'd kill anyone who attempted to stop me.

I closed my eyes and dropped to my knees. The road bubbled around me. Reason told me to get up and get out of there. Enforcers would be here soon, and I'd kill them. I couldn't stop myself. I didn't want to. Suffocating madness embraced me. Laughter boiled inside my head and bubbled from my lips. Yes, this was what I needed. Why fight the inevitable? It was time to let go.

I fell forward onto my hands. Rivulets of flame spilled from my fingers, seeking fuel. Camera flashes jabbed at my vision like bee stings. Whispers, curses. A glass bottle smattered beside me. "Demon!" I snapped my head up, locked the vocal stranger in my sights, and lunged.

Akil scooped me up and flung me over his shoulder in a fireman's carry. A guttural roar tore from my lips. I let loose a flurry of talons and teeth, biting, kicking, snarling. My wing thrashed. The air tightened suddenly, squeezing from my lungs. Static energy washed over me, and in the next breath we were in the open-plan expanse of Akil's Battery Wharf apartment where I'd seen Carol-Anne's body.

He dropped me on my feet. A barrage of words spilled from him: something about control. I locked my hand into a fist, drew my arm back, and punched him in the face hard enough to feel bone crack beneath my knuckles. He grunted and reeled back. I threw a ribbon of fire at him. He spat blood and snarled while my obedient flames coiled around his waist and then disappeared as though absorbed by his clothes. Fire wouldn't work on him, but I was beyond rational thought. I lunged, hit him square in the chest, and slammed him against the granite bar. He huffed a foreign curse. I was on him. I sunk my teeth into his throat and tasted hot, spiced blood. All my thoughts focused into a pinpoint of all-consuming rage. I was a machine with a single purpose.

Akil thrust his hands out and threw me back. I bounced off the couch, tumbled to the floor, sprang off my feet and dashed for him again. I wanted more blood, more destruction. I'd tear his throat out. I'd burn this apartment, this building, and everyone in it.

He backhanded me, snapping my head back. Pain burned across my cheek and jaw. In the momentary distraction, I lost my footing and fell. He stalked forward, eyes ablaze, hands fisted at his sides. I kicked his leg out from under him. He went down onto a knee, his muscles already tensing to spring forward. *Bring it. You lying bastard.*

Twisting like an eel, I leveraged my wing under me and pushed off the floor. Akil pulled up short. Had I been thinking, I'd have realized he was capable of more than this sparring session, but I was too far gone to care. I swung a fist, he ducked, twisted, and struck viper fast, punching me in the gut. My breath whooshed out of me, but as I buckled, I saw my opportunity and hooked my arm around his neck, yanking him back against my chest. My teeth found his shoulder and pierced his hot flesh once more. He roared and bucked beneath me. Then a vise-like hand caught my leg and tugged. I clung on like a pit bull, fangs in too deep to be wrenched free. He danced back and rammed me into a wall. I snarled against his hot, spicy flesh, ground my teeth into the wound, and swallowed the gush of rich blood.

The stakes changed when he brought Mammon to the party. One minute I was clamped onto Akil's back, the next I sat lodged between Mammon's enormous wings. His blood boiled in my mouth, and finally, my humanity reasserted itself. I pried my teeth from his leathery skin, suddenly and acutely aware I was clinging to the back of a Prince of Hell.

He reached a muscular arm back, clamped a huge hand around my upper arm and shoulder, plucked me off him as easily as removing a tick, and tossed me aside. I hit the floor hard and rolled before twisting onto my front, breathless, bruised, snarling and snapping my rage.

Mammon, a mountain of rippling black muscle and sizzling embers, eyed me with delight. He shook his wings out and rolled his massive shoulders. Hot ash rose from the fire licking across his skin. When he took a step toward me, a low warning growl rumbled through my entire body. Ash rained from my skin. Red-hot hunger slithered across his otherwise black eyes. I shivered with a peculiar mix of adrenalin, desire, and unease. *What the fuck was I doing?* This was real. I was here. In Akil's apartment. Facing off with a Prince of Hell. Mammon's infinitely dark eyes read me, waiting, almost baiting me with the promise of violence. I straightened up to my full height—he still loomed over me—and shook my demon off. She retreated with a wicked slice of laughter that pulled my human lips into a smile.

Mammon tilted his head. His tongue licked across black onyx lips, and he dissolved away, leaving a bedraggled and abused Akil behind. He reached behind his left shoulder and hissed a curse. "You almost tore my shoulder open." His voice was muffled, the words not quite clear. Crimson blood streamed down his neck and over his shoulder, soaking into his shirt, but the wounds had already closed. He pressed the ball of his thumb to his nose and frowned when his hand came away bloody. "And broke my nose." That'd be the reason he sounded as though he had the flu. I tasted his salty blood on my lips and suppressed a groan. My demon stalked my thoughts, asserting her desires over mine. To bloody another demon was a power trip. To bloody a prince had my demon panting with lust. Holy hell, I'd virtually propositioned

Mammon, the outcome of which didn't bear thinking about.

I wiped my mouth, alarmed by the blood on my lips. "Why didn't you tell me Sam was an Institute spy?" My voice had turned cold and flat. Good. I didn't have it in me to outthink or outmaneuver Akil. Let him believe I didn't care. Splatters of blood speckled my clothes. The hot-copper smell filled my head and flipped my stomach over. I was a mess, through to the bone.

Akil gave me a bored look, as though disappointed I'd blame him. "It wasn't significant." He shrugged his jacket off and laid it over the kitchen counter. Peeling off his shirt, he balled it up and tossed it in the trash. I'd torn several deep gashes in his chest, taken a chunk out of his neck, and torn open his shoulder. Yeah, I'd completely lost it. But I'd come back. That was a good thing, right?

"What do you mean it wasn't significant? Don't pull that shit, Akil. I'm barely under control here."

"I'd noticed." He gripped the bridge of his nose and, with an audible grinding of bone, set it right with barely a twitch.

I swept a hand back to tuck my hair behind my ear. My fingers shook. Now that I'd noticed the tremors, my entire body decided to join in. I clamped my arms around me, trying to crush the quivers away. "You knew all along. Was that why you killed him?"

Akil's glances revealed an uncharacteristic concern as he rinsed a towel beneath a tap and wiped the blood from his face and chest. "His betrayal would make a convenient excuse. Would you think differently of me had his deceit been my singular motive?"

I blinked. *Yes, I would*, I thought but didn't reply. The man Akil murdered had been a stranger to me, but Akil had still killed a man. Just because Sam worked for Adam, didn't make it right.

"It matters not why I killed him, just that I did. If you're looking to absolve me, don't waste your time. I took pleasure in it. He was a pretender in your bed. My only mistake was not killing him sooner. The Institute tests my patience. They wanted you. They still do. Their insolence—"

"Is astounding. Yes, I know. You told me that once." I backed up and pressed a hot hand against my forehead. "Akil... You should have said."

"And ruin the only taste of freedom you've experienced?"

I dropped onto the edge of the couch, mouth open. Had he just told me he'd lied to protect my illusion of freedom? He looked back at me, eyes so damn understanding that it hurt to meet his gaze. I laced my hands in my hair and slumped forward. The world was wrong. Everything I relied on, the truths I'd come to cherish, were unraveling around me.

"The Institute has a hit out on Stefan," I grumbled. "He's gone wild. Dawn is probably terrified and alone somewhere in the netherworld. Levi wants to offer me up to Asmodeus on a platter. I'm losing control." I hissed in a sharp breath. "I was going to kill that man... on the street. It was all I could think of. I wouldn't have stopped at him either." I lifted my head and found Akil standing in front of me, holding two glasses of wine. Smears and dribbles of blood marred an otherwise perfect chest. Cuts crisscrossed his arms. He had blood in his hair and a smear across his cheek.

"I know."

"You stopped me."

"Yes." He hitched his bare bloody shoulder. "And experienced your wrath first hand. Which was... uncomfortably arousing."

I groaned and hid my face in my hands again. "Damien's soul-lock is getting stronger. I think he helped loosen the reins on my demon."

"Indeed, as I warned you he would." The couch shifted as he settled beside me.

I sat back, took the wine from Akil, and gulped it down without stopping for breath, then handed the empty glass back to him. His lips twitched. "Why me?"

He roamed his heated gaze across my bloody and torn clothing. "If you ceased battling your other half and embraced the truth of what you are, you'd have your answer."

"I'm just a wretched half-blood girl caught in a storm."

Akil tasted his wine and smiled. "Muse, you are the storm."

Chapter Twenty

I woke in Akil's bed, thankfully alone. He'd found some clothes I must have left behind years ago —boot-cut, low-rise jeans and loose V-neck sweater—and left them out for me. The clothes were a tight fit. I'd gained some muscle in recent months. The fact he'd kept the clothes at all disturbed me on a level I didn't dare think about. I had a long list of things that were best not to dwell on. Losing control, failing Dawn, eyeing up Mammon for violent and bloody demon sex, breaking Akil's nose, and how I wanted to rip Adam's spine from his flesh and beat him with it.

I ditched my trashed clothes from the night before— retrieving Ryder's cellphone and my sidearm—showered, helped myself to breakfast, and found a note left on the kitchen counter. Akil had handwriting you'd expect to find in an antique tome, consisting of elaborate flourishes that seemingly flowed into one another with no room to breathe. I eventually deciphered his archaic patterns. He'd written *"be discreet"* and *"keep control."* Beside the note, he'd folded *The Boston Globe* newspaper. A surprisingly sharp image of Stefan and me flexing our demon muscles adorned the front page. The headline read: Demons Slaughter Enforcers.

I headed home, my head filled with uncertainties and the residue of emotional fallout. Levi would come for me. Of that I was certain. My father unfortunately hadn't forgotten about me. Plus, I'd broken out of Levi's cage. He wasn't finished with me either. Dawn was, in all likelihood, with my psycho-brother, and I didn't know enough about Val to go after her. Even if I could find him, I wasn't strong enough to avoid his sex-on-legs mojo. If he tried that shit on Dawn, I'd go nuclear on his immortal ass. I could drain the fire from him. And technically, he wasn't permitted to kill me. Still, I needed a plan before I went charging after Val.

What do you do when you're swimming with sharks? You make sure you're the biggest, most badass thing in the pool. I was already a primetime topic—even made the front page. A demon celebrity for all the wrong reasons. Could I use that? Should I encourage it?

Arriving outside my apartment, I noticed the door was ajar and instinctively reached for my gun. Val? No, he couldn't enter without an invitation. Akil? He wouldn't bother with traditional means of entry, not now he had his own personal invite. He was more likely to appear while I was in the shower.

I gave the door a shove. It creaked open and revealed Stefan draped in my couch, boots propped up on the coffee table, and Jonesy curled in his lap, belly up, receiving tickles under the chin.

An unexpected surge of joy tugged a smile across my face. Then I remembered the circumstances surrounding our last meeting, and my smile died. I slammed the door closed and holstered my weapon. "Are you insane? They'll be watching my place."

"Well." He sighed, and lifted the pliable Jonesy off his lap, "I wasn't about to interrupt your sleep-over at Akil's."

But he didn't look angry, more mildly amused. "How did you–?"

"You've still got Ryder's cell. Plus, someone snapped you going feral in the street and sent it to the news stations. Akil's image was blurred, but I don't know any other guys in suits who could throw a flaming demon over their shoulders and disappear into thin air."

I snaked my arms crossed and tried to read him. His smile held a tight line, and his focus was off, as though he looked through me, not at me. I shifted my element and tried to gauge his power, but he was shut down, his demon behind lock and key.

"Akil kidnapped me."

"He stopped you from hurting anyone." He looked away, seeming to admire the framed symbols on my walls. "How many Enforcers did I kill?" His voice had leveled, like still waters with something dark lurking underneath.

My throat tightened. "Seven," I whispered.

A grimace tugged on his features, and at the same time, a brief lick of his element danced over my skin. "Something is very wrong with me. I can't stop the demon—"

A knock at my door startled a yelp out of me. Stefan's irises sharpened to an azure blue.

I held up a hand. "The Institute doesn't knock." I opened the door.

Lacy waved a newspaper in my face. "Holy crap, Charlotte Henderson, is this you? Are you a demon?" She grinned. "You must tell me everything. Do you have wings? I can't make it out in the pictures. They're all fuzzy, but it sure looks like you, just kinda... y'know, if you were burned to a crisp."

"Lacy, it's sort of a bad time."

She flicked her hair out of her face and gave me a knowing smile. "Is Akil here?"

I winced. "No."

"Aww, c'mon... You're, like, famous. You have demon friends. Did you kill those Enforcers?"

"No." I gasped.

"That's cool, I knew you wouldn't. When I read it, I thought, no way, that's not Charlie... Hey, who's the ice dude? There are more pictures online. They've enhanced them an' everything. Are his wings really made of ice? You two looked, kinda... y'know, cozy."

"Lacy, I'll answer all your questions. Okay? Just don't mention you know me, please. I mean it. I like it here. I don't want to have to move again."

"'Course, you're my friend, Charlie, and if I get to meet some hot guys, bonus. Are you an' Akil, like, an item? I was thinkin' maybe, if y'know, if it's cool, you could give him my number?"

Stefan opened the door wider, rested his forearm on the frame, and gave Lacy the 'you-have-to-be-kidding-me' stare. "It's Lacy, right?"

She blinked up at Stefan, mouth open, eyes wide. "Uh-huh."

"Akil likes to call hell his home. Maybe you've heard of Hell? Fire and brimstone? Eternal damnation? There are demons there who will tear off your skin and wear it as an apron. Akil is a Prince of Hell, so what do you think he'd like to do with your pretty skin, Lacy?"

She closed her mouth. "Equal rights for demons, dude. Don't discriminate." She showed Stefan her hand, palm out. He growled, low and threatening.

"Okay, you two... Lacy, please give me a few days for all this to settle down and for me to work out some kinks... and I'll happily teach you all about the dos and don'ts of demons. I highly recommend you don't piss them off."

"Sure." She grinned, glared at Stefan, and then stalked away.

Stefan slammed the door and loomed in front of me. "Do not tell me you invited Akil into your life again?" His eyes flashed electric blue.

"Do you think I'm an idiot?"

"She asked if he was here... *inside your apartment.*"

Now he gets pissy? Now he cares? I scowled back at him. "He coerced his way in via my landlord, alright? You know he's in denial about... everything."

He straightened and drew back. "You smell like him. It drives me crazy."

"I smell like him?" I cringed. "Do you know how weird that sounds?"

"I can't help it. My demon..." He growled again and turned his back on me. A coil of power I hadn't realized had tangled itself around me, unraveled as he strode away. "My demon's messed up, Muse. He's in my head the whole time... I can't shut him out like I used to. The things he wants... I want..."

"I thought you said you wanted the freedom." I said quietly.

He stopped and bumped a clenched fist on the back of the couch. "I do, and that's the problem. The Enforcers, that was just the start."

"That was an accident."

He turned. "Was it? You seem so certain. I wasn't thinking. I just... acted. It wasn't until later, when I came down off the power-trip, that I knew I'd killed them." He scowled. His shoulders slumped. "And I didn't care."

"Don't say that."

"It's the truth. I used to know where the demon ended and I began, but the lines are blurred. I'm starting to want what he wants."

Everything he said felt familiar in ways I didn't want to admit to. "What does he want, exactly?"

His gaze danced about the room, as though seeking the right words, and sucked in air between his teeth. The resulting hiss sounded almost demon. "Revenge... on the Institute." He closed his eyes. "My father, Akil, the netherworld. Everything." He twitched his head and dropped his chin. When he opened his eyes, the slippery touch of raw elemental energy crawled over me. "I'm not decided about you yet. We–I swing from revenge, to... something else."

"Maybe you just need to vent." My words were as pathetic as they sounded. No amount of venting—like we had at the park—was going to help.

His smile quirked. "Vent? I'm terrified of what I'm capable of, Muse. Right now, standing here, I know there's ice in the atmosphere miles above us. I can draw the cold down and freeze the air in your lungs before you could summon your demon to stop me. These symbols don't do anything. I don't need to draw from the veil. It's in here." He curled a hand over his chest. "You felt it."

I had when he'd driven his power into me in place of a kiss. My demon purred her pleasure. I mentally slapped her back. "Okay. Maybe I can help you. We could go to the mountains. Get away from everyone. You could throw your power around all you wanted without hurting anyone."

"I'd hurt you." His steeled gaze confirmed it. "I'm afraid of what we could do together. We're too dangerous. It's worse when I'm around you. My demon gets... distracted."

I knew that feeling. My demon was doing the same, purring and pacing, strutting around my head like a cat in heat. "I know you won't hurt me."

"I know one thing, I can't be around people. There's no way I can stay in Boston. Enforcers will be watching the lake house. There's only one place I can go where I can't hurt anyone."

My breath hitched. "The netherworld." He gritted his teeth and didn't deny it. "If you go back there, your demon will win." *I'll lose you again.* He couldn't go. I'd already experienced a world without Stefan, and it was an insipid place. He reminded me what it was like to be alive. He loved life. At least he used to. His dark half and his lust for mischief had twisted into a thirst for revenge.

"I think I have to."

I shook my head. "It took Akil ten years to make me human. If you go back there, you might never be human again."

"What choice do I have? I killed seven people, Muse. Seven. I stole their lives and I did it"—he clicked his fingers—"like that. I don't want to be that demon."

"Stefan—"

"No, Muse. If Ryder comes after me, I'll kill him." His voice fractured. "I will. My demon will. It's all the same."

I worried my lip between my teeth. "This isn't right."

He sunk his hands into his hair and blinked too-bright eyes up at the ceiling. "Tell me about what's right and fair. I fought my entire life to control this thing inside me, and I failed."

"No." I was losing him. He was going away from me. "You didn't fail. We just need to figure out a way to control him again." The words tumbled breathlessly from my lips. "Akil tamed me..."

"You were a young girl, Muse." His wan smile humored me. "He had years. You barely had enough control of your element to light a candle. I'm too far gone. I have too much power."

"I'm not giving up on you." *Shit.* Tears blurred my vision. I gulped the knot in my throat. "Just... just don't do anything. Not yet, okay? There must be a way."

"There is." His smile softened. "I walk away." This was goodbye.

I staggered back and bumped against the counter. It was all my fault. I'd driven him through the veil to begin with. I'd started everything. "No. Please don't. I'm sorry." Panic ripped away my fears and doubts, and the words I'd wanted to say since he'd returned spilled from my lips. "I tried to get to you. I would have followed you to the netherworld if I could. I only wanted to live when I told you to get rid of Akil. I didn't mean for this to happen. What you saw outside the lake house between me and Akil that night, it wasn't what it looked like. I didn't bring Akil back. I brought you back. Akil was just... there. I needed him for the bastard inside me. When you found me in the library with Nica, I tried to save her. Damien was too strong. I did everything I could. I tried to do the right thing. I'm not perfect. I fuck up—too often. I don't know what I'm supposed to do. I'm scared too. I don't know what's happening to me. I didn't... I couldn't..." Cool tears skipped unchecked down my cheeks.

He stood granite still, eyes glistening. I'd told him everything, the truth, all of it. But it wasn't enough. The truth couldn't change the past. He clenched his jaw and stayed demon-still, not daring to close the distance between us: just a room, but it felt like a canyon.

"Say something," I blurted. "Dammit, shout at me, curse me, fight me if you want to. Just tell me you won't go."

"You'll be alright." His eyes said '*Goodbye.*'

"No, no, don't do this..." I stepped forward. He recoiled.

"Don't... Don't come near me." He held out a hand. "I'm..." His image shimmered, element surging. "Please, stay back, Muse."

This was insane. It was wrong. It wasn't fair. "You won't hurt me."

"I will," he snapped, and then more softly said, "I can't control it."

Gritting my teeth, I chained my emotions down. If he walked away now, I might never see him again. "Okay... Alright. But wait. Just... don't leave yet."

"If I wait, it will only get worse." His words settled around us like snowflakes.

I shook my head, dislodging tears. "Not yet. I..." I had to keep him there with me. I would find something to help him. Akil would know a way. I'd do anything. "I need your help. You asked me once for help. You wanted to kill my brother. You know what he's doing, don't you? You know he trades half-bloods."

"Yes." He replied gruffly. "I'd planned on asking for your help, but then I crossed the veil with Akil, and nothing mattered after that."

"Val has a little girl. Dawn. She was Levi's, but Akil stole her and dumped her on me. I can't abandon her. Val took her. She's a half blood like us. I have to get her back, and you're the only person I trust to help me."

He fluttered his eyes closed and inclined his head, fighting an internal battle. When he spoke again, his demon shadowed his words, lowering the timbre to a jagged growl. "If I do this, you let me go. You don't try to stop me."

I pursed my lips. I wouldn't let him go. I was as stubborn as he was committed. He just needed time to think it through. That was all. He'd change his mind. He'd battle his demon and win like I had all those years ago. He would because he was Stefan, and he was my hope that everything would work out in the end. He would survive because he always did. And if he could, then so could I. Two half bloods of opposing elements. Two hopeless dreamers.

He sighed. "I know where to find Valenti. I'll take you. We'll get Dawn. But you return with her to Boston, and leave me behind. That's the deal."

I held his arctic gaze with fire in my eyes. I'd leave him there over my dead body.

Two sharp knocks at the door shattered our negotiations. I swiped drying tears away and stalked to the door. I'd have to be curt with Lacy, lay down some scare tactics. I tugged open the door, a warning on my lips. Ryder shunted me aside. I reeled back and caught sight of the black-clad Enforcers outside my apartment, armed to the teeth behind riot gear.

"Easy... easy big fella..." Ryder trained a gun on Stefan. "No sudden moves, and nobody gets hurt."

There are moments in life when events undo in front of you like the thread of a scarf, and no matter how you try to stop them, it all falls apart as though it's inevitable. Fated. That moment in my apartment unraveled as time slowed. I watched, oddly detached, as Stefan's entire body sparkled with ice dust. He dropped his stance, lifted his lips in a snarl, and I knew he would kill Ryder, right there, in front of me. He'd do it before Ryder could pull the trigger. A glimmer of thought would end it. Ryder was a dead man.

Instinct drove me forward. No hesitation, no stumbling, or slipping. I grabbed Ryder's shoulder and yanked him back. He twisted, trying to shake me off. With dreadful certainty, I stepped in front of him. And the world blanched white for a second. Just a blink. When color bled back into my vision, I couldn't make sense of it. Warm liquid spluttered from my lips. Silence smothered me. The world was quiet. At peace. And Stefan stood in front of me, so close I could have leaned in and brushed his lips with mine. Ice dusted his face. His eyes sparkled like they had at the park when we'd both been free—just for a little while. He pressed a hand to my face and said something, but the words tore from me. I was falling. An intangible dark pulsed in my peripheral vision, an inescapable truth.

Stefan pulled away. I was so very cold. I wanted him back, but my mind drifted. Looming shadows devoured my untethered thoughts. His expression shattered. His face twisted with horror. He staggered. A slither of light slipped across the dagger of ice gripped in his hand. A splash of deep red coated the serrated blade. Streams of blood dribbled over his clenched fingers. My blood?

He'd stabbed me.

From behind, strong arms coiled around my waist. I sank to the floor, falling against the warmth of the man who smelled like gun oil and hot metal. Heavy eyelids fluttered, but I couldn't tear my gaze away from Stefan. If I looked away, he'd be gone. He lowered his gaze to the dagger in his hand, as though only just realizing what he'd done. When he said, "I'm sorry." I didn't hear the words, but I read them on his lips.

Dark lapped at my mind, breathing in and out, washing over me, drowning me. I clawed at the suffocating pressure and tried to fight my way back to the surface, but the pressure closed in, and after a while, my limbs wouldn't respond. I drifted. *So cold.* I drew my thoughts into the warmth inside me. And let go.

Chapter Twenty One

They'd kept me sedated. Of that I was damned certain. I drifted in and out of consciousness and growled at the white-coats when they came near me, but I was so very weak. I couldn't escape them. It felt like hours I'd been that way, but when I finally had enough strength to swing my trembling legs from the bed, my muscles clenched with atrophy, and I suspected it had been much longer. My body quivered under the effort of movement. Cool beads of perspiration broke over my skin. I could walk. I could escape.

My bed was the only one in the spearmint-green room. A wall of one-way glass drew my eye. I'd been there enough times to know I was inside the Institute's medical facility, and they were watching, always watching.

I tore the IV from my arm, applied pressure to staunch the blood, and searched my room for clothes. I couldn't very well escape in a flimsy hospital gown, but the room was barren, more like a morgue than a clinic.

Ryder burst through the door, and I nearly jumped out of my skin, not least because he carried a bunch of pink carnations and a grin so wide he must have gotten laid while I was out for the count.

I scowled at him. Ryder and flowers? "Did someone die?" My voice clawed its way out my parched throat. Shit, just how long had I been out?

He dumped the flowers on the end of the bed. "Yeah, you." He tucked his thumbs over his belt. Rocking back on his heels, he wandered his wide-eyed gaze over me and then muttered a curse and swept me into a bear hug.

"Ah, easy." A twinge of pain needled me in the ribs. "Ryder." He squeezed tighter. "Kinda need to breathe here."

He pulled back. "Dammit, Muse, you died in my arms." He swept my bangs back from my face and searched my eyes. "I tried to get you out the apartment so you could summon your demon, but the Institute took over. The fuckers told me you'd died. And here you are. Shit, don't do that again." He glared at me, eyes flicking back and forth, tracing my expression, as though committing every nuance of my face to memory. Finally, he seemed to realize he was still clinging to me and stepped back.

"Well, I'm okay." I tried to smile but winced instead. My side throbbed. I pressed a hand over the heat of the wound and felt the sticky bandage taped to my side from below my breast to my hip. "What happened?"

"You'll have a bastard of a scar."

I winced and tried to stretch out the pain. "Scars are my armor."

"You saved my ass, Muse." He scratched at his chin and then chewed on his thumbnail. "He was gunning for me. He'd have gutted me right there..."

Stefan. My vision blurred. I gripped the bedside table. The Enforcers had stormed my apartment. Stefan stabbed me. I steeled my thoughts, packed all the unwieldy emotions down into a reinforced mental box, and rammed the lid on. When I met Ryder's stare, my expression was blank.

"Did you kill him?"

"No. He opened the veil and stepped through. He's gone."

I blinked, heard my demon roaring, smacked her down into the box, and tied a pretty pink bow on top. Stefan had gone through the veil thinking he'd killed me. "How long ago?"

"Two weeks. The whole world thinks you died. The Institute released a statement. The demons who slaughtered their enforcers had been terminated. End of story. Charlotte Henderson is no more. Adam only told me you were alive two hours ago. I had thirteen days of thinking you'd bled out in my arms. Fuck, don't ever do that again, lil' firecracker."

"I'm dead?" I might not have believed it, if it wasn't for the excess moisture in Ryder's eyes.

"As good as."

I should have felt something. Anything. "I want to go home." Why was I numb?

He smiled. "Adam wanted to keep you here. Yeah, don't give me that look. I told him you'd be happier back home. At least, you wouldn't try to kill him. He's flexed some Institute muscle and forced your neighbors to sign a non-disclosure contract. If they talk about you or what they've seen, they'll find themselves in a whole world of trouble."

Ah, hell. I hadn't wanted to get them involved at all. I lifted a trembling hand and rubbed my eyes. "What about Akil?"

Ryder shivered. "He's dropped off the grid, probably gone back to hell. Good, fuckin' riddance. Psycho tracked me down, damn near broke my arm, and demanded I give him a second-by-second break-down of what happened." He rubbed at his arm. "He wasn't best pleased with what I had to tell him."

Akil thought I was dead. Stefan thought he'd killed me. Asmodeus would stop looking for me. So would Val, and Levi. I was... free? I touched my chest. No, not free. Damien still thrummed through me. But almost free. Was that even a thing? Almost free? No, you can't be almost free. Free is an absolute.

I sighed out a weary breath. Did Dawn think me dead too?

I'd been dead to the world for two weeks. Two weeks in netherworld time was more like two months. I'd seen Stefan's face. The horror and guilt had crushed him. "I need some time..."

"Sure yah do. Let me buy you a drink, though. Maybe a round of pool? Might even let you win this time."

He was getting all mushy again. "Jeez, Ryder, who knew you had a heart behind all that swagger?"

He screwed up his face. "Yeah. I know. Don't go spreadin' it around. Seriously though, we need to talk. The night after you died, some weird shit started goin' down. The number of demon incursions fell off the chart. The Institute number-crunchers said it was a glitch, but the sightings, events, they're dwindling by the day. Demon chatter says something's up beyond the veil. We've got a few demons in the cells, but they won't talk. They're scared."

As he explained, I reached out a probing thought and poked at the veil. Usually, it rippled in the back of my mind, a constant that I ignored like the background noise of the city. When I reached for it, it should have pulsed and rippled. But when I reached for it then, it shivered and settled like the waters of a millpond. It didn't move. Didn't dance. Didn't twitch.

I repressed the shock, kicked it into the same mental box with everything else, and nodded. "You're right. That's not normal. Something's up, and it doesn't feel good."

Chapter Twenty Two

A month after I'd been declared dead, I stood in the ladies washroom at The Voodoo Lounge, frowning at my pale reflection. The music thumped the air and drummed the inside of my skull. I'd had a headache before I'd arrived at the Lounge. Now it was pulsating mass of agony, as though Damien had shifted from my soul and settled behind my eyeballs. My stomach heaved. I gulped back pools of saliva. *How many drinks did I have?* Demons in people-suits brushed by me and muttered various slurs. The club had been packed to bursting point every night since reopening two weeks ago. I was here to find out why the Lounge was bustling. And I was fucking it up.

My reflection looking back at me in the mirrors above the rows of sinks was a stranger. I had my straight-as-nails hair cut above the shoulder and dyed bottle-blond. A pink and black short skirt ensemble accentuated curves I didn't know I had. Lacy had assured me the outfit was as anti-Charlie Henderson as I could get. She was right. I hardly recognized myself. I had blue contacts in too. I'd melted the last pair when a demon got frisky a few days ago. He'd told me he'd rather live out his days in the Institute cells than go back across the veil. He'd fought like his life depended on it. Once, I would have killed him, but I let him go. Ryder didn't know.

What the hell was I doing here, surrounded by demons, and dressed-up like some demon fangirl?

My reflection frowned at me. Yeah, that was right. This was my idea. "Let's check out The Voodoo Lounge," I said. Word in the demon-chatter said the place was jumping since the veil had fallen quiet. The demons were getting twitchy, grouping together, flocking. *Safety in numbers.* The Enforcers wanted to know why. The last time I'd been in the Lounge, Levi had trapped me in a cage. Who was running this club, and exactly what had the demons spooked so badly they would rather die than go home? I also had a darker motive for my visit, something I'd yet to fully admit to myself. I was looking for trouble, itching for a fight. I hadn't slept properly since waking from my near-death experience. Blood soaked nightmares soiled my dreams. My demon hungered. So did I. If I didn't find trouble, I started it. Ryder had already called me out on being careless while on duty. My head wasn't in the game.

"Honey, too many flamin' Zambuccas?" The woman— if one could call her that—might have appeared normal if not for the two furred tails twitching around the hem of her skirt and the fangs crowding her mouth. She laughed and left me hunched over the sink, trying to keep my churning stomach contents down.

Ryder didn't know I'd been getting acquainted on a nightly basis with a bottle of wine. Not that he'd judge me. We all had our vices. I recognized the signs. I was slowly sinking in quicksand. The weight of despair pulled me under. I should have been happy. Ninety percent of my problems had evaporated overnight. The world thought I was dead. I was now happy Carla Gordons, who dyed her hair sunshine yellow and wore cherry red lipstick. I didn't want it. I wanted to go home, curl up in my bed, and hide. Carla wasn't me. I wasn't a coward. I didn't run. I didn't hide. But I was running, and each time I reached for the bottle, I was hiding. The darkness inside me throbbed harder with every passing day. *The whispering dark...* Damien's hideous laughter haunted me.

My phone chirped in my pocket. Snarling a curse, I answered it as yet another demon bumped into me and grunted something derisive. "Ryder..." His name was more a growl than an acknowledgement.

"Hey... Just checkin' in. Everything okay?"

"Peachy."

"You don't have to do this, Muse. I can send another Enforcer in." We both knew that wasn't happening.

"No, I got it." I needed to be here, among demons.

"Okay, I'll call in an hour. Get something we can use."

"Gotcha." I jabbed the end-call button, splashed water on my face, and left the bathroom, heading for the dance floors.

The night wore on, and my mood soured. I managed to get a few tidbits of information out of a semi-conscious demon slumped over a table. It was bad across the veil. The princes were laying down their laws. Pick your allegiance or die. The demons who could escape had, but not all possessed the skill to cross the veil without assistance. Some bartered with higher demons for safe passage, but many didn't make it that far. The princes forbade it. I tried to get out of him why the princes were battling when they'd had centuries of relative peace. He mumbled something indecipherable about the veil, titles crumbling, and the *fall of wrath*, whatever that meant, before proceeding to drink himself under the table.

Frustrated, I wandered the dance floors, scanning the sea of demons. My demon paced back and forth inside my mind. I couldn't bring her to the show, not without revealing who I was. I could dye my hair and paint my nails pink all I liked, but my demon didn't change. A half blood was rare enough. A half blood missing a wing? They'd know me the second I dropped my humanity.

My phone buzzed in my jacket pocket. I plucked it free and ducked to the side of the dance floor, almost falling over a crate as the crowd spat me free. Except it wasn't a crate. I ignored Ryder's call and crouched down beside the metal cage.

"Dawn?"

She was curled up in the middle of the cage, her filthy slip of a dress barely covering her grazed knees. She blinked doe eyes out from behind matted bangs. "Muse?"

"Move back." I summoned a slither of heat into my palms, gripped the bars, and tried to pour it into the metal. White glyphs flared beneath my touch, sending my jolt of heat back up my arms. I cursed and let go. "It'll be okay. I'm getting you out." I wouldn't leave her there. If I had to tear the club down around us, she was getting out of that cage.

She hugged herself tighter. "No. He'll hurt me."

"Who?" I pressed my face close to the bars. How could anyone do this to a little girl? I knew the answer. I'd had it done to me. They didn't see a girl. Dawn was property. The demons in this club barely gave her a second glance. Just a half-blood toy in a cage, an abomination.

"He's inside my head. He drowns me, but I don't get wet. Just go. He'll hurt you too."

Drowns but doesn't get wet? A shiver trickled across my flesh as the memory of experiencing exactly that bubbled to the surface of my thoughts. She had to be referring to Leviathan. Beneath the multicolored lights and deafening beat of the music, I couldn't see anyone resembling Levi. The club was too full of demons and their mingling elements to even try to sense him. "Is he here, Dawn?"

She bit into her lip and nodded. "The one with the black wings brought me back here. I don't like him. I don't like any of them."

Black wings? *Valenti*. My twisted excuse for a brother had handed her back to Levi. "Did the black-winged-one hurt you Dawn?"

She shook her head. "He said it wasn't right for half bloods to be free." She blinked, dislodging a silent tear. "The water prince likes it here. He told me he likes to make the demons thirsty. I get so thirsty. All I want is water. Then he drowns me..." Her tiny body shivered. "But it's not real."

"I know, honey." I had to get her away from here. I searched the edges of the cage and found a padlock. Bolt cutters would get it open. Ryder would have those. "I can get you out, but I need tools. I'll be back real soon, okay? I promise."

Her eyes saddened, and she turned the torn rabbit over in her arms and hugged it close. "I want it to end. I want to hide."

I closed my fingers around the bars. "Hiding won't make it go away. Hiding just delays the inevitable. Unless we do something about it." I offered her a hopeful grin. "I let my friend down once and didn't get to him in time. That's never happening again. Do you hear? I'll be back later, and I'm getting you out. And if Levi shows up, I'll boil him dry."

She blinked and nodded. "Okay, Muse."

* * *

I called Ryder from the parking lot beside the club and told him everything. He picked me up in the tired Mustang ten minutes later and drove a few blocks away before parking.

"Okay, listen up..." Twisting in the drivers seat, he gave me the no-bullshit glare. "The club closes at four hundred hours. I've checked local security footage. By five, the staff have gone. The security is non-existent, probably because nobody is stupid enough to break into a club owned by a Prince of Hell. So that's what we're doing. We break in. Cut open the cage. Grab Dawn. And get the hell out of there before anyone knows we've been inside. You sure you can deal with Levi if he shows up?"

"Yup." Maybe, mostly... definitely. If I could suck the fire out of Akil, I could most definitely turn Levi to steam. I had to. I wasn't leaving without Dawn. "Sounds like a plan."

He grabbed a gun from the back seat, checked the chamber, magazine, and handed it to me. "You're toting demon-killing soft point rounds, etched with glyphs. One shot to the head will take down any lesser demon, but the princes are tough bastards. It'll slow a prince down, but it won't kill him."

Cool. "You tested it on a prince?"

"I planted a few in Akil a few months back, but he took 'em like they were bee stings. Happened a few blocks from here."

Oh. I ejected the magazine and examined the rounds, deliberately avoiding Ryder's keen stare. I'd healed Akil's wounds that night. Ryder's bullets were more effective than he realized.

"You up to this?"

"Huh? Yeah. Sure." The adrenalin had ousted much of the alcohol in my veins. A blast of fire from my demon would combust the rest. Unfortunately, my demon couldn't help my fragile state of mind.

I briefed Ryder on the conversation I'd had with the wasted demon. Until a few months ago, the princes hardly featured on the lips of demons at all. It seemed they'd thrown off their complacent attitude and gotten their hands dirty. Akil would be in the midst of it. Perhaps I should have been concerned, but given his recent behavior, he clearly wasn't as weak as he allowed everyone to believe. He was different, he'd said so himself.

Memories of the garden event summoned thoughts of Stefan. I quickly trampled those before my past dragged me down toward the yawning pit of despair I tried to crawl out of on a daily basis.

"Have you thought about what you're going to do once you have Dawn?" Ryder asked, anchoring my thoughts in the present.

"Take her home."

He gave me a look that said, *try again, firecracker*. "Don't blow your cover. If you take her back to your place, you might as well paint a target on the top of your building saying, *Muse isn't dead*."

"Damn." I hadn't thought that far ahead. Dawn was hot property. Every badass demon I knew wanted a piece of her.

"Hand her over to the Institute."

"Ryder, no way. We've been through this."

"Yeah, I know, and I'm still right. Look me in the eye, and tell me half bloods aren't dangerous."

He had me there. "Adam doesn't have a great track record with half bloods. He'll ruin her."

"Muse, c'mon... she's a little half-blood demon girl. If she survives to adulthood, it'll be a bloody miracle. You only made it because Akil kept you safe."

I flinched back. "I don't belong to Akil."

"That ain't what I said."

"Is that what you think?"

"Muse, don't dump your shit on me, alright. Dawn doesn't have an asshole like Akil besotted with her. She won't last on her own. Her only chance is the Institute. You know it's true. Stop trying to find her a happy ending. There ain't no happy endings for half bloods. The best place for her is the Institute."

"Did you know Adam has two other half bloods squirreled away somewhere? He's buying or breeding them, rearing them like pets, and turning them into weapons. You think he'd care about Dawn at all? He ordered the death of his own son. I'm not giving her to him. I'll take her away somewhere. I'll drop off the grid. I've got nothing else. I'll keep her safe, Ryder, and don't you dare try and take her from me."

I'd tested his loyalty to the Institute before. There were times he should have bundled me back to the men in white coats, but he hadn't. That didn't mean he wouldn't though. From the hardened military-grade stare he'd fixed on me, he clearly wasn't negotiating.

"The Institute can't have her," I said. "Dawn deserves a chance at freedom, and maybe you're right. Maybe half bloods don't get happy endings. That's why I have to give her what nobody else can. Freedom."

His lips parted, and those old eyes steeled. "Then you'll both die. If she doesn't get you killed, she'll blow a fuse one day and nuke the neighborhood."

My scowl tightened and brought a snarl to my lips. "You've given her up as a lost cause already, haven't you?"

"No. I want what's best for the girl. If you stopped thinking with your heart, you'd see that."

"Have you given up on me, too?"

He spat a curse. "I'm here, ain't I?"

"Yeah, now. What about tomorrow or next week when I screw up, which I will, because I'm only human. What then? You gonna tie me up and bundle me off to the Institute too?"

He narrowed his eyes. "You know the answer."

"Yeah, I do." Crossing my arms, I slumped in the seat. The answer was yes. Ryder was the only man I knew—demon or otherwise—who never lied about what he was. "That morning at my apartment, you would have shot and killed Stefan."

He flinched and turned his face away. "Yeah, and it would have been the right thing to do. I screwed up. Hesitated. It won't happen again." Slowly, he faced me once more. A muscle twitched in his jaw. "He nearly killed you."

A sharp smile sliced across my lips "It must be easy, seeing in black and white." His glare contracted. "Sometimes, there is no right thing. Sometimes wrong wins, and that's okay. Life can't be distilled down to right and wrong. It's all about that messy gray area in between and how we deal with it. I sure hope I'm not the one staring down the barrel of your gun when you figure that out."

He humped and glared out the window. It was going to be a long few hours until 5am.

Chapter Twenty Three

The last time I'd broken into the Lounge, I'd been with Akil, and Levi had flushed me down a hallway. I chalked that up to him having the element of surprise. This time I was ready. I had no wish to repeat that experience and planned to get Dawn out before the Prince of Envy realized we were on his turf. In all likelihood, he wouldn't be on the premises. Surely princes had better things to do than stalk empty clubs? If not, I was ready to flash-fry his ass.

Dawn's cage was right where I'd left it. Ryder's flashlight beam washed over her. She gripped the bars, eyes wide. Swirling protection symbols flared beneath her delicate hands, and a peculiar quiver of power jolted through me. *Not Levi's element.* I shook it off while Ryder cut the padlocks.

I swept my gaze across the shadows coating the dance floor, gun in hand, anti-prince rounds locked and loaded. I'd shoot the slippery bastard between the eyes before he could say, "Boo." Bam. No talking. No evil monologue. That's how things go wrong. Levi was too destructive. Give him an inch, and he'd take a mile. That wasn't going to happen. I'd pepper him full of bullets and hope they killed him. At the very least, it'd ruin his pretty human-suit and slow him down.

Dawn burst from the cage and clung to my leg. I sunk a hand into her hair. "It's okay, honey. We're gettin' out of here."

Breathless whispers slipped from her lips too quietly for me to hear. I crouched down. Her wide eyes pleaded. She shivered and whispered. "He's here..." Her breaths fluttered across my cheek.

Ryder dropped the bolt cutters. They clattered against the floor. "Fuck. Muse. What the fuck?"

He lifted his gun at arm's length. Tremors wracked his grip. He aimed at Dawn, then brought the weapon up, and tracked me with it as I straightened. Perspiration beaded his pale face. "This ain't me. I'm not doing this!"

Ushering Dawn behind my legs, I mumbled, "I know." I searched the dark. I couldn't see Levi, couldn't even sense him.

"Fuck, Muse. I can't—I can't stop it."

Ryder's disjointed hand angled the gun around. His arm followed until he held the muzzle at his temple. His expression twitched. He drew his lips back and snarled. "Get the fuck out of my head!" His eyes darted, searching for the source.

"Levi..." I growled. "Are you a coward now?" My voice bounced around the empty club. "Not going to show yourself?" Any second, I'd hear a gunshot, and Ryder would be gone. Adrenalin surged through my veins, threatening to pull the fire in its wake. "You don't need to kill my friend."

Ryder dropped to his knees with a strangled cry. He was fighting it. He'd die fighting if I didn't act fast.

Dawn whimpered and huddled in close. "Dammit, Levi, face me!"

Water vapor coalesced on the dance floor. I aimed my gun and narrowed my sights down the barrel as the steam adopted a female outline. The vapor spun up, like a reverse waterspout, and She-Vi stepped out. I pulled the trigger. The blast cracked the air. The gun kicked in my hand. The bullet splashed through She-Vi's forehead and smacked into the wall somewhere in the shadows behind.

She-Vi laughed.

A knot of dread tightened in my gut, even as I fired again, and again. Well, damn. I'd been so convinced the rounds would at least slow Levi down. It hadn't occurred to me they'd sail right through his watery vessel.

"Burn the bitch!" Ryder hissed.

She-Vi's brow jumped. "Summon your element, undead half blood, and I'll redecorate these premises with the contents of his skull."

My demon rattled her mental cage. She wanted out. The lure of the veil, albeit quiet, lingered within my reach. How quickly could I open it, draw from beyond, and throw flame at Levi? I was fast, but not bullet-fast. Given time, I could boil Levi dry from the inside out, but not before he killed Ryder. God, what had I done? I'd been so desperate to free Dawn, I hadn't even considered Ryder's vulnerability – his human mind.

"Half bloods are intriguing." She-Vi's singsong voice rippled through the dark. "Demon and human. Both and neither. Humans are puppets of flesh. All of them." Levi stalked to one side then the other, pacing, observing, weighing the three of us. "Humans dance for me." Her double-eyelids flickered. "They break like toys. I discard them, find more. Those break. They come here and drown themselves in drugs and alcohol to forget. Their fragile minds shatter. It's tiresome. But half bloods... Half bloods break and come back for more. My little half blood was learning well before Carol-Anne took it upon herself to flaunt my pet in front of Mammon. My little one, my Dawn, has spirit. There's no sweeter taste in the mind than a crushed spirit." She stopped pacing and lifted a hand, curling her fingers into a fist. "Like you, Muse. You were dead. The infamous half-blood daughter, Mother of Destruction. Ruined, spoiled, broken. Tortured..." She tasted the word on her lips. "And then deceased. Much was argued after your demise. Mammon believes it. Asmodeus believes it. The Court of Dark believes it. Nonetheless, here you stand: changed, hungry, raw. And yet you are the same petulant human, once again stealing what is mine. Valenti's sister, no less. And he had the gall to chastise me for losing my little pet. Your persistence is commendable. One might begin to believe the whispers cloying the air around you, Muse. Perhaps your father, Lust, is not wrong."

"Take me to Asmodeus," I said, hoping to bargain my way out. "I won't fight you. Just let Ryder and Dawn go." Levi had been tasked with my retrieval. I'd worry about my own chances of survival once my friends were safe.

She-Vi chuckled. "Why would I let them go? Dawn belongs to me. Half bloods must be owned. That is the way of things. And this puppet... Ryder? He is nothing. I would kill him now if his mind did not harbor such delicious intricacies. This one is a killer, a hard man, and yet so perfectly simple."

"Bitch!" Ryder snarled. "If you wanna mind-fuck me, come over here and let's get personal. Go deep, I like it rough. See what you find in there, princess."

She-Vi's body shimmered. In the next step, Levi was all masculine and muscle again. He cocked his head and observed Ryder curiously.

"Well, fuck me." Ryder spat a harsh laugh, gun muzzle grazing his temple. "Now if that ain't an instant turn-off, I don't know what is."

Levi's double-eyelids blinked, but otherwise he didn't move. Ryder appeared to fascinate him. Maybe it was his no-bullshit stance on life. He had a military past. Perhaps those memories intrigued Levi. While I coiled a slither of energy into my body, Ryder locked his fury-laden stare on Levi. To reach for the veil, I'd need to call my demon, but I didn't have time to do both. Levi would sense my demon as soon as she broke over my skin. He'd blow Ryder away.

Dawn's tiny hand slipped into mine, and a curl of slick energy touched my palm. I tightened my grip, afraid to look down at her for fear of catching Levi's attention.

"It's okay," Dawn said. Only she didn't. Her voice plunged through my thoughts like a beam through the dark. "I will unmake him." The crawling touch of her power dragged up my arm, spilling pins and needles in its wake. I flinched. The human part of me wanted to recoil and sprint away from her, as though something about her tiny body repelled me. Her power bloomed beneath my feet. A wash of energy rose over me, knocking me aside. One minute, I stood beside Dawn, my skin trying to crawl away from her, the next I was face down half a dance floor away, ears ringing, body dashed by countless needles of pain. I pushed up on my hands, wincing as a sudden pain scurried around my skull. Raw energy tickled my skin, itching madly. I had to fight not to dig my nails in and scratch the unwanted element out of me. Whatever element she wielded, my humanity ran screaming.

I twisted, half scrambling to my feet and saw Dawn, or rather, saw her demon. She was a nightmare of liquid green and oil black suspended a few feet off the ground, back arched, arms out. Dark-light bled through her emerald skin. A mass of oily, black barbed vines lashed about her head, each moving independently. Vines sprouted from her back, tangled around her, exploded outward, and knotted through the mangled miasmic cloud that had once been Levi. Dawn had literally unmade him, torn into him, pulled him apart, and thrown him back together into a frothing soup of blood, flesh, and water. The vines picked, plucked, and stabbed, working like a thousand needles.

My breath caught in my throat. I could taste her element like poison polluting the air. Panic rattled around my skull. Every muscle strummed tight with the need to run. It was only my stubborn need to protect Dawn that rooted me to the spot, that and my demon's morbid fascination.

In the dancing green light, I caught sight of Ryder pressed against the far wall. Gun clutched at his side, he cringed back from Dawn but didn't look away. I knew, without doubt, that he'd kill her if she lost control.

One of Dawn's vines snapped at me, cracking like a whip at my feet. I flinched back as more separated from the river and peeled toward me. "Dawn..." They still came, rippling above the dance floor, eager and hungry. "Dawn?" I back-pedaled. "Dawn!"

She didn't see or hear me. Her all-green eyes were locked on Levi's mess, her little head cocked to one side as her tendrils knitted parts of Levi back together and then unraveled him all over again.

The slick touch of her power snaked around my ankle and tugged my leg out from under me. I fell hard on my ass. The abhorrent crawl of Dawn's power yanked my demon out of me, plunging fire through my flesh. Dawn swung her blazing green eyes on me, dropping what was left of Levi. Blood and bone splashed across the dance floor. Her whip-like tendrils reared up behind her tiny body. Countless eels of energy hovered in the air, poised to strike.

"Dawn... I know you're in there, honey." My demon slur couldn't hide the quiver in my voice. "Don't let it rule you." Her dark energy swelled, replacing the air with a sour, elemental soup, heavy with energies not of this world. She was so little. How was she supposed to fight the desires of the demon riding her? Her demon might have been physically small, but the power she wielded wasn't. She hadn't even drawn from the veil.

Her element broke free and lunged for me. I thrust out a retort of fire, blasting her back. A gut-churning scream pierced the roar of my fire. Dammit, I was hurting her. I recalled my element, and realized my mistake as soon as the eels plunged through the fizzling embers and coiled around my legs. Her element, whatever dark power it was, knotted around my limbs and tightened. This couldn't be happening. Would she unmake me as she had Levi?

A gunshot punched through the air. Dawn collapsed with a cry. Her demon-form shattered. The black eels coiled around me splintered and dissolved, leaving behind a film of sticky black tar.

Shaking off my demon, I got to my feet and stumbled to Dawn as Ryder approached her. "Jesus, Ryder, you shot her." Blood pooled beneath her fragile body. I gathered her into my arms, snatched up her rabbit, and glared over her shoulder at Ryder. "Goddamn it, she's just a little girl."

He had the decency to look horrified before his training kicked in. "She's dangerous." He jerked a thumb at the pile of flesh and blood that had once been a Prince of Hell. "You wanna end up like Legolas over there?"

Dawn buried her head against my neck. This wasn't the time to rage at Ryder, but I'd be having a few sharp words with him once we were safe. "We have to get out of here." She'd killed a prince. Holy hell, killing a prince would surely trigger alarm bells in the netherworld. Plus, every demon in the local area would have sensed her power-drain.

Ryder offered me a hand. I ignored it and pulled Dawn close while staggering to my feet. "Let's get her to the car. I need to see how bad the wound is."

"I just grazed her," he grumbled. "I should have killed her."

I glared at him as we made a dash for the doors. "What the hell has gotten into you?"

"She was gonna kill you, Muse."

I uttered a string of colorful curses and shoved through the door of the club into a wall of bright light. The full weight of half a dozen spotlights blinded me. My demon reared up, poised for a fight. She tried to wench my control away. I staggered back with a snarl, fighting instincts and alarm.

"*RELEASE THE HALF BLOOD.*" A voice boomed somewhere behind the barricade of blinding light. Enforcers. A rich melodic growl bubbled up from my demon. I swung an accusing glare at Ryder. He'd set me up.

Hands raised, gun still palmed, he backed up. The bastard was retreating to join his ranks. "It's for the best."

Like hell it was. I glared hard into the lights and made out a handful of cars, maybe a dozen Enforcers, all armed, all ready to shoot me down if I made one wrong move.

"Muse..." Dawn mumbled.

"It's okay. It's going to be okay." And it would be okay. Because they weren't having her. "I want you pretend you're somewhere safe. Somewhere warm. Think of the beach."

"I've never been to a beach."

My heart broke for her, and I nearly dropped the reins of my demon right then. "When we get out of this, I promise to take you." I set her gently on the road outside The Voodoo Lounge and straightened to face my enemies.

"STEP AWAY FROM THE HALF BLOOD."

Screw you.

I stepped around Dawn's vulnerable form and lifted my hands. My eyes had adjusted to the stark whiteness. I could see the Enforcers much clearer now. Some, I knew. Adam wasn't there. Ryder stood off to the left on the fringes of the cadre. His steely eyes watched me while the others appeared more interested in Dawn. Ryder knew where the real threat lay. He stilled, lifted his chain, and shouted an order.

In a second's thought, my demon slammed into me. I planted both feet and closed my eyes. The veil opened with a precise mental swipe, and freedom whispered in my ear. Yes, this was right. My fire danced with me, roaring loud, swallowing the sounds of gunfire. Bullets slapped against my molten skin. I tasted melted metal in the blaze. Doubt didn't exist. Fear had fled. When Damien's poison seeped out of its hiding place and flushed through my veins, it didn't matter. They would not have Dawn.

The veil pulsed, and with it, pleasure strummed through my quivering demon muscles. I had more, so much more to give. Levi's words, Mother of Destruction—words I'd almost missed—briefly flitted through the inferno of my mind before skipping out of reach. My demon cared nothing for those words. Or those people. Or Ryder. But she recognized the half blood cowering on the floor behind us. She recognized power, and Dawn's little human body threw off enough power to render my demon feral.

I worked fire and flame like a conductor directs an orchestra. A flick of a wrist, a glance, a twitch. It was easy, quick, and wondrous. Wildfire ran free. When the gas tanks on the cars blew, shrapnel pummeled my molten skin. I soaked up the pain, twisting it into pleasure. Screams, sirens, gunshots, alarms: they meant no more to me than birdsong at the break of dawn. I expected the madness, when it came, to be a violent thing. I'd thought Damien's embrace would shred my thoughts and flay my soul, but the truth couldn't be further from my fears. The insanity, the chaos, was instead peaceful. All I had to do, was let go. I wondered why I'd ever fought it.

Akil's words drifted through the placid lake of my thoughts, 'If you ceased battling your other half, and embraced the truth of what you are, you'd have your answer.'

It became clear as I stood in front of Dawn and flushed flames through the street, washing them clean of Enforcers, that freedom was within my grasp. Once free, nobody could stop me. Not the Institute. Not Akil. I was the mother of fire, and fire destroys. I was destruction.

Chapter Twenty Four

Chewing on my thumbnail, I paced the tiny front room in Jerry's modest apartment. Dawn slept on a battered old couch, a blanket pulled up under her chin, bunny tucked under an arm. We'd fled the scene, and I'd called Jerry from a payphone only once I was sure the Enforcers hadn't sent back up after us. He hadn't asked questions, but he didn't need to. The street we'd left behind was ablaze. Fire crews had descended on The Voodoo Lounge. I'd walked away from a hellish nightmare of my own creating. There were bodies back there. I knew it. There had to be. When I'd summoned the fire, I'd let it gorge itself. To make matters worse, Damien's poison had crawled into my skin and stoked my lust for chaos.

I'd heard their screams...

What if Ryder had been one of them?

"You're going to wear a hole in my carpet."

Jerry's deeply delicious voice coaxed my thoughts back into the room. I looked down. There wasn't any carpet, just well worn floorboards. Lifting my head, I fixed a neutral mask on my face and gave Jerry the picture of restrained stoicism. His backlit, muscular frame filled his kitchen doorway.

"Coffee?" He grumbled.

I nodded, not trusting my voice. I hadn't spoken to him, not since the call. I was afraid of what I might say. My gaze fell to Dawn. I'd been protecting her. And that would have been just fine, but it wasn't entirely true. Not all my motives had been as honorable. The demon shifted inside me, resettling, her urges sated. I'd let go. And I'd liked it.

Watching Dawn's chest rise and fall, a resolute calm settled over me. I couldn't go back to the Institute. I'd burned that proverbial bridge. I didn't want to anyway. Not like this, so close to madness. I would take Dawn, and we'd go away, just the two of us. But I didn't want to leave the life I'd made for myself. I liked my home. I enjoyed chatting with Rosa about her time in England. Lacy was like a breath of fresh air in my otherwise stale existence. After Stefan had blown my workshop to smithereens, I never thought I'd find somewhere to call home again, but Southie was as close as I was going to get. To keep Dawn safe, I'd have to walk away. To keep my neighbors and friends safe, I couldn't go back. What would Stefan do in my shoes? As soon as I wondered as much, I smiled. He'd already done it. He'd walked away to keep those he loved safe.

I moved to the kitchen doorway and leaned against the frame. Jerry's mountainous bulk filled the tiny galley-style room. I watched him fix two coffees, tracing my gaze over the swirl of tattoos marking his scalp. "You always been a demon doctor, Jerry?"

"Nah. I was a warrior in another life." His deep voice filled the kitchen just as well as his muscle-bound body. Warrior was an obscure word. I was about to ask him what he meant when he planted a steaming hot cup of coffee in my hand. "Get that in you."

I had to crane my neck to meet his eyes. For a warrior, he had curiously beautiful eyes. Beguiling. He regarded me with detached indifference. "Have you ever killed anyone?" I asked. It's not the sort of question you can ask in passing. *How was your day? Have you killed anyone lately?* But Jerry was different. I might not have known him well, but I recognized strength when I saw it and not just physical strength either. He'd helped me before. He knew about half bloods. He'd seen a lot of things, knew a great deal about demons. There was more to him than a backstreet vet.

That fact was made all the more clear when he didn't react at all to my question. The mask of tattoos didn't move. He raised his mug, took a sip, glanced through the doorway behind me, and then leaned his bulk back against the countertop. "Well, I guess you aren't as dead as the Institute made out, huh?"

"Looks that way." I tasted the coffee. Strong. Black. It would deliver the kick of caffeine I'd surely need to keep marching forward. I'd have welcomed a shot of whiskey with it.

Jerry's gaze roamed over me, assessing my new post-death transformation, complete with blond hair and short pink skirt. "Not sure about the pink and black..."

I arched an eyebrow. "Says the man wearing a mesh tank-top over gray sweatpants."

He snorted a laugh but quickly sobered. "That lil' girl asleep on my couch is Carol-Anne's half blood, Muse. How'd you get her, and what happened at the Lounge just now?"

I flinched, not entirely surprised that Jerry knew who Dawn was. Clamping both hands around my mug, I brought it to my lips. Hot, aromatic steam wafted over my face. "I think I killed them," I mumbled. I'd said the words. They were out there, as though speaking them made the truth all the more real. I'd expected to be afraid of the facts, but a cold weight of acceptance settled in my gut. Was this what Stefan meant when he said he didn't care? A part of me cared. That part cared so much that I was afraid to acknowledge it for fear I might break down and let the demon in. I could crawl into the corners of my mind and hide while she took control. She wanted to. She hungered. It would be easier that way. I hide, and she wins.

Jerry slowly blinked. Even his eyelids were marked. "You've changed since you asked for help to control your demon months ago. You're not that same woman. I see that. There's steel in you now. If you killed, that's your burden. It's how you deal with it that will define you." His steady tone and even stare could only come from experience.

I nodded. "I think Levi might be dead."

His eyes narrowed to slits.

"Yeah." Keeping my gaze trained on him, I gulped coffee, and welcomed the heat searing my tongue. "I don't suppose that's going to go unnoticed for long."

He rubbed the palm of his hand over his shaved head. "You killed a Prince of Hell? A creature that can't be killed? An immortal chaos demon?"

My eyelids fluttered as I looked down. The lie felt right. Dawn didn't need the fallout from that coming down on her. If she had any hope of escaping all this crap, she'd need to stay off the demons' radar. "Yeah. He had it coming. Nobody puts half bloods in cages. Not anymore."

Jerry shifted, planted his coffee on the counter, and crossed his thick arms over his chest. "Shit. You really are something." A smirk broke out across his lips, brightening his eyes and lessening the effects of those intimidating tats. "You know what they've started calling you across the veil?"

Whore. Abomination. Filth. I'd heard it all. "I can guess."

"The Mother of Destruction."

Jerry's words slammed into me. I attempted to hide my reaction by freezing my expression somewhere between mild curiosity and indifference. The result probably looked as though I was having a stroke. Levi had called me the same. When demons start calling you the Mother of Destruction, shit gets real. Titles have power in the netherworld. They're not just words. They're a purpose.

I blinked and laughed. "That's insane."

"Yeah well, you're dead, so I guess you got a posthumous rep or something. Although, from what I hear, didn't you nuke a few hundred demons not so long ago?"

I recalled that event well. The ash-strewn images, boiling flames, and acrid smells stalked my dreams. I'd leveled a few netherworld buildings and turned on the Prince of Greed too. "Yeah." It wasn't something my human half was proud of. My demon, on the other hand...

"Alright. So let me get this straight." He lifted his hand and started checking off my sins on his fingers. "You ruined the Prince of Greed, one of the First chaos demons... You killed the Price of Envy, also immortal, although not-so-much. You nuked a flock of demons. Killed your owner. Wiped out a cadre of Enforcers?" He raised his eyebrows. "For such a little thing, you've got some serious issues."

I choked on a splinter of bitter laughter. It was so ludicrous that the only sane thing I could do was laugh. "You offering to be my therapist?"

"I would if I wasn't scared of you." He flashed me pearly white teeth.

A rich bubble of laughter burst from me. There I was, a tiny half-blood thing dressed in pink and black, standing in front of the formidable Jerry, and he's telling me he's afraid of me? I laughed so hard I had to put my coffee down. The demons believed me some kind of harbinger of destruction? Hilarity flirted with insanity. Laughter wracked me so damn hard my sides hurt, and my eyes watered.

"Laugh it up, Muse." Jerry spluttered between bursts of his own laughter. "'Cause once the princes realize you're alive, they're gonna be coming for you."

Chapter Twenty Five

The bus ride to Salem was a painfully slow experience. Dawn had receded into a quiet shell and refused to speak to me. I wasn't entirely sure if the silent treatment was due to what she'd done or my own monumental fuck-up. As I watched the scenery outside the bus windows change from urban sprawl to leafy green trees, I was also acutely aware that my brother would soon realize Levi was dead. Would he suspect his supposedly deceased half-sister? He knew about Blackstone—where Dawn and I were headed. It wouldn't take him long to find us. Once inside, we were safe. It was the only sanctuary left. I couldn't risk exposing my neighbors to the likes of Val. I needed to get away, to regroup and collect my thoughts. Blackstone was my last chance to figure out my next move. The Institute would be looking for us. Jenna had likely told them about Akil's house in the country. That meant I'd have to plan my next move quickly.

Security lighting puddled around Blackstone. Dawn and I had trudged up the driveway, wrung out, saying nothing. Her power coiled around her and throbbed like the dark thing clenching my heart. What a pair we made.

The night was quiet and calm. It soothed my wrung-out thoughts, but my demon stalked too close to the surface of my mind for comfort. The devil on my shoulder, she whispered, coerced, and tingled my human senses. I would need to shut her down if I wanted to pretend everything was fine and dandy. Another confrontation like the last could tip the scales of my control indefinitely.

I'd expected Blackstone to be empty, but as we rounded the bend in the driveway, I saw that someone was clearly home. A sleek, black and silver Lamborghini had gouged out four grooves in the loose gravel before being discarded outside the house. I glanced at the car as we passed. Low to the ground, shaped like an arrow, its sleek lines and undulating curves gave it the appearance of travelling a hundred miles an hour while parked.

Two steps past the Lambo, a wall of heat blasted across my skin. I jerked back, pink human flesh firing off pain receptors in my brain. A rich curse followed. If I taught her nothing else, Dawn would have a colorful new vocabulary. Between us and the house, a wall of almost tangible heat blocked our path. I could call my demon, but I really didn't want to risk having her back in my skin so soon.

Let me out. Let me play. This heat is nothing. We hunger. We devour. We destroy.

I gritted my teeth and gave her the mental equivalent of a shove. *Back off, bitch. I'm in charge.* She snarled. I snarled. Before I could further entertain arguing with myself, I stepped into the wall of heat and drew it into my flesh with an inward breath. Once more, it came easily, eager to join the bubbling chaos simmering inside me. With the heat gone, Dawn followed in my footsteps, silent and calm. I sensed Akil's unique elemental touch slithering around my ankles. It was weak, though. My demon purred. I licked my dry lips. Yes, we would like for Akil to be here. A snarl crawled across my top lip.

"Muse?"

Dawn's quiet voice cooled the lust burning through me. I glanced back at her. So small. So fragile. So freakin' powerful she could unravel my DNA if I pissed her off. "It's okay." I mustered a smile. "I think Akil is here. Do you sense him?"

She nodded, big human eyes widening. Killers shouldn't look like little girls. Was it wrong that I could look her in the eyes and feel sorry for her while also fearing her? She was terror, camouflaged in the body of a nine year old. What must she be thinking? How would her young mind process what she'd done? Did she care?

After entering Blackstone with the hidden key, I followed the beckon of Akil's element and came to an abrupt halt in the lounge doorway. Dawn peeked from behind my leg and sucked in a tight yelp.

Mammon lay sprawled in front of a cold fireplace, wings draped over him like a black sheet over a corpse. The marble floor had cracked beneath him, likely from heat stress. The walls around the room bore the scars of an inferno. The ceiling had a layer of soot so thick it looked like the night sky. I could only assume the fragments of fabric and metal scattered here and there were the immolated remains of the furniture.

"Is he alive?" Dawn whispered.

"Yes." The sound of his bellows breathing confirmed it, but the lava veins tracing across his skin barely glowed. I inched closer when Dawn's hand on mine stopped me.

"It's okay," I said. "I don't think he'll hurt me." I would have welcomed my demon, but the symbols etched into the construction of Blackstone held her back. Sneaking up on an unconscious Prince of Hell while wrapped in my fragile humanity wasn't the best idea I'd had all day. One swipe of his hand could cave in my skull. "Dawn, it might be best if you went to your room. Do you remember where it is?"

She nodded and hurried out of the room. Only once she was safely out of earshot, did I turn back to the Prince of Greed.

"Mammon..." I whispered.

Seeing him sprawled in front of the fireplace seemed deeply wrong, like birds on the ground or rivers flowing upstream. Mammon had always been a force of nature, a natural disaster that threatened with his mere presence. To see him face down on the floor and vulnerable disturbed both halves of me on a deeply primal level.

With heavy steps, I shirked around his wing tip and traced my gaze across his muscular shoulder, over his bicep, his forearm, hand... and flicked it to his open eyes. *Dead eyes. Black. Empty.*

My breath caught, and my heart fluttered. What was wrong with him? How long had he been like this? Who could have hurt him? "Mammon?" I inched closer and crouched on my heels beside his hand. The heat rolling off him should have been unbearable, but I felt his power as little more than the warmth of the sun on a summer's day. "Akil?"

His black eyes blinked and widened. He snorted air, breathing it into him. The entire musculature of his body quivered. I had a moment to realize I should get out of his way, when he lunged with alarming speed. I sprang back, stumbled, and fell on my ass with a grunt. Mammon knocked me flat on my back. He braced powerful arms either side of my head. Rigid thighs fenced me in, and his vast obsidian body arched over me, muscles rippling, but he didn't touch me. Jesus, I'd never been so close to him while so completely human before. My head swirled, eyes stinging. Tears slipped over my lashes and dried on my cheeks. His gaze pulled me in while at the same time repelling me, urging me to look away.

Mammon bowed his head and inhaled at my neck. My skin briefly cooled as he drew the hot air into his lungs, but the heat quickly returned when he sighed the breath out again. His vast wings settled either side of us. I struggled to swallow, my mouth as dry as sandpaper while my throat burned. If he fell on me, he could easily crush me and would most certainly burn me.

I gave my demon a mental tug, but she butted up against invisible barriers. A ripple of power spilled through me, just enough that it no longer hurt to *see* him, and a violent tremor shocked through his body. He snarled. Black lips undulated over fangs the size of my fingers. I told myself if he were going to kill me, he'd have done it already. And then it occurred to me that killing might not be the first thing on his mind. I flicked my gaze down the crevice between our bodies. *Oh shit.*

"Okay, big guy, I can't summon my demon here, remember? I'm just little ol' me, crunchy on the outside, chewy in the middle. Please don't act on those thoughts in your head right now." I'd have shoved him back if his skin wouldn't have caused me third degree burns. I seized a breath of sweltering air and summoned some authority. After what I'd dealt with over the last hell-knows-how-long, I could sure as hell tame a sexed-up Mammon.

"Mammon, Prince of Greed." I held his stare, denying the headache punching through my skull. "Back off."

He thrust his head forward, too close. A blast of heat tightened the skin on my face. I cringed and turned away. Tremors rolled from the tips of my fingers to my toes. Okay, so maybe using the authority-voice had been a very bad idea. I'd forgotten he liked it when I fought him.

He pushed up, herculean arms acting like hydraulic rams to heave his bulk off of me. Sprawled on my back beneath him, I could do little but watch with a mixture of awe and fear as Mammon peeled apart. The hand that went to his head flickered from volcanic black to tanned bronze, claws receding and then punching from his fingers again. His body reshaped, drawing the parts of Mammon inside, and then remaking and reshuffling demon flesh into human skin. It took time. Seconds, minutes, I don't know how long. I couldn't move, inexplicably fascinated as lashings of power knotted together, peeled apart, then tangled into the shape of a man.

Akil collapsed, naked and trembling beside me. Perspiration glistened on his chest, beaded over slick muscles, and trickled into the valley of his navel. I forced my focus higher, where he rested the crook of his arm over his face, hiding his expression. His breath sawed through gritted teeth.

I blinked, stunned into silence. He was okay. At least he was alive. That was good, right? I got to my knees, pinching my clothes away from my sweat-soaked skin. The stifling air inside the house crowded me. I needed to get away, to get some cool air into my lungs.

"You were dead." Akil's barely human voice grated from the back of his throat. He turned his head toward me, and I wasn't sure if his face was wet with perspiration or tears. It had to be sweat because the alternative was unthinkable.

I opened my mouth to explain but found my voice had abandoned me. Where did I start? Stefan, Dawn, Levi... the dead Enforcers. He couldn't help me with any of it. They were my mistakes. My problems. Akil couldn't save me from myself. Somewhere down the line, I'd stopped expecting him to.

"I should go." I climbed onto unsteady legs and, wiping the dampness from my forehead, I stumbled for the door.

Akil choked on a dry laugh. The ragged sound of it stopped me a few steps from the doorway. Turning back, I swallowed hard. He still laid on the floor, a goddamn picture-perfect man, apart from the shivering and twitching and the haunted wrung-out look in his eyes when he turned them on me.

"You should stay. You need to stay."

"No." Staying was a terrible idea. Every second I lingered, the urge to wrap him in my arms grew more immediate. "I thought the house was empty. I didn't realize you were here. Quite honestly, I've not thought about you for weeks." I could talk the talk, but when I watched him drag himself to his feet, stagger and sway like a drunk, my conviction fell to pieces. My demon stalked too close to the surface. Raw emotion teased around the edges of my control. I battled old urges and shoved the demon back, only for her heat to spill through me again. She wanted to go to him, to dance in the fire. "I can't do this." I turned away.

Akil's solid embrace fell on me from behind. I immediately lashed out, only to find myself planted against the wall. His deliciously spicy, otherworldly scent burned my senses. I tensed to shove back, but he pinned me still, rigid naked muscles smothering me. A growl rumbled through him, like distant thunder. A warning. It stirred my instincts. My responding growl came easily. "I told your alter-ego Mammon to get the fuck off me. If you don't let me go, I'll fight like a demon until you do. In the condition you're in, I might even have a chance."

He bowed his head and sucked in a breath just as Mammon had done moments before. His broad chest expanded against my back. I *would* fight him, but given his current state, I wasn't entirely sure if fighting would help me.

"Listen well, Muse." His words slurred behind a melodic accent, barely English, certainly demon, "I am revealing a fragment of my soul to you, here and now." He hesitated, as though waiting for me to interrupt or perhaps contemplating his next words. "I am chaos eternal. I desire everything this world and the next offers. I am greed. I hunger." A snarl punctured his words. "Oh, how I hunger... I want the pathetic mortals of this world to bow before me. I want all that they own, all they desire, every marvelous creation of theirs, but there is only one thing in this world that I need, and that, Muse, is you." He leaned closer, rapid breaths whispering on my neck.

A flush of heat washed over me. I twisted in his embrace and pressed my back against the cool, hard wall. Akil planted his hands either side of me. Amber-rimmed eyes bored into mine. I'd peered into Mammon's eyes in much the same position before, only now we were vertical instead of horizontal. "This can't end well, Akil. You know that." No matter what he said, it would always end the same. He'd try to evict Damien. He'd slip his power into the heart of me and seduce my soul.

He licked his lips and said very carefully around sharp teeth, "You are killing me, Muse."

A shiver trickled through me. Fear? Maybe. Desire, lust? Certainly. He was too close, crowding me, filling my senses and clouding my thoughts. In those moments, he was all I knew, my anesthetic, and it was bliss. I needed to forget. I wanted to push the pain of reality away, to drown the horror of my own capabilities in the overbearing presence of Akil. But if I let him, he'd steal the last thread of my humanity, pluck it right out of me, and toss it away. Did he know how close I was to losing my mind? Could he sense the lure of chaos whispering to me? I gently planted my hands on his slick chest and soaked up his feverish warmth. His body quivered, and those micro movements just about undid me. When I flicked my gaze to his face, the raw emotion I saw seared my conviction. He bowed his head and sunk his hand into my hair. He pressed his scalding cheek against mine. I couldn't slow my racing heart or pull back the sharp intakes of breath. I didn't want to.

"I lost you," he whispered. His lips brushed mine, and the promise of a kiss fizzled between us, so damn close I locked my teeth together, refusing to succumb. His element flushed over me, a rapid wash of heat that summoned a storm of emotion from the darkest depths of my half blood body. I gripped his broad shoulders, intent on shoving him off, but my arms wouldn't obey. I dug my nails in, hoping to hurt him, but his growl sent a wave of sparkling lust flooding through me. A short gasp escaped my lips as the reins of control slipped away. He nipped at my mouth and swept the tip of his tongue out, testing my resistance. I had none to give.

"Akil–" Desperation clipped my voice. I was about to break, and he knew it.

He lunged in and captured my mouth with his. That tiny part of me that knew this was wrong faded into the background, smothered beneath a roaring need to have him chase away the horrors stalking my thoughts. I laced my fingers into his hair and pulled him into the ravaging kiss. I attacked him as though starved. His lips burned, his teeth nipped, and his tongue swirled. This couldn't happen. In seconds, he'd try to dive inside me to dislodge the dark parasite coiled around my insides. He'd rip out my cancerous parasite and take my humanity with it. I couldn't let him do that. This wasn't right. So why wasn't I pushing him away? If I told him to stop—really told him—he would. Why wasn't I saying the words? That damned demon lust was too fresh. Too real. Was it her, or was it me? What was the point in fighting my nature? Lust was in my veins, part of my DNA. My demon father was the Prince of Lust. My humanity only went halfway, and my demon had hold of me like never before. She pushed at my control, leaning into my restraint. She had the scent of freedom now and refused to yield.

I broke the maddening kiss, breathless and trembling, and dropped my head back, closing my eyes. "I can't." He trailed scorching kisses across my jawline, fluttering them down the curve of my neck. His hand eased under my top, slid around my waist and clamped against my lower back. He tugged me against him with an animalistic groan and pulled me close. His naked body smothered mine. Even as I knew it was wrong, I melted against him with a shuddering moan.

"Akil..." I closed my eyes, not wanting to see the delicious plain of his chest or the way his arms tensed, muscles tightening. I could feel him though, the heated strength of him, the hardness of his body against the softness of mine. Nerves fluttered low, shortening my breath. "You suffocate me."

"Stop thinking and feel. Let me love you."

Finally, a bolt of anger fired through me, driving back the smothering desire. I shoved, half mad with lust. He leaned back, giving me space to breathe again. "Love?" I snarled. The wicked play of firelight in his eyes pooled wet warmth between my legs. He licked his lips and pinned me in a predatory glare, making it quite clear he had every intention of devouring me once the foreplay was over. What did he know about love? "I can't do this, Akil. Don't do this to me. You know my demon wants you. Don't tempt me like this. I'm not in my right mind. I'm losing control—"

His fingers speared into my hair, locking his palms against my cheeks, forcing me to glare into his eyes. "Stop lying to yourself. This isn't your demon's doing, and you know it. Let me make love to you. Permit me this." He molded his body against mine, driving the hardness of his erection against my hip. "Not as demon," he whispered. "No element. No power. Just as a man." His lips brushed mine. His breathless whispers sawed, rough with hunger. "I need to feel you as a man does a woman. You have no idea what it costs me to say these things to you. You cannot fathom what it means. I need you. I lay the truth before you. Would you turn me away? Right here and now, Muse, I am but a man."

My fragile heart stuttered. Tears welled in my eyes. His words burned like nothing else could. How did he know how to break me so completely? How could he know what

I needed? I didn't want him a demon. But as a man? When his lips met mine again, he teased and explored with reverent hesitation. He eased my jacket from my shoulders, the heat of his touch seeping through my clothes to sizzle against my sensitive skin. This was my last chance to pull away, and the decision was mine. I couldn't deny what I felt for him. I wanted him, both halves of me wanted to hide from the world inside Akil's embrace. I could forget the hideous thing crippling my soul, forget the sins hooked into my conscience, forget how everything I touched turned to ash.

I rode my hands over the silken hardness of his chest, skipped my fingers over his shoulders and captured his face. "Damn you, Akil." Drilling my gaze into his, I was already lost. I fell into his kiss, locked my arms around his neck, and dragged him down. My demon purred her approval. Otherworldly heat sizzled beneath my skin, and where Akil's hands explored, desire sparked.

He gathered me in his arms. A flash of static energy sprinkled my flesh, and in the next moment, we were in the bedroom. I registered the dark wood and opulent furnishings in my peripheral vision before Akil's growl hooked into my wandering thoughts and drew me back to him. He backed me up to the bed, fingers teasing up my thighs, sinking beneath the hem of my skirt and riding higher. I dragged my nails down his back, smiling against his mouth as he tensed and bowed me against him. His power had gone, his element snuffed out. I touched his fevered flesh and felt only the trembling of a man in the throes of desire.

I pulled him down and whispered against his neck, "I'm not the same woman you screwed over, Akil. The woman you tried to force my demon from, she's long gone. Do you believe you can tame me?"

"No." His gruff reply was more growl than word, but I heard it clearly enough.

I shoved him back a few feet and watched with perverse delight how his body revealed his need to have me beneath him. Jesus, he couldn't be real. He was too damned delicious to be real. In the low light, his primal masculinity stole all that remained of reason from my mind. I slid my tongue across my lips. He tracked the tiny movement. Removing my clothes, deliberately taking my time, I basked under the heat of his gaze as it roamed and devoured. He trembled by the time I kicked my boots off and stood before him in all my human nakedness. There was a time he'd despised my humanity, wanted only my demon, but there was no sign of that now.

He stalked toward me, gathered me in his arms, and claimed me with a kiss. Arching against him, I threw my head back. His skillful tongue swirled down my neck. I was lost to lust, buried too deep in the madness to care about anything but Akil. Swirling his tongue around a nipple, he licked and teased, spurring my lust higher. He hitched my thigh around his hip, his fingers digging into my flesh before diving into the wetness of my core, stirring my needs into frenzy. Inhuman growls escaped me. I bucked against him, needing him inside. His dark laughter ratcheted my madness higher.

I speared my hands into his hair and snarled a warning. "Stop playing games."

His soft hazel eyes glistened with unspoken promises. His smile spoke of the wicked things his mind had conjured. He cupped my behind and lifted me against him before lowering me onto the bed. He prowled up my body, timeless wisdom burning in his eyes, but no power. His eyes had never been more honest. With the fire gone, he was just a man. I peered up at him through half-closed lashes, drenched with need. As Akil towered over me, the vision of male perfection, ageless, netherworldly, I saw a weakness in him I'd never witnessed before: a knowledge in his eyes coupled with a fraction of regret, not for me, but for himself. He noticed my expression change, but before I could voice what I thought I'd seen, he nudged my knees apart and plunged into me, arching my back and stealing a ragged groan of ecstasy from the depths of my ruined soul.

* * *

I woke entwined in Akil's arms, captured against the unyielding strength of his body. Sunlight streamed in through the wall of windows. Akil's steady breath betrayed him as awake, as did the press of his erection against my leg. I purred and stretched beneath the sheets, deliciously languid and broken. Peeling open heavy eyelids, I stilled. Akil's glare brought an abrupt end to my dreamy post-sex state. He stared down at me, head propped on his hand, face stern and eyes cold.

"What's wrong?" I asked.

"The Prince of Envy is dead. By your hand."

"How do you know that?"

He tapped his temple. "I hear them, my brethren. Their reach rarely extends beyond the veil, but the death of one of their own has them grieving. Their voices are distracting. It is part of the reason I spend my time here, away from their whispers." So he had Prince FM playing in his head. It didn't escape my attention how he'd referred to the princes as them not *we*. He didn't include himself among them. Why? "They are furious," he added with a scowl.

"What makes you think I killed him?"

The corner of his lips—lips I'd nipped and teased last night—curled up. "Because I know you. When I last saw both you and Levi, he'd trapped you in a cage. Once Stefan's ice thawed, Levi was quite adamant he would draw you out, using Dawn as bait. Your apparent-death didn't change his plans for the half blood girl. He was a fool, blinded by prejudice and thankfully quite ignorant of the power of half bloods. Are you going to deny your involvement in his demise? I'd like to listen to you try."

I quickly darted my gaze away and dropped my head back on the pillow. If he looked into my eyes, he'd see the lie. "Yeah, that was me."

"How?"

"It doesn't matter—"

He gripped my jaw and tried to pull me to face him, but I growled and jerked my chin free.

Muttering a demon curse, Akil rose from the bed. "Your timing is somewhat imprudent." Liquid sunlight flowed over the smooth skin of his back. I propped my head up, brazenly admiring how his muscles flexed and rolled.

I could still taste him on my lips, still feel the throb of his touch on my skin. "Levi deserved it. He had Dawn in a cage. He'd toyed with her like she was worthless." My voice fractured, prompting me to clear my throat. I'd been a demon plaything. Memories bubbled but didn't surface.

He turned to face me, his expression a hard mask of disapproval. I arched an eyebrow and allowed the sight of his nakedness to fend off the reality I'd been trying to hard to forget. I didn't take much effort to recall where on his body I'd teased my tongue, or dragged my nails down his honeyed skin. "Don't go."

Even as I said the words, he flicked his wrist and clothed himself in tailored suit and amethyst colored shirt. "You don't kill a Prince of Hell and walk away, Muse."

I sighed, mourning the loss of his body. "That's exactly what I did." Flinging the sheet back, I trailed a fingernail down the valley of my waist to crest my hip. His gaze wandered before he remembered himself and shot me a scowl. "Oh, c'mon." I scoffed. "They call me the Mother of Destruction. I was living up to expectations."

His eyes narrowed. "The Mother of Destruction? Who told you that?"

"Levi. Right before I kicked his not-so-immortal ass into the underworld."

Akil snaked his arms crossed. A muscle jumped in his jaw as he ground his teeth. "You have no idea what you've done." Ah, but his lips fought a smile. "You killed a member of the Dark Court. A member of the Court hasn't fallen for a millennium. Not since the Queen..." His eyes glazed over for a few seconds. He shook his head and focused on me. "They aren't going to let this go unpunished, Muse." I'd seen Akil angry, and the expression on his face wasn't anger. The slant of his voice suggested pride. Being demon and a being of chaos, I imagined my crimes were tantamount to heroism in the netherworld. Chaos followed me wherever I went.

"I killed Enforcers too. I don't suppose Adam'll let that go unpunished either."

Akil's expression ticked, surprise widening his eyes before he shut it down. He spat out an ancient word that could only be a demon curse. "Your return and my… lapse." A curious rumble emanated from the back of his throat, not quite a growl. "This is… unexpected. When David Ryder told me how you'd died, I believed him. How is it possible he lied?" He growled, the surprise back in his eyes. "The Enforcer looked me in the eyes and lied. To me."

A taste of your own medicine. "No, he didn't lie. He believed I was dead. Everyone did."

Akil closed his eyes and sucked in a shuddering breath. He opened them again. "Why didn't you come to me?"

Because I no longer needed him. I sighed. This whole mess wasn't going away, despite my best attempts to pretend it was. "I thought you were in the netherworld. Were you here? All this time?" Had he been mourning me? Was that why he'd been virtually comatose when I'd found him?

He tilted his head curiously, perhaps really seeing me for the first time, taking in my bottle-blond hair, slim frame, and no doubt putting that image together with the black-hearted demon who killed a prince and set a dozen Enforcers ablaze.

I squirmed a little under his penetrating gaze. "What was I meant to do? I've got demons queuing up to slit my throat. Val, Levi, not to mention the vile bastard rooting around my soul. I had to keep that little girl safe, the girl you dumped on me, by the way. When you can't beat 'em, join 'em, right?" My fake bravado was almost enough to paint over the cracks in my fragile emotional state. Although the way Akil's gaze penetrated, I wondered if he could see right through those cracks into my swirling darkness. He couldn't know the gut-wrenching fear I was harboring for my waning humanity, could he?

"Where is the half-blood girl?"

"In the room down the hall."

A faint smile crept across his lips, and his attention wandered again. This time, I felt the skim of his gaze like the touch of his hands. He knew it. The hungry look in his eyes told me he'd like nothing better than to relive the erotic memories we shared. "You are a vision of temptation."

I returned his smile. I'd felt something in him as we'd lain together as man and woman. In all the years I'd slept with Akil, we had never reveled in one another like we had in those hours. Sex had always been a raw act, a physical need, not an emotional one. I'd never woken nestled protectively in his arms as I had moments ago. He'd never told he wanted to love me the way a man does a woman. Last night was different on so many levels, and some of those levels terrified me. He had said he wanted to 'love' me and then corrected himself by adding 'make love to me'. I wasn't naive enough to believe he loved me. I'd been down that road before, but he felt something. His reverent touch had confirmed as much, and considering where I'd come from and who I was, my heart just about shattered with pride at being the tiny, insignificant half blood standing beside a Prince of Hell. My demon purred in agreement, I allowed the verbal equivalent to ripple at the back of my throat and watched Akil's gaze splinter with fire.

He nodded at my unspoken words as though sensing my thoughts. "There are matters I must tend to. The Dark Court asks after me. If the rumors are to be believed, the Mother of Destruction is not dead."

"Will you tell them I'm sprawled naked in your bed?" I purred.

His smile twitched. "In case you hadn't noticed, I am the master of half-truths. I can manipulate the Court. I've been doing it for years." He grinned, baring sharp white teeth before vanishing in a burst of static.

It didn't escape my attention that he hadn't answered my question.

Chapter Twenty Six

Time alone with my thoughts was the last thing I needed. It wasn't long before the anesthetic effects of sex with Akil wore off, and I was faced with some cold, hard facts. Fear of what I'd become gnawed my bones. My demon stalked happily around my head while guilt, remorse, and disgust churned my gut. I found a bottle of red wine in the cellar and sat at the breakfast table, glowering at the corked bottle and the empty glass beside it. I should have been stronger. I knew that. My demon was my responsibility. I was meant to be something better than this weak-willed woman I seemed to be, and yet I sought out means to forget what I was slowly becoming. *A monster.*

I poured the wine. Akil was no different from the wine in that glass. He could offer me temporary reprieve, but it didn't solve any of the problems. In fact, he complicated matters with his dark words and even darker needs. I needed help, the kind that wouldn't come from drinking myself silly or sleeping with the sweet-talking Prince of Hell. If I was the Mother of Destruction, I was surely running headlong down the path of self-destruction with no means of escape.

I huffed out a breath and spread my hands on the countertop. Stefan was the only person who could possibly understand how much I terrified myself. Shit, the things he must have been thinking after killing those Enforcers. We were both so terribly damaged that our only hope had to be found in one another. If only he'd agreed to run away with me where nobody could hurt us and we couldn't hurt anyone. We could have fled, escaped all of this, but to what end? Dawn would have been trapped in a cage. I could never have left her. What ifs weren't going to change anything. Stefan was gone and, in likelihood, had turned full-demon by now. The same fate awaited me if I didn't get a grip.

Was this Dawn's future? There had to be a way out for her. She was powerful beyond anything I'd ever witnessed before. She wielded an element I didn't even begin to understand and did so with deadly efficiency. Had it not been for Ryder's intervention, she might have killed me. That was a sobering thought. Akil had said she was powerful, but Dawn was something else. No wonder the princes squabbled over her. She could kill an immortal. That made her demon kryptonite. But that erroneous accolade now rested on my shoulders. I trailed my gaze down the dark hallway, knowing I should check in on her... but finding myself hesitating. She'd have questions, and my answers weren't going to be happy ones.

There were two other half bloods out there somewhere, subjects in the Institute's Operation Typhon. Were they just as damaged? Were they strong? Did they beat the system? Had they needed help like I did?

I picked up the wine glass and admired the swirl of burgundy liquid. I'd tried to help Stefan once. *Half bloods don't get happy endings.* I'd destroyed any hope I'd had with him, despite my best efforts. Was I just delaying Dawn's inevitable destruction? No, I had to believe the little girl asleep down the hall could have a good life. It was too late for Stefan and me but not for her.

I tasted the wine, let it roll around my tongue, and swallowed. *The Mother of Destruction...* What did it mean?

An alarm chimed somewhere, alerting me to movement outside. I checked the CCTV feed on the little flat-screen TV in the kitchen and saw Jenna striding toward the back door. The Lambo was the only car in the drive, evidently Akil's. I sighed. They'd found me.

I answered the door before she had chance to ring the bell. Glass of wine in hand, bed-hair, and dressed in some old ill-fitting old clothes of mine, I must have looked as bedraggled and bemused as I felt.

She arched an eyebrow. "I thought I might find you here."

I raked my gaze over her. Her jacket bunched around a sidearm at her hip. I leaned out and checked the driveway and then the pale blue wash of sky. "No backup?"

"Just me. May I come in?"

I couldn't summon my demon inside the house. She knew that. In a straight up fistfight, she'd probably win. I was fast. I had some tricks up my sleeves. Ryder taught me well, but I didn't have her years of training. "I don't think that's a good idea."

"Is Akil here?"

I leaned against the doorjamb and sipped my drink. "What do you want?"

"To talk with you."

I wondered if Akil had stashed any whiskey in the house. "How many did I kill?" I echoed the very same words Stefan had asked me.

"None, miraculously. But it was a close thing. Two are in the hospital. Their burns won't kill them, but..." she shrugged a shoulder.

I clutched the doorjamb as my vision wavered with relief. "Are you here to take me in peacefully? Avoid a firefight? Is that it?"

"No. I er..." She moistened her lips and looked away. "The Institute doesn't know I'm here, okay. Something's happened. I need your help."

I laughed. "Believe me, I am the last person on this earth you want helping you." I stepped back, giving her room to step inside. "If you knew what was good for you, you'd turn around and walk away. Get as far away from me as possible."

"I don't think I can," she said quietly.

She'd come all this way to talk to me? It didn't ring true, but I was beyond caring. I checked the tree line again, expecting to see Enforcers spilling from the forest. The fresh morning air was sweet on my tongue, the pine-scented breeze cool. I listened hard but heard only the undercurrent of the breeze. "Fine." I closed the door and showed her to the kitchen. "I'm having breakfast." I lifted my glass. "Want some?"

"Muse..."

I shrugged at her motherly tone of disapproval. "Yeah, I'm a wreck. I know it. You don't have to beat around the bush."

"What happened to you?" She tucked her hands into her pockets and squared her shoulders.

"The same old shit. Don't worry about me. I'll survive. I always do. What did you come all this way for?" I leaned against the breakfast table.

Jenna settled against the countertop, gaze evasive, body restless. "Do you remember when your brother tracked me to the mall in Salem then brought me here?"

I tapped my nails on the table. "Yes." It wouldn't be long before Val showed up again. If the Dark Court suspected I was alive, Val would soon hear about it. He wasn't a prince, but he was well connected.

"He er..." She swallowed and bowed her head. "When you tried to save me from him, after he... Y'know, when you were unconscious..." She shifted her stance and sighed. "Damn. Listen, I'm not easy, you understand? I don't usually..."

I narrowed my eyes. "Spit it out, Jenna."

"That day. Before he took your little girl and while you were out cold, Val... Ah, damn, he worked me over with whatever magic he has. Okay? I mean, he really went to town on me. Dammit, this is harder than I thought..."

"He got to you." I recalled how my brother had crowded Jenna against the car, smothering her with his netherworldy presence.

She sighed. Tears glistened in her eyes when she looked up. Until that moment, I'd never really felt much of anything for Jenna. She was the infallible Enforcer, Stefan's 'friend,' the type of woman I wanted to be. Driven, passionate, committed, perfect. Now, as I looked at her, I saw another life torn apart by demons and felt a tangible weariness drag me down. When would it end?

"My god, Muse," she whispered, "it was... wrong, but I wanted it. I still do. He –" Her throat moved as she swallowed. "He comes to me. He's been coming to me since that day. Jesus..." She chewed her lip. "He asks me things about you, the Institute, and I tell him because I can't bear for him to leave me without..." She swiped at a tear. "...without him screwing me."

"Oh, Jenna..." The bastard. "I'm so sorry."

She gave her head a few sharp shakes. "I thought maybe I could deal with it on my own and stop him somehow, but he's too strong."

I retrieved a glass from the cupboard and poured her a generous helping of wine.

Her hand trembled as she took it. "He came to me last night." Her focus wavered, memories clouding her eyes. "I can't help telling him things. The way I am with him, I'm not fully aware of what I'm doing... until afterward."

Lust was a madness. I knew it well. "What did he say?"

"He said Dawn was missing and that the Prince of Envy was dead. He knew in his blood it was you, and he asked me if you were alive. I told him." She gulped back a few mouthfuls of wine and wiped the back of her hand across her lips. "I'm so sorry. I had to find you. This was the only place I could think you'd go."

I spat out a curse. "What did you tell him about the Institute?"

She sobbed. "Everything. And what I didn't know, I found the answers to because I wanted to please him." She groaned. "It makes me sick, knowing what I've done, and I still want him. How can that be possible?"

"It's not you. It's his power. He's the Prince of Lust's first-born son. You didn't stand a chance, Jenna."

"He asked about Operation Typhon and half bloods, Muse." She saw me tense. "I didn't know what it was to begin with. I asked Ryder. He said it was a breeding program for demons. Something about creating weapons. He's the weapons guy. He should know, right? But he clammed up. I asked Adam. He denied it existed."

The fact that Ryder knew about Operation Typhon didn't entirely surprise me. His name had been all over the file I'd got a glimpse of. I trusted Ryder more than I trusted myself, but Jenna's words had me rethinking my opinion of my old friend.

Jenna's gaze said she knew more, and it wasn't going to be good. "Go on."

"I broke into Adam's office. This isn't me. I wouldn't have done it, but... I need him."

"It's okay." I shivered. Val's hideous power sickened me. "Tell me everything."

"I stole the file and gave it to him."

I groaned. "Did you read it?"

"Some of it. The Institute has been experimenting on half bloods in a big way. It's not just you and Stefan. There are others and more in other cities. But they're killers, Muse. It's terrible. They're caged animals, not really human."

Nausea pooled saliva in my mouth. I gulped it back, swallowing with it the rising tide of rage. "Val knows this..."

"His name is in that file, but they don't know much about him. I probably know more." She threaded her fingers through her hair.

"He controls the half bloods in the netherworld. Trades them like cattle." I downed my wine and refilled my glass. "When he learned that I was going to be sold to the Institute, he put a stop to it. I can only imagine what the Institute is doing offends him. Everything this side of the veil offends my brother. The fact he must breathe the same air as humans pisses him off."

"What will he do to the Institute?"

I met her gaze. "I have to worry about what he'll do to me before I can worry about the Institute. I killed Levi. I have Dawn, and we know he wants her back. He was working with Levi. I don't care enough about the Institute to help them dig themselves out of a hole of their own making."

She nodded, her eyes unfocused again as she chewed on her lower lip. "What am I going to do?"

"We'll think of something." I had no idea. Val was a terrible force to be reckoned with. One touch of his wings had rendered me unconscious. He'd dangled lust in front of my eyes, and I'd gladly thrown myself at his feet, as weak as a kitten. I couldn't imagine the horror Jenna had been living with, knowing he had her under his control and liking it. He'd be coming for me. And for Dawn.

"I need to check on Dawn." I left Jenna alone with her thoughts and wandered through the sprawling house, trying not to think about the physical and emotional numbness spreading through my body. I should be relieved. I hadn't killed anyone. That was good news. So why didn't I feel like shouting from the rooftop? Grim realization tugged the corners of my lips down. It wasn't a relief because I'd already accepted my demon was very capable of killing. Therefore, so was I. The lines between us were eroding.

Dawn's room was empty. The bed had been slept in and her bunny lay sprawled on the pillow, but she was gone. "Dawn?" The house was too damn big. I checked each room, my anxiety notching up a degree with each passing minute. She had to be here. She wouldn't have left. Not without the bunny. Nobody could get into Blackstone. The symbols kept all demons out, apart from Akil. I called her name, the pitch of my voice increasing as dread pooled in my gut.

The touch of Akil's element tugged through me as he called his power from somewhere inside the house. I turned on my heel and jogged back through the house until I found him in the kitchen, pinning Jenna to the wall, hand locked around her throat.

"Akil, put her down."

He snarled. "I don't take kindly to Enforcers on my property." Heat haze rippled the air around him.

Jenna's wide eyes locked on me. She groped for her gun, but Akil captured her hand and pinned that to the wall too. Leaning in closer, he breathed in through his nose, drawing her scent into him. "She has Valenti's scent on her." He swung his gaze back to me. Embers fizzled in his eyes, a sure sign he wasn't happy.

"I know." I sighed. "She came here for help."

He yanked her to him, growled through sharp teeth, then threw her to the floor between us. "She's his minion and the reason he waits outside."

I hissed, my fear for my brother like acid in my veins. "Val's outside?"

Jenna staggered to her feet, wild eyes finding me. "I'm sorry." She wheezed and spluttered, gasping air. "I couldn't have denied him even if I wanted to. I was supposed to lure you out, but I couldn't do it. Please believe me." She gave me a wretched stare, her self-disgust evident in the savage downturn of her lips.

I couldn't deal with her right now. Val was outside and... "Dawn's gone."

"Yes," Akil replied, smoothing back his hair. "Her departure was necessary."

"Oh god... What have you done?"

"I did the right thing, as I told you to do weeks ago. She's far too volatile to be allowed to roam free. If any of the other princes claimed her, they'd very quickly turn her against the rest of us. She is chaos, Muse. You saw as much when she killed Levi. Yes, I know it wasn't you. You might well be the Mother of Destruction, but that little girl is raw chaos inside the body of a nine year old human."

No, he couldn't be telling me this. This wasn't real. "Akil, what exactly have you done?" My hands clenched at my sides, fists aching as my muscles strained.

Firelight played in his eyes. "She's with the Institute."

My balance tilted out from under me, and my vision blurred. Staggering back, I fell against the countertop. "No. No, Akil. You aren't telling me this. The Institute?" I slumped forward and concentrated on my breathing because, if I didn't focus on something other than the rage bubbling up from the depths inside, I was going to lose control. I heard myself repeating "No" over and over, even as my element thrashed inside me. "She's just a little girl... Just a little thing... She deserved a shot at freedom, you son of a bitch."

"She's gone. There is nothing more to be done."

I swung my head around and snarled, welcoming my demon as close to the surface as she could get. "Get her back."

He blinked and held my stare. "This is not negotiable."

"You're afraid of her, aren't you?" I grinned. "The mighty Prince of Greed is afraid of a nine year old girl."

"She plucked an immortal chaos demon apart at the molecular level. Yes, I'm afraid of her. I happen to enjoy living, even after all these years. A whelp of a girl isn't going to threaten my existence."

"You selfish bastard. She wouldn't have hurt you. She only hurt Levi because he was going to kill Ryder and hand us both over to Asmodeus. She trusted you."

"That was her mistake." He arched an eyebrow and gave me a bored look. "Did you witness her killing Leviathan?" He saw the answer on my face. "Then you know how wild she is. Look past her human vulnerability, and see the demon inside her soul, Muse. It would be remiss of me to let a threat like that walk free."

She would have killed me. I already knew that, but I'd tried to convince myself that I'd understood her. "Do you have any idea what they'll do to her?"

"She is in the only place the demons cannot reach her."

I shoved off the counter and strode up to him, crowding his personal space. Jenna watched from the sidelines as I faced off with the Prince of Greed. "Take me there. Now."

"No." He glowered down at me, fiery eyes fierce with defiance. "If you go there, all you will accomplish is your own incarceration. Is that what you want?"

"I don't care about me, Akil. I'm already lost."

Jenna chose that moment to bolt for freedom. I cursed and lunged after her. Akil snatched my wrist, pulling me up short. "Let her go," he growled.

I tugged, but his unyielding grip held me fast. "Goddamn you, Akil. She'll tell Val where Dawn is. You think he's going to let the Institute stop him getting what he wants? He'll send Jenna in. She'll get Dawn for him. I have to stop him. I have to get her out of there before they ruin her like they did Stefan, like they did me. Let me go, Akil. Just let me go."

A flicker of acknowledgement narrowed his eyes. He exhaled a curse and released me. I ran after Jenna, only slowing as I approached the open back door. I couldn't see her outside, nor could I see my brother. But that didn't mean he wasn't there. I stepped out into the blazing sunshine, expecting to feel the touch of his power, but the absence of his element told me all I needed to know. He was gone. He could flit between vast distances just as well as Akil. He might already be at the Institute, manipulating Jenna.

I climbed into Akil's Lamborghini and jabbed the start button. The car burst into life with a hungry, resonating growl. The instruments lit up. I flicked the paddle shift into gear and spun the car, kicking up a wave of gravel in my wake. Akil could try to stop me at any time. We'd fight. I'd win.

The supercar twitched under my control, champing at the bit as I planted my foot to the floor. *I'm coming for you, Dawn.*

* * *

A plume of black smoke marred the pale blue sky over Boston. I spotted the cloud a few miles outside the city limits, but as I crawled the Lambo through the early morning traffic and the cloud bellowed higher, an unsettling sense of dread crawled across my flesh. I flicked on the radio. It didn't take long to locate a news broadcast. A warehouse complex was ablaze. I flicked to another station. The reporter was giving a breakdown on an international company charged with policing the demons: the Institute.

Disregarding traffic laws, I demanded everything the Lambo could give me and plowed through the clogged main routes. Akil must have left Dawn at the Institute while I slept, no more than a few hours ago. What had happened in that time? This had to be Val's doing.

I abandoned the Lambo as close to the Institute as I could get, outside a barrier of fire trucks and fought my way through a crowd of onlookers. Black smoke blotted out the sun. Thick, rolling shadows rippled across the walking wounded huddled around ambulances. It was chaos. There had to be hundreds of people spilling from the Institute doors.

I searched the faces for any signs of Ryder or Adam but couldn't see them.

"Ma'am, you can't go any further." A stocky fireman in all his firefighting gear blocked my path.

"I work there. I can help."

"There's nothing you can do."

A crackle on his radio drew his attention. I skirted around him and bolted between two fire trucks. Two rigs had extended their ladders over the flat roof of the warehouse complex. I couldn't see any flames, but smoke rolled skyward with no sign of letting up. I called my element and immediately felt the blast of heat inside the building and something else, the sickly, abhorrent touch of Dawn's unique power.

A line of firefighters helped a steady stream of smoke-damaged people spill from the doors. I strode up to them, very much aware of my unassuming appearance. They weren't going to let me inside. I didn't need to see their eyes behind their visors to know that.

In the next step, I threw a second skin of flame across my body and plastered a crazy grin on my face. They all recoiled. The wounded scattered. One of the firefighters barked into his radio, "There's a woman, a-a demon woman coming your way."

"Have you vented the smoke?" I asked, my demon-voice barely more than a growl.

The guy peering back at me gave me a wary nod. "What you gonna do?" He hedged, clearly not sure if he should try to stop me from entering the building.

"Fire demon." I quirked an eyebrow. "I'm going to put the fire out." That was the plan, although I'd technically never tried to extinguish a fire anywhere near the size of the inferno raging inside the the Institute. "You goin' to let me pass?"

He stepped aside.

Smoke immediately hindered my advance through the building. I pulled my element into me, not needing to add to the heat already pulsing against the walls. A few stragglers hurried by, coughing into rolled up shirts, their eyes wild with fear. Shoring myself up with a courage I didn't know I possessed, I kept low and ventured deeper into the building.

A closed door blocked my path. From the bubbling paint and terrible weight of heat throbbing the air, the inferno raged beyond. I planted my feet and called my demon, letting her slip inside my skin and protect my fragile human flesh beneath her lava-veined skin. My wing jutted against the ceiling. I drew it in behind me and sucked in a deep, smoldering breath. Time to see if I could tame the flames. Dawn was in there, alive, if the touch of her power was reliable. She'd be terrified.

I closed my hand around the door handle and shoved.

A wave of super-heated air blasted my body. Fire lunged for freedom and gobbled up the ceiling. I sent out a sharp flicker of power, curling my element around the wild roaring heat and drawing it to me in a motherly embrace. The wildfire coiled around me, answering my call. Power fizzled through my limbs and danced across my skin. A groan escaped me as the fire seeped into my demon flesh.

As I walked on, the flames danced around my blazing body, eager to please. The tunnel of fire beckoned. Blazing energy boiled across the walls and smothered the floors. The dark pollutant around my heart throbbed with the beat of the flames, devouring the rush of heat, feeding its addiction. I was walking a thin line of control. So damn thin it might as well have been a tightrope. My demon rode high, turning me into a beast of molten heat, the walking, living, breathing soul of fire. And I was hungry.

I stumbled against a wall, my hand sinking into the charred plywood. A snarl bubbled from my lips. Ahead, the heart of the fire beat for me, calling me closer. It hungered too. It wanted freedom. So did I. I rolled my shoulders and spread my ragged wing, absorbing the heat through every inch of my flesh. Fire lapped at the pleasure receptors in my brain, firing off my ingrained lust for chaos. It was wicked and divine. All the things my demon wanted, I wanted. I was demon.

I threw my head back and laughed. We walked on, demon and woman soaking up the power, reveling in the simplicity of madness.

Charred timbers rained around me. Ashes swirled in my firestorm. Walls collapsed, floors buckled, and I laughed. The roar of the fire gobbled up my laughter and raged higher. It taunted, beckoning me closer to its heart.

The Institute was lost. Nothing was coming back from this blaze. I felt a curious tease of pleasure ripple down my spine at that knowledge. I could help it on its way. Blast the building to ash. I'd done it before in the netherworld. I could raze the Institute, grind it to dust beneath my feet. If I reached for the veil, I'd feel what it truly meant to destroy. Giddy with power, I chuckled. It was what they deserved. They meddled with demons, cavorted with chaos. *Well, chaos always wins, you sons of bitches.*

I sensed something human to my left, behind a blackened door. Someone was alive inside. The blaze tempted me. I didn't care for these people. They were nothing, fuel for the flames. But my humanity had not yet died. I stumbled against the door and almost tumbled inside as it gave way beneath my superheated flesh. Fire licked at my wing, teasing me further into chaos, but as I swept my gaze around the room I recognized the wall of books and the old, claw-footed desk.

Adam lay sprawled on the floor, a limp hand reaching toward the door. I cocked my head and looked down at the man I despised. I could hear his heartbeat flutter in his chest and his short rasping breaths. He would die here. All I need do was turn and leave. Demon desires tugged me away. The flames beckoned. The firelight's embrace called. I stayed in the doorway, unable to move.

"Adam..."

His fingers twitched. His heavy eyelids blinked. He rolled his eyes up to me and saw a fire-bathed demon looming over him. I smiled, baring fangs.

"Muse," he rasped, hand reaching.

A splintering crack above us snapped my attention to the ceiling. Fire pooled above. Melting plastic dripped to the floor, and then the entire ceiling ignited, flooding a wash of tumbling orange flame above us. I thrust an arm out and funneled the hungry fire through my fingers, down my arm, and into my body.

"Go!" I snarled.

He tried to heave his bulk off the floor but collapsed, breathless and unfocused. Dammit. It was taking all my control not to walk away. My demon wanted more than that. She wanted to bury him in flame. It was all he deserved. Nobody needed to know how I'd ushered him toward death. *But I'd know.*

"Go, Adam. Go now–" A roar was the only warning before the ceiling and its framework collapsed, slamming me to the floor under the weight of debris. I clung onto consciousness despite a jagged tearing pain assaulting my senses. If I lost consciousness, the fire would roar back to life. I had hold of its reins for now.

I clawed at the floor, grating sharp claws through the melting carpet. Black boots. I blinked, and looked up at the man those boots belonged to. A firefighter peered down at me behind his visor and oxygen mask.

"It's a demon. Leave it behind." A voice barked through his radio.

"No." Adam shouted. A wracking cough almost robbed him of his ability to walk. He leaned heavily on the firefighters hurrying him from the room. "Don't leave her."

I wanted to tell the firefighter to help me up. That I could stop this, but it only came out as a growl, probably cementing the notion in his head that I was little more than an animal. I locked my gaze on his eyes behind the soot obscured visor. *Help me.*

The voice crackled through his radio again, telling the crew to fall back. The building was lost.

He muttered something that I missed and then crouched beside me and heaved the metal gantry high enough for me to wriggle out. He headed for the hall.

"Come with me," he said, voice muffled through all his breathing gear. His bright eyes pleading.

I shook my head. "There's a girl here." I could still feel Dawn's power. She wasn't far. "Go." I felt his gaze on my back as I walked into the flames.

* * *

I devoured the fire with every step. Dangerous laughter played in my mind the whole time. It was glorious. I couldn't escape the sensation of wonderment. Like a proud mother, I admired the destruction the fire wrought even as I corralled the wayward flames to me.

Dawn's power loomed up ahead in what had once been the cafeteria. As I rounded the ruined corridor, I saw her demon form suspended amid her threads of chaotic tendrils. Black eels of power whipped and thrashed around her, containing her inside a pulsing bubble of dark energy.

Her eyes flicked to me, and treachery burned there.

I tugged on the fire devouring the room and snuffed it out in one sweeping gesture. Smoke drifted and rolled between us, shirking her aura. I caught the unmistakable odor of burned flesh, but I couldn't see the bodies, just dunes of debris, fragments of ashes, papers, and shredded clothes.

"Dawn..." I stepped closer. A lash of power snapped out at me, clearly a warning. "It's okay. I won't hurt you."

"I was wrong." Her innocent voice had twisted beneath the riding power of the demon. She didn't sound like Dawn. She sounded like madness. "I trusted you and Akil. You said not to. You said he was bad. But you trust him, and I trust you."

The dark boiled around her, dangerous and deadly. I had no doubt she could kill me and probably do it in an instant. I might not even see death coming. "I'm sorry. I didn't know what he was planning."

"He said you should have brought me here. Is that what you were going to do? I don't like it here." Her face clouded with shadows. "I unmade them, Muse, and it felt good. That's not right, is it? Is that what you felt when you burned those people to save me? Am I meant to be empty? I'm scared." She sobbed, and then a grin slashed across her face. "I want to do it again."

I clamped my jaw closed. "Dawn, I can help you manage your... gift." Right, like I managed my own. "We have to leave. The building isn't safe. The fire still hungers. Let me get you out, Dawn. Let me save you."

She tilted her head to the side and assessed me. I shivered with the overflowing currents of energy breezing through my veins. Ashes rained from my skin. Around me, the fire whispered promises of destruction. If I didn't save myself soon, I'd be as lost as this building was.

She puffed out a sigh and slumped forward. Her demon fell back from her skin, leaving the vulnerable little girl behind.

"Come..." I shoved my demon back. She snapped and snarled as she fought me for freedom. Gathering Dawn against me, I guided her back the way I'd come. The flames had died down. Behind us, the walls groaned and the ground trembled.

Chapter Twenty Seven

We stumbled out into a sunlit backstreet, coughing and wheezing smoke from our lungs. EMTs crowded, sirens wailed, people cried. I hugged Dawn close and snapped at the EMTs to get back. We were fine. Others needed their help more than we did. A grumble shook the air around us like thunder. A cloud of ash spluttered skyward as the warehouse complex collapsed in on itself. A savage spike of glee twitched my lips as I turned away. I shouldn't have enjoyed the destruction, but I did. Had it not been for Dawn, I'd have been dancing in the debris.

Dawn's voice reached me through the clamoring madness in my head. "I don't know what I am."

A street away from the simmering remains of the Institute, I planted her down on a curb, away from the crowds, near a closed grocery store, its graffiti-covered shutters pulled down. Crouching in front of her, I cupped her face in my filthy hands and smiled. "It's okay because you're not alone. I won't ever let you go again. I can help you manage your demon. We'll work together, two half bloods, just you and me." I'd lost Stefan. I wasn't losing her. I tucked her hair behind her ear. And maybe, if I could save her, I'd save myself too.

A delicate smile skipped across her lips.

"Muse. Back away. Do it slowly."

I swung my stare over my shoulder and fixed it on Ryder. He had a gun palmed in his right hand, finger hooked over the trigger and Dawn in his sights. Determination hardened his sharp eyes.

"Ryder..." I stood slowly, as he'd said, and turned my back on Dawn to face him. "What are you doing?"

"She killed everyone in the cafeteria, Muse. Jesus..." His hand trembled, aim wavering. He flexed his fingers and regained control of himself. "She pulled them apart, turned then into confetti."

"Ryder..." I licked my dry lips, my throat hoarse. "You can't do this. She's just a little girl." A quiver of power slithered through me. I looked to the right, across the street. Akil stood at the curb, hooded eyes locked on me.

"She ain't no little girl." Ryder blinked rapidly. His lips turned down, and he shook his head slowly. "The Institute is gone because of her. Do you know what that means? The only thing stopping the demons from flooding this city is dust. She's demon, and she's a killer."

"It wasn't her fault." I lifted my hands, palms out. "Akil..." I glanced back, but he'd gone. "Akil brought her here. He had no right."

"It doesn't matter who did what. She slaughtered them. Shit, Muse. I saw it all on the cameras. She's a monster. Half bloods don't get happy endings, Muse. You're too damn fucked up. Every single one. Even Stefan, in the end. Y'know, I thought you might be different, but it ain't possible. The demon inside you calls the shots. Doesn't it?"

Dawn stood beside me, her little hand resting on my thigh. She looked up at me with those doe-eyes, wise beyond her years. "I am a monster."

"No, honey." My heart stuttered to hear her say it. "You just need a friend, that's all."

"I don't want to be this way."

I don't want to be that demon. Stefan's words drifted back to me.

A whimper betrayed my internal battle between the need to save her and the need let her go. I knew, deep in my bones, that Ryder was right. I'd witnessed her power, and she truly was a terrible thing. But I'd come so close to saving her, to freeing her. She was a half blood caught in a storm just like me.

"Please..." I stepped in front of Dawn, shielding her behind my legs. "I will take her away from this, from everyone, somewhere she can't hurt anyone. There must be a way to control her demon." Even as I said the words, I wasn't sure I believed them.

Akil flitted into existence in my peripheral vision. "The princes will find her. They were ignorant of the power residing in half bloods. That is no longer the case."

Ryder breathed hard. His wide eyes flicked between Akil and me, probably alarmed to find Akil backing him up. "Fuck, Muse, get outtah the way. Don't make me shoot you too."

"I can't let you do this, Ryder." I lowered my hands. He would shoot me. I'd always known it. If it came down to this, staring down the barrel of his gun, he would pull the trigger.

He trembled. A sheen of perspiration glistened on his face. He smiled, but it was a bitter, worn out ghost of a smile filled with regret. He snarled at Akil, "Get Muse out of here."

I shot my hand out, halting Akil as I drilled my stare into Ryder. "Akil, don't you dare."

"She can't be saved, Muse." Akil's smooth voice sounded entirely reasonable.

I smiled and tugged on my demon's reins. "Then neither can I." I tasted the flames on my lips, felt them lick across my body. *Let the demon win, and nothing can hurt me again.*

Ryder fired. The bullet smacked into my shoulder, engulfing my entire right side in a blast of agony, spinning me. My demon recoiled, leaving me human. I collapsed face down on the road. The smell and taste of my own blood coated my nose and throat. And then, as if the world felt I hadn't been dealt enough of a challenge for one day, I looked up to see my brother in all his netherworldly glory leering down at me. Vast black wings draped me in shadow. His milky-white body gleamed like marble. "Thank you for delivering her to me, sister-mine."

"Dawn, run!" I screamed.

Ryder's gun rang out. A splash of crimson burst across my brother's chest before his flesh soaked up the wound. His muscles rippled and spat out the deformed slug. It bounced on the road between us, reminding me not to fuck with immortals.

Val stepped around me, apparently deciding I wasn't worth the time or energy. I tracked his formidable demon form as Ryder continued to empty a clip of bullets into him. They buzzed about Val, no more bothersome than flies.

Mammon barreled into Val – seemingly out of thin air. His obsidian muscles rippled as he tackled Val and shoved my brother through the storefront shutters with all the finesse of a wrecking ball. Inhuman growls, snarls, and roars resounded inside the store. There was no way on this earth Mammon would let Val take Dawn.

I struggled to roll onto my side and hook my legs under me. I couldn't stand. I could barely sit up. My entire right side throbbed with a mind-numbing pain. Blood soaked my clothes, gluing them to my feverish skin. Through the haze of agony, I fixed Dawn and Ryder in my sights. Ryder loomed over her, the muzzle of his gun inches from her forehead. His aim didn't waver. His hand had never been steadier. Dawn tilted her head up and looked into his eyes. She didn't run, didn't beg, didn't call her demon. She could have done all of those things. She could have killed us all without even drawing from the veil. She was chaos, but in that moment, chaos was controlled by a nine-year-old human girl. She blinked up at Ryder and said two words.

"Thank you."

He pulled the trigger.

"No!" I reached a hand out as the gunshot cracked through the air and echoed down the street. My demon tried to clamber into my skin, but physical and mental anguish drove her down.

Dawn fell back. Her tiny body crumpled in a heap at Ryder's feet. She lay still. The touch of her element had vanished. A strangled cry—somewhere between a scream and a growl—tore from my throat. I smothered the blazing pain under my rage and somehow managed to get to my feet, only for my legs to crumple, dropping me to my knees.

Ryder staggered under the weight of his own guilt and turned away from Dawn's body and from me. He gave a wrenching groan of agony. I didn't care. I wanted to gather Dawn's fragile body into my arms, but I couldn't get to her. I fell forward onto a hand, lifted my gaze through my hair, and whispered, "It's okay, Dawn. Everything is going to be okay. You're free now."

The tears came, sliding down my soot-covered cheeks. It wasn't right. It wasn't fair. She could have survived. She could have lived. She didn't deserve this.

After perhaps minutes, hours, I don't know, I was aware of Akil's warming presence close behind me.

"Valenti has fled," he said softly. "The Enforcers are coming."

I bristled. My demon prowled just below the surface. "Get away from me."

I expected an argument, but in the next breath he was gone. He had brought Dawn here to this hellhole. It was his fault. All of it. He could have stopped Ryder, and he hadn't. He'd wanted her dead too. Everyone wanted her dead. Nobody cared enough to try to help her. What was wrong with this world?

Eventually, the sounds of the city coaxed me back to reality. Ambulance sirens *bipped* through the crowds a street away. Clouds of gray smoke bellowed skyward, but the inferno devouring the Institute was dying. I felt its death in my veins.

I watched, detached and numb, as a black-clad firefighter walked toward me, helmet tucked under his arm. His short chestnut hair was plastered against his head. His face sported smudges of ash and soot. I might not have recognized him if not for the calm blue eyes: the same firefighter who'd helped me in Adam's office.

He crouched beside me, looked me over with a sensitive appraisal, and noted the blood soaking my top.

He gave me the most heartbreaking smile. "There's no use in you dying here."

I wasn't sure I had the strength of mind to reply. Behind him, the EMTs wheeled a gurney closer, and behind them a handful of Enforcers bore down on us. Tears blurred my vision.

He tugged his gloves off and held out a hand. "C'mon, let's get that wound looked at."

I shook my head and bit my lip, trying to stop its quivering. "I can't leave. I promised her."

He glanced over my shoulder to where Dawn lay and nodded. "You're banged up pretty bad. Maybe it's time you looked after yourself?" His sincerity spoke of understanding. I examined his features, searching for hostility, but he wasn't Institute, and he wasn't demon either. He was just a normal guy who wanted to help, no strings attached, no ulterior motives. I closed my eyes, fearing what it meant to let Dawn go. I'd pinned more of my hopes on that little girl than I'd let myself believe.

As the firefighter closed his hand around mine and tugged me to my feet, a veil of forced indifference settled over me. I managed a few steps before falling against the ambulance crew. The blissful embrace of unconsciousness stole me away.

Chapter Twenty Eight

The Stone's Throw bar had never seen a crowd quite like it. I jostled through the throngs of people, taking note of the armed Enforcers among them. My arm throbbed; a week and it still burned like a bitch. The painkillers were wearing off. I'd been popping so many pills I virtually rattled as I walked.

Ben Stone acknowledged me and gestured to one of his new bartenders to fix me a whiskey. I probably shouldn't have been drinking while my veins were buzzing with drugs, but really, in the scheme of things, I had other things to worry about. Like being a single thread away from disaster.

While I waited at the bar, I couldn't help dragging my gaze across the symbols spray painted across the walls and ceiling. The Enforcers were here en masse, and judging by the incident wall set up along one side of the room, they were here to stay. A map of Boston sat center stage. I couldn't see much, tucked away in the corner as I was, but I noted the locations of a dozen or more fat red circles pimpling the map.

The bartender handed me my drink. I paid, brought it to my lips, and noticed a hushed quiet descending over the crowd. The crawling itch of dozens of pairs of eyes skittered down my back. I took a sip and welcomed the sweet heat of the alcohol as it burned my throat and eased the tiredness in my muscles. I took my time, and all the while, the silence settled over the crowd until only the mumblings from the TV disturbed the quiet.

Licking my lips, I placed my drink down and leaned my good arm on the bar. When I lifted my gaze, upward of seventy Enforcers glared back at me. *Way to make a girl feel uncomfortable.* At least I'd ditched the pink and black persona in favor of my more typical knee high boots, skinny dark washed jeans, and my 90's throwback leather jacket. They'd see the gun holstered at my hip. Not that it would do me any good against a mob of demon killers.

I don't know what they expected me to do. Sprout horns and a wing, and roar at them?

Adam Harper's deep voice broke the stalemate. "Muse, join us..."

His Enforcers collectively grumbled their displeasure, but none would argue with the boss. They slowly resumed their conversations, turning away from me in the hope I'd skulk off with my tail between my legs. If only it was that simple.

I carried my drink to where Adam's voice had originated from to find him standing with half a dozen others around two tables pushed together, strewn with maps of Boston. Ryder hung back, leaning against the far wall, thumb tucked over his camo-print pants. His untucked shirt bunched around his gun. He chewed on a toothpick while training all of his attention on the documents. We hadn't spoken since he'd executed Dawn a week ago, and that was perfectly fine with me.

"Are you up to speed, Muse?" Adam asked.

All eyes turned to me. I might have squirmed under their collective no-nonsense stares if any of this actually mattered to me. As it was, not even whiskey could warm my cold heart. I'd shut all the emotional shit away.

"No." I said, surprised at my steady tone. I slid my gaze to Adam. I hadn't seen him since the firefighters hauled his ass out of his burning office. He was lucky to be standing there. My fingers twitched with that knowledge. I'd promised Ryder once that I'd never hurt Adam or the Institute. Well, I'd kept that promise. For what it was worth.

I rolled my sore shoulder beneath my jacket. "I've been in and out of the clinic." They didn't need to know I meant Jerry's place and not the general hospital.

Ryder lifted his hooded gaze. He plucked the toothpick free, picked up a file, and tossed it across the table to me. Fat black letters printed across the cover spelled out the contents: Operation Typhon.

I reached out, instinctively seeking answers, and then paused, curling my fingers into my hand. "What's going on?"

Adam straightened. "We're down, but we're not out. Demons have renewed their incursions with vigor, scouting parties before an all-out invasion. They're breaching the veil in record numbers. Boston PD is swamped with reports. Witnesses are reporting vigilante groups setting themselves up as would-be Enforcers, believing we're not up to the task of protecting this city. We have emergency plans in place, including new premises and several inbound teams, but it's taking time, and the vigilantes are out for blood. They're getting themselves killed." Adam dislodged his glasses and pinched the bridge of his nose. "The calm of a few weeks ago was a lull. What we're experiencing now is the outer fringes of an incoming storm. I've received reports of half a dozen Class A demons in Boston, Muse."

I was a Class A. So was Akil. We used to be the only ones. It looked as though that was changing. "Shit just got real, huh?" I found it hard to sympathize with the assholes who brought this all on themselves.

Adam pushed his glasses back on and gave me the disapproving fatherly stare. "Some, we suspect, may be princes." He puffed out a sigh. "We need you."

One of my eyebrows hiked up of its own accord. "Is that so?" Bet they could have done with Stefan too. What a shame Adam ordered the death of his son and their best Enforcer.

"We need your connections." He tapped a black and white photo of Akil. "We need your expertise." He flicked open the cover of the Operation Typhon folder to reveal an image captured on the Institute's internal video network. A one winged demon stood in a hallway, arms out, wing flexed high above her head, summoning the fire like a magnet calls metal. "And we need your power."

Well, damn. My gaze hooked up on Ryder. He wasn't happy about this, and considering his rigid glower, I could assume it wasn't his idea.

"What makes you think I'm going to work for you after everything that's happened?" I met and held Adam's eyes.

"We're not the bad guys here, Muse. The demons are. If they go unchallenged, if it's true, and there are princes on this side of the veil, people will die. Good, normal, everyday people. This is just the beginning, and you know it. Do it for the people of Boston, for your neighbors, your friends. You're a good person. You know what this means, and you can do something to stop it." His Adam's apple bobbed as he swallowed.

I flicked my gaze across the stern faces of the others crowded around the table. I had no friends here. Most of these people would happily put a bullet in my head, Ryder included. But this wasn't about the Institute, not any more. The demons were coming. "I'll help you. But I'm not dishing out your justice, Adam. I'm not needlessly killing demons for you. I will provide you with intel about the princes, because if you're right and they're here, then you're gonna need more than me. You'll need something not far off divine intervention." Perhaps Dawn could have turned the tide. She'd had the power to kill an immortal. But she was gone.

Jenna eased into the group beside me. A warm smile briefly lightened her lips. I failed at hiding the sharp intake of breath. She nodded, understanding my hesitance. "Playing both sides, Muse. Just like you."

"That's a dangerous game, Jenna." My brother was not to be messed with. Once he tired of her, he'd destroy her in ways I didn't even want to think about.

"I know." She regarded her colleagues with pride bright in her eyes. "We're the frontline. If we fail, they'll be nothing left of Boston."

"Can we count you among us?" Adam asked.

"No." Their collective gasp brought a smile to my face. "But I'm not against you. I promise you that much."

The Enforcers talked strategy, but none would look me in the eyes. I listened, soaking up their camaraderie. I was no longer part of their world, but I never really had been. Always on the outside, that was me. Nowhere to call home. Half demon, half human, wholly fucked. I finished my drink, grateful for the warmth spreading through my otherwise cold soul, scooped up the Operation Typhon file, and moved to leave when Adam's heavy hand clamped around my good arm. He drew me to one side, away from his devoted employees.

"What you did, I won't forget it."

I flicked my gaze down to his hand, which he promptly removed as though I'd scolded him. "Just because I saved your ass, it doesn't make us best buddies. I'm not your hero, Adam. I'm your enemy. Don't ever doubt that." I turned away from him before I really told him what had crossed my mind back in his office. He was a smart guy. He'd have figured as much.

Outside, I stole a few moments to deliberately breathe the slightly briny air of Boston into my lungs and soak the ambience of the quiet street into my pores, letting the city sounds and smells subdue my rattling anxiety. I didn't imagine the creeping sense of unease. If Adam was right, then whatever was happening beyond the veil had reached a tipping point, and those demons who could get out were scrabbling for freedom. Unfortunately for them, the Boston streets weren't demon friendly. They never really had been, but now gangs and death squads awaited newly arrived demons. People would die. Both sides were losing what was fast becoming a bloody turf battle. The body count was rising. Before long, the press would catch on. The fuse was burning down to a whole load of explosive material and the Institute was woefully underprepared, outmanned, outgunned and vulnerable. I admired their tenacity even if it would get them all killed. Never let it be said the Enforcers were cowards. They knew they were fighting a losing battle, but they were going to take the demons down with them.

I closed my arms around the Operation Typhon file and hugged it to my chest. Inside, there would be information about the other half bloods. *They're like animals*, Jenna had said. The Institute was going to need them, but could they be controlled? From what I'd learned about my half-blood comrades, the answer was no. We didn't have a great track record for control. At least if I stepped out of line, Ryder would shoot me down.

A tight sizzle of heat trickled down the back of my neck, alerting my human senses to the wholly demonic presence behind me. I could have ignored him and walked away, but walking away from the Prince of Greed wasn't an easy step to take.

"Am I going to find your name all over this file?" My voice carried through the crisp night air. Distantly, a siren wailed, but even the very real noises of the city couldn't detract from the netherworldly throb of power he radiated, especially when I felt the tease of his fingers through my hair.

I gasped and snapped my head around, expecting Akil to be standing right behind me. He emerged from the shadows of a blocked-up doorway, as though those curtains of darkness had created him. In the subdued light where color fled, red embers sizzled in his eyes. The fall of his expensive suit accentuated a body I'd recently become intimately reacquainted with. He didn't approach as I'd expected him to, but stood back, reading me, likely waiting for the accusations that burned on the tip of my tongue.

His gaze flicked to the file in my hand, a cursory glance, guarded with indifference. "The contents of the file is irrelevant, as is the past. The Boston Institute is rubble and ash. Their meddling delivered them their well-earned justice."

He was entirely too nonchalant. I'd bought the blasé bullshit from him for ten years. Not anymore. The infinitesimal widening of his eyes, the slight flare of his nostrils, the slippery smile that hardly touched his lips: they all added up to a hint of something like smug satisfaction.

I glanced at the closed doors to Stone's Throw. A murmuring undertone of voices drifted through the still night air. At any moment, my little chat with a Prince of Hell could be disturbed. My fraternizing with Class A demons wouldn't go down well. "There are upward of seventy Enforcers behind those doors. Any one of them would give their right arm to capture you, and you're standing not ten feet from their back door. Are you trying to get caught?"

His heated gaze stayed trained on me with laser-like intensity. "Do you really believe seventy or seven hundred Enforcers could capture and hold a demon of my caliber?"

And there were seven—scratch that—six smug-ass princes just like him eyeing up our world. Hell help us. I licked my lips and watched as the movement caught his molten gaze. He'd scored me with that gaze as we'd lain together, wrapped in the trappings of lovemaking. Was that what he was thinking? Undressing me with his eyes? I couldn't pretend the sex hadn't meant anything, but neither could he. The change between us simmered like an electrical current in my veins. I had the distinct impression I'd somehow dragged him down to my level, and he'd elevated me to his. And there we were, standing on mutual ground, eyeing each other with sharp intent and dark knowledge. I'd seen him lost to grief, heard him beg to be loved, and while he may not have said those exact words, I knew what I'd felt in his fevered kisses and urgent touch. In all likelihood, he didn't understand what was happening between us. An immortal chaos demon could not love. He was incapable of wrapping his egocentric mind around it. Love was impossible for him, and yet... Those things he felt, they were alien to him, and I bet that drove him wild. I let a satisfied smile sit easily on my lips. His fire-touched eyes narrowed, but his smile stayed, curious, uncertain. He looked at me as though I were a puzzle, and the very fact he couldn't figure me out drove him to distraction. Good. He could know exactly how it felt to have the one you love shut you down. He'd done it to me. I was foolish then, naive and weak. That half blood girl was long gone. Whatever I was becoming, I was on a par with him. Equal.

When I spoke, my tone implied an equally blasé and nonchalant attitude. I'd learned from the best. "Things are different."

"Indeed." His statuesque masculinity served to remind me of the demon I was facing off against. Akil's human vessel was a trap, but which one of us had been caught?

"You could have stopped all of this from happening, but you didn't lift a finger. It's your fault Dawn's dead. As sure as Ryder pulled the trigger, you killed her." My calmness didn't sound right to my ears, but the glassy undercurrent mirrored in my thoughts was exactly what I needed. It felt good not to care for his reply as though he couldn't hurt me, no matter what he said or did. I was beyond that.

"Dawn's demise was necessary." Still, he didn't move, and he watched me as though he might actually care about my reply.

"How did you get her in? Did you just drop her off at the door and shoo her inside like you did at my apartment?" She'd been so eager to learn, brimming over with wonderment. The little girl Akil had left in my care with her mismatched socks and tatty rabbit could have been saved.

"I gave her to David Ryder. In this instance, he and I were in agreement. Did you know he has a teenage daughter and an ex-wife?" Akil's lips tightened as he saw disbelief on my face. "You do not ask enough questions of those around you, Muse. I make it my business to intimately know my enemies. David Ryder is a private man with many secrets. Humans find it difficult to look innocence in the eye and see the potential for madness. He knew Dawn was dangerous but failed to acknowledge the depth of chaos corrupting her young mind. He hesitated to administer the delightful drug they use to subdue demons. Perhaps he listened to you and gave her the benefit of the doubt? As a father himself, I imagine he let his own feelings cloud his impeccable judgment. Regardless, he made a mistake. He is, after all, only human."

I briefly closed my eyes, understanding the stalwart determination in Ryder's expression right before he'd pulled the trigger. He'd been the one to take her in. The deaths inside the Institute were on his hands. Maybe he had listened to my incessant belief that she could be saved. I'd asked him not to judge her on what she was, and she'd killed within hours. I should have handed her over when I had the chance, when Ryder first asked me to. It would have been the right thing to do. But I'd let my own past obscure the truth of what she was.

I opened my eyes. "Don't you feel anything?" I asked quietly. "You sent a little girl to her death."

He dipped his chin and peered at me through dark lashes. A predator's glare. "She knew what she was. She acknowledged her fate and accepted it. If I feel anything, it's a sense of achievement."

"How could you be sure they wouldn't use her against you?"

"Chaos cannot be controlled."

I drew in a measured breath as the truth of his words presented itself to me. "You knew Ryder would hesitate. You knew she'd tear it down around them..." Not a question but a realization. "You handed her over like a Trojan horse." Ryder was right all along. He'd even said as much to me while standing in my kitchen right after Akil had left her with me. "You used a nine year old girl to bring down the Institute." It made sense now. "From the second you showed up on my doorstep telling me to *do the right thing*, you thought I'd give her to Adam, or at the very least, that they'd find her with me." Slippery son-of-a-bitch. This hadn't been about saving Dawn at all. He'd condemned her the second he stole her from Carol-Anne. *Kill two birds with one stone.* Dawn and the Institute. Both threats to his existence. And to look at him now, his understated confidence and the glint of infinite knowledge in his eyes, you'd think he'd done the world a favor.

He had never looked more reasonable than he did standing on that street outside Stone's Throw. "I believed you'd do what needed to be done."

"You don't know me at all, do you?" How could he think I'd subject any half blood to the Institute's attentions, especially a little girl? "You thought you'd leave her on my doorstep, and I'd send her to her death? What kind of monster do you think I am?"

"You're smarter than this, Muse. You are fully aware of the devastation half bloods can summon. Need I remind you of Stefan's downfall? You must, by now, appreciate your own potential. You should have handed her over to David Ryder. You should have done the right thing. You failed her by filling her head with hope when there was no hope for that half blood."

"You're insane."

"No. I'm right." He held my glare, eyes midnight black. "I could have delivered her into the hands of the Institute myself, but they'd treat her with less suspicion coming from you. When it became clear you had no intention of doing what must be done, I found other means to achieve the required outcome. Dawn was volatile, a threat. She could not be allowed to remain within Leviathan's grasp. Any one of the princes would have exploited her. I took advantage of an opportunity and put into motion the only possible outcome. Had I thought I could control her, I'd have secured her in my care long ago."

The same as he'd done with me: saved a wretched half blood girl from her abusive owner, mentored her, manipulated her "...and groomed her as your weapon later? Is that what you sought to do with me? Is that why you kept me all those years? Were you nurturing a weapon? Is that still your plan, even now?"

He broke the stare and looked away, perhaps searching for the right words. Whatever he was thinking, he barred it from his face. "Fire—our shared element—consumes. We are forever hungry, you and I. Fire devours, leaving nothing but ash, remnants devoid of life. Fire is the definitive destroyer. The demon you harbor has the potential to be wonderful in ways you do not yet fully understand. I see brilliance in you, but the time has passed where my attentions could be ignored. The princes know you now." The streetlight sparkled in his eyes and cut shadows across his face, making him appear leaner, sharper, harder. When those fire-lit eyes found me again, he swallowed. "Yes, you were to be my weapon. I am guilty of all those accusations and more. I find myself inexplicably disarmed in matters concerning you. I grew impatient and made mistakes... although those mistakes had the desired effect of awakening your latent abilities. Unfortunately, the resulting incarceration in the netherworld dampened my plans somewhat." He smiled. I didn't. With a sigh, he declared, "I admit my original intention was to use you as a weapon against my enemies. Is that truthful enough for you?"

At one time, his confession would have sent me spiraling into rage. The truth should have shocked me. I waited for the gut-wrenching fear to consume me, but nothing happened. The dark touch of Damien wrapped around my soul, gave an acknowledging squeeze. I'd not felt its touch since lying with Akil, but it was there now, an ever-present threat, a beast stalking the remnants of my shredded humanity, waiting, growing impatient. *Hungry.* My head was crowded with dark dreams and impossible wants. Some were my own desires. Others belonged to other netherwordly inhabitants of my body and mind.

I stole a step closer to Akil and would have walked right up to him had he not stepped back. I cocked my head, frowning. "When I saw you at Blackstone, by the fireplace, you were grieving, Akil. You believed me dead, and it cut you up. I know what I saw, and I know what I heard in your voice when you asked me to love you. What am I to you now? Just your weapon or something more?" My tone told him not to screw with me. I wasn't in the mood for lies, and this wasn't about hope, or some love-struck fanciful dreams. If Akil felt anything for me, I could use it.

I already knew the answer, but I waited for the lie he would surely tell and scrutinized his expression for any hint of him working to formulate a response. He eyed me steadily, breathing slowly. A muscle pulsed in his jaw. Amber fringed his eyes, revealing the demon poised inside his human avatar. At one time, it might have startled me to realize how he fought with the truth. He wanted to lie. I saw that much, but the foundation of our relationship had changed. Lying was no longer an option. We'd progressed too far beyond lies.

"I..." the words caught in his throat. He dipped his chin and lifted his glare, peering through his dark lashes, his gaze baking me in elemental heat. "You mean something else entirely." It pained him to say it. He couldn't have looked more disconcerted if he shuffled from foot to foot with his cap in his hand. As it was, he stood rigid, locking his vulnerabilities behind a mask of stubborn denial. He'd told me once the Prince of Greed didn't recognize denial. *He does now.*

I smiled. There was no need for me to rage at him. It wouldn't change a thing. It didn't matter anyway. The past was irrelevant. The wretched half blood girl, the silly little whelp he'd planned to exploit, was now *something else entirely*. I'd outgrown him, and I had him exactly where I needed him: under my control.

From the slight pinch around his eyes, he hadn't expected to see the slow crawl of a smile slip across my lips. Acknowledgement darkened his gaze. He'd expected me to yell, to accuse him of using me. Maybe he wanted me to beat my fists against his chest. I might have done all those things once, but my smile told him more than he could have imagined. I'd accepted my fate. I knew what I was, what I was becoming, if I hadn't already crossed that line. I didn't fight the thing inside me—the half of me that danced in the dark—not any more. Cool, hard acceptance shuttered my emotions, sealing them off from my humanity. I stared back at him, mirroring his guarded-yet-fractured mask of indifference. He now knew what it felt like to have a piece of his soul at the mercy of another. I had him. The tables had turned. A fundamental shift in our relationship had altered everything. He was the demon sprawled in front of his fireplace, drowning in grief. Those birds were on the ground again. Waters were once more running up stream. The Prince of Greed was mine.

"New titles are born. Old titles die." He inclined his head, as though bowing, submitting, subservient. "You are ready." And with that, he vanished in a burst of static.

Chapter Twenty Nine

I fumbled with my keys outside my apartment. What had just happened? Akil had admitted why he'd kept me safe and why he'd saved me all those years ago. Dawn's fate could easily have been mine. We'd both been pawns in Akil's game. I'd survived, whereas he'd led her like a lamb to the slaughter. All those years, I'd looked up at him with wide innocent eyes—the same way Dawn had looked at me. I'd have let him take my hand and walk me to my death once too. He'd only let me live because he believed me powerful yet pliable. I was his means to an end I didn't yet understand.

None of that was particularly surprising. Typically demon, Akil acted only in his best interests. But his admission that he'd felt something for me wasn't typical. He should have brushed my death off like a spec of dust on his impeccable attire, yet grief had ravaged him. He was chaos eternal, incapable of feeling much of anything besides hunger. But clearly he did feel. I wasn't comfortable with that revelation, and neither was he. Chaos demons were deadly enough without adding emotion to the mix.

The terrifying part was how he'd just left me. The finality of his words. The peculiar way he'd bowed out, as though saying farewell, as though his part in this game was over. *New titles are born. Old titles die.* He'd given me the truth, and yet he'd left me with a gut-churning sense of unease. As usual with Akil, his answers revealed more questions. Questions I wasn't sure I wanted the answers to. The way he'd looked at me: pride, acceptance, lust, love? Maybe even a little fear? A Prince of Hell feared me. What kind of monster did that make me?

With a growl, I shoved all thoughts of Akil into the broiling mass of emotion walled up in my head. I'd deal with it all later, after I'd drowned myself in a bottle of wine and forgotten everything for a little while. Damn Akil and his Machiavellian ways. The dark coiled around my heart gave a tight squeeze in agreement, briefly clenching my chest and shortening my breath. I snarled back at it and grumbled a few colorful words as I worked the correct key into the lock and shoved inside, too preoccupied to notice the door wasn't locked.

My grumbling curses froze on my lips when I looked up and saw Stefan leaning against my kitchen counter, open tub of Ben & Jerry's in one hand, spoon in the other, eyebrow raised, licking ice cream from his lips. My heart stuttered, my mouth fell open, and I knew I was dreaming. He could not be there, all smart-ass smiles and dazzling blue eyes.

"There's no Ben & Jerry's in the netherworld. It's a crime." His gravely demon brogue instantly roused my demon half. She gave herself a mental shake, her visceral hungers and curious anxiety merging with mine.

I dropped the file. Papers spewed across the floor. My keys slipped from my hand and clattered beside my feet. I gawked at him, drinking in the wonderful sight of Stefan in my kitchen. His scuffed red leather coat had darkened to the color of dried blood. The cool blue shirt and loose, low-slung jeans seemed unremarkable beside the sword sheathed at his hip. When I noticed his crooked half smile that said 'you know what, it's gonna be okay,' it was too much. The emotional steel rods I'd driven through myself while facing off with Akil turned to liquid and drained away. My knees buckled. His arms swept around me before my addled brain could register the fact he'd moved. A cool snap of power arced between us and wrenched my breath away. He held me close, body pressed against mine.

Wide-eyed, I stared with abandon and found myself falling into his brilliant gaze.

He chuckled softly, the demon turning the laughter wicked. "I've always wanted to catch a swooning woman. I just never thought it'd be you."

I barely registered his words as I reached a trembling hand up and touched his face with my fingertips then slipped them lightly down his jawline. He felt real. Not a ghost, but solid, warm, and very much alive. A spritz of energy fizzled up my fingers. I slid the tip of my finger across his lips. His mouth twitched around a smile. He was really here. I wanted to blurt out how I'd ached deep in my bones to see him one more time, how I'd wanted him back but dared not dream I'd see him again, and even if I did, how I was afraid of what he might have become. But my voice had abandoned me. I couldn't say a single word.

He raised an eyebrow. "You could have let me know you weren't dead."

I slid both hands over his face, committing the slightly abrasive texture beneath my fingers to memory. There were more fine lines than I remembered. My thumb brushed the corner of his lips, lips I wanted to kiss. But I was so afraid that if I did, the spell would be broken, and he'd be gone again. After losing him for the second time, and then losing Dawn, I'd come to understand that hope didn't belong to the likes of me. If Stefan couldn't beat his demon and I couldn't save a lost little half blood girl despite all my shallow promises, then what chance did I have?

But Stefan had beaten his demon. He must have. He was here and looking back at me with mild curiosity. The hope I'd given up on sparked back to life. I clutched at his coat, knuckles whitening.

"Speechless?" His words sounded like a purr. "What is the world coming to?"

My mouth moved. I tried to snatch at the words in my head. My tongue tried to wrap around the necessary sounds, but my brain appeared to have detached itself from my vocal cords. All I could do was swallow and blink like a dumbstruck fool.

He lowered his gaze. Fair lashes shuttered his eyes. His smile faded, and a jolt of panic snapped through me. He was going to say he had to go. He would say the words. I knew it. This wonderful moment was already ending. I couldn't let him go, not again.

I pulled him into a raw, desperate kiss, exposing my soul as my lips met his. I didn't care that he stilled against me, that his arm stiffened as though he would push me off him in the next breath. I needed to feel him, to taste how real he was. When his lips parted and his responding hunger molded with mine, I very nearly came undone. My legs were all but useless, but it didn't matter. Stefan held me him like we'd never been apart, as though we'd never part again. I drove my fingers into his hair and pulled him so close I might gladly drown in him. Vaguely, I registered the clatter of the spoon against the floor. He slid his hand down the curve of my back and cradled me against him, hauling me in close enough that the heat of his body warmed the cold in mine.

He broke the kiss, only to roam his lips across my cheek. "You're crying." His cool breath tickled across the tracks of my tears.

I really was. "Please, don't stop. Don't say... anything." I couldn't bear to hear why he'd returned and why now, knowing it wouldn't be good. I never got a break. My world was one disaster after another—the Mother of freakin' Destruction—and this would be no different. *Half bloods don't get happy endings.* But I refused to hear it. I was not letting him go. I would not hear the terrible things he had to say. Instead, I wanted to forget it all: the horror of my own failure to save a little girl and the wretched realization of my own capabilities. Forget that I was cursed. Forget Akil's prophetic words...

"This is a mistake," he whispered.

"Don't." I growled, the sound borrowed from my demon.

His sharp breath hissed, and his entire body tightened with restraint. He fought even now, struggled with his own demon. I could see regret in his evasive gaze and the guarded expression on his face. He didn't want this. He would push me away. I fluttered my eyes closed, knowing in the next few seconds he would say something pertinent, and we'd pull apart. But for now—this singular moment—it was perfect. If I could have trapped time in a glass jar and kept it forever, I would have.

"I'm sorry." He captured my mouth once more, driving his tongue in deep. A demonic growl resounded through him, possessive and wild. Elemental energy simmered around us. A tantalizing quiver of chaos energy skipped across my flesh, sprinkling goose bumps in its wake. Stefan's hunger mirrored mine. He teased in his maddening way. Our bodies moved as one, thrust together as though inseparable. He tasted like ice cream and chaos. Sweet, delicious, and wonderfully alive. I purred my pleasure, demon and woman, both hungry. The chilling touch of his element coiled around us, igniting the fire slumbering inside me. My demon stretched beneath my skin, basking in the power he radiated.

He pulled away all too soon, withdrawing carefully, his gaze skittish and head bowed away from me. I let him go, even though every part of my muddled mind screamed for him to stay. Slumping against the counter, I touched my lips and tasted the chaos sprinkled there, fizzing like popping candy. Stefan moved away, turning his back on me, shoulders bowed. He didn't need to say a thing. His body said it for him. He didn't want this.

"Do you have any idea how difficult it is for an ice demon to light a campfire in the netherworld?" he asked, cool, and calm, as though we hadn't just tried to devour one another.

"Huh?" The residue of arousal tingled across my skin. I licked my swollen lips and blinked rapidly. Muddled thoughts reeled about my head. Why was he talking about campfires? I swept a hand back through my hair and swallowed hard. Holy hell, he was really there... Not demon, not dead.

"Try impossible." His coat buckles rattled as he reached down and scooped up the ice cream tub, placing it on the side. "Which is a problem when trying to cook demon meat. You don't wanna know what raw Sasori demons taste like. Also, don't eat the dark meat. It's poisonous. I found that out the hard way." He leaned back, hands braced against the countertop either side of him. "You'd think after a few years there, I'd have learned a few things about surviving in the netherworld." A glint of light reflected off an elaborate fractal-etched rapier at his waist. Seeing him armed with a sword reminded me of how my brother likes to appear tooled up and ready for battle. "I'm craving food, real food, like ice cream. And coffee. And French fries." He ground out a restrained groan and raked a hand through his hair. "But mostly ice cream." The heated look in his eyes when he finally met my gaze told me food wasn't the only thing he craved, so why push me away?

"I don't think those things are classed as real food," I said in a quiet voice, bumbling along with the bizarre conversation while my thoughts still spun, and my body burned to have him close. His kiss hadn't been a half-hearted response to my advances. It could have gone further. I wanted it to. But apparently, he didn't. Like an idiot, I'd forced myself on him.

I averted my gaze and busied myself scooping up the contents of the file from the floor. *Your father is the Prince of Lust... You and Akil deserve each other...* I could guess why he'd stopped things before they spiraled out of control. His words from months ago still wounded me, even after all this time. It shouldn't matter. Coming from anyone else, those words wouldn't have mattered.

I dumped the file on the coffee table, aware that a quiet tension simmered between us. He still threw off power—nothing like the embrace I'd felt minutes before when he'd been pressed against me, but enough to distract my demon.

Facing him, I flicked my hair out of my eyes and planted a hand on my hip, grateful for the kitchen counter between us. I didn't trust myself not to pounce on him and couldn't bear it if he pushed me away again. Who was I kidding? Stefan wasn't meant for the likes of me: the Mother of Destruction. He was better in every way. A shining star. I'd already ruined his life, killed his sister, and condemned him to hell. The longer he stayed with me, the more I'd destroy him.

"I think you should go." I couldn't meet his eyes. He'd see the truth there. I wanted him in every way a woman wants a man. My demon wanted him in ways I couldn't even wrap my thoughts around. The intensity of my own desire terrified me. Was it lust? Was that all it was? My father's legacy living in me? No. If it had been just lust, I could have escaped it. Lust was simple. Yes, it was madness, but it was an uncomplicated madness. This need to have Stefan close, to bury myself in his embrace, to hide in his arms and snowflake kisses, it wasn't demanding, or selfish, and it definitely wasn't simple. I wanted to share everything with him, to spend precious time with him, time when demons weren't trying to kill us, and the Institute wasn't watching. Just the two of us. I couldn't escape these feelings, and that made them all the more terrifying because clearly he didn't feel the same.

"Is that what you want?" he asked. "You come back from the dead, kiss me like the world's ending, and then tell me to leave?" He managed to sound amused.

I bit my lip and nodded. "It's not safe here... with me."

He wove around the kitchen counter and stopped in front of me, a wall of red leather and cool temptation. Light glinted off the sword's guard and I realized I'd seen it before. Kira-Kira. *His mother's sword.* I flicked my gaze up through my lashes and immediately lost my thoughts under the intensity of his eyes. The cool touch of power was back, prodding at my demon, taunting her with its proximity.

"I came back to warn you." Severity hardened his voice and dragged it down to a deep demon growl.

A knot of dread tightened in my gut. "How long have you known I was alive?" I didn't want to hear his warnings. Whatever it was, it would ruin everything. I knew it as certainly as I knew he would leave me again. He stood so close, and yet there was a chasm between us. He was already gone. We just hadn't said the words yet.

"A few weeks—netherworld time. I wasn't going to come at all. But the Princes..."

"Why?" My emotions bled through that one word. "Why weren't you going to come? I needed you. Everything is falling apart. I'm... I'm out of control, or I'm terribly in control. I can't tell which. I nearly killed Adam. I could have. I wanted to. You've no idea how I ached to see that bastard burn. And before, there was... Something happened... I thought I'd killed people."

He held my stare, his expression guarded, bordering on resigned. When he brushed my bangs from my eyes, an electric shower of sparks shivered beneath that lightest of touches. "But you didn't do either."

He was too close. All I could think about was the cold burn of desire and the overwhelming need to hold him. "It doesn't matter," I said quietly, "because when I believed I was a killer, I didn't care. I accepted it. I never would have believed I was capable..." My humanity was failing me. Damien's touch had already poisoned too much. I was drowning in the dark. I just didn't have the good grace to go under one last time. "Dawn's dead. I couldn't save her, just like Ryder said. In the end, she thanked him, right before he killed her." I searched his gaze for any sign of judgment, but all I saw was hard acceptance. "I know why you left. The same fate awaits me. But I can't run back to the netherworld. Not now. Not ever. There's nowhere for me to go, nowhere to run. There's no way out. I'm trapped against a wall. Ryder should have put a bullet between my eyes. I see it on his face when he looks at me. He knows the truth, Stefan. He's just waiting for me to fuck up. We don't get happy endings. I am destruction. Akil's weapon..." I paused, sucked in a breath, and said, "And I feel... nothing."

Stefan's expression finally registered a change and darkened. "Akil's weapon?" He tried to capture my gaze, but I flicked it away. "What do you me—"

"You're right." I ground out the words while biting back a knot of emotion. "This—us was wrong. It was a mistake, just like you said. Every time I'm with you, bad shit happens." I remembered his words and repeated them back to him, "I'm sorry we met." The longer he stayed, the more I'd ruin him. I'd drag him down into the darkness inside of me and drown us both. I suddenly knew with absolutely clarity that I could never be a part of Stefan's life, not if he was going to survive. He sure as hell could beat this madness. He had the tenacity, the instincts, and the passion. But the likes of him weren't for me, not the Mother of Destruction. I'd ruined everything. I'd promised Dawn freedom and got her killed. Stefan's sister, sweet Nica, had died because of me. Stefan lost his whole world, because of me. Ryder'd had to execute a young girl because I'd failed to do the right thing. Destruction was my name. Holy hell, the demons knew me better than I did. Maybe Akil was right. I really was the monster he thought me to be. "You need to go."

"I'm not going anywhere." He turned away and picked up the Operation Tyhon file. "Wanna know why?"

I didn't imagine the drop in temperature or the trickle of power dancing against my skin. He appeared to be controlled, but the leeching touch of his power said otherwise. If I reached an element touch out to him, I feared what I'd find. My humanity—what was left of it—tingled a warning, raising the hairs on the back of my neck.

He flicked open the file, eyes narrowing as he skimmed the contents. "I have debts that need paying. Wrongs to right. My father, for one. The Prince of Greed is another. Your brother. The Institute..."

His words sounded dangerously like revenge woven together with a thread of something I regularly coveted: madness. "The Boston Institute is gone," I said carefully.

His smile cut deeper. "Not while Adam lives."

"Stefan, this doesn't sound like you." My breath misted in the air. I hugged myself, bracing my hands against my upper arms.

"Doesn't it?" He lifted his head and pierced me with his ice-born glare. "I thought I'd killed you. When I realized what I'd done..." He dropped the file onto the table, gaze locked on me. "When I watched you die in Ryder's arms, it destroyed me."

There was that word again. Just a word. But it spilled fear into my veins and seemed to pull a cold blast of air into the room around me. Shivers quivered through my exhausted body. "But you're here. I'm here. What you thought you did doesn't matter. The past is irrelevant." I inwardly winced, realizing I'd paraphrased Akil's words. *The past is irrelevant. The Institute is insignificant.* It occurred to me that Akil had taken out the Institute just as half the netherworld demons decided to make Boston their new home. That couldn't be a coincidence. Was Stefan's presence here also just bad timing, or was he in some way connected to the change in the netherworld and the influx of demons?

"You told me once we're the products of our past..." Stefan said with a wistful air of sadness.

I had, when he'd first taken me to the lake house, before he revealed the depth of lies he'd told me to protect his sister, before a lot of things, none of them good. I didn't know what to say to him. Nothing I could say would change the weight of the past pushing down on us.

He was in front of me so suddenly I gasped and jolted back, shoving against his chest. Instincts demanded I escape, but his hands clamped down on my shoulders, fingers digging in. Pain bloomed in my wounded shoulder muscles. I flinched and tried to pull away. "Stefan, please... you're hurting me."

He bowed his head, pulling me tight against him. This wasn't anything like the warm embrace we'd shared moments before. His body trembled with chilled restraint. A blast of cold stole the breath from my lungs. A dusting of ice tightened my skin.

He brushed his cheek against mine, his demon purring, "I came to warn you. The netherworld is dying. The princes are rallying. You are not prepared." He sighed and slumped against me as though speaking the words relieved him. "I am the Prince of Wrath. And I've never needed your help more than I do right now."

I gasped and pulled back. His words pierced my soul like splinters of shattered ice, and everything I'd felt for him, every tiny flicker of hope I'd cherished, scattered, chased away by terror. His hands tightened on my shoulders, gaze drilling deep. The demon that was Stefan damned me beneath his glare. The colors of the veil danced in his eyes, but further inside, deeper, I witnessed a soul cowering behind a barricade of ice. Brittle fractals sparked across his cheek, lanced into his hair, and sliced across his lips, cracking, spitting, as it smothered his expression in a mask of lacy frost. The restrained power I'd felt pulsing inside him since his return suddenly broke out and washed over me. I groaned and arched back, torn between fighting him and the terrible urge to answer his power with my own. The flood of ethereal energy slammed my humanity down. My demon roared inside my head, thrashing against her restraints in a bid to devour the source of chaos inside him. I tried to swallow a wail of despair, but it tore from me in an anguished cry.

The Prince of Wrath glared down at me with terrifying certainty. He'd come for vengeance. On his father, on Akil, on anyone who'd ever wronged him. Including me.

I looked up into his diamond-eyes and knew it was too late for Stefan.

I'd already destroyed him.

The reaching tendrils of Aki's power encircled me before I even knew he was nearby. Ice and fire wove around me. The opposing elements tightened against my skin and vied for supremacy. I heard Stefan's snarl just as I was wrenched back out of his vice-like grip and pulled into a chasm of darkness. For the briefest of moments, I was nowhere. It was time enough for panic to clench around my heart and my demon-hitch-hiker to spill its poison through my veins. It was only the scent of cinnamon and cloves among the suddenly embracing warmth that prevented me from losing my mind to fear. *Akil.* I stumbled out of the dark and fell into his arms. Or I would have, had I not spun and slapped him so hard his teeth rattled.

I shoved off him and staggered back, trying to get my bearings as the room around us sharpened into focus. The lounge at Blackstone. It had undergone some re-decorating: new leather couches, a new coat of paint so fresh I could still smell it drying. My demon shunted my humanity to one side and snarled at her failed attempts to be free. I threw that snarl at Akil. "Take me back!"

He worked his jaw and fingered the flushed mark on his cheek. "You're getting stronger." He spoke with pride in his eyes.

I didn't have time to deal with his ego. Stefan needed me, and Akil had just stolen me out of his arms. "Take me back right now."

He arched a dark eyebrow, managing to look both bemused and haughty. "You are capable of many things, but suicide is not one of them."

I glowered. "Stefan wasn't going to hurt me."

He sighed, his shoulders slouched, and his eyes lost some of their luster. He appeared to age a few years in a few seconds. "He killed you once, Muse. In that very apartment. By some miracle, you came back to me. You're mortal, and I'm not making the same mistake twice."

I clutched at the cool leather of the couch I'd bumped into, needing something to keep me upright while my legs threatened to give out. My head still wasn't quite grounded, thanks to the unexpected reality-hop. An ache throbbed behind my eyes, and my parasite's sickly touch still burned in my veins. It was all I could do not to double over and hurl all over Akil's polished, marble floor.

I sucked in a deep breath. "I have to go back."

Akil shrugged off his jacket and tossed it over the opposite couch. He unbuttoned his shirt cuffs and rolled his sleeves up. All the while, his gaze seared me as though we were about to engage in combat. "You don't seem to understand the danger you're in. Let me be perfectly honest with you—"

"That'll be a first."

He ignored me. "No more half-truths. You *are* a weapon. The princes are aware of this pertinent fact, due to your antics over the past few months. Titles are shifting. Half bloods are rising. An immortal prince dies. Another has his title ripped from him by an upstart half blood ice demon who doesn't know any better. The netherworld is dying. The veil weakens." Akil scooped up a TV remote from the coffee table and flicked on the vast ultra-thin TV mounted on the wall. "Lesser demons are bleeding through. And you, my Muse... are the eye of the storm."

I blinked, wondering if I should be feeling something, but my body was numb and my thoughts hushed. The TV played a newsfeed. I got a glimpse of the reporter, but no sound. Akil had muted the volume. I didn't need to hear what was being said because the Hellhound sprawled on the road outside a McDonalds restaurant really didn't need an introduction. There were a number of things very wrong with that picture. People aren't meant to be able to see Hellhounds. But that fact didn't appear to have reached the members of the crowd taking pictures with their smartphones. Also, Hellhounds don't die. From the glassy red-eyes and lack of breathing, that one sure appeared to be dead.

"Oh."

"Indeed."

"What's going on?"

"The princes are coming. I've deterred them as long as possible, centuries in your time, longer in theirs. Unfortunately, the netherworld is dying. My home is no longer able to sustain the demons. And as with all immortals, the princes tire of that which they possess and hunger for that which they can acquire." He sighed. "Chaos is forever hungry."

This was big. Bigger than me. Bigger than the Institute, than Boston. "It's bad, isn't it?"

"It is. And inevitable."

I turned away from the TV and found him standing close enough that I had to look up to meet his gaze. "How much of this was your doing?"

"None." He swept a lock of hair from my face.

Why did I find that hard to believe? "Right. And I'm Mary Poppins. Wait while I get my umbrella, so I can beat you to death with it for never giving me a straight answer to anything. Cut the crap. Give it to me straight. I've earned that much from you."

He smiled. "You have. I told you once of the King and how the Queen killed him. You remember?" I nodded. "Good. The King and Queen—control and chaos—together maintained balance in the netherworld. When the Queen killed her counterpart, chaos reigned, and the beginning of the end of the netherworld was born. Unbeknownst to the remaining princes, the King lived in hiding. He was weak—"

"Okay, I've heard enough. Is this the part where you tell me you're the King? Because really, my head's already spinning from Stefan's revelation..."

He fought with a grin. "No. I'm flattered, but no. I'm *just demon* remember."

"Just demon," I echoed and didn't believe it for a second. I'd thought Akil had killed Sam in a jealous rage, but I was wrong. He'd killed an Institute spy to protect me. I'd tried to point fingers at him, accusing him through rose-tinted glasses of being inhuman. Well, he was demon. I was just too much of a dumbass to accept it. And now he was telling me about a King who wasn't dead but had been weak, hiding on this side of the veil. So pinch me if I didn't quite believe him. Akil hid the truth in lies.

"Are you quite finished scowling?"

"Not by a long shot."

"As I was saying, the King was weak. He came here to regain his strength while the princes believed him dead. I know where he is. I helped him, in fact. We will need the King if we're to protect the human realm from the Princes."

I think I liked him better when he was wrapping me up in a bubble-wrap of lies. "I'm hearing a lot of plural talk in there."

"Well, you are the Mother of Destruction. I was hoping you might like to help save your city. But you do get a choice. Where you go, destruction follows. You merely need to choose which realm you reduce to rubble in your wake."

He made it sound as simple as whether I should have chocolate sprinkles on my cappuccino. "Yay. A win-win situation," I replied, dryly. This night was just getting better and better. "Okay, say for a second I take your word as the truth—which, by the way, I don't—why on this earth should I listen to you? You just used a little girl to wipe out the Institute. Convenient timing. From where I'm standing, that sure looks like you're on the side of the princes. Also, there is the fact you *are* a prince with a reputation for manipulating the truth."

"Sacrifices must be made. The Institute was ill prepared. They played at being protectors, but it's not nearly enough."

"Are you telling me you did it for their own good?"

"Back any creature into a corner, and it will fight. Now the Institute gathers, galvanized. More of their ranks will come to Boston. They ready their soldiers. I disturbed the nest so that they'd wake in time to see the truth and prepare."

I pinched my lips together, biting back the urge to tell him people had died when he'd decided to rattle the Institute. He would tell me they were collateral damage. "And what do you get out of this? What does the slippery Prince of Greed gain? Because if I've learned anything, it's that you don't do anything unless it benefits you."

"I get my city back." He smiled a broad wolfish smile. "I have no desire to see this world burn. I'm content with playing these humans for the fools they are. Boston is mine, and I will not suffer any demon, prince or otherwise, who dare attempt to steal what is mine."

That sure sounded like the Akil I knew. I slumped against the couch, suddenly bone-tired. The news report, the plea from Adam to help the Institute, Stefan's breathless cry for help, and Akil telling me I'm somehow caught in the middle of it all were too much. "And Stefan? He's really a prince?"

Akil straightened, squaring his shoulders. "Impossibly, yes."

"You knew?"

"I did."

"For a long time?" I sighed as he nodded. "Why didn't you tell me?"

"He's beyond saving, Muse. He became prince not long after he believed he'd killed you. From what I understand, he laid waste to parts of the netherworld, attracting the attention of the princes. He made short work of Wrath. It should not be possible, a half blood as a prince..." He sucked in a breath, hissing air through his teeth. "Once

Wrath fell, my brethren retreated. The damage was done. Had I told you, you'd have gone to him, and he'd have killed you again. Wrath is not just a name, Muse. It's a title. Wrath is his purpose. There's nothing you can do for him, but you can help stop the princes. Stefan will be among them, should he choose to be."

No, he wouldn't. He'd come to me, asking for help. He knew what he was, but he was still in there—that kiss hadn't been cold—and he needed me. I was sure of it. "Damn, Akil, this is a lot to wrap my head around. I need space to think."

"While you do that, may I suggest you help your former colleagues patrol the streets? The princes have begun summoning their lesser cousins. Their presence will rouse chaos, and where chaos reigns, the remaining princes will follow. Should chaos swell beyond control here, the veil will fall. Control the lesser demons, stem the flow, and buy yourselves time to regroup because, make no mistake, when the princes arrive, they will destroy Boston, and they won't stop at one city."

Stopping lesser demons was something I was definitely capable of. "And what are you going to do? Go and find this phantom King?"

He smirked. "You've already met him."

"I'm pretty sure I'd remember meeting the King of Hell. Forked tail, cloven hooves, goat legs, plays the fiddle?" Akil chuckled. "You're not going to tell me, are you?"

"No. While he is weak, it is better you do not know."

"You don't trust me?" I almost laughed when he frowned. "That's rich, coming from the Master of Lies." I snorted, then abruptly asked, "Is it you?"

"No. Again. You appear to be having difficulty hearing the truth."

"That's because, coming from you, truth and lies, right and wrong, they all sound the same."

"They are all a matter of perspective."

"Urgh..." I groaned. "I think I liked it better when you told me everything and nothing. Can we go back to that?"

"We are both too much changed to return to how things were."

I stood and raked my hands through my hair. "You know what would be handy right now? A half blood who could kill princes." I clicked my fingers. "Oh damn, you just sacrificed the best weapon we had against them." Scrunching my nose up, I asked, "Whose side are you on again?"

He gave me a sideways glance, arched an eyebrow, and twitched his lips. "Not the best weapon by far. I have that right here."

"Yeah, well, this blunt weapon of mass destruction is going back to Boston to find Stefan. The end of the world can wait. I can drive there, or you can take me back right now so I can at least try to convince the Prince of Wrath to fight on our side."

"Stefan is beyond listening to reason. His demon rules him."

"He'll make that call."

"I don't like it." A flicker of fire touched his eyes.

"I don't like you much either, but I can't seem to get rid of you, so how about we stop talking and start doing?"

Akil eyed me cautiously. "Stefan and I... The Prince of Wrath will not stop until his debts are paid." I read that as it was intended. Stefan would kill Akil. Stefan was more powerful with the weight of another world behind him. He had the potential, the motive, and no reason not to. When Akil and Stefan threw down, I had no doubt who would walk away. Stefan's only weakness was his mortality. I swallowed and denied those thoughts purchase. "Then stay out of his way, at least until I can talk to him."

Akil's eyes sparkled while at the same time managing to rake me with a sympathetic gaze. "You can't save half bloods. The trappings and foibles of your humanity provide you with great strengths but also insurmountable weaknesses."

"Yeah, yeah, half bloods don't get happy endings. I get it. I've never been one to follow the rules." I flashed him a bright smile and held out my hand. "Take me back."

He glowered at my outstretched hand and made no move to take it. "The safest place for you is here."

"It's about time you trusted me, Akil. Isn't this what it's all been about? What were you keeping me for, if not to use against your enemies?"

His gaze softened. "Once, yes. Now I find myself in the alarming situation of fearing I may lose you again and caring."

I instantly shoved that unnerving revelation to the back of my mind, ramming it down into the existing mental box marked *'deal with this shit later.'* I could not even begin to consider what his words meant. Not with everything else crowding my head.

I stood, grabbed his hand, and met his curiously pained expression. "Surely the Prince of Greed and the Mother of Destruction can kick some demon-ass back to the netherworld. It might mess up your street-cred, but I'm sure an ego the size of yours can take it. Once we've averted disaster, you can go back to being the slippery, back-stabbing son-of-a-bitch I know so well."

He allowed himself a faint smile. "Boston is mine. I protect what is mine with every weapon at my disposal. No member of the Dark Court will take that which I possess." The fierceness behind his words wasn't lost on me.

"Good. Hold onto that thought." The enemy of my enemy was my friend, and right then, Akil was the only friend I had. It wouldn't last. He wanted me so he could pry Damien out of my soul, take his place, and wield the weapon he'd been fashioning for himself since he'd first seen me all those years ago. Words like 'love' and 'care' were cheapened when falling from his lips. He was the spider in the web, but I saw him now.

He looked askance at me, narrowing his eyes. He was an ageless chaos demon, and he wasn't buying my thinly veiled enthusiasm. "Why do I feel as though I'm the one making a deal with a devil?" He closed his fingers around mine.

I flashed him a sharp-toothed smile. And now we were equal.

EPILOGUE

CONFIDENTIAL SUBJECT REPORT

FAO: VP Sabine Sturgill, New York Hub.
Source: Adam Harper, HO, Boston Hub.

OPERATION TYPHON UPDATE (Previous file
destroyed due to security breach).

SUBJECT EPSILON – a.k.a. **Dawn**.

STATUS: Contained & holding.

Comments: Operation Typhon progresses
despite the recent destruction of our Boston
hub. We are now in possession of Subject
Epsilon, a.k.a. Dawn. Regrettably, there
were unavoidable casualties, due in part to
how we acquired her. All necessary. Epsilon
is securely contained on site at the
Middlesex Fells facility. From various
reports by field Enforcer, David Ryder,
Epsilon exhibits an element as yet untapped,
but which could prove vital if Class A
demons do breach the veil, as reports
suggest. While demon chatter claims Subject
Beta (Muse) terminated the Prince of Envy,
Enforcer Ryder has confirmed Epsilon was
responsible. Epsilon has the potential to be
an invaluable asset. Her detainment is of
the utmost importance. Her current status

must remain confidential. Her continued existence is officially denied.

Note: David Ryder is aware Epsilon lives. This was an unfortunate necessity as Enforcer Ryder played a large part in her capture. While his devotion and commitment to our cause continues to be exemplary, it may be necessary to apply emotional pressure. I advise a trace be planted among his estranged family should his devotion lapse.

SUBJECT GAMMA
STATUS: Contained & holding. No change.

SUBJECT DELTA
STATUS: Contained & holding. No change.

SUBJECT BETA - Muse, Charlie Henderson.
STATUS: Consistently volatile and unpredictable. Borderline demon. Beta's allegiances have yet to be proven. She has the potential to be a valuable ally, but her relationship with the Prince of Greed is undesirable. She will cooperate while she believes she is in control, but her actions of late border on needing a termination order. If it were not for her connections in the netherworld, we would have allowed her to perish at Subject Alpha's (Stefan's) hand. Demon chatter indicates her father, Asmodeus, has shown an interest in acquiring her. She is currently under his 'protection.' This makes her useful and invulnerable to all but her father. We will continue to rally Beta to our cause and utilize her connections among the demon hierarchy. However, should she lose control of her demon —which I believe to be an imminent threat—a termination order will be issued.

Note: Demon chatter refers to Beta as the Mother of Destruction. This title is not to be dismissed as idle gossip. I suspect there are events in her recent past of which we are unaware. These events have increased her standing among demons. I strongly advise Enforcers focus on extracting the meaning behind this recent shift in Beta's status.

SUBJECT ALPHA - Stefan Harper.
STATUS: Failed. Termination order in effect.
Note: Sabine, I am perfectly capable of neutralizing the threat Subject Alpha poses. I have no emotional connection to my son. Thank you for your offer, but your assistance, while of course appreciated, is not necessary. Subject Alpha will be terminated.
SIGNED: *Adam Harper.*
END REPORT
* * *

The Veil Series continues in 'Drowning In The Dark', coming early 2015. Read on for an exclusive first look.

An exclusive look at the first two chapters of 'Drowning In The Dark' Book 4 in The Veil Series, due early 2015.

Excerpt Chapter One

Demon claws sliced into my waist, sending sparks of pain dancing up my right side and stealing a ragged cry from my lips. I twisted away, more instinct than thought, and cracked my fist across the demon's brittle jaw. His face fractured like glass, which would have been a victory, had the shards of bone not pierced my knuckles. Jesus, it was like fighting barbed wire. I saw the right hook coming, his claws spread wide, and realized I may have underestimated my quarry and overestimated my current abilities. I ducked, snatched my dagger from its sheath at my ankle, and lunged upward, driving the blade deep into his gut. He grunted. My gaze met his opaque eyes. He grinned, slippery blue lips drawn back over jagged teeth. Hot blood spilled over my hand, but from the look of glee on his crumpled face, you'd think he'd won. I was missing something. His brittle laughter confirmed it.

"They're coming, half blood," he growled around his fangs.

"Yeah, I got the memo. The princes are coming, blah blah. Tell me something I don't know."

His hand shot out like a viper strike. I yanked the blade from his gut, recoiled from his scalpel-like claws, and arched away, but my balance wobbled. Overreaching, I staggered. My stomach flip-flopped. Fear churned my gut. The big grin on his bony face morphed into a hideous, toothy snarl. He lunged and slammed his not-so-lightweight body into me. My back hit the alley dirt, knocking the breath out of my lungs. This would be one of those times when calling the fire would solve my misbehaving demon problem. I could kill him in an instant. A flicker of a thought was all it would take. But I wouldn't stop there. The alley would look nice draped in fire. That overflowing dumpster back there would go up like the 4th of July. The buildings would catch next. My fire would lick the sky, devour the neighborhood, and gobble up every living thing in the immediate vicinity. Insane laughter bubbled through my thoughts.

The demon coiled his hands around my throat. His legs straddled me. I took a swipe at his arm with my blade. His skin peeled apart, blood dribbled, but he didn't loosen his grip. I sliced again, while my lungs burned. His grip on my throat tightened. My vision clouded. The edges of his half-broken face blurred. My demon snarled inside my mind and rattled her mental bars. *Let me out...* she urged. *Let me play. We will make short work of this beast. We are destruction. We taste his death. Ashes in the air. Let us devour.* It was pretty crowded in my head. Next, my personal parasite spilled his poison into my veins. His darkness polluted my limbs, stoking my thirst for fire. I couldn't hold out much longer. The fire would come. My demon would break the reins of my control, and this time, I might not come back. This could be it: the very last time I held the reins of my control. Was it over so soon? Would I lose my battle in this alley?

Demon spittle dribbled onto my face. My head lolled to one side. Among the fog of impending unconsciousness, a dark figure walked toward me. I didn't need to see clearly to know him. His element flooded ahead of him. Heat. A terrible, breath-stealing, skin-crawling heat. Fire without the flames. The demon with his hands around my throat jerked his head up. His chokehold vanished as foreign words spilled from his lips. He scrambled off me, but stayed kneeling, skinny shoulders hunched.

Akil's image shimmered behind a veil of heat-haze. The air around his body rippled and strummed. He wore a double-breasted overcoat over his trademark suit, as though he might actually suffer from the cold on this chilly Boston evening. Only Akil could stalk back-alleys and still look like he'd stepped off the pages of GQ magazine.

As my demon attacker mumbled and growled in an ancient and exotic language, I concentrated on filling my lungs with air, ignoring the odors of mildew, fish, and urine. The air tasted pretty sweet to my oxygen-starved lungs.

"Return to the netherworld," Akil ordered, his tone level and direct. He didn't expect to be disobeyed. He stopped in front of the prostrate demon, handsome face perfectly neutral.

"It won't do any good, sire. They come. There is nothing there but death."

Akil's dark eyes flicked to me. I wiggled my fingers at him. It was all I could muster.

"Perhaps you misheard because I'm certain you didn't just deny a direct order from your prince." A smile flirted across Akil's lips, and fire brimmed the irises in his otherwise hazel eyes.

"No, sire." The demon ducked his head.

"Good." Akil flicked his fingers, and a ribbon of light rippled open beside him. *The veil.* "Be on your way."

"Now? B-But…"

Akil plucked the demon off his knees and shoved him through the twitching slither of light. The veil stitched itself closed moments later, and Akil turned to me. "Before you say a word about not needing my help, I observed your altercation for several minutes before intervening. Had it gone on any longer, I'm quite certain you would be dead."

"Dead is such a strong word." My voice came out littered with scratches and hitches, dashing my attempt at bravado. I rolled onto my side, wincing as the wound in my side flared, and climbed to my feet. Akil watched me stagger and right myself. He knew better than to help me.

"Nice coat. Do you always kick demon ass dressed like an Italian supermodel?" I brushed loose dirt from my jeans and tee. When I caught sight of the bloom of blood and the warm metallic scent of it hit me, I gulped back a knot of fear. It *had* been too close.

Akil blinked into existence right in front of me. His heat wrapped me in a quilt-like embrace. I attempted to deny how his warmth soothed my rattled body and mind, but it was a losing battle. Exhausted, battered, bruised, and bleeding, I was in no condition to argue with him. I'd not seen him in weeks—not officially—but I knew he'd been on the streets, eager to kick any wayward demons back to the netherworld, or hell as it was fondly referred to. According to Akil, Boston was his city, and nobody would take it from him, not an influx of demons, and certainly not the other princes. I wasn't entirely surprised to see him. I'd had my suspicions he'd been watching me from afar.

He hooked a finger under my chin and tilted my head up. "Why did you allow that demon to best you?"

I fluttered my eyes closed, the disappointment on his face too much. "I'm afraid."

"Of what? Not him."

"Damien." My parasite. I opened my eyes in time to catch Akil's glare narrowing. "He constantly pulls on my control. And my demon… She's impatient. She whispers to me the whole time. If I let her go, Akil, I'm afraid I might not come back." I'd lost control a few weeks ago, almost killing an angry mob and nearly tearing Akil's arm off in the process. He'd stopped me from doing both, but it had been too close for comfort.

He drew his hand back. Our gazes locked for a few seconds before he dipped his lower, over my lips, my chest, to where his fingers peeled the sticky hem of my top away from my waist. "You know how to remove the soul-lock. I'm sure you don't need me to say it again."

Right, by letting Akil dig him out. I'd been thinking about it every night when I woke screaming, drenched in cold sweat, body aching and mind shattered beneath a flood of revolting images—Damien's memories. Yeah, I'd thought about it a lot while drowning myself in whiskey. Damien was killing me as sure as if he was standing over my shoulder, driving a dagger into my back. I needed

Akil's help. I was losing this battle. I'd been losing it since the beginning. And I didn't have much time left.

"Could he ever come back?" I asked quietly. "The part of him that's in me, could it ever become solid again, flesh and blood real?"

Akil searched my face, delaying, until he finally gave me the truth. "Yes. There is a way. But you need not concern yourself with it. Without your consent, it could never happen." I gulped back the burn of disgust. I wanted my owner out, gone for good. I'd have gladly cut him out with a rusted razor blade if I could. "You cannot continue like this, Muse." Akil's deft fingers probed my side, drawing a hiss from my lips. "If you refuse to summon your demon, you will likely die the next time you find yourself in harm's way. I may not always be here to save you."

I bowed my head, simultaneously resting my forehead against his chest while he pressed his hand over the wounds and fizzled heat through my flesh. "I think... maybe... I guess..." I sighed. "You're right. I have to do something. I'm ready." His body tensed, and his hand over the wound stilled. "You need to take him out of me, Akil. Please. I can't live like this anymore."

He laced his fingers into my hair and tipped my head back. I could have fought him, but what was the point? We both knew this had to happen eventually. He didn't look as happy as I thought he would. He studied me, his sculpted face marred by suspicion.

"I expected you to, y'know, gloat or something. You've wanted this since he soul-locked me."

"Much longer, actually. But I–"

His teeth snapped together, and he jerked, as though struck, then shoved me away from him. I almost fell over my own feet trying to stay upright. Stumbling against the wall, I spluttered a curse. "What the hell?"

He'd spun around and faced the mouth of the alley, his back to me. I saw them then, six black-clad men and women, assault rifles raised and trained on Akil as they closed in. Laser dots bounced around on his back. I searched the roofline and spotted the snipers above us.

Worse, more special-ops jogged in from my left behind
Akil. And I recognized one instantly. Ryder led the smaller
team, rifle shouldered and aimed at Akil's back.

"Shit, Akil, get out of here." I shoved off the wall and
strode into the line of fire, exuding a confidence I didn't
have. "Don't do this, Ryder." I called over the sound of
hammering boots on asphalt. Akil would kill them all.

"Get outtah the way, Muse," Ryder barked. "We will
shoot through you."

Akil's element lashed outward, surging past me and
rushing toward Ryder's group. "Dammit, Ryder, you
wanna be responsible for more deaths?"

"Ain't gonna happen." His men were closing fast. It
would be a bloodbath. Five in his group, a couple on the
roof, six approaching Akil from the front. It wouldn't be
enough. A hundred wouldn't be enough. What the hell was
Ryder thinking?

Akil's element spluttered beneath my feet. I felt it
choke and gasped, spinning around to see Akil drop to one
knee and brace himself against the ground, head bowed.
Heat throbbed around him, beating the air in relentless
waves. He should have been upright, smug and confident –
at the worst, he could have called his true form Mammon –
but something was very wrong. "Akil?"

The Enforcers gathered around him. His shoulders rose
and fell as he breathed hard, but he made no move to attack
them or protect himself. A deep inhuman-growl rumbled
through him. He snapped his head up and scored a few
Enforcers with his powerful glare, but it only seemed to
make them more determined. They closed ranks, moving
tighter.

I stole a few steps closer when Ryder grabbed my arm
and pulled me to him. "Stay away if you know what's
good for you." He shoved me back, fierce determination
making his glare hard and cold.

"Ryder, he'll kill all of you. Are you insane?" Akil
might be down now, but it was likely a trap. He was
probably hoping to lure them in so he could catch them
together. I strode forward. "Let him go before it's too late."
I didn't want to see anyone hurt, especially Ryder. We'd

had our differences, but he didn't deserve to screw it up like this. "You can't capture a Prince of Hell. Ryder, please, c'mon... before he brings Mammon..." My words trailed off as Akil's gaze found me. Lips pulled back in a snarl, eyes bright with amber, he glared at me, accusations burning in his gaze. What? Did he think I had something to do with this? "Akil... Don't hurt them. Let them go." Another growl rumbled through him.

"He's not going anywhere, Muse." Ryder raised his rifle, aimed, and pulled the trigger. The sharp crack bounced around the alley. Akil took the hit in the shoulder. He spun around, his body moving liquid fast, but it wasn't enough. They opened fire. The deafening noise of gunfire drowned out my shriek of alarm. I sprang forward, only for Ryder to grab me and shove me into the arms of three of his crew. I kicked, yanked, writhed, and bucked, but the goons held fast.

When the gunfire ceased – a horrible unearthly quiet settled over the alley. The smell of hot metal, and acrid gun smoke burned my nostrils and laced my throat. Ragged breaths sawed out of me. I couldn't tear my gaze from the group huddled around a pool of blood. He couldn't be dead. Could he? Why hadn't he fought? Why didn't he summon Mammon? He'd once told me seven hundred Enforcers wouldn't be enough to take him down.

The crowd of special-ops parted. My knees buckled. Akil lay on his side, shredded clothes dark with blood. His glassy gaze stared into the middle-distance, seeing nothing. Blood dribbled from his parted lips. This couldn't be. My demon surged forward, driving a growl ahead of her and out of me.

Ryder turned to me. "Don't even think of bringing her to the party, Muse." He thumbed over his shoulder at the snipers above. I saw them and followed their aim to see the red fireflies dancing on my chest. "Unless you want your demon packed away for another day."

He glanced back, smiled, and nodded. "Job well done, everyone. Bag him, and let's get outtah here."

"You killed him," I snarled, battling with the terrible desire to spill fire into my veins and burn everyone in the alley—turn them to ash and dance with their remains in the breeze. It was insane, but that didn't make the thought any less appealing. "He was helping us drive the demons back." I clamped my teeth together, hissing each breath between them even as I felt my fangs lengthen. "Why do this?"

Ryder finally looked at me, and saw me—not another demon getting in his way, but me, once his friend. "Look," he lowered his voice, "he ain't dead. He's just chock-full of PC-Thirty-Four and a bit beaten up. He'll be pissed, for sure, but he won't be able to do a damn thing about it."

They'd drugged Akil. They'd *drugged* a Prince of Hell. Panic speared through me. "Give him the antidote. Now. Before he comes 'round. Let him go. Do that, and you'll live. Otherwise, Ryder, when he wakes and realizes what you've done, you're a dead man. And not just you. Everyone here. Shit, maybe the whole city for all I know. Don't risk it. Walk away now. Tell Adam you failed."

Ryder beamed and backed up. "Hell, no. This is the best night of my life." He nodded in the direction of Akil's lifeless body. "That bastard deserves everything he gets, and now we have him. Happy days, Muse." He winked, and strode away.

"Ryder! Don't do this. You'll get them all killed. You can still make it right!" I kicked at the mountain of a man to my right, stamped on his instep and tried to clamp my sharp teeth down onto the hand gripping my shoulder. Ryder grumbled a warning. *Screw him.* I snapped my head back, caught something soft on the outside and bony inside, heard one of them spit a curse, and drove my elbow back. The blow, when it came, cracked across the back of my skull and sent me spiraling into darkness.

Excerpt Chapter Two.

Ben Stone eyed me from behind his bar, his hands busy drying glasses. "Bit early for whiskey, Charley."

"Bite me, Ben. I've had a rough night." I eased my sore body onto a barstool. "What time does Adam get here?"

"Seven-ish." He still eyed me, like a stepbrother trying to decide whether he should care or not. "I serve coffee now. With real beans. Maybe you'd prefer caffeine to alcohol?"

"No offense, but the syrup you serve isn't coffee." I glared. He really didn't want to push me. "I tried to take down a demon last night when he decided to wipe an alley floor with me and sharpen his claws on my insides. I then promptly had my Prince of Hell lover shot to shreds in front of me by my ex-friend and intend to speak with said ex-friend's boss in about"—I checked the clock on the wall behind the bar— "ten minutes. So would you just cut me some slack, and serve me a drink? I'm a big girl. I can handle whiskey at seven a.m."

"That's what I'm worried about."

"Your conscience is clear. You said your bit. Now, where's my drink?" Yes, I was being short with him. He didn't deserve it, but I'd had virtually zero sleep. I felt as though I'd been put through the wringer. Somewhere, there was a Prince of Hell fuming at the hands of the Institute. If he hadn't laid waste to their base of operations yet, he would soon. I had to find him. Fast. Adam was getting an earful the second he stepped through the Stone's Throw's doors.

Ben delivered my drink with a side order of judgmental expression. He knew I was a wreck. I knew I was a wreck. Surely we were past all the arched eyebrows and tut-tuts by now?

As the bar began to fill with Institute staff—most of them filing out the back to their temporary safe house—I wondered where Ryder had taken Akil. Obviously, the Institute had another base of operations somewhere, yet they still used Stone's Throw as an unofficial office. What had once been a forgotten bar Ryder and I frequented after work had turned into the Boston hub for all things demon hunting. The back wall looked like a psycho's pin-board, except the photos and maps were all demon related. The Enforcer's rallied here, and Adam dropped by three days a week. Today just happened to be one of those days. I'd mostly avoided the days he graced the bar/office for fear I might boil his insides. In fact, I'd not been to the bar much at all since the events a few weeks ago when Ryder had shot a half blood girl in the head, thereby destroying her short, tragic life and driving possibly the final nail in the coffin of my control. The only thing keeping me sane was stalking the streets, killing demons who stepped out of line or bumping illegal demon-immigrants back through the veil. I didn't sleep. Not any more. *He* was there, stalking my dreams. I was on a downward spiral, one I'd finally accepted I needed Akil's help to break free of. Well, that wasn't happening any time soon.

Ryder walked in with several Enforcers in tow, Jenna the raven haired no-bullshit beauty, being one of them. The group clearly still buzzed from the previous nights' exploits, bouncing on Enforcer happy-pills until they saw me. Ryder peeled away from them, wove around the empty tables, and hitched himself onto a stool beside mine.

I waited for him to comment on the whiskey in my glass. He picked up a coaster and teased the edges with his fingers, his smile dying. "A hundred demons came through the veil last week alone, and those are the ones we know about. New York caught or killed dozens more. We ain't got the luxury of being picky—not no more, Muse. We gotta use everything we have. If that means grabbing the Prince of Greed, we do it. One Prince down. Five to go."

Technically four, if you didn't count Stefan, the newly crowned Prince of Wrath. Ryder didn't know about Stefan's recent promotion. Few did. Akil knew. Would he tell the Institute? No. It wouldn't come to that. He wouldn't let it. Shit, Akil would make them pay if I didn't get to him and talk him down.

"Akil was helping us."

He lifted mocha-brown eyes to me and ran a hand through his hair. His chin bristled with stubble, but he looked good, in a don't-give-a-damn kinda way. His eyes were bright, his gaze sharp. I knew that look. He was ex-military, and he liked nothing better than to get his teeth into a mission and feel like he was doing the world a favor. His scuffed tan-leather jacket looked as though it had seen as much action as he had.

"I'm not getting into a bitching contest with you about Akil, Muse. He's fucked you over more times than I can count. He's the Prince of Greed, for fuck's sake. Get over your Stockholm Syndrome, and move on. You'll live longer."

His words hit me like a punch in the gut. How dare he sweep me up in a statement like that? He knew what Akil had done for me. I'd thought Ryder knew me, *really* knew me, the way friends should. I snatched up my glass and threw whiskey in his face just as Adam walked through the door. Ryder spluttered, knocked the glass out of my hand, and stilled himself. His right hand clenched in a fist that trembled with the effort of restraint.

I shot to my feet, sneering into Ryder's face. Ryder's groupies loomed near the back of the bar, hands on their holstered weapons. Jenna included. "You bastard," I growled. "I thought you were different. I thought we understood each other."

"Get the fuck outtah my face, Muse, before I do something I'll regret." He delivered his threat with enough bravado to deter me, even with whiskey dripping from his chin.

"What happened to you?"

"Me?" He dragged a hand down his face and flicked moisture from his fingers. "We're at war, and you're on the wrong side. Get your shit together, or get out of Boston."

Adam's presence loomed to my left. He was a big guy, built like a lumberjack in Abercrombie & Fitch apparel. Casually classy. He loitered in my peripheral vision, radiating authority the way Akil radiated heat. Behind him, three Enforcers watched me like hawks hovering over their prey. Six others hung back. All they needed was an excuse, and I'd be full of bullet holes. I blinked—grossly outnumbered—and backed away from Ryder. This wasn't over. I threw him a glare that told him as much and then steeled myself against Adam's stare of abject disapproval.

Adam nodded once and beckoned me away from Ryder. Whiskey churned in my gut as I obliged. Ryder's words couldn't have hurt me more if he'd stabbed my in the chest. I knew things were bad between us, but I hadn't realized how deep his hatred went. I shouldn't have been surprised. I hated him right back for what he did to Dawn, the half blood girl I'd tried to save and he'd killed.

"Everything okay?" Adam pulled out a chair and gestured for me to sit. I snorted and crossed my arms. "Sit."

"No."

"Very well." He sat and leaned back in the chair, stretching his long legs beneath the table. "This is about Akil. Let me make something perfectly clear, Muse. You will not be seeing Akil unless you're under the influence of P-C-Thirty-Four."

His words sucker-punched me right where Ryder's had already wounded me. My head spun, and my vision blurred. I sat in the chair and slumped forward, sinking my fingers into my hair. A dull ache throbbed up my right side, and the whiskey in my stomach threatened to force its way back up my throat. "I can't do that."

"This is not something we can negotiate. You're too volatile, and he's too valuable."

There was no way in hell I was letting Adam stick a needle in me and pump me full of PC34 again. Not going to happen. Ever. Not even for the demon who had saved me from myself on many occasions and in many different ways.

I lifted my head and despised the fact he'd see the tears brimming my eyes. I couldn't do a damn thing to stop them, so I snarled. "Akil was on our side. He's been on the streets like us. He no more wants the princes here than we do. What you've done... You don't understand how bad this is. He'll never let you live, Adam. He despises the Institute and how you meddle with demons. Until you did this, he's tolerated you, but that's not an option anymore. He'll destroy you."

"He's contained—and he's not going anywhere, Muse. Not for a very long time."

The thought of Akil strapped to a table and at the mercy of the Institute scientists was almost enough to tip my thin control over the edge. "Is he conscious?"

"Yes." Adam blinked slowly.

"Has he said anything?"

He didn't reply as he assessed me, obviously working over a few possible replies in his head before finally saying, "He's demanded to see you."

My heart flipped, but Adam's concerned expression trampled on the new-shoots of hope.

He sighed. "He believes you're involved in his capture. He claims the real reason you didn't summon your demon in that alley was to lure him into action. He's not saying much, but when he does, he's quite... vehement."

Fuck. I clamped my teeth together. I could see how, from Akil's point of view, it might look like I'd been involved. "And you haven't said anything to put him right?" Adam didn't reply. How could he sit there, so freakin' calm? If it wasn't for the anti-elemental symbols adorning the walls, I'd be dancing in the fire and giving him third degree burns by now. "How did you know he'd be in that alley?" I leaned back and crossed my arms, locking my trembling fingers into fists.

"Akil usually resurfaces around you. I had you watched."

"Where are you keeping him?"

"A secure facility."

"Is he... alright?"

"He's recovering from the assault better than expected, considering PC-Thirty-Four is subduing his demonic nature."

My jaw ached. A terrible pressure throbbed in my head. They could have killed him. Had they used etched bullets, they'd have destroyed his human avatar. Akil as I knew him, would have died. Mammon would have lived. He was truly immortal. But I didn't care about Mammon. I cared for Akil more than I'd realized. They'd taken him from me. He was mine, and the Institute had ripped him out of my arms. Worse, they'd defiled a Prince of Hell. A demon growl rumbled up my throat.

Adam's eyes widened. "Do I need to be concerned about you, Muse?"

"I'd be concerned about your affairs, Adam. Best get that Will & Testament written up while you're still breathing." They had no idea what they'd captured. Akil wasn't just another demon. He was chaos eternal. A force of nature. "You're an idiot. You all are. You had a Prince of Hell working toward the same goals as you—a direct link to the others—and you've managed to royally fuck it up. After what you've done to him, he'll never help you. You won't get anything out of him. You might as well let him go before he escapes. Which he will. Trust me." I looked around the bar and allowed my stewing anger to raise my voice. "You're all as good as dead. You just don't know it yet."

A dozen Enforcers glared back at me. They hated me. All of them. Fine. I was done with them. With everything and everyone. Ryder didn't even look over. I got a great view of his back and knew exactly where I stood with him. I shook my head at Adam. "Don't come crawling back to me, Adam, when you have the princes breathing down your neck. It's over. I can't help you any more."

He nodded, not in the least concerned. He would be.

'Drowning In The Dark' #4 The Veil Series – Coming Early 2015.

Want More?
Visit the **website** for exclusive access to character bio's and **Muse's personal blog:**
www.theveilseries.co.uk

The Veil Series has a **Facebook** page where you can comment on the books, read character interviews, enjoy exclusive updates and artwork, chat with likeminded readers and the author:
www.facebook.com/theveilseries

If you enjoyed Darkest Before Dawn, please **review the book on Amazon and Goodreads.** Every review helps more readers discover Muse.

ABOUT THE AUTHOR

Visit: www.pippadacosta.com
Twitter: @pippadacosta
Facebook: www.facebook.com/pippadacosta

Born in Tonbridge, Kent in 1979, Pippa's family moved to the South West of England where she grew up among the dramatic moorland and sweeping coastlands of Devon & Cornwall. With a family history brimming with intrigue, complete with Gypsy angst on one side and Jewish survivors on another, she has the ability to draw from a patchwork of ancestry and use it as the inspiration for her writing. Happily married and the Mother of two little girls, she resides on the Devon & Cornwall border.

ACKNOWLEDGMENTS

To the fans of the first book, Beyond The Veil: Thank You so much for joining me on Muse's journey. Your heartfelt reactions to Muse and her story made all the difference and kept me writing into the wee hours.
To my still-suffering husband:
You married a writer; sorry about that.

FEEDBACK

Your comments are extremely important to me. Please do get in touch, even if it's just to say 'Hi'. Your reviews are like gold dust to authors. You don't need to wax-lyrical, just a few words will do.
Show your love and keep writers writing.

53560753R00164

Made in the USA
Columbia, SC
17 March 2019